# *Croc Country*

Kerry McGinnis was born in Adelaide and at the age of twelve took up a life of droving with her father and four siblings. The family travelled extensively across the Northern Territory and Queensland before settling on a station in the Gulf Country. Kerry has worked as a shepherd, droving hand, gardener and stock-camp and station cook on the family property Bowthorn, north-west of Mount Isa. She is the author of two volumes of memoir, *Pieces of Blue* and *Heart Country*, and the bestselling novels *The Waddi Tree*, *Wildhorse Creek*, *Mallee Sky*, *Tracking North*, *Out of Alice*, *Secrets of the Springs*, *The Heartwood Hotel* and *The Roadhouse*. Kerry now lives in Bundaberg.

**Also by the author**

*Pieces of Blue*
*Heart Country*
*The Waddi Tree*
*Wildhorse Creek*
*Mallee Sky*
*Tracking North*
*Out of Alice*
*Secrets of the Springs*
*The Heartwood Hotel*
*The Roadhouse*

# KERRY McGINNIS

# *Croc Country*

MICHAEL JOSEPH
*an imprint of*
PENGUIN BOOKS

MICHAEL JOSEPH

UK | USA | Canada | Ireland | Australia
India | New Zealand | South Africa | China

Michael Joseph is part of the Penguin Random House group of companies
whose addresses can be found at global.penguinrandomhouse.com.

First published by Michael Joseph, 2020



Cover photographs: landscape by Australian Scenics/Getty Images; crocodile by Songsak Wilairit/EyeEm/Getty Images; birds by Scott Gibbons/Getty Images and Timothy Christianto/Shutterstock
Cover design by Louisa Maggio © Penguin Random House Australia Pty Ltd
Typeset in Sabon by Midland Typesetters, Australia

Printed and bound in Australia by Griffin Press, part of Ovato, an accredited ISO AS/NZS 14001 Environmental Management Systems printer

A catalogue record for this book is available from the National Library of Australia

ISBN 978 1 76089 694 2

penguin.com.au

*This one is for Bill and Judy Bandidt,*
*for friendship above and beyond.*
*Thanks heaps, guys!*

# *Chapter One*

Tilly Hillyer woke with a jerk and a small cry, her heart in overdrive. It didn't happen so often now, but on occasion the dream still returned, making a peaceful night's sleep something of a lottery, with horror the consolation prize. It was so vivid and immediate even after the passage of two years – the tiny falling figure, bulky in its life jacket, tumbling endlessly through space into the rushing darkness and the waiting water.

An old tag of poetry, from schooldays or something she'd once read, popped into her mind as she panted for breath . . . *at one stride comes the dark*. Yes, she thought, it had been like that. As if the night had roared out of the mangroves to devour—

'Enough!' Tilly sat up, thrusting the cotton blanket aside. Once upon a time the world had been a different place but life had folded in upon itself, leaving her apart and separate from the *then*. *Now* was where she was at and the rest was a fairytale whose happily-ever-after ending she had been denied. She was suddenly aware of the bird calls beyond the window, as if her present life, which the dream had temporarily pushed aside, was demanding attention.

It was daylight then, time to rise. Life didn't stop for anyone's tragedy. Gerry and Francie were gone, and Tilly had passed through all the painful stages of grief that survivors suffered and it was unhealthy – and pointless – to let that nostalgic *once* drag her back into the depths through which she had already lived. Sophie, at any rate, would tell her so.

The thought forced a wry smile from Tilly. 'Pointless' was her cousin's favourite maxim. Anything deemed so was best ignored in her view, be it unnecessary directives from head office in Adelaide or fretting over the weather. *What is, is, Till, and you just have to live with it.* You could call it tough love but by whatever name, Tilly couldn't deny that Sophie's brisk, can-do attitude had been the lifeline she needed to raise herself from the nadir of despair. And the same woman would soon be wanting breakfast, as would Matt and Luke, the other two members of the ranger station for which Tilly cooked and house-kept here in the isolated wilderness of the north-western Gulf Country.

It was Sophie who had wangled the job for her when her world had collapsed. 'You need peace and space and somebody to look out for you, Till,' she had said. 'That'll be me. And you need a job. You've got to eat, girl. So take it. You'll get through this, love.' Her brown, blunt-fingered hand had clasped Tilly's own. 'Not in a month or a year, or maybe even two, but someday, I promise, you will be happy again. Losing a child must be like losing part of yourself but things *will* get better. It's a long road you've embarked on and the only way to get to the end is to just keep moving, one step at a time.'

The dull anger – at life, at fate, at Gerry – that had simmered deep inside Tilly ever since the tragedy had made her snatch her hand away. 'How would *you* know? You've never had a child to lose.'

Sophie hadn't taken offence. 'Because you're strong, love,' she had said. 'You were out here living in a fisherman's shack with no mod cons – how many town girls would pull that on? You'll make it, Till. Trust me.' She had encircled Tilly's tense shoulders in a brief hug. 'And I'll be there every step of the way to help you along.'

Showering, Tilly reflected that her cousin had been true to her word. She owed Sophie everything from her sanity to the roof over her head, for she had lost more than her husband and baby daughter in the tragedy. Her home had gone, along with *Esmerelda*, the fishing boat Gerry had operated from their base on the McArthur River, whose waters emptied into the Gulf of Carpentaria. She had never returned to their humble building of concrete and tin or the wide reaches of the treacherous river. Sophie had packed for her and organised the move to Binboona, the conservation park run by the Wildlife Protection Association, which lay well to the east of her former home, on the Territory side of the border in the rocky escarpment country of the western Gulf. The property of Binboona, eight hundred and fifty square kilometres in area, ran from the ranges to the coastline. The wildlife reserve had once been a cattle station but was now managed by Sophie and overseen from head office in Adelaide. Dedicated to the preservation of wildlife and the natural habitat, the WPA sanctuaries were dotted across the continent from the deserts of Central Australia to Western Australia's wild Kimberley coast, precious oases in the struggle against the growing wholesale extinction of species.

Living at Binboona was not as easy as at their comfortable home in Cairns, but she had grown accustomed to the differences: partial power, a weekly mail service, a hot water system that relied on one stoking a fire . . . The isolation didn't worry Tilly, while the injured and orphaned animals she helped care for had been a blessing in disguise in those early weeks, her empty hands and heart touched by their suffering and helplessness. And as time had passed she had come to know and like her three companions. At the beginning, Sophie had been little more than an acquaintance. A generation separated them: Tilly was twenty-eight and Sophie in her early forties. Matt Mercer, the older of the two men, was quiet and diffident, giving away little about himself though she guessed him to be somewhere in his late thirties. Luke Aldyce, with his wild head of hair and university education was a mere boy of twenty-two, in love with his vocation, endlessly enthusiastic about the country and its native creatures, both feathered and furred.

Gathering up her dark hair into a ponytail to keep it out of her eyes, Tilly tidied the bathroom and then went through to the kitchen to start the day. It was a large room, bearing the old-fashioned stamp of its 1960s origin in its furnishings; Binboona's available funds were spent on the land and the fauna they protected, not the lifestyles of those doing the protecting. Thirty years on from its inception, the large double-ovened wood-burning range still dominated one end of the room, while the original kitchen cabinets and the long pine table, whitened from years of elbow grease and sandsoap, served the rangers as it had the stockmen of earlier years.

Some things had changed, of course. The kerosene fridge had been replaced by a coldroom and freezer, and Tilly cooked with gas. These days the old stove served as a planter stand and a place to stack the nature magazines Luke was addicted to. The homestead held five bedrooms and quite a comfortable living room where the television lived, but, especially in the cooler months from now, May, through to September, everybody tended to spend their free time in the kitchen.

At first she had wondered if Sophie was behind this, an organised effort to keep her from brooding on her loss, but she had come to see that the banks of louvred windows above the sink and either side of the door provided a good view of both the Nutt River fronting the homestead and the bird basin that Luke had erected near the old gate posts. A pair of binoculars rested permanently on the rickety cane table next to its matching chair, and her own idle moments were frequently passed there absorbed in the avian life of the area.

Placing the kettle over the gas ring, Tilly peered through the window at a cluster of tiny finches flitting about the basin's rim. They took off as the screen door slammed behind Sophie.

'Morning, Till. I was up early, thought I'd do the joeys for you.' She set the empty feeder bottles on the sink, then removed the long thin teats to rinse them under the tap. A quick sideways glance and she frowned. 'You look a bit peaky. Bad night?'

Tilly's hands stilled on the bacon packet. 'Not really. I had the dream again, that's all.' It embarrassed her to admit it; she wasn't to *wallow*, Sophie had said, but who could help their dreams? 'But listen, I just now saw a Gouldian finch on the basin! It was only there for a second or two among the others, then your coming scared them off.'

'Are you sure?' Sophie peered in turn. 'You couldn't have been mistaken?'

'Not unless there's a thumb-sized parrot out there. What else is that colour and size?'

'We'll count it as a sighting then. Mind if I borrow your kettle to scald these bottles?'

'Go ahead. How are the joeys this morning?'

'Doing really well.' Sophie smiled with satisfaction. Hers was a round, weather-beaten face with a dimple in one cheek and hazel eyes, their corners much creased from squinting into strong light. Solidly built and of average height, with grey strands beginning to show in her brown hair, she was capable, self-sufficient and a dedicated conservationist. Over the last two years Tilly had come to love her dearly, and not just for her unstinting support. Her cousin had filled the void left by the absence of Tilly's mother and her closest friends from whom she'd drifted apart, separated by the length of the continent.

'That's good,' Tilly responded and nodded at the margarine container thawing on the sink. 'There's Mickey's meat. I forgot to get it out of the freezer last night. Just slipped my mind, sorry.'

'He can wait a bit.' Sophie finished with the bottles. 'You realise we'll never get rid of him now – butcherbirds aren't stupid. Why hunt their own tucker when it comes free from the humans?'

'His song's worth it,' Tilly protested. Luke had brought

home the injured bird some weeks beforehand and he'd settled in well. 'You think he'll fly again?'

'I don't see why not. The bones have mended. When his feathers regrow he'll be right. Shall I ring the bell for the boys? I think Matt's down the river checking the trap. I haven't seen Luke yet.'

'Yes, please. I heard him go out earlier.' Tilly piled the toast onto a plate and pulled the milk jug from the fridge. 'It's ready. Will you be wanting lunches today?'

'Mmm.' Sophie took a piece of toast to the door and clattered the donger against the steel pipe that served as a dinner bell. 'The boys will. I'll be in the office all morning. Mail day tomorrow. You need anything in the tucker line? I'd best order it today if so.'

Tilly sipped her tea, putting down the cup as the screen door opened. 'Morning, Matt.' To Sophie she said, 'I'd better have a tin of yeast.' Air freight was expensive, so ration orders came by truck from Darwin, but small items could be got out on the weekly mail plane. Tilly tried not to let the place run out of essentials, but yeast was a perishable product that one couldn't order in large quantities. At Binboona they had their own hens, a plentiful supply of fish, meat from the neighbouring Spadgers Creek Station, and the garden supplied them with most of their vegetable needs. The bush provided a few more: Luke, in particular, was an enthusiastic promoter of bush tucker, some of which Tilly had forcefully rejected, declaring, 'Anything slimy, muddy or weird from the mangroves is not coming near my stove! You want to cook that, you can build a fire outside.'

'Morning.' Matt rinsed his hands at the sink before taking

his place at table. 'No fish, Tilly. Couple of young terrapin got in and took the bait.'

'Oh well, a tinned-tuna bake dinner instead, then,' Tilly said philosophically. 'What would you like in your sandwiches?'

'Anything.' His ginger head settled lower over his plate as he added quietly, 'They always taste good.' He wore his usual jeans and longsleeved shirt, and she could smell the suncream on his exposed skin. A redhead, she reflected, really had no business in an outdoors job, but he was vigilant about sun protection.

'You're easily pleased,' she said as the door opened. 'Ah, Luke – morning. Any preference in sandwiches?'

'Hi, Tilly, boss, Matt. Oh, let's see. Roast beef and pickles?'

'Uh-uh. No meat. How about cheese and pickles, or egg and lettuce?'

'Whatever. Good-oh, bacon.' He helped himself liberally, adding tomato and mushrooms before piling three slices of toast on the side.

Sophie eyed his plate with amusement. 'You sure that's enough? I wouldn't want you starting the day hungry.'

He grinned, his narrow face alive with the mischief that twinkled in his eyes, brilliant blue against his dark hair and smudge of beard shadow.

'Growing boy, boss. So, Mickey flew this morning. Not far, just from his perch to the ground. He flapped his wings a few times – bit doubtful, like – then spread 'em and wobbled down. He needs a few more feathers still.'

Sophie beamed. 'That's great news. Right, so, today. One of you needs to go across to Spadgers Creek to pick up some meat. You'd better do that, Matt. And Luke, you might take a swing down along the coast road, check things out. The station rang last night. Bruce Hansen says there's a fire burning somewhere along it – he thinks it might be on our country.'

Tilly was surprised. 'How? It couldn't be a lightning strike, not in May!'

'No,' Sophie agreed. 'Has to've been lit. Fishermen, illegals, tourists even. What matters is stopping it before it spreads. Bit hard to pinpoint from eighty-odd kilometres away. Give me a call on the radio once you know. Bruce said he'd send the grader across if we needed it. Oh'—she looked at Tilly—'and I almost forgot. We've got a guest coming sometime this week. A botanist from the uni in Darwin. He'll be staying for a bit, camping round the sanctuary and making the homestead his base, so he'll need the spare room, Till.'

'Okay, I'll get it ready for him. You don't know what day he's coming?'

'It was a message on the answering machine. Bit light on details. His name's'—she wrinkled her brow—'Colin . . . Carl? Something starting with a c. We'll find out when he gets here.'

'Okay.' Tilly piled cup and plate together and carried them to the sink. 'Your lunches will be ready in ten, boys. Luke, you didn't bring your thermos back.'

'Sorry. I'll get it. It'll be in the vehicle.' He folded his last slice of toast about the rest of the bacon and took a large bite as he left the room, calling, 'Back in a tick, oh slave driver.'

When they had all dispersed, the men to the vehicle shed and Sophie to the office, Tilly cleared away and washed up, then moved on to the morning's tasks, the first of which was feeding the injured animals. Mickey's mince had thawed by then. She had a margarine container of diced carrot and apple for the possum, and another of cubed meat for Harry the brolga, whose injury was permanent in that he had somehow managed to snap off the front half off his top beak.

'Like he'd stuck it in a dog trap,' Luke had said angrily when he'd brought the young, malnourished bird back to the homestead soon after Tilly's arrival. 'I can't see how else it could've happened.'

Traps were illegal within Binboona's boundaries, of course, but there was little the rangers could do about enforcing the rule. They would have needed to find proof first, and then the culprit – something they all knew to be impossible. Lacking the ability to dig or even to drink properly, Harry would certainly have starved if it hadn't been for the ranger's intervention. He'd be a permanent guest, Tilly mused, tossing him his breakfast, one piece at a time. She'd tried letting him take it from her hand, but his enthusiastic lunges hit her fingers as often as they did the target, as if the damage done to him had also addled his judgement. The possum, being nocturnal, required no effort beyond removing last night's empty container from the cage and replacing it with the full one. It was almost ready for release, the injury to its front paw having healed and the fur almost grown back.

The garden was her next chore. Wearing a wide straw hat and gardening gloves, Tilly entered the netted enclosure, methodically watering her way along the rows, picking a lettuce for lunch and, when the hose had been coiled out of the way again, filling the crown of her hat with beans. It was a productive piece of ground and she enjoyed the work. In Cairns she had grown tropical shrubs and African violets, but since taking over the plot from the men's hit-and-miss efforts, the vegetable garden had prospered.

'You've got a natural green thumb, Till,' Sophie had said admiringly.

'I like it.' She found a soothing rhythm in gardening, a thoughtless peace where for a little while she could forget everything but the task before her. With her hands in the earth, time seemed to flow over her without the constant reminders that accompanied the rest of her day. Only in the garden were the ghosts of the lost absent from her thoughts. Sitting back on her heels, Tilly smeared a muddy glove across one cheek to brush away a stray hair and looked about her with satisfaction. Weeding carrots was finicky work but she'd got most of them out, thinning the rows as she worked.

Resting for a moment, she surveyed her small netted kingdom and the reach of land beyond that stretched all the way to the river bank. There were no fences or garden beds around the homestead, though the gateposts near the bird bath showed there must once have been. Of the original station garden only the lemon tree had survived. Some natives had grown up and been left for shade, and there was one immense tree towering above the house whose name none of them knew. The grass that Matt usually mowed ran to the edge of the little spring-fed and pandanus-lined creek behind the homestead from which they drew their water.

Out front, the land dipped to the jungle-like edge of the Nutt River, where sweeping paperbacks intertwined with swarming creepers, palms and pandanus thickets that almost screened the water from view. It was a big river, the

Nutt – deep and brown and dangerous, home to the estuarine crocodiles that could often be seen sprawled like drying logs on the muddy edges of its banks. Open forest country stretched beyond the water, a dry vista of grass, landscaped with bloodwood, stringybark and white-trunked gums. A blue-winged kookaburra was just now cackling his heart out from the branches of one.

With a last glance at her row of weeded carrots, Tilly stood, clapping her earthy gloves together. She just might add to the order for yeast, she thought. Surely the WPA could buy her a packet of flower seeds? She had a sudden desire to see a tub of them near the front steps. Cosmos, perhaps, or marigolds. Something bright and pretty to lift all their spirits at the end of the day. And if management considered them an unnecessary expense, she'd damn well pay for them herself.

# *Chapter Two*

Tilly stripped off her gloves, leaving them in the basket beside the door, and went to wash, thinking she had best get on with preparing the spare room. A glimpse of her mud-smeared cheek in the mirror brought an involuntary smile that faded as she studied her face. She had not looked at herself – not really – for months. There was no call for make-up out here and sunscreen could be applied by touch.

Now, placing her hands on the vanity top, she leant curiously towards the reflective glass, her gaze tracing the lines of her face with its high cheekbones and long chin. There were shadows under the blue-grey eyes and her cheeks were thin enough to look hollow. She pulled the scrunchy from her ponytail and saw that her hair needed a trim; the ends when she examined them were split and uneven. Sophie cut the men's hair – maybe she could take a bit off hers, too? Tilly'd lost weight and she looked – what? Older, haggard, sad? All of the above, and dirty.

Abandoning the introspection, she reached for the soap, then paused, cocking her head to the sound of an arriving vehicle. It pulled up and there came the clunk of a car door closing, followed shortly by another. Luke and Matt were long gone and wouldn't be back until late. It must be their visitor from the university, only it sounded like he had somebody with him.

'Hell's bells!' Hastily she washed her face and brushed her hair, thankful to hear Sophie's footsteps in the hallway on her way to meet them. She wondered where they could find another bed for the extra body. There might be a spare stretcher in the old men's quarters that they could set up on the verandah. Otherwise whoever it was had better have a swag. Catching up the scrunchy to secure her hair, she heard her cousin calling her name.

'Coming!' Tilly almost bumped into Sophie as she exited the room. 'What's up? I know he's earlier than we exp—'

'It's not the botanist. It's a couple of detectives from Darwin. They want to talk to you.'

Tilly stared at her. '*Me?* Why?'

'They didn't say. Just asked if you were here and said they needed a word.' Sophie frowned, concerned. 'Do you want me to stay? I've no idea what it's about.

'Neither have I.' Her heart suddenly leapt and she pressed a hand to her chest, face paling, made giddy by sudden hope. 'It couldn't be,' she whispered. 'They haven't – oh, Sophie, they haven't heard something about Francie? She . . . did some boat find her, save her?'

Sophie put an arm around her. 'Don't, Till. Don't go there, you'll only hurt yourself. Francie's gone and it's no good letting yourself hope. That's a one in a million chance and you know it . . .' She paused. 'They didn't look like they were bringing good news.'

'Well, but why . . .?' Tilly's wild leap of hope fled, leaving her feeling drained and slightly sick. Numbly she entered the kitchen where Sophie had left the two men. They hadn't sat down; one stood by the table while the other peered out of the window above the sink. Both faces turned towards her and she was aware of a hard scrutiny from each. The closest, who was also the tallest, spoke first.

'Morning. Mrs Matilda Hillyer?'

Tilly nodded. 'That's my name. What—?' she began but she was interrupted.

'I'm Detective Sergeant David Burns.' He tipped his head sideways, 'My colleague, Detective Constable Wayne Wilmot. We'd like to have a bit of a chat with you about your husband. Shall we sit down?' He pulled out the chair where Matt normally sat. 'Please.' He gestured towards another seat as if the place belonged to him. To Sophie, he said, 'Thank you, Ms, erm . . .'

'Barker. Tilly's my cousin and I'm staying.' Sophie seated herself in Luke's place and patted the chair beside her. Tilly took it, as the constable moved to sit beside his superior.

Clearing her throat, Tilly said, 'What's this about, Sergeant, and why now? Gerry's been dead for two years.'

The man's hard eyes, a curiously pale grey, bored into hers. 'Are you quite certain about that, Mrs Hillyer? I understand there's room for some . . . confusion, shall we say? His body was never found. And he did owe rather large sums of money. Isn't that correct?'

Tilly gaped at him. She heard and understood his words but they made no sense. Before she could say so, Sophie's voice cut harshly across her bewildered silence. 'What exactly are you suggesting, Sergeant? The matter was fully investigated at the time, I can assure you. There was a full-scale search – of the sea and the coastline. They had boats out for a week looking for his body. It's all in the coroner's report.'

'And yet Gerald Hillyer still managed to disappear off the face of the earth.'

Sophie cast up her eyes. 'God give me strength! His two-year-old daughter fell overboard. He went in after her, plucked her from the water and put her in the runabout, and the tide took both it and him. We're talking about a fast ebb in shark- and croc-infested water, man! Of course they didn't find his body. Be a bloody miracle if they had, in my opinion. He was probably taken in the first ten minutes. I'm sorry, Till.' Her eyes shot daggers at the officer as she turned to her cousin. 'You shouldn't have to listen to this. What is the point of it anyway? Why are you here?'

'It might be better, Ms Barker, if you let Mrs Hillyer speak for herself,' Burns said. He turned back to Tilly. 'So you haven't had any contact with your husband – seen him, spoken to him on the phone, received any written communication from him since his alleged death? And before you answer, please remember that lying to the police is a serious matter.'

Tilly gripped the table's edge, eyes enormous in her pale face. 'Are you suggesting . . .? How can you even think – I don't believe it!' Her voice rose wildly as the enormity of his meaning sank in and she shot to her feet. 'Gerry *loved* his daughter! He dived into very dangerous water to save her! What are you saying? That he let her drown *because he owed money?* That he *planned* it? You . . . you . . . Get out!' she screamed, livid with rage.

The constable tapped his superior's arm. 'Sarge, maybe you're . . . I mean, there's nothing to prove—'

'And you can get out too,' Tilly spat at him, a flood of scarlet flushing her formerly pale cheeks.

'You're done here,' Sophie seconded her. 'I'm asking you both to leave. You're way out of order. Go strangle some kittens or something,' she added contemptuously. 'That ought to be right up your alley.' Marching to the door, she swung it wide and stood there holding it, waiting for them to pass through.

'We have inquiries to make,' Burns said, as he stepped past her, though whether in explanation or apology neither woman could tell. 'Not everybody likes them.'

'Yeah, well, if you're planning another visit you'd better bring a solicitor with you,' Sophie snapped. 'She won't be speaking to you again without one.' She returned to Tilly's side and they stood listening to the doors slamming and the sound of the engine turning over. When the noise had faded to a faint hum she blew her breath out, saying comfortingly, 'I doubt they'll be back, Till.'

Tilly dropped bonelessly onto her chair. 'How could they even *think* . . . *Why* would they think—'

'Of course he didn't! Where are their heads at anyway?' Sophie demanded rhetorically. 'Do they seriously imagine he was going to swim all the way to the islands dodging death at every stroke? And what then? It's not as if it wasn't the first place the searchers looked. The man's a cretin! The copper, I mean, not Gerry.'

Immersed in her own thoughts, Tilly ignored this outburst. 'He would never have left Francie, Sophie. He adored her, he gave his life to try and save her. Oh, I was angry with him, because he was supposed to watch her. He *promised* he would, but you know with kids you only have to look away for a second—'

'I know, love. I know. Come on, now. Don't let that idiot get to you. It's pointless because he was talking rubbish. Probably fancied a drive on a nice day and thought hassling you was one way to justify it. What you need is a good strong cuppa.' Sophie, filling the kettle, prattled on, though Tilly hardly heard her commentary: behind her anger and bewilderment, and the reopened wound of her grief, it had occurred to her to wonder why, two years after the event the police should suddenly suspect the veracity of the inquest's findings.

The rest of the day passed in a blur. At one moment Tilly would find herself standing with a plate or a sheet in her hand, stalled like a rundown wind-up toy while her mind went over and over that morning's meeting, analysing the sergeant's words and his hard, inquisitive eyes. Next she would be at the sink with no memory of the interim period, or rubbing furiously at a spot on the table, reliving it all again. The moment, indelibly stamped on her memory, when she'd stepped from the companionway onto the deck and had seen the bright bundle that was Francie falling overboard. And being plunged back into the useless self-recriminations that had accompanied her mourning.

If only she hadn't left the deck to step below! Or that she had returned five seconds earlier. If only she'd learnt to steer and work a boat – she and Gerry had been married four years, for God's sake, and the boat was their livelihood. But she'd never been more than a day passenger on the *Esmerelda*. She'd just coasted along, leaving everything to him, and her ignorance had contributed to their deaths.

Once upon a time, before that dreadful day, she had been a mother, a wife. She had been happy – and then in the blink of an eye everything had changed.

Sometime during the afternoon Matt returned with a cooler of meat. Tilly put the kettle on for him, then in the same mechanical fashion with her mind elsewhere, sliced and cubed and bagged the hunks of flesh for the freezer.

'Everything okay, Tilly?' Matt's forehead creased as he watched her. 'You're very quiet.'

'Yes, of course,' she said brightly. 'So how were things at the station? Who did you see?'

'Pretty busy, actually. The stockyard was full of horses. I expect they'll be mustering soon. I spoke to Bruce, and the cook. He's new – a bit strange, I thought. Mad-looking eyes. Talked non-stop. Only got one hand too.'

'Really? How does he manage?'

Matt shrugged. 'He seems to get along. He's got some sort of a fist fitted to the stump, inside a glove, like.'

'I suppose it would help kneading dough,' Tilly said doubtfully. Some of the stations still baked their own bread. 'I guess people who lose bits of themselves learn to compensate, because they have to.' As she had, she thought. But the amputation she'd suffered was invisible to the casual viewer.

'I saw the tracks out front,' Matt said. 'Who was it? The closed sign's still up for visitors.'

'Oh, just the police.' Hastily, to prevent him asking what they had wanted, she added, 'I wondered, Matt – is it worth reporting the fire to them? Not that they're going to catch anyone for it, but—'

'What would they do?' he scoffed. 'The wind's died, but driving back I never saw smoke. Probably gone out by now.'

'I'm sure you're right.' Tilly collected her knife and cutting board and carried it to the sink. 'Well, that's the meat done. I'd best feed the chooks. Just leave your cup and plate with the rest of it, Matt. I'll clear up when I get back.'

Luke returned at sundown. Tilly, who had been giving the joeys their evening feed, paused to hail him as he climbed out of the vehicle and stretched his long body before reaching back in for the thermos and his lunch pack. His hands and forearms were scratched and dirty, and there was a rip in one sleeve of his shirt.

'How was the fire, Luke? Is it still going?'

'Yeah, but it's contained, just creeping along slowly now. I did a backburn, so there'll just be logs and stumps alight come morning. Looks like it started behind the shoreline and spread a fair distance inland. I got there in time to burn back into it from the old track along the coast, put out a few spot fires where it'd already crossed over, and Bob's your uncle.' He caught up with her, slowing his long stride to keep pace. 'What's for dinner?'

She laughed. 'Do you ever think of anything but food? There's syrup pudding for dessert – how does that grab you?'

'You're a wonder,' he said fervently. 'You ought to have seen us before you came. Sophie can't cook worth a damn and

Matt and me are no better. I tell you, it's a miracle we didn't starve.'

Tilly rolled her eyes. 'You didn't look exactly malnourished as I recall. So how do you think the fire started?'

'Oh, someone lit it. A boat had come in. There's a stretch of sand between the mangroves where the track runs in, and they'd beached it there. The tide hadn't washed their footprints away when I arrived. Most likely fishermen down from the islands, or maybe Indonesia – probably illegals after trepang.'

'Or people smugglers?' Tilly suggested. 'Wasn't there something about a boatload of Chinese people put ashore on the Kimberley Coast maybe five years back? Which is practically murder when you think of the isolation and distance from anywhere. It was just luck some of them found that station.'

'Pretty damn silly to light a fire if they were trying to sneak in the back door,' Luke objected.

'There is that, of course. Do you want a cuppa before dinner?'

'I'll wait,' he decided. 'I need to shower first anyway. Might have a beer after that though.'

Nobody was late to bed that night. Once she had cleaned up in the kitchen, Tilly readied the bottles for Sophie to give the joeys their evening feed. The next task was preparing the possum's breakfast. Matt, busy setting out the board and having failed to find a playing partner in Luke, then invited her to a game of chess.

She pulled a face. 'You know I'm not up to your standard.'

'Don't matter. Call it practice.' He shrugged.

Sighing inwardly, Tilly took a seat across the kitchen table from him. Not that she had anything better to do. The others had found their own pursuits, Sophie lost in a book and Luke watching a football game on TV, by the sound of it. She pushed a white pawn carelessly forward, and when her turn came around again followed it with another, seeing not the board but the hard glint in DS Burns' face as he asked if she'd had contact with her husband. Even if it were possible that Gerry still lived, why would the police be involved? Just supposing he had somehow miraculously survived, was that in itself a crime? Matt was waiting on her; she moved a knight at random and saw his fingers, with their light dusting of blotchy freckles, grasp his king and tip it over.

'No point,' he said when she looked up. 'Your head ain't in it.'

'I'm sorry, Matt.' She hadn't wanted to play but now she felt bad about spoiling it for him.

''S'okay.' He was setting the pieces back on their squares, removing some and shifting others about the board. 'I can nut out problems instead.' Cradling his chin in one hand, he became rapt in contemplation as Tilly rose and left him. Everybody had their little quirks, she thought, and Matt's was chess. He knew all the famous end-games by heart and often worked them through, trying to find alternative moves to those the masters of chess had played.

By nine o'clock the lights were out, but Tilly's thoughts kept her wakeful. As a rule, physical tiredness had her falling asleep the moment her head touched the pillow but tonight she tossed and turned, unable to forget DS Burns' suspicions. He couldn't just have plucked the idea out of the ether, she reasoned, so something, somewhere, must have started him questioning the accepted account of Gerry's death.

Had some look-alike involved in criminal activity been wrongly identified as her late husband? Didn't they say that everyone had a double? Tilly had never met her own, but there had been two instances she could recall when she had herself mistaken someone in the street for another person, so it was possible. Much more likely than Gerry having survived that night. Unbidden, her mind returned her to it, to that instant on the edge of darkness when she had asked him to watch their toddler because she was going below for a moment.

'Okay, babe.' She could see him at the wheel, the rakish, handsome face glancing from the binnacle to the child near his feet, his body silhouetted against the low smudge of mangroves looming ahead, and the two buoys that marked the entrance to the channel into the river mouth. Had it been as much her fault as his? She had known, hadn't she, that he was concentrating on steering the boat? But it was only a minute of his time she had asked for – three at the very most. Was that too much to expect? She had been quick, her returning feet clearing the companionway a scant two minutes later, just in time to see Francie tumble overboard, like a chick falling from the nest.

Tilly had screamed her daughter's name and heard Gerry's startled, guilty cry, 'Christ!' – or was that the moment she had loaded her own guilt upon him? And a second later he had dived after the toddler while the *Esmerelda* had lost her forward motion and began wallowing in the darkness and the outrushing tide.

Chaos had ensued then so that now, in the aftermath, it

was hard to disentangle the actual events from the terror that had surrounded them. She had rushed to the rail as he surfaced and he'd yelled something – 'Get the wheel!' perhaps – as he was swept sternwards. But she had ignored him, screaming her daughter's name. She had seen him slash free the painter of the small boat they were towing, and a part of her gibbering mind understood that when he reached Francie he couldn't hope to both hold her and swim against the tide. Straining her eyes, she had glimpsed the yellow of the bobbing life jacket and had breathed, 'Oh, thank God! Thank God!' as Gerry reached it.

He'd lift her into the boat. She'd be safe. Until that moment she had forgotten that a far greater danger than drowning lurked in these muddy, offshore waters. But her relief was short-lived, for the unmanned *Esmerelda* chose that moment to heel sideways and she had lost sight of them. They'd be all right though, both safely aboard. It wasn't the easiest thing to climb into a boat from the water but Gerry was strong – he would manage. All she had to concentrate on was driving the *Esmerelda* to a point where she could pick them up without running them down.

Would it have made a difference if she had remembered and activated the EPIRB, the emergency beacon, right then? Or put a call through on the radio? She had been desperate not to lose them and when it became plain that she had, precious time had already ticked away. Help had come but by then it was too late.

The night and the ocean, or something worse, had swallowed her little family and the endless litany of *once upon a time* had begun.

*

The fishing fraternity had rallied to her wild distress, quartering the seas about the islands until dawn. Rough, kindly men with salt-scarred skin plotted where the tides would carry a small boat, forced thermos tea upon her and organised a search of the islands' shores. The police had arrived at daylight, and a light plane owned by a local charter pilot had flown a grid pattern over the waves. He was later joined by a small helicopter borrowed from some station muster. Together they had crisscrossed the Gulf waters around the Sir Edward Pellew Group of Islands and further out into the vast soulless blue where the plane reported no sightings beyond a prawn trawler, whom the police had immediately co-opted into the search. The helicopter pilot, however, who was young, and new to the north, brought back an excited description of the many big crocs he'd seen hauled up on the silty banks fronting the mangroves.

Tilly's nightmares had started then, peopled with scaley monsters devouring her child. Two days later her mother had briefly appeared, crying as she held her sobbing daughter, but Elaine Williams couldn't stay. Her husband suffered from dementia; he had slipped away mentally from his family several years before and needed constant supervision. She had placed him in respite care for the brief duration of her visit and both of them knew she must return.

'They're gone, love. There's nothing more you can do here, so come home with me,' Elaine had pleaded.

Tilly had refused. 'I can't leave them, Mum. I can't. There's a chance still,' she cried fiercely. 'There is! There must be!'

That was when Sophie, contacted by Elaine, had stepped in instead. And now, when her life had shakily resumed its imperfect rhythmn and the scar over her injury was beginning to heal, the day's visitors had torn it open again, bringing back the full horror of the event – along with the unanswered question she had been too angry and confused at the time to even think of, let alone ask.

Why were the police looking for a dead man?

# *Chapter Three*

The morning came with its wakening chorus of birdcalls, and when Tilly stepped out onto the verandah to view the brightening east, she found Mickey waiting on the balustrade, his throat pulsing with song. 'You clever thing! How did you get up there?'

As if to answer her, he flapped his lopsided wings and glided down to her feet, cocking his head to look at her with a bright dark eye.

'All right, food's on its way. Just let me get the kettle on first.'

She fed him before starting on breakfast. The others were up; she could hear the shower running and one of the men had gone to start the pump, for water suddenly shot from the sprinklers dotted across the grass, startling a flutter of finches off the basin. Mostly double-bars and a few crimsons, she noted: no Gouldians this morning. Breakfast ready, she made lunches for all three, for they would, she knew, be working at the campground today, preparing it for the influx of visitors scheduled from the middle of the month onwards.

Binboona was designated as bush camping, which meant basic showers, fireplaces and compostable toilets. No dogs, cats or generators allowed. The rangers kept the long grass cut around the camping area, supplied firewood and serviced the hot water boilers in the showers. Customers could also book a walking tour with a ranger. These varied from bird-watching strolls beside the river to serious treks into the bush along the edge of the escarpment. Though she had never seen them, Tilly had heard there were springs and caves in the area as well, a vast section of rocky pinnacles known as the Lost City and some rocks where Aboriginal paintings could be seen. These had been fenced off, Sophie had told her, to protect them. They were very old, the ochre in places faded into no more than a shadow on the sandstone.

'I'd like to see that part of the place – the caves and the City – one day,' Tilly had said, but so far it had never happened. Everyone was busy during the dry season and in summer there was the heat, the insects and boggy roads to dampen one's taste for exploring. Last summer had been her first in the Gulf and she hadn't enjoyed it. Perhaps this year she would go home to Mallacoota to see her parents – well, her mother; her stepfather had travelled so far from them he might as well have been in another country.

Tilly had no siblings and, as a child, had found her stepfather incomprehensible. An enigmatic man, he was given to bouts of depression followed by fervent but short-lived enthusiams as unsettling, by their frenetic nature, as his previous gloom. He had been an unreliable parent, his path strewn with broken promises and sudden rages. She had learnt early not to depend upon him, and they had become as strangers long before dementia claimed him. But her mother loved him – or she had. Perhaps it was only duty that held her now. Tilly sighed, wondering in her secret heart if she still loved Gerry. If he were to turn up on the doorstep now, after all the anger and grief and heartache she had suffered, would she be able to forgive him and fall into his arms? She honestly didn't know.

Sophie's arrival from the joeys' pen put an end to her ruminations. Her cousin was frowning as she rinsed and sterilised the bottles.

Tilly slanted a look at her. 'Something wrong?'

'The little feller's scouring a bit. I've put him in a new bag. Maybe you could mix an egg through his next feed? See if it helps.'

'Will do. But you said he was fine yesterday. Is the Pretty Face okay?'

'Seems to be. Course the little one was always weaker. Well'—she dumped the last teat in the sterilising fluid—'if he makes it, he makes it. We can only do our best.' But she would feel it if the joey died, Tilly knew. For all her tough, no-nonsense approach to living, Sophie loved the orphans they raised and took every death as a personal failure.

Luke came in then, dark hair damp from the shower. 'We gonna need the chainsaw today, boss?'

'Yes.' Sophie filled her cup from the teapot and sat down. 'Both whipper snippers too, and plenty of fuel. You can't even see where the firepits are. We might take the paint as well and give the stones a touch-up.' The campground sites were marked by whitewashed rocks that faded over summer. 'Do you want a job, Tilly?'

'Why? What do you need done?'

'The airstrip markers. When the mail plane's been, I wondered if you could drive along the strip and chuck 'em on the back and bring them in? If we're going to paint, they're due a coat as well.'

'Yes, of course. If there's another brush I could do that this afternoon.' She made a rapid assessment of the day's tasks. 'I haven't much on once the baking's done.'

'Luke can have a look before we leave. There should be an old one in the supplies, and there's turps in the shed. You don't have to be too particular, just so long as they're visible from the air.'

'Okay,' Tilly said, pleased by the idea of doing something different.

After breakfast Luke vanished into the big shed next to the engine room and reappeared with a cobweb-infested brush and tin of white paint with a much-battered top.

'I loosened the lid,' he said. 'You'd never get it off, else. And it's water based – you won't need the turps.'

Tilly rolled her eyes at him. 'I'm not quite useless, you know, but thanks anyway. Just leave it on the verandah.' She was on her way to feed Harry and the possum, and for no reason, save that the morning was fresh and blue-skied, with a waft of wattle blossom in the air, her heart lifted. It was suddenly good to be alive and part of a team, with tasks to perform and animals to care for. She hummed a little as she placed the possum's dish inside the dark box Matt had made for him within the netted shelter.

'Wake up sleepyhead. Here's your breakfast.'

*

Tilly was painting when the vehicle arrived. She was in the big shed, squatting beside the last of the airstrip marker tyres and applying a second coat to it, when the rumble of the engine broke into her concentration. Her immediate thought was that the bullying Sergeant Burns had returned and her heart jolted uncomfortably. Cravenly she wished Sophie was around for support, but a moment later caught herself on the thought and stood up, paintbrush in hand. She had nothing to fear from the man; it was he who was in the wrong, badgering her as he had, and she would tell him so – before giving him his marching orders.

Jamming the lid on the paint tin, Tilly stalked from the shed, forgetting the brush in her hand, and was brought up short by the sight of a totally different four-wheel drive parked near the house. The driver was standing with his back to her at the foot of the verandah steps gazing upwards. 'Hello, the house,' he called. He was tall and lanky, clad in the sort of multi-pocketed khaki that Luke wore, with a felt hat topping blond hair that curled over his shirt collar. He wore flat-heeled boots of the type that Bruce Hansen, manager of Spadgers Creek Station, used for driving, and one of his tanned forearms sported a bandage.

'Were you looking for me?' Tilly asked.

He wheeled about in surprise and she made a small grimace. 'Sorry, didn't mean to startle you. Are you him – the botanist who rang? Sorry,' she repeated. 'I didn't get your name.'

'Oh, it's Connor. Connor Doyle, and you must be Ms Barker?' He looked momentarily confused, apologising in turn. 'You don't – I mean, I was expecting someone older.'

'She is. Older. I'm Tilly, not Sophie. I'm the cook housekeeper for the ranger station. We didn't know what day you were coming, but I made up your room in case – there is just you, I take it?'

'Just me,' he agreed. He had a pleasant-enough face, somewhat long-nosed, she thought and his brown eyes seemed incongruous with his light hair. He was very tall – what her mother would have described as 'six foot up'. 'What were you painting?' he asked and Tilly glanced down in surprise at the brush she held.

'Oh, just some old tyres for the airstrip, but I've finished. Come in and I'll make you a cuppa. There's nobody else home, I'm afraid. They're all out at the camp, setting things up for the early tourists, you know.' She gestured towards the house and he followed her up the steps. 'Here we are. Make yourself at home, Connor, I'll be back in a tick.' She went out to the laundry to slosh water into an old feed tin and dump the brush. There was paint on her hands and her jeans; she scrubbed the former, decided there was nothing to be done about the latter, and feeling strangely shy, for it had been a while since she'd entertained visitors, returned to the kitchen.

Connor was standing at the window with the binoculars to his eyes. He turned as Tilly entered, saying, 'Brilliant idea, the bird basin. The little 'uns'll feel so much safer there than drinking from the river.'

'That was Luke's intention. One of the rangers – he built it. He told me he caught a big catfish once that had a bush canary in it. He must've snapped it down from the surface when it came to drink. We see all sorts on the basin, finches, flycatchers . . . Would you rather tea or coffee, Connor?'

'Oh, tea please, if it's no trouble. So Luke's keen on birds?'

Tilly smiled. 'Keen on everything that swims or grows or flies. The environment, and protecting it, really matters to him. Well, it does to Matt too, and Sophie of course, but Luke's still young and his enthusiams tend to bubble over. But I understand botany's your field?'

'Yep, field work and research. What about you?' His gaze, she noticed, had fallen to the wedding ring on her hand. 'Is the other chap your husband?'

'Matt? No,' she said composedly. 'I'm widowed. I am related to Sophie Barker though – she's my cousin. I got the job through her.'

'I'm sorry. You're very young for that.' He laid the binoculars aside and drew a chair to the table where Tilly had poured his tea. 'Thanks. So how do you find it here? Not too quiet for you?'

'No.' Sitting down, she offered the cake she'd cut and stirred her own tea. 'I'm used to it and I love caring for the animals the others find – injured ones and orphans. We have a couple of joeys at present, a possum that Matt found with its foot jammed in the crack of a hollow tree, a brolga and a butcherbird who broke his wing somehow. I expect we'll never get rid of *him*.'

'No, real opportunists, they are,' Connor agreed. He had a friendly smile and seemed to be enjoying the cake. Tilly took a piece herself to encourage him. 'Was the brolga a chick?'

She frowned. 'Full grown but damaged. The poor thing's lost half his beak. He nearly starved before they found him. Luke thinks it was a dogtrap that did it. I suppose it's possible – there are any number of dingoes about and

I understand that their scalps are worth quite a bit. Poor Harry will be a permanent resident, I think.'

'Harry?'

'It's what I call him.'

'And he's doing okay? How long have you had him?'

Tilly moved her fingers counting the months. 'September last year, I think. When the tourists were still about anyway. Which is why they couldn't work out who could've set the trap. Too many people camping and coming and going, and it's a big place. There are just three rangers after all, so there's only so much they can patrol what with the tours and the talks . . . Education is part of Binboona's remit,' she explained conscientiously. 'But honestly, some people! They'd cut down the last living tree if you let them, and kill the last creature if it brought in money.'

'So you're a conservationist too?' he said with a faint smile.

Realising that her voice had risen, Tilly flushed. 'I suppose I am,' she said stiffly. 'Look, I have to get on. I'll show you your room, shall I, and leave you to settle in and look around? Dinner's around six-thirty if the others are back then, later if not. I expect you carry your own, but there are reference books on the local flora and fauna in the lounge, and a very good map of the property on the wall in Sophie's office. It shows all the roads, and where both the river crossings are. I'm sure she wouldn't mind if you want to check it out.'

'Thanks, I will.' Connor stood, pulling his chair in and picking up the hat he'd removed. 'I mostly camp on the job, so it's very good of you to take me in. I'll try not to make too much extra work for you.'

'That's all right. It's what I'm here for.'

'And,' he said, 'I'm all for conservation too. You people do a great job. I'm sorry if I sounded flippant just then.'

'Don't worry about it. Not everybody thinks it's important, so I guess we get a bit defensive.' She smiled at him, collecting up the cups, and turning to the sink as he left.

# *Chapter Four*

Within days of his arrival Connor was fitting easily into their little group, mixing companionably with the men and spending time studying the office map, learning the camp site and its approaches, and the various roads across the property. Some were the wet-weather tracks that never saw the old-fashioned grader the rangers had inherited from when Binboona had been a station.

'Emergency use only, them,' Matt told him. He was the one who drove the antiquated grader. 'They follow the high ground and grading 'em would turn them into creek beds. Best left be. That way if you've gotta, you just might get a four-wheel drive through the bog.'

'Do you often have to?' Connor, tracing the line on the sheet, lifted an enquiring brow.

'Now and then,' Sophie said. 'Last year some idiot was up-country after we'd closed the camp down. Wasn't supposed to be anyone on the place and we got this radio message to say he was crook and needed help.' She shook her head disgustedly. '*Other* side of the river of course, and we'd had early storms so the crossings were flooded. The boys had to winch him across and use the wet-weather tracks to get him out. Took eighteen hours all up.'

'Most of 'em up to our knees in mud, being eating alive by mozzies,' Luke added feelingly. 'The ground was too soft for the grader and his mate was a bloody useless driver. Damn near overturned the vehicle in the river, then stalled it just as it reached the bank. It sank like a stone. Had to leave it and bring 'em out in our vehicle.'

'I don't remember that,' Tilly interrupted. 'You're sure it was last year? I didn't hear a word about it.'

'You were in Darwin,' Sophie said. 'And by the time you got back the cyclone was coming in, remember? So we had more to think about.'

'Of course. What was wrong with the sick man?'

'Dunno.' Luke shrugged. 'Bellyache. The doc thought it might've been a bleeding ulcer. We never heard because he never came back or contacted us.'

'Yeah?' Connor sounded surprised. 'Not even to collect his vehicle?'

'The river got that,' Sophie said. 'I daresay it's somewhere at the bottom of the Arafura Sea now. You can tell people until you're blue in the face, but they see the country in the dry and they won't believe what a metre or more of rain'll do to it. Ulcer or not, we saved his life and his mate's, because no way would they have made it out without the boys' efforts.'

Connor grunted. 'And no thanks?'

'Not a word.' Sophie shook her head. 'Course, they shouldn't have been here in the first place. Everyone who visits is supposed to check in. We're not a charity. There's no free camping allowed.'

'So how did they get across the river?'

She shrugged. 'Came in from the east on a station road, I expect. Probably shooters. There's hundreds of miles of old tracks on Binboona, put in for mining exploration back in the fifties. Hunters can sneak in and use 'em and be gone again before we know they're here. They come after pigs, buffalo – even crocs although they're protected. Of course we don't allow firearms,' Sophie said angrily, 'but it happens. We can't be everywhere.'

'No, of course not,' Connor touched a line on the map. 'This track here will get me across the river? I might poke down to the coast tomorrow. It's mangroves, I suppose – any beach at all?'

'Yep. East of the river mouth.' Luke showed him. 'I was there a day or two back, checking out a fire, so there's not much growing in this area here. But this long inlet to the east'—he tapped it—'wasn't burnt so there there should be plenty of vegetation. You looking for anything in particular?'

'Tree orchids – there are a few species native to the area,' Connor said. 'Then the general health of the flora, and any noticeable weed infestation, that sort of thing. There must be boats that come ashore from up in the Straits – half the country's environmental problems are carried to our shores by foreign boats. It's not only plants, of course – insects, reptiles . . . The Indonesian gecko, for instance, must've got here on a boat.'

Sophie nodded. 'We've plenty of them.'

'But what can you do about weeds?' Tilly asked. 'Once

they're established, I mean? You can't pull them all up – not thousands of them.'

'No, but if we know about them, the research johnnies can work on a possible solution. It's how the CSIRO beat the prickly pear back in the thirties. They found an insect that killed it off. That was well after it had invaded huge areas of grazing country and nearly wrecked an industry. These days we'd rather nip things in the bud.'

'Before they seed,' Tilly said.

His lips twitched, acknowledging the joke. 'Exactly.'

'Well, I expect you'll want your lunch then. Will you be camping or coming back?'

'I'll be back, I think – if that's no problem?'

'It's fine,' Sophie answered for her. 'Come and go as you need to, just let Tilly know about the meals.'

'Of course,' he said, 'and thanks. They'll be a treat. I get pretty sick of my own cooking.'

'The tucker's great here,' Matt said loyally then ducked his head, pretending a sudden interest in the map.

That evening Luke snapped off the television when the news ended and proposed a game of cribbage. Connor readily assented, though Matt, setting out his chessboard mutely, shook his head.

'What about you, boss?' Luke looked at Sophie, who shrugged.

'I suppose. I haven't played for years though. Join us, Till?'

Tilly declined. Cribbage had been Gerry's game, and she was suddenly, unbearably, reminded of winter nights in their old fishing shack with Francie in her cot, the wood stove warming the room and Gerry's handsome face alight over the cards as he cried, 'Eights the weight!' or 'Seven in heaven!' He knew all the calls and played with a fierce enthusiam she had loved but never matched. Swallowing, she shook her head. 'I won't, I think. I don't much care for cards.'

She had thought that would end it but Connor had turned courteously to enquire, 'Would you rather play Monopoly?' There was a set in the games cupboard that came out in the Wet when there were often full days to kill. He must have seen it when Luke got out the card pack.

'Oh, no.' She shook her head. 'Scrabble's better, but that's okay. I don't have to play.'

Luke groaned. 'Too slow, Tilly. We'll be here all night.'

Sophie grinned. 'You mean she's got a better vocabulary than you. Scrabble it is then.'

Trapped, Tilly temporised. 'Well, what about Take Two? That's quicker, and good fun. Like a crossword but played with the Scrabble tiles. You draw your letters and have to use them all up before you get any more. When someone does that, they say, "Take two", and everybody must. Every time a player uses all their tiles everybody gets two more. When they're all gone the first one to finish wins.'

'That's a new one,' Connor said. 'Where did you learn it?'

'My mum. We'd play of an evening when I was little, waiting for the boats to come in.'

'You can't have been that little if you could make crosswords,' Luke objected, and she pulled a face at him.

'Okay, so I was ten or twelve. And spelling was my best subject, smartypants.' She tipped the Scrabble tiles onto the kitchen table as she spoke. 'Turn them face down, then we shuffle them.'

'So what boats were they?' Connor asked. 'Where's home for you, Tilly?'

'Here,' she said. 'But I grew up in Victoria at Mallacoota. Dad had an abalone licence. When I was a kid we always seemed to be waiting on him to come home.'

'Ah. I've never had much to do with boats.' He flipped tiles with his long fingers. 'He still around, your dad?'

'He's got dementia,' she said shortly. 'Okay, we all start with seven tiles.' She drew hers towards her across the table. 'Turn them up – and go.'

It was as she had said, a good, fast game. For long moments the only sounds in the kitchen were groans of despair and the click of plastic being shuttled about, then Sophie cried triumphantly, 'Take two!'

'Jeez!' Luke complained, he had only three of his seven in place but he took another pair then cried, 'Hey! Hang about,' as Tilly, who had got an 'e' and an 'r' in her pick added them to an already formed word and immediately said, 'Take two,' again.

'Keep up, Luke,' Sophie encouraged with a grin.

Sophie won that game and Tilly the following one. Matt smirked at Luke as Connor congratulated her.

'It's practice,' she said dismissively, 'and knowing when to re-arrange.' She glanced at Luke's attempts and leant across. 'Like this.' Demolishing his first line she reset it, which left a blank tile and the letters 'n' and 'i'. 'There you go,' she said, arranging the three tiles above the 't' in 'tiller'. 'You can't afford to cling to words you've already made. Not if you've got leftover tiles. See?'

'Yeah?' Luke sounded unconvinced. 'What's "int" when it's at home?'

'Hint or pint. It's like Scrabble, the blank tile can be whatever you want.'

'Crazy game,' he said. 'Gimme cards any day. So, what's on for tomorrow, boss?'

Sophie snorted. 'You have to ask? We'll cart and saw firewood and get on with the whipper-snipping. That grass is tall enough to hide tigers in, let alone snakes. Which still leaves the river trail. Also the signs around the camp need touching up. The paint on some is so faded they're scarcely legible. We've enough paint left, I believe.'

'I could do that if you bring them back here,' Tilly offered. 'Or I could have a day out and go over there?' She felt a surge of energy as she spoke, the first in a very long time. It would be a change, a fresh experience in what she suddenly saw as her humdrum existence. How long was it since she'd last had an outing, time away from the old homestead and the endless round of little chores that filled her days? 'I'd like to,' she said firmly, and Sophie, as if recognising and approving the sudden resolution in her cousin's voice, nodded acquiescence.

'Good. Then the job's yours.'

# *Chapter Five*

The following morning, Tilly, cutting lunches for all of them, was stirred from happy anticipation of her plans by the realisation that she lacked transport. The other three would leave immediately after breakfast, Sophie in one four-wheel drive, and the two men in the other. She, however, had her own work at the homestead to attend to first – there were the usual kitchen chores, the animals and the garden, which meant she wouldn't get away before nine-thirty at the earliest.

'Perhaps I could take the motorbike?' she said doubtfully. But it was a temperamental beast of a thing that even Matt had trouble with, and the limited practice she'd had with bikes had been on sealed roads.

'Can you ride?' Luke asked. 'You hit a patch of bulldust with it and it'll stack you, sure as shooting.'

She sighed in frustration. 'Maybe I won't risk it. Damn! I was looking forward to going, too. I don't suppose you could wait for me?' But she knew as she asked that it was impossible. Any hour now their first campers could turn up and their custom was essential for the economic future of the sanctuary.

'It needn't be a problem,' Connor said unexpectedly. 'I can take my time. I'll wait till you're ready and drop you off at the camp. How far away is it?'

'Could you?' she said eagerly. 'It's only five kay. I could leave by nine-thirty. It's not going to muck up your day too much, is it?'

'No problem,' he said laconically. 'I'll wait. Give us a shout when you're ready.'

It was actually closer to ten before the last chore was done, Tilly having rushed through her preparations for the evening meal. The vegetables she'd diced for a stir-fry now rested in a covered bowl in the fridge and she'd whisked the junket recipe for icecream into trays, stirring a jelly one-handed as she rinsed off the milky utensils with the other. All that needed doing then was to pop a tin of peaches in the fridge and pick up her lunch.

'Ready,' she announced to Connor, who was finishing a cuppa at the table.

'You're not having tea?'

Tilly shook her head. 'That's okay. I've held you up long enough. Only I did want to get everything done. There'll be the animals to feed tonight, eggs to collect – all sorts of stuff to do when I get back.'

'Can't the others help you?' His glance had fallen on a thermos draining on the sink. He rose to pour the contents of the teapot into it, saying, 'You can have it later.'

'Oh, well, thank you. And no, they have their own work. Why should they do mine?' She lifted her chin. 'Sophie might be my cousin, but my job here is real. I pull my weight. I wouldn't stay otherwise. It wouldn't be fair on the rest of them.'

'Of course. I didn't mean to suggest—' He held the door as they emerged onto the verandah, abandoning the sentence. 'You come from Mallacoota, you say. However did you get this far north?'

'My husband was a fisherman,' she said reluctantly. 'We had a boat in the Gulf and a house in Cairns, but Gerry and I spent the winters out here until he died. Look, do you mind if we don't talk about it?'

'Sorry. I didn't mean to upset you. Well, here's the old boneshaker – hop in.' He shoved his lunch behind the driver's seat and handed her the foam box in which hers was packed. 'And the thermos. You can push it under the seat if you think you'll remember it.'

'Thanks. I will. You should have it, actually.'

'I'll be right. I've got a billy,' he said, engaging the gear. He waved an expansive arm. 'And there's any quantity of wood to boil it.'

'So long as you don't start a bushfire.' She smiled. 'Luke thinks the one where you're heading today probably got away from a boatie. You'd think the country would be too green but it still burns. Of course the grass shoots again immediately this early, but Luke worries about the little birds. The wrens and the finches and the like. It's nesting season for them now and they build in low bushes and shrubs – and they burn up in fires, you see.'

'Ah.' Connor nodded. 'I remember you said he was keen on birds.'

'Oh yes. He can name them all. He does the talks for the slide shows when the camp's full, and he takes the twitchers along the river walk in the early mornings. He keeps records for Birding Australia too. We all make notes of the birds that come to the basin for him. If he keeps up his studies he'll be a professor of ornithology one day – if there is such a thing.'

'And Matt?' Connor changed gears and quirked an eyebrow at her. 'What's his particular interest?'

'Oh, engines, I think.' Tilly mused. 'He's such a quiet man, you have to guess. But he knows the bush and he can fix anything. Binboona couldn't do without him, Sophie says.'

'And you, Tilly – do you plan on staying out here?'

They were coming up to the gate in the camp enclosure and he braked to a stop. She pulled at the stiff door latch and shrugged. 'Who knows?' He asked a lot of questions, she thought, lifting out her lunch and thermos. 'Thanks for the lift. This'll do me. I can hear them working from here. See you tonight.' Lifting the thermos in salute she turned her back and climbed through the gate. The dust rose under her feet as she padded down the road and the noise of the receding vehicle mingled with the throaty snarl of the whipper snipper up ahead.

Tilly had often visited the camp, which was fairly basic, although Sophie had spoken of plans to enlarge and upgrade it by providing cabins. As it was, it consisted of a large semi-cleared spot amid the scrub, dotted with camp sites. A road looped in a wide circle around them, and the ablution block stood in the centre of the space beside a wide shade roof over a concrete floor. There was a tank on a high stand, with a hot water donkey below it behind the shower rooms, next to a small heap of firewood. There were laundry tubs under an open-sided roof with a clothesline stretched beside it. Close to the gate next to another clearing was a weatherproof box where the visitors' log was kept, along with the various leaflets about the camp listing the birdlife and flora and a warning that the nearby Nutt River was home to estuarine crocodiles. A pile of indestructible old railway sleepers had been converted into bench seats near the box and it was here that a series of slideshows were shown through the season to entertain and educate visitors while spreading the conservation message and the importance of the work done by the sanctuary rangers.

Tilly found the vehicles with the Binboona logo on their doors parked beside the ablution block, Matt's already loaded high with a supply of wood for the water heater. It would be taken back to the homestead to be doled out daily to the camp, for as Sophie said, 'You can't get it through people's heads that it doesn't take a raging inferno to produce hot water.'

Looking around, she spotted Luke and her cousin, whipper-snippering in a cloud of grass stems and dust.They wore gloves and safety-glasses with bandanas covering their lower faces, and were working slowly outwards from the centre, the cut grass lying in patterns behind them. There was no sign of Matt. He was probably down at the river installing the pump: the laundry taps when she tried them were dry. Meanwhile, somebody had wrenched the signs from the ground and slung them in a heap under the laundry roof where she could work in the shade. The esky holding their lunches was also there, along with a plastic crate containing brushes, turps and paint tins.

Tilly found a rag to wet from the water container, scrubbed

the dust off the top sign whose faint lettering read '*To the river walk*' and, selecting her paint tin, settled to her task.

When the shadow of the roof stood squarely beneath it, the others joined Tilly in the shade, mopping sweaty faces and drinking hugely from the water canister. The silence after the racket of the petrol motors was bliss. The twittering of small birds fell busily into the stillness and the sudden caw of crows overhead was as loud as a shout. Matt returned silently out of the bush, a shovel on one shoulder and his boots caked with mud. The Nutt was perhaps a long stone's throw from the camp site and the pump floated on a raft tethered to the bank which, just there, was too steep and scrubby to access with a vehicle. The wet season saw the pump's removal to a shed at the homestead and its annual reinstallation, Tilly had gathered, was a difficult task. Matt sat down with a *whoof* of relief and Tilly passed him his lunch.

Sophie's head tilted as she listened to the rush of water hitting the tank bottom. 'Seems it's still working then?'

'Yep. Took a while to prime. Doesn't help there's a croc slide right beside where we put her in. Let's hope the noise scares the bugger off.'

Tilly gasped and looked quickly at the mud on his boots. 'You will be careful, Matt!'

He ducked his head, smiling his brief smile at her. 'Course.' He glanced at the painted signs propped against the tin wall. 'You've got a few done then.' It was like Matt to shift the conversation away from himself.

'Uh-huh. Connor dropped me off a couple of hours back.

He seems very keen on the place, doesn't he?' She looked at Sophie. 'Are there really tree orchids here? I've never seen any.'

'There are.' Her cousin nodded. 'Not that you'd notice them unless they were flowering. I've seen some at the springs up near the caves. Very ordinary-looking plants, hard to spot too, in that they grow high up in the fork of trees. When they flower you smell them long before you notice them. Their flowers are mostly small too.'

Tilly sighed. 'I'd love to see one. Are they rare?'

'Well, not common anyway. Connor'll have to cover a fair bit of country and he'll need good eyesight to find 'em.'

'He has binoculars.' Tilly folded her lunchwrap and stowed it away. 'And a very fancy-looking camera in his vehicle. Maybe he'll get some photos.'

'Yeah, of weeds,' Luke teased. 'The new invasion from the north creeping south to strangle the native born. Look out, Mitchell grass! You and your mates better head for the hills.'

She gave him a withering look. 'You wouldn't laugh if your precious birds were threatened by something from overseas.'

'Tilly's right,' Sophie said soberly. 'Disease, extinctions, infestations – it's what we're here to control, or stop if we can. Laugh if you like, Luke, but losing habitat starts with the flora. Connor's work is as necessary as ours.'

'He seems nice,' Tilly said, 'and very interested in you all. He was asking me lots of questions about you. I'm sure he could help you with your bird records, Luke. How many species are on the list so far?'

'One hundred and seventy-two. But I'm not claiming anything on his say-so until he's proved he knows the difference between a crow and a tree-creeper.'

'Well, you can teach him if he doesn't,' she said lightly. 'It seems like he'll be around long enough.'

By day's end the water tank was full, and Tilly had repainted all the signs. She spent the last hour with a pitchfork helping Luke clear the cut grass from the camp sites.

'Thanks,' he said when they'd finished. He took the fork from her hand to toss onto the vehicle tray, and gave a tired grin. 'Bet you didn't know what you were letting yourself in for by coming along today.'

'I've enjoyed it,' she said truthfully, wiping her sleeve across her damp face. She smelled of dust and sweat and her shoulders ached, but the day had been deeply satisfying. She was tired, yes, but she felt more alive than she had in a long while. 'I'll be sorry to get back to just cooking and cleaning again.'

'And people,' he reminded her. 'You'll be knee-deep before the week's out.'

'Yes, I suppose.' Sophie had phoned Bruce at Spadgers Creek the previous night telling him that the camp would be open this week. Bruce would remove the 'closed' sign from the noticeboard on the boundary and what would start as a trickle would soon become a flood of campers. 'When do you plan to release the possum?'

He considered. 'Might do it tonight – he's ready.'

'That's good.' Once the camping season began you needed eyes in the back of your head with the animals. People either wanted to love them to death or else put themselves in danger of attack. Wild animals bit and scratched, and even bottle-fed marsupials could turn on humans, while signs about trespassing and privacy were simply ignored. 'I suppose we can hang the joey bags in the laundry until they need to be out more, which only leaves the birds.'

He nodded. 'Good thinking. They can look out for themselves. You riding with Sophie?'

'I guess so.' Tilly stifled a yawn. Shower first, she thought, then start the garden sprays, feed the animals and ready the evening meal, which she'd follow up with an early night. Ranger work was exhausting.

Connor was back when they arrived home. They saw his vehicle first, then his lean figure seated on the verandah. He was using the binoculars to watch the segments of visible river where the water had changed to pewter in the failing light.

'Good day?' he asked as the women climbed the steps laden with lunch boxes and thermos, and to Tilly, he said, 'I made tea, and helped myself to the cake. I hope that's okay?'

'Of course,' she said. 'And I enjoyed the day. Can't stop to talk now though. Do you mind if I have first go at the bathroom, Soph?'

'Go ahead. I'll shower while you're getting dinner.' To Connor she said, 'So, you found your way about okay?'

'And back again, yep,' Tilly heard him reply as she hurried to her room. It was actually a little later than she had planned on. She yanked her clothes off, then stepped under the shower; she'd meant to wash her hair but it would have to wait. The hot water was bliss on her tired shoulders but she rationed herself to a few moments only before stepping out and drying off. The others would be just as eager for the bathroom so she pulled on a housecoat and sped to her room to dress, tutting in frustration when the hand reaching for her hairbrush encountered an empty space.

Tilly stared blankly at the dressing table, then discovered the missing item on the far side of the table. She must have put it there in the morning's rush, unusual for someone as set in her ways as she was. Gerry used to tease her about her little routines . . . Tilly banished the thought. This was no time for woolgathering. She felt with her toes for the flat sandals she'd left beneath the bed and tutted again, eventually getting down on her knees to locate them, pushed almost out of sight. It was always the same when one hurried, as if the universe was aware of your haste and determined to frustrate you.

Her seedlings had survived the afternoon's heat. Uncoiling the hose, she sprayed the beds then hurried across to the animal enclosure where Mickey greeted her with reproachful cries. 'I know, I know, but you're not actually starving. Besides, you could easily find your own,' she scolded. Unlike Harry, who stalked across to stand tall before her, spreading his wings demandingly, the missing half of his beak rendering what should have been a stately sight a pathetic one. With the joeys' bottles empty she was done, for the possum was going dinnerless. Being hungry would provide the impetus for him to leave when Luke released him later that night. Possums were like butcherbirds, she had learnt: they tended to know when they were on a good wicket and would hang around indefinitely.

As she rinsed her hands at the tap, Tilly took a moment to watch the early stars pricking out against the darkening sky. A full moon was rising and the regular pulse of the diesel drowned out the cries of the flying foxes flickering dimly above the treeline along the river. Light burnt in the windows of the homestead, spilling onto the verandah, and she could hear Luke and Matt wrangling good-humouredly over something on the news. Through the kitchen window she saw Sophie setting the table. They'd all be hungry. She hurried inside to start dinner.

# *Chapter Six*

Two days later the first of the season's campers turned up, motoring hesitantly into the compound to pull up beside the homestead. Everyone save Tilly was out for the day. She greeted the burly-looking man in thongs and t-shirt who hooked at his slipping shorts as he got out. She could see a woman's face in the passenger seat, and the faces of two tow-headed boys craning through the lowered window.

'Morning,' the traveller said, glancing around. 'We're looking for the camp.' He gestured back at the way he'd come. 'The sign said it was this way?'

'And so it is – just another few kay down the track.' Good-humouredly she went into her spiel. 'You've got no dogs or cats hiding in there? No nets, traps or firearms? Just the kids – oh, they're allowed.' She smiled at the man. 'If you'd just step into the office and sign in? It's a safety measure – we need to keep track of who's on the property.' She led the way to the minuscule office at the end of the verandah, took the camping fee and watched him scrawl his name, address and vehicle registration. 'That's great, thanks. You'll find a ranger down at the camp, and there'll be firewood at the site, hot water in the showers, and the ground has been cleared at the camp sites. Whenever there's enough of a crowd, we hold a slide night – usually weekly – and there're leaflets detailing the walks you can do. Okay?'

'What about fuel?'

'No chance,' Tilly said firmly, making a mental note to put the padlock back on the bowser. They left it off through summer as a matter of convenience, but this was only the first of the many enquiries she'd be fielding. 'What we have, we need.'

'Fair enough, I suppose. So the closest fuel'd be the Alloway Roadhouse back up the track?'

'That's right. Now'—she followed him out to point—'see the two sheds there? Drive between them and you're on the road that runs to the camp. I hope you have a lovely stay.'

'Thanks,' the man said. His wife smiled from the passenger seat and the closest boy called eagerly, 'Hey, Miss! Is it on the river? Can we swim?'

'It's not far,' Tilly replied, 'but it's full of crocs so you definitely can't. Not unless you want to be eaten.'

'Told ya,' his brother crowed, and a moment later the vehicle moved off. The rangers, Tilly thought, would reinforce the warning, and there were signs posted about the dangers. Thankfully, Sophie said that they had never had a death at the camp, though a German tourist had been taken on the Adelaide River the previous year. She shuddered, shutting her mind to her thoughts, and went to locate the padlock for the bowser.

*

Another two vehicles turned up the following day and then, overnight it seemed, the camp was in full swing. If Sophie or the men chanced to be home they saw to the travellers, and once even Connor, pumping petrol down near the shed, had a four-wheel drive coast to a stop beside him. Tilly, about to step outside, saw him hook up the hose and go across to talk to the driver. It seemed quite a long conversation. Ten minutes later he was still there, leaning against the vehicle, his right hand moving to illustrate some point. Then he shook his head and pushed himself upright while jerking a thumb towards the house. The vehicle made a U-turn, but instead of stopping, it drove off back the way it had come while Connor stood, hands on hips, watching it leave.

Curiosity got the better of her, and when the engine note faded, she crossed the lawn to speak to him. 'What was that all about? Were they lost, or was he after fuel?'

'Ah, Tilly.' Connor pushed the padlock closed and handed her the key. 'I didn't see you coming. No, they had a dog. I told 'em they couldn't take it into the camp and they were arguing the toss. It was a house pet, the woman said – it'd stay inside the tent, nobody would even know it was there. I told 'em it wasn't on and the rangers would throw them out. They saw reason in the end. Not before I got an earful though,' he added ruefully.

Tilly shook her head. 'Some people. Didn't they read the sign? Thanks though. If they argued with you, they probably wouldn't have listened to me.'

'Probably not.' He tipped his hat to scratch beneath it. 'I reckon that woman'd get stroppy with a charging rhino. Right, I'll be off then.'

'Where are you headed today?'

'Up river,' he said. 'I want to check the country around the escarpment. What can you tell me about the springs? I believe there're several somewhere near by.'

'Nothing,' Tilly confessed ruefully. 'Much as I'd love to see them, I've never been there. Luke says they're very pretty, lots of moss and ferns. He said there're fish in the springs – only small, but still fish. Probably lots of different plants too.'

'Every habitat has its own species,' he agreed. 'Okay, see you tonight.'

'Have fun.' She smiled, turning away.

Later in the morning, another vehicle's approach brought her out into the yard again, but it proved to be only Matt, returning from Spadgers Creek where he'd gone to pick up the store order the carrier had delivered there.

'Had your lunch yet?' she asked. 'I was just about to put the kettle on for mine.'

He shook his head. 'I was gunna eat but I got held up. Couple of tourists coming out from camp blew a tyre back a ways. I stopped to give 'em a hand. Thought I'd come on home to wash before I ate.' He held out his dirty palms. 'Dead useless, the bloke, and his girlfriend wasn't much better.'

'Ah, the ones with the dog. Connor turned them back. They must be illiterate too – the sign plainly says no pets allowed in camp. Connor says the woman abused him over it.'

'Yeah?' Matt followed her up the steps into the kitchen. 'I didn't see no dog, and she hardly opened her mouth. Neither of 'em were very chatty. Come from the south, he said.

Looked it, too. He'd still be fightin' the tyre if I hadn't turned up.'

'How strange.' Tilly wrinkled her brow. 'Maybe it was a small dog and you missed seeing it.'

'Must've been stuffed under the seat then.' He wet his hands at the sink and sprinkled Ajax liberally over them. 'The spare was under the load so we had everything out. Marvellous what them southerners carry.' He spoke the term scornfully and Tilly grinned.

'I'm one of them too, you know.'

'Yeah, well,' he said, suddenly absorbed in his hand washing. 'You're different. You fit in, like. I dunno why blokes like him even bother.'

'Well, they can't have been the ones Connor spoke to.' She dismissed the subject. 'So I must've missed seeing a vehicle. Damn! Okay, whenever you're ready. I've made the tea.'

They sat down at the table, Tilly with the salad she'd made herself and Matt with his sandwiches. He was usually such a silent companion that she seldom initiated conversation and was surprised to be dragged from her own train of thought by a unexpectedly personal question.

'When you was growin' up, Tilly, were you a happy kid?'

'Oh,' she said. She looked across at him, snub nose, brown eyes, ginger hair, a slight flush working its way over his face as if aware he was breaking some sort of protocol he'd set himself. His glance slid away from hers but he was obviously waiting for an answer. 'I suppose,' she said slowly. 'Why do you ask?'

'Just wondered, like. Only you never talk about it.'

'Well, neither do you. You've never said if you have siblings, or whether your parents are still alive. Are they?'

'There's just me. Orphan, I am. What about you?'

'That's sad. I'm an only too. My dad ran an abalone boat, though he went after rock lobsters too in season. He wasn't actually my father, I just called him Dad. He married my mother while she was pregnant, only he didn't know about that until after the wedding. He stuck around and looked after us, but he and I have never been close. I don't suppose you could expect it – she did deceive him, after all.'

'Yeah, bit rough on 'im,' he said slowly. 'Was he kind to you?'

Tilly considered the question. She had rarely analysed the relationship – it was as it was, and long before dementia had taken Les Williams' mind, she had given up trying to change him. 'He wasn't mean to me,' she said slowly. 'I was fed and clothed and schooled. He just didn't go the extra distance. I never got a hug from him. There were no treats or special outings. He never turned up for the school concerts. I suppose he saw me as a responsibility but I didn't really matter to him. He's got dementia now – hardly even knows my mum, never mind me.'

Matt put down his sandwich, face creased in a frown. 'She stayed with him, but? It sounds like he held it against her that she was up the duff and never said.'

Tilly shrugged, not liking the way he'd put it. 'I expect she was grateful. Back in the mid-sixties it was a big deal for an unmarried girl to get pregnant, especially a Catholic one. She was a convent schoolgirl, my mum. And she seems to love him – she never talked about it, but yes, I'm sure she cares for him. Without me I think they might have been truly happy. I left as soon as I could, and I don't go back much.'

'So you stay out here instead?' He eyed her consideringly. 'Don't you get lonely?'

'Location doesn't make any difference to that,' she said shortly. 'Anyway, enough about me. What about you, Matt – you're what, thirty-something? How come you're not married?'

His gaze slid away from hers again. 'I am. It were a mistake. We split,' he muttered.

'Oh.' Tilly could think of nothing more to say. In silence she chewed her last piece of carrot and gathered up her plate and cutlery. 'We're a sad pair then, aren't we? Will you be here for smoko?'

'Yeah.' He smoothed out the plastic that had held his lunch, then immediately crumpled it again, mumbling, 'Gotta get those stores unloaded,' and left without another word.

Tilly shook her head. Being an orphan might explain Matt's oddness, she supposed, and his shyness and reticence. She could see how what had perhaps been a defence brought about by loss could have grown into habit, like the way he had of never meeting a person's gaze full on. She had, she reflected, learnt more about him over the meal than in the previous eighteen months. Who would have thought he was married? Hard on the heels of that came the memory of him asking if she got lonely. She examined the thought: the only reason she could conjure up for him doing so was that perhaps *he* did.

A sudden suspicion wormed its way into her mind, and her hands stilled in the sink. But no, they were workmates, nothing else! Surely he couldn't be interested in her? She hoped uneasily that it wasn't so. It would make life here very awkward if she had to rebuff him. She needed this job and, besides, had nowhere else to go. She grabbed at the cutlery in the suds and felt the blade of a knife slice into her finger.

'Damn it all!' She snatched her hand back. It wasn't a deep cut. She watched the bright scarlet drops stain the soapsuds and sighed, overcome by a sudden gloom. The revelation, if such it was and not just vanity on her part, was nearly as unwelcome and troubling as the recent incursion of the police into her life.

An hour later, as if the stray thought had brought them, the police returned. Tilly had just overseen another camper's registration when the next vehicle pulled up behind her. She turned, smile in place, but the friendly greeting dried on her lips as she saw the driver's face.

'What are you doing back here? You can leave at once, Sergeant. I won't listen to another word of your absurd accusations.' With relief she saw Connor's vehicle approaching down the track and turned back to the house, hearing the police vehicle's door open behind her. He couldn't stop her, she told herself – he wouldn't dare lay hands on her.

David Burns didn't, speaking urgently across the vehicle body instead. 'Mrs Hillyer, I just want you to listen a moment. Please, it's important. Look, I'm sorry about the other day. I got hold of the wrong end of the stick, thinking you must be involved. If you would just give me five minutes of your time – that's all it will take.'

Connor arrived then. He must have read something of the situation through her body language, she thought, for he'd left his door open in his haste to come immediately to her side. 'Everything okay, Tilly?' And to the strangers, 'Who are you?'

'Police,' she said. Some of the tension drained from her now that she was no longer alone. 'If I've done nothing wrong, I don't have to talk to them, do I?'

'I can't see why you would,' he agreed.

'It's every citizen's duty to help the police,' the sergeant snapped. 'Who are you anyway?'

'Connor Doyle, botanist.'

Burns glared at him. 'Well, it's Mrs Hillyer's time I need, not yours. Five minutes, that's all, and then we're gone.'

'And if she doesn't want to speak to you?'

Burns drew in a long breath. 'Of course I can't force her. But I'm respectfully requesting a few moments of her time, that's all.'

'I am still here,' Tilly interjected. 'Not that I'm not grateful for your help, Connor.'

He rubbed his neck. 'Your decision, Tilly, but I suppose it can't hurt to see what he wants.'

She nodded brusquely. 'All right then. So what is it?'

The constable had got out of the cab and now passed a folder to his superior. He glanced at Tilly and then the homestead. 'Can we go inside for a moment?'

'No.' Hostility vibrated through the refusal. She would not invite them into her space, but the sun was very hot, which made her hesitate and relent enough to add grudgingly, 'You can come onto the verandah.'

The three men ascended the shallow steps with her, grouping themselves about the table there with Connor at her side. The sergeant opened the folder and dealt half-a-dozen photographs onto the cane table top. 'These men,' he said. 'Have you ever seen any of them before? With your husband, maybe, or around his boat? Or any of his mates' boats for that matter?'

Anger flared in her at the mention of Gerry, but she bit back a retort and stared at the pictures. They were glossy black and white blow-ups, some a little grainy and blurred, and she realised the subjects had been unaware of the photographer. Like in the cop shows on TV – a long-range lens and some undercover operator sneaking about. Then she gave a little gasp of surprise and blurted, 'That's our boat!' The lines were unmistakable and if they hadn't been, half the name was visible between the heads of the two men standing before it.

'Yes,' Burns agreed levelly. He didn't move but she felt him tense beside her. 'Do you recognise either of the men? Have you ever seen them before?'

'No. But I wouldn't. I never knew Gerry's crews. I rarely went out with him.' Except for that last fatal day that had started as a pleasure trip to the island and turned into a nightmare. Tilly thrust the thought away. 'There was a sort of camp on the river where all the crews bunked when they were ashore. He met them there, and after a trip he'd clean up there and have a drink with them, but he never brought them home. They were a rough lot, he said. Not fit company for his girls.' Her voice wobbled then, and she coughed fiercely to quell the emotion. 'Look, I don't know what you're trying to prove, Sergeant. My husband was a fisherman but I knew nothing about his business. Not even,' she added bitterly, 'that he was in debt and didn't actually own his own boat.' Her eyes swept over the spread of photographs. 'I've never seen—'

She stopped and leant to pick the last one up, a profile shot of a man wearing a baseball cap above a heavy brow and hooked nose.

'Yes?' Burns fairly vibrated beside her. 'You know him?'

'I think . . .' Tilly frowned, staring at the snap. 'I saw him once. We stopped at the Alloway Roadhouse for a cold drink and Gerry bought fuel. He – that man – was talking to him at the bowser. I saw him when I came back to the car for my bag. I'm sure it was him.'

'Did you hear any of their conversation?'

'No.' Tilly let the picture drop. 'He left before I got close enough. I asked Gerry who he was, what he'd wanted, but he was a stranger to him. Just some bloke looking for work, he said.'

'And this was when?'

Tilly furrowed her brow. 'Three – no, two years ago. Ninety-four, it was. Yes, early in the year because we were hauling the trailer. That's why we needed the extra fuel. We were bringing the gear up for the season. Three months before . . . before the accident.'

Connor said crisply, 'Okay, Sergeant, I think you've had your five minutes.' He picked up the photos, tapped them into a pile and handed them to Burns. 'It's a long drive back to town.' He nodded a dismissal, then held the screen door for Tilly. 'Would you like me to put the kettle on?'

She flashed him a grateful glance as the two officers, plainly unwilling to go, turned reluctantly to the steps. 'That's okay, thanks. Tea's my job.'

# *Chapter Seven*

In the kitchen they settled into their accustomed seats with the tea before them. Tilly left the fruitcake on the board she'd sliced it on and now pushed the whole thing Connor's way.

'Have something to eat. Thank you for getting rid of them. I don't like that sergeant. Last time he was here he was perfectly horrible.'

'He's been before? When was that?'

'Before you came.' Her blue eyes sparked in angry remembrance. 'He as good as accused me of colluding in faking Gerry's death. As if I would risk my child! And why would I anyway? I was so angry! Sophie threw him out.' Her knuckles whitened over the spoon she was gripping. 'He made it sound as if Gerry had done it on purpose – let her fall so he'd have an excuse to cut the runabout loose and take off, leaving Francie to drown . . .' She broke off gulping. 'He made me so furious!'

Connor's hand patted hers and withdrew. 'I'm sorry. Look, I'm a bit lost here, I don't understand any of this. Who's Francie?'

Tilly blinked away tears before they fell. 'Didn't they tell you?' But they wouldn't, she thought. Luke and Matt were too loyal, and Sophie would consider it none of his business. But he had backstopped her with the police, providing support when she needed it, so she found herself telling him about the accident in which she'd lost both daughter and husband.

He listened without comment and when she had finished said simply, 'I'm sorry.' There was nothing more you could say, she knew. The more appalling the event the fewer words there were to cover it.

'It was my fault,' Tilly said tiredly. 'I mean, if Gerry had watched her more closely it wouldn't have happened, but once it had, I was useless. If I'd bothered to learn about boats . . . but I've always hated them. Because my stepfather had one, I suppose. I didn't know what to do, how to put it in gear, or steer it. If I'd been able to go after them at once . . . But it was dark and the tide was running . . .' She sniffed and shook her head. 'I think of her, you know, out there in the dark, all alone, screaming for me. She'd have been so frightened . . . They never even found the runabout. She'd have perished if she didn't tumble overboard first, and with Gerry, drowned or taken by a croc—' She shuddered, then sighed deeply, face haunted, the blue-grey stare bent beyond the bright kitchen to a darker horizon.

Connor patted her hand again awkwardly, the fleeting touch unacknowledged. 'I'm sorry.' He seemed to feel the futility of the repeated phrase. 'I still don't get why the cops are involved, unless'—he gave a deprecatory cough—'your husband was fiddling his tax or something like that?'

'What?' Tilly gave a sad crack of mirth. 'That's funny, it

really is. Tax was the least of it. Gerry owed money all over. I had no idea. Some men came to see me – to threaten me actually. It turned out that the boat wasn't his. I had to sell it and our home in Cairns, and it still wasn't enough to cover his debts. Thank God my name wasn't on the business or I'd be liable for the rest. So no, I doubt he was cheating the tax man. Anyway, Gerry wasn't like that. His catch was legal, he was as honest as anyone else, so why they would even *suspect* . . .? That's what makes the whole thing so weird. And those photos? Why would Burns suppose I'd know anything about those men?'

'I don't know. Only you said it was your boat in the pic, didn't you? Maybe he can't find anybody else to ask. How many people live on the river?'

'Hundreds!' Tilly said tersely. 'Through the season, that is. Besides the regular commercial fishermen like Gerry, the place was always overrun with anglers, all trying to catch a barra. They never stay long and they change all the time, so whoever took those pictures was probably snapping grocers and mechanics and bank managers, not terrorists, if that's what Burns thinks they are.'

He frowned. 'Why would they be terrorists?'

'Well, terrorists, drug runners – I don't know. Whatever the flavour of the month in cop-land is, I suppose. Anyway,' she said, standing up, 'I have to get on.' She pushed her chair in, then paused in the act of turning away. 'I've been meaning to ask – have you found your tree orchids yet?'

'What? Oh, not yet. Well, there was one maybe, but it was pretty high up and branches were in the way. I couldn't get a clear view.'

'That's too bad,' Tilly said. 'When you find one, I wish you'd take a photo. I'd just love to see it. There were a lot of orchids in Cairns, but mainly the big showy ones – cymbidiums and cattleyas. They're lovely, of course, but it would be great to get a look at some of our native ones.'

'I'll have to see what I can do then. Payment for all the cake.' Connor raised his brows.

'Thanks.' She managed a wan smile. 'Orchids are my favourite flowers. Even the weird-looking ones.'

Sophie, learning of the sergeant's return, was annoyed. 'It amounts to harassment,' she said. 'I've a good mind to complain on your behalf.'

'No, don't. Burns sort of apologised for last time, and he left when Connor told him to. Really, Sophie, I'd rather just forget about it all. I don't think they'll be back. He wasn't asking about Gerry this time, but other men I'd never set eyes on, except for one – and I've no idea who he was, so there doesn't seem much point.'

'Well, if you're sure.' The militant light faded from Sophie's eyes. 'What are those drums out front?'

'Oh, they're planters. Matt cut a forty-four in half for me. Remember those flower seeds I got with the ration order? Well, the seedlings are finally up in their trays and that's where I'll be planting them out. Just to add a bit of colour to the place.'

Sophie shook her head. 'The wallabies will eat them, you know.'

'I'll put some netting round them.'

'Whatever. I suppose it might work. Luke's doing a slide-show tonight so I'll run his dinner down to him. Give me a shout when it's ready.'

'Is he coming home after?' Tilly asked.

'No, he took his swag this morning, and some baked beans for breakfast. He'll be right. There've been a few takers for the river walk tomorrow morning. He'll do that at first light, then come back.'

'Okay.' Tilly glanced at the sun; the days were shortening but she calculated that she still had time to barrow a load of dirt into the drums before the start of the evening chores. Tomorrow she would transplant the seedlings, and then it would only be a few weeks before the blooms appeared – supposing she could find and rig up some netting to protect them. Sophie was right: the wallabies were drawn to anything green and there was no fence to stop them. Still, she was optimistic as to her chances. It was truly amazing what could be found in the old station sheds.

The following day, having found some rusting wire mesh, she was obliged to pause in her work of erecting it when a vehicle pulled up behind her. Sucking a pierced finger, she went across to see them, only to find them rolling away from her approach.

''S'okay,' the driver called breezily. 'Between the sheds, right?' A patterned shirt sleeve showed in the window and she glimpsed a cadaverous face with pale eyes and acne-pitted cheeks. He waved airily and sped off.

She had time only to register the vehicle's colour and catch the briefest glimpse of its passenger's profile before it accelerated away. She called, 'Stop! Wait!', running a few steps after it, but the engine drowned out her words and she came to a stand, staring after it as its speed picked up, her heartbeat gradually returning to normal as the dust of its going subsided.

'Not ones to hang around,' Connor observed. Tilly jumped and gasped at the unexpectedness of his voice behind her. 'Sorry,' he apologised. 'They're in a bit of a hurry, aren't they?'

'Yes.' She turned, a hand pressed to her chest, wondering if she was going mad. 'You startled me. I thought you'd gone.'

'I reckoned I'd lend a hand with that, first.' He nodded at the stiff coils of netting. 'You seemed to be having a bit of trouble. What are you trying to do with it?'

Tilly grimaced as she pulled herself together. 'Well, thanks for the *trying*. I thought it would be easy enough, but it isn't. I've just transplanted my flowers. I want to rig something up to keep the wallabies off them when they grow. They swarm the place in winter, keeping the grass down *and* anything else they can get their teeth into. It's good, really, the boys only have to mow through summer. But it makes it a bit hard to grow stuff.' She was babbling, but it seemed the only way to control the sick thumping of her heart. Because, her brain told her, she couldn't have glimpsed what she thought she had. It was quite impossible and yet . . . She shut down the thought and concentrated on the present.

'Right.' Hands on hips, Connor regarded the problem. 'First, you need some fencing pliers, and some wire. Where'll I find that?'

She showed him where the tools were kept. He sorted through them until he found what he wanted, then watched anxiously as he waded through rusting coils on the old wire dump to one particular lot. 'There could be snakes,' she called.

'There's some perfectly good wire here, right on the edge. Won't that do?'

'Wrong gauge,' he said elliptically, carrying on. When he had what he needed, they returned to the roll of netting at the steps where he quickly fashioned two cylindrical cages about the drums, securing them by means of several short lengths of the wire doubled over the bottom of the netting and hammered into the ground.

'That should do it,' he said testing the structure with a good shake.

'Thank you, Connor.' Tilly looked ruefully from the finished work to her inadequate hands. 'I'm afraid I'm useless with tools.'

'So "mechanic" isn't listed in your work resume?' He lifted an eyebrow.

She laughed derisively. 'You have to be joking! No, I tried a few things during my backpacker period. Worked in a cinema, and a greengrocer. Even picked tomatoes once, at Bowen back in Queensland – that's a terrible job. Never again!'

'Why's that?'

'The smell. It's just tomatoes, but it's overpowering when it comes by the truckload. It must have been two years after I left before I could bear to eat one again.'

'Bowen, eh? I've been there. Is that where you met your husband?'

'No, that came later, further north.'

It had been at the Cairns markets. She could see herself now, legs bare in her pencil-strap sundress and floppy yellow hat, gazing at the piles of exotic fruit. She'd bought feijoa, guava, rambutan and two mangoes, not even knowing which part of them you ate but determined to find out. As she turned from the stall, the bottom of her calico hold-all had parted, spilling its cargo onto the ground. She'd tutted crossly and a voice behind her had said, 'Whoops! I've got it,' and its owner helped her pick it up. 'I'm Gerry,' he'd announced, before masterfully inverting the bag and fixing the hole with a length of twine from his pocket.

'It'll pull out,' she had demurred, stunningly aware of his extreme good looks and lithe, suntanned body.

'Not if we eat a couple first,' he'd replied. So they had done so, sitting at a picnic table under the palms amid the flowering hibiscus and bird of paradise bushes, with the blue heave of the sea beyond. He carried a stock knife in a pouch on a plaited belt and had sliced the cheeks from a mango: her first taste of the golden ambrosia known as the queen of fruits, and the first incipient stirrings of attraction. She had never been in love before . . .

Tilly blinked, mourning for that lighthearted younger girl in her weightless summer frock with life's promise still unfilled before her. 'Well,' she said, pushing the memories away, 'thanks muchly, Connor. Now I'd better let you get on. Don't worry about them,' she said as he bent to retrieve the tools and leftover wire. 'I'll put them back.'

'It's fine. I'm going that way anyhow. And it was a pleasure, Tilly.' He headed for the shed and finally she was free to retreat indoors. Her sense of shock had lessened and her heart had quietened, because of course she was mistaken. Half a second, maybe less, wasn't long enough to identify anyone, especially someone whose face had been in profile and turning away at the time. Still, rooted before the basin, repetitively washing her hands, Tilly couldn't forget the unpleasant sensation in her chest as the vehicle had sped off before she could address the passenger – whose half-averted profile, she had to admit, had been a dead ringer for Gerry's.

# *Chapter Eight*

The following day, contrary to Sophie's expectations, Luke didn't return to the homestead until late afternoon. Tilly, occupied with her own thoughts, failed to notice his absence until she was sitting down to her sandwich lunch. Due to the nature of their work, the rangers were often late so she thought no more about it, and when he eventually turned up just on sunset, she greeted him with a question. 'I expect you must be starving?'

'Hmm?' He blinked as if woken from a dream. 'Oh, hi, Tilly. What did you say?'

'I asked if you're hungry.'

'Not really. I had a cuppa at the camp. And lunch too, so that's fine. Look, do you think you could cut my hair tonight? It's a bit shaggy, don't you reckon?'

Tilly was a little surprised, for this was normally Sophie's task carried out on a Sunday, but she considered the question. 'I expect so, if you're happy with short back and sides?' She had regularly cut Gerry's hair and that of any of the fishermen who had asked while they had been in the camp. 'It'll be hand clippers though, nothing fancy.'

'That's fine. Sophie,' he confided, 'does a sort of pudding basin job. I thought you might make a better fist of it. Just not too short, please. It'd be great if you could do it after tea.' Seeming to feel the oddness of the urgency, he added lamely, 'It's driving me mad at the moment.'

'Okay, then.'

When the washing up had been done, Tilly took a sheet from the linen chest and told Luke to bring a chair out onto the verandah. Moths were circling the light bulb and the breeze from the river nipped at her bare ankles as she parted his dark hair and pinned a section of it up.

'What are you doing?'

'Checking for nits,' she teased, 'and dandruff. Thankfully you don't seem to have either. So, how short do you want it?'

'I'm beginning to think this was a bad idea,' he said. 'Look, nothing too drastic, eh Tilly? More a tidy up, like.'

'Don't worry, I've done this before. Since when have you worried about your appearance anyway?'

'Well, a feller doesn't want to look a freak,' he grumbled.

'Your birds won't mind,' she said lightly as she combed and snipped, then the penny dropped as she made the association. 'Oh, so that's why you were late home! How long is she staying?'

The back of his neck reddened, then he laughed. 'This is your famous female intuition, is it?'

'Huh-uh. This is a young man acting out of character – it can only mean you fancy some girl. Don't worry, your secret's safe with me. How about I put some extra cake in tomorrow's smoko? You could ask her to share it then.'

'That'd be great. Not that I'm saying . . . I just like your cake, Tilly.'

'Course you do. Right, keep still if you value your ear.'

The following morning, as Tilly handed Connor his thermos and packed lunch, he surprised her by asking, 'D'you ever get a day off? I'm heading down to the coast today. I wondered if you'd like to come for a drive?'

'Well, I'd love to,' she said regretfully, eyes turning to the tiny office on the verandah, 'but I can't. I have to be here to check in the visitors.'

'Ah, I forgot about that. Pity. I was looking forward to the company.'

'You can have it.' Sophie looked up from the sink where she was sterilising the joeys' bottles. 'Go on, Till. You haven't had a day off since your last trip into Darwin. I'll be here. No reason I can't book them in.'

'Are you sure? Well, thanks, Soph. Oh, wait a minute – what time do you think we'd be back? Because there's dinner . . .'

Connor considered. 'Mid arvo-ish. That suit you? We could make it earlier if you wish.'

'No, no, that'll be fine. I'll just make my lunch and grab a hat. Five minutes, no longer.'

'Take your time.' He settled his hip against a corner of the range and began leafing through one of Luke's magazines as she reached for the sandwich makings she had only just put away.

*

The drive to the coast was neither quick nor smooth going, but Tilly thoroughly enjoyed it. The novelty of a morning free of chores, and the changing scenery as the track led them north from the palm-fringed river country through the paperbark forests to the coastal flood plains, kept her interest piqued. The road was dreadful: they bumped and jerked their way over stony ledges and gutters, through drifts of ashy sand where the paperbark trunks stood like sentinels blocking her vision, to the bone-hard jolting of the bulldust patches where the pale dust rose like fog behind them.

'Sorry about the road.' Connor grimaced as the wheels fell into a hole concealed beneath deep bulldust.

'Heavens, it's not your fault. You get used to it, anyway. Not that I've been on this one before,' Tilly added truthfully.

'So you don't have much opportunity to get away from your base?'

'Not through the season. And when the tourists stop coming, it's either too hot or too wet for unnecessary travel. I've been out once or twice late in the year with the rangers when a fire's come in close to the homestead, but that's at night, and country I'm familiar with.' Tilly drew in a satisfied breath. 'This is all different.'

'You really like the bush then?'

'I do now. The first time I came out to the fishing camp at McArthur I was petrified. I worried about snakes, of course. And crocs. And the sheer *bigness* of it all. The land seemed so empty. Well, it is,' she admitted fair-mindedly, 'but I came to see that it wasn't necessarily a threat. I mean, the sky is big, and I suppose a meteorite could fall out of it and kill you, but it's not like it would be on purpose, is it?'

'Of course not.' A smile tugged at his lips. 'So you're saying you regard the bush as a passive entity, not an aggressive one?'

'Mmm – maybe "indifferent" is a better word. It's been here forever. When you think that those rocks,' she pointed as they passed an outcrop of boulders, their surfaces pitted by weather, 'would've been lying there when William Dampier was stooging around the north coast – well . . .'

'Or even when the pyramids were being built,' he suggested. 'You're right. As a species we haven't really made much of an impression on this bit of the earth's surface – a few tracks that half-a-dozen monsoons would swallow up as if they'd never been. A pristine canvas. Just as it was, in fact, before the first white man set foot on this country.'

'Well, I hope our work means a bit more than that!' Tilly protested. 'We're here to protect the wildlife. The land couldn't sustain itself without its birds and animals, you know.' She caught herself. 'Sorry, I was forgetting that you're a botanist, and know all about the interrelated chain of . . . Dear me, I'm beginning to sound like one of Luke's lectures!'

'That's all right. Those who believe in what they're doing have a right to be passionate. So, does Matt lecture too? Somehow he doesn't strike me as the type.'

Tilly smiled. 'I think he'd sooner cut his tongue out! No, Matt's better with his hands than his voice. He's our fixer – everything from the radios to the vehicles. I think he grew up on a farm, but that's just an impression. He never talks about himself. I've always assumed he had an unhappy childhood – only because he was asking me about mine,' she added quickly, 'so I could be quite wrong about that.'

'And was yours happy?'

'That's what he asked too. Why's everybody suddenly interested in my past?'

Connor shrugged. 'Just making conversation. You all seem to mesh quite well together, though you're obviously all different. Is that hard – living as isolated as you all do, I mean?'

Tilly shook her head. 'Not really.' She pondered the matter, squinting a little, eyes thoughtful as she considered her answer. 'It hadn't crossed my mind before, but we all give each other space. That's probably why it works. That and having our own interests. Sophie's passionate about the job, Luke's got his birds, and Matt his tinkering and his chess.'

'And what about you, Tilly? What keeps you going?'

Sensing his genuine interest, she tried to answer honestly, though the question was closer to the bone than she liked. 'I think it's knowing they all care about me,' she said slowly. 'Sophie's more like a favourite aunt than a cousin, but the boys have sort of adopted me as – well, a sister, I suppose. It's been'— she searched for a word that fell somewhere between 'hard' and 'devastating' to describe the past two years— 'difficult, you know.' *Once*, her heart mourned, *once upon a time* . . . She shook the memories aside, saying, 'They've been there for me from the start. Like family. So,' she added, firmly changing the subject. 'What about you? Where did you grow up, and were *you* a happy kid?'

'I was a lucky one.' Connor swung the wheel to skirt a fallen branch. 'I'll shift that on the way back. My father died when I was a nipper, but my grandfather filled the gap. He was pretty young still, and as I was only three when my father went, and Gramps lived in the next street, I just transferred the bond I'd had with my dad to him. He turned up for everything – birthday parties, footy practice, parenting night, the time I got into trouble at school . . . Most of the kids thought he was my father.'

'And your mother never remarried?'

'Nope. Dad was her one and only, she always said.'

'That's sad,' Tilly observed. 'What did your grandfather do?'

'For a living? He was a nurseryman.' Connor grinned. 'I was potting plants by the time I was ten. It was a fun way to fill the weekends, till I got older. It sucked a bit then, of course, I had other interests, but I never got over my fascination for plants.'

She nodded. 'Yes, our interests broaden as we grow, and teenagers rebel. But you obviously came back to it?'

'Mmm. I took biological sciences at university and majored in botany. I've never regretted it.' He pointed ahead where the suddenly sandy track curved through tall, clumpy grasses and low scrub. 'The coastline's just through there. Fancy a stroll along the beach?'

# *Chapter Nine*

The Gulf was flat, the tide out. Pausing where the sand began, Tilly drew in a lungful of warm, salty air and scanned the wide, curving bay whose shores were as flat as the distant sea. Sunlight winked on wet sandbars and the shallow channels between them where sea-water lingered. There was no breeze. Insects buzzed amid the stalky grass clumps and the hardy convulvulus vines sprawling over humps in the sand. The wind must build them, she thought vaguely; there seemed no other way to account for their existence. On the horizon, sea and sky met so closely she had to blink to tell the difference.

'Well, I can't see that many boaties would get in here,' she observed. 'You could wade out for miles, it's so shallow.'

Connor shook his head. 'There'll be spots where it's deeper. Channels to navigate. In any case, not everything that comes has to be physically brought. See that tree?' He turned and waved inland at the broad dark shade of a substantial-looking tree with a girth far larger than Tilly's arms could encompass. 'Its seed probably got here the same way that mangroves and coconuts do – brought by the sea itself.'

'Really?' Tilly wandered back for a closer view. 'It must be old to be so big. What is it?'

'A tamarind. From somewhere in Asia.' He assessed its size. 'Could be over a century since it grew its dicots.'

'Its what?'

'First pair of leaves. They're called cotyledons, but if there are two, and there are in this instance, they're called dicots.'

'Oh,' Tilly said. 'Okay, Mr Botanist. A century – really? I didn't think anything lived that long in the north. A case of quick growth and early death, like poincianas and wattle and – other stuff,' she ended lamely, temporarily unable to name more. 'I don't know much about plants,' she confessed.

'Still, you grow a mean garden. Anyway, I'm starving. What about lunch? I'm thinking that shade looks pretty good.'

'Yes, I'm hungry too. I'll fetch it,' she said as he moved towards the track. 'You go look for your unwanted immigrants.' His eyes flickered, not catching the reference, and she laughed gently at his mystification. 'Your foreign weeds, Connor. We can't have them taking over, can we?'

'Not on my watch,' he agreed.

It was pleasant in the shade. The ground beneath the tamarind was bare and one exposed root made a comfortable place to sit. A myriad of small green pods covered the tree and Connor pulled one off, breaking it open to show Tilly the half-formed seeds.

'You can make a paste from it. They use it a lot in Asian cooking,' he said. 'This one's immature, but when the pods are ripe the insides are quite pleasant to chew. A bit astringent.'

'Oh yes, I remember trying it,' she said. 'There are lots

of Asian restaurants in Darwin and Cairns, and Gerry loved eating out.'

'Darwin, eh? My favourite town. Did you spend much time there?'

'Just quick visits. Gerry would mostly sail the boat across through the Straits, then I'd fly to Darwin and he'd pick me up. Sometimes, if there was gear to bring in, we'd drive. And then do the reverse when the season ended. He wouldn't leave the boat up here through the monsoon.'

'Too risky,' Connor agreed. 'These are great sandwiches. You weren't a chef, were you, in one of those fancy Cairns eateries?'

Tilly smiled. ''Fraid not. I didn't train for anything. I guess you learn what you have to, to get by. And I enjoy it – like you enjoy plants.'

'Well,' he said, wadding the plastic wrap from his sandwiches and draining his cup, 'maybe we ought to be starting back. I've a couple of creek banks I need to check out on the way. And I don't want to make you late. It's been nice having company though.'

'I've enjoyed myself,' Tilly replied, getting up, 'despite the road! I think I'll have a dig at Matt about it. He's in charge of the grader.'

'A man of many parts,' Connor quipped. 'Anything he doesn't do?'

'Not much if it's mechanical. If he'd finished high school, I'm sure he could've been an engineer. Or maybe an inventor. Binboona would be lost without him. Sophie says so, and she ought to know.'

*

Connor didn't hurry their return. They stopped twice beside the banks of steep, narrow creeks still trickling with wet season run-off. Growth along them was vividly green in contrast to the russet and gold of grasses on the flats.

'You'd think they'd have dried up by now,' Tilly said. 'Nothing's fallen from the sky since the start of April.'

'It's seepage water, coming from the higher ground,' Connor explained. 'The country's a sponge, so it takes some draining when the rains finally stop. Ah,' he said with satisfaction, 'I thought there was a chance . . .'

'What?' She stared around at the rampant growth, wary of snakes.

'Look up. Hang on while I grab the glasses.' He brought them from the vehicle and offered them to her. 'In the fork of the ti-tree there – what do you see?'

She focused the binoculars, saying, 'I can't . . . oh, yes, I've got it. Wait! That's not an orchid, is it? There's not much to it.'

'It's showier when it flowers, though still pretty hard to spot. It's a dendrobium. They call it the Onion Orchid because of the little bulb it grows. You'll have to come back later in the year though to see it in bloom. Round late August should do it.'

'Well, thank you, Connor.' Tilly handed the glasses back. 'I didn't expect you to go out of your way to find one for me, though. I suppose a photo wouldn't be possible? You can barely see it with the naked eye.'

'I'm afraid not. I'll just have a quick squiz a little way up the creek. Moving water can spread a lot of seeds. If you'd rather wait in the vehicle . . .?'

Eyeing the long grass and the saw-edged fronds of

pandanus, poking out like green spears, Tilly agreed. Waiting, she squinted up again at the growth in the tree hollow. A couple of leathery looking shoots were all that was visible. She'd never have noticed it, but botanists, she supposed, knew where to look. It was warm in the vehicle; no breeze blew and the silence was broken only by the drone of flies. She watched a dragonfly with azure wings hover above a weed and pushed the hair back from her face. Connor was taking a long time. Tilly stared along the creek but there was no sign of him returning. Bored, she flipped the catch on the glove box, finding the usual stuff: vehicle manual, tyre gauge, a stubby pencil, a torch, a crumpled box of tissues, and a slim handbook on northern orchids. That would do. Opening it, she settled to read until Connor returned.

Their second halt was much briefer, and as Connor had promised her, Tilly was home by mid-afternoon. He dropped her at the front steps, then drove off to refuel and garage the vehicle. Sophie, coming out of the office, relieved her of the thermoses.

'Did you have a nice day? See anything interesting?'

'We found an orchid.' Tilly dumped her lunch box on the table. 'Well, a handful of dryish-looking leaves in the fork of a tree, actually, but still an orchid. Connor said they flower later in the year. What about you – many visitors?'

'Yep. The camp's full. I've rung Bruce, asked him to change the sign. I thought we had one more camp site, but turns out it was occupied. You must've missed one.'

Guiltily, Tilly remembered. 'Yes. I meant to tell you. There were a couple of men who drove straight through. Well, they sort of stopped, then took off again when they saw me. I was going to let you know.' Only she had been so shocked by that brief glimpse of the passenger that she'd forgotten to keep track of the numbers. Apart from safety concerns and camp fees, that was what the compulsory registration was all about. Shamefaced, she said, 'I'm sorry. Did you have to turn someone back?'

'Yes. Luckily Luke was at the camp when they arrived there. I have to say they weren't pleased.'

'I imagine not.' It was a forty kilometre drive into Binboona from the station road and another five to the camp. 'I'm really sorry, Sophie.' Tilly considered explaining but the imagined sighting would only worry her cousin who, she was aware, closely monitored her emotional wellbeing.

'Oh well. Perhaps we need a gate between the sheds. People are generally good, but there's always one. I'll get Luke to check which rego we haven't got and have a word with the driver. We should really have the right to levy fines, but that would raise a scream, I suppose. Do you need a hand with anything?'

'I'm all organised thanks,' Tilly said gratefully. 'And thanks for the time off, Soph. I really enjoyed it.'

Her cousin's weather-beaten face broke into a smile. 'I'm glad, Tilly. High time you had a bit of pleasure in your life.'

Luke must have made his point with the guilty camper, for he was full of remorse the following day when he pulled up before the homestead and clumped up the steps to the office. Tilly, drying her hands she'd snatched from the sink, appeared as he reached the verandah.

'Yes? Can I help you?'

'Just come to apologise,' he said gruffly. 'The ranger bloke said you have to log in when you come. Didn't realise. Also, I thought the camping was free. Sorry about that. So I'm here to pay up, and to log in before we leave. You want I should do it now?'

'Oh.' She had instantly recognised the acne-scarred face, and craned her neck to see the passenger who, suddenly aware of her presence, leant forward and waved. She stared bemused at the young tow-headed man whose lips, as if conscious of her observation, were twitching into a tentative smile. 'What?' she said, then recovering, 'Right. Yes – pay and sign in. I'll get the book. Better late than never, I suppose.' She must be losing her mind, she thought uncertainly. How could she possibly have imagined . . .?

The man was still talking as he pulled out his wallet while she patted the desks distractedly in search of the pen. 'The point is,' she interrupted severely, then lost the thread of what she'd started to say. She saw him looking at her and strove to collect her wandering thoughts. 'What you did – it leads to . . . I mean, the fees apart, we need to keep track of how many campers we have. Yesterday someone drove all the way in here and we had to turn him away, because my boss didn't know that your camp site was taken. It cost that poor man ninety kilometres of travel and now he probably has a very poor opinion of the place.'

'Yeah, well, I'm sorry. Never thought . . . It won't happen again.'

'Good.' She couldn't, Tilly supposed, keep chastising him. In a friendlier voice she asked, 'So, where are you from?'

'Huh? Oh, Mackay, North Queensland.'

'I know it. What about your mate?'

'Further south. Right, that it?' He laid down the pen and settled his rather grubby felt hat more firmly into place. He had a growth of dark stubble, a prominent nose, muddy brown eyes presently examining the office, and copious body hair, judging by that on his sunburnt arms and the dark mass showing in the open neck of his cotton shirt.

'Yes, thank you.' Tilly stepped back from the door and let him precede her to the steps. She cast a last puzzled look at the pair of them as the vehicle pulled away, then returned to her work at the sink. She'd obviously suffered some sort of amnesiac attack if she couldn't even remember her dead husband's appearance. It *was* the same vehicle, the man had admitted it. Which meant . . . what? She was losing her marbles? The passenger had been the very antithesis of Gerry – younger, fairer, totally different.

Drying off her hands, Tilly marched back to the office and checked the book just to be certain, but the registration the man had entered matched none of the other vehicles logged into the camp. It was official then: she must be so stressed that she had begun seeing things. Thank God she hadn't said anything to the others or they'd be making her a reservation at the nearest funny farm.

Later that afternoon, Matt returned to the homestead with another load of firewood, which he tossed off into the compound behind the shed. Tilly, feeding Harry his dinner, greeted the man as he walked past carrying the chainsaw.

'Good day, was it? Looks like they're having a run on the hot water.'

'The donkey's workin' overtime,' he agreed. 'There's some of the buggers want morning showers, some evening ones, and they're giving the tubs a fair workout too.'

'Where's Luke?'

'Slide night.' He shrugged. 'I reckon he'll stay at the camp. That bird of his is leaving tomorrow.'

'Oh, poor Luke. What's she like?'

He grunted. 'Young. Legs and shorts. More of her on show than not.'

Tilly sighed. 'Really, Matt! You can do better than that. Is she pretty? Have you talked to her? Where's she from?'

'I dunno, never asked. Not as pretty as you,' he said deliberately, his gaze immediately sliding off hers.

Willing him not to say more, Tilly said lightly, 'Well, thank you. By the way, that chap Luke chipped about not stopping? It had an effect – he pulled in this morning before leaving and apologised. Signed the book too. A bit late, but still.' She tossed the last cube of meat, saying, 'That's it, my feathered friend. No more till tomorrow.'

Matt stood there watching her leave. She grimaced as she went, feeling his gaze on her all the way back to the steps.

# *Chapter Ten*

The following morning, with the grey light barely showing in the east and before the earliest bird had uttered a sound, a vehicle roared between the sheds and pulled up by the homestead. Tilly was awake but relishing the last fifteen minutes in the warmth of her blankets. Pulling a robe around her and with only her bedsocks to cushion her feet from the freezing vinyl, she hurried to the kitchen just as Luke erupted into it.

'Luke! What on earth . . .?' Gazing beyond him, she saw he'd left the Toyota running, lights on and with its driver's door swinging open, the logo on it catching the light spilling from the kitchen window. 'Something wrong?'

'It's Jane.' His eyes were wild. 'She's in a bad way. Her dad's bringing her in. Ring the flying doctor.'

'Right, of course, but I have to know what to tell him. What's happened and when?'

'Christ, what difference does when make?' he bellowed. 'She needs a doctor. Like, now!'

'All right, settle down, Luke.' An air of calm entered the room with Sophie. 'You're not helping by yelling. Tilly's right.'

She scooped her hair back from her face and finished tying the cord on her dressing gown. 'First we need to see her. Is that them now?' Lights cut through the crepuscular dawn as the second vehicle pulled in. 'What's the patient's name and age? He'll want to know that.' She'd pulled the pad from beside the phone and poised a pen over it.

Luke groaned, gritting his teeth as he raised and lowered his hands. 'It's Jane. Jane Wellaway. She's nineteen. Her father woke me, said she was having trouble breathing. Her face is all swollen, and so's her right arm. She's sorta drooling, like she can't swallow and she's been sick. I think something bit her. There looks to be a mark on her hand – there's a lump there, like a really big one, hard as a rock. I put a pressure bandage on her arm, just in case.' He swallowed, suddenly looking very young and frightened. 'If it's snakebite . . .'

'We don't know that,' Sophie said briskly. 'Could be a scorpion.'

Tilly ran to hold the door open as a partly bald man, wearing shorts and a t-shirt, with a strained look on his weathered face and his arm around a young woman's shoulders, half-carried her into the room.

'Here.' Luke seized a chair. 'Put her here, Don. How is she?'

'As you see.' The girl seemed hardly conscious. Her limbs flopped loosely and her head drooped, a thin stream of saliva issuing from her lips. The man wiped it up with a handkerchief, speaking softly to her, then looked at the women. 'Please – she needs medical help.'

'We're getting it,' Tilly said soothingly. Sophie had dialled and was stretching the phone cord to allow the fingers of her other hand to grasp the girl's limp wrist. Eyes on the clock, she waited for the doctor to come to the phone, lips moving silently as she counted. The affected arm was dreadfully swollen, Tilly saw, and the visible area of the girl's face was puffy.

The pulse taken, Sophie made a note and nodded at Luke. 'Get Matt or Connor up. Somebody needs to check the airstrip. One good thing, it'll be sun-up soon so we won't need the flares.'

'I can do that.' Luke started for the door.

'No,' Sophie said firmly. 'One of the others. In your present state you could drive over a buffalo without seeing it.' Turning her head back to the phone, she began to speak. 'Morning, doctor. Sorry for the early call. We have a patient for you – a tourist, Jane Wellaway, aged nineteen. She's presented in a semi-conscious state . . .'

Luke left, and a few minutes later Matt appeared fully dressed, passed through the kitchen without a word and drove off in the former's vehicle. Connor arrived next, also clothed.

'I heard the racket. What's up?' he murmured to Tilly, who was filling the kettle at the sink.

She nodded at the girl and her father. 'They're from the camp. It's Luke's friend – she's been bitten in the night.' Suddenly realising that she was still in her pyjamas, Tilly slipped away to pull on jeans and a fleecy top, and exchange her bedsocks for footwear. Then, remembering the Wellaways' state and the chill of the kitchen, she took a soft blanket from her bed to swathe about Jane and asked Luke, returned and waiting fretfully for the phone call to end, to find a jumper for Don.

'One of mine'll be a better fit,' Connor said, eyeing the

young man's rangy body. He fetched a rollneck pullover, then began prosaically pulling plates and cutlery from their shelves and drawers to lay the table.

'Thanks,' Tilly said. 'I see your wife has you well trained.'

'I'm not married, but some men *are* house-trained, you know,' Connor said mildly. 'We're not all slobs.'

'Of course not,' she agreed hurriedly.

'Okay.' Sophie put the phone down and turned to Don. 'They're on their way. The doctor thinks the swelling sounds more like an extreme allergic reaction to something – a scorpion or centipede, maybe even a green ant – than snake venom. He said if she's conscious enough to swallow, we could try giving her a couple of tablets to relieve the swelling. I've got the number here. But not if there's any danger of choking.'

Don, frowning fiercely and supporting his daughter's head, said, 'Number? What number?'

'All the drugs in the medical chest are numbered,' Sophie explained. 'What do you think? Could she swallow?'

'No,' he barked. 'Look at her. She's comatose.' Then he shut his eyes and drew a deep breath. 'I'm sorry. Not your fault. You're very kind. How long?'

Sophie grimaced. 'An hour maybe, bit more? He's coming from Darwin, but they have to get the pilot out to the airport, do the checks . . . it all takes time. Look, would she be better lying down in the recovery position, perhaps?'

'I'll get a mattress.' Luke vanished before Don could speak and shortly the patient was ensconced on the floor, covered by a blanket. She roused briefly as she was lifted, mumbling, 'Daddy' and something else Tilly didn't catch. Her eyes were swollen almost shut but even so, Tilly thought, one could see the prettiness beneath. Luke, hovering over her, restlessly cracking his knuckles, was obviously deeply concerned.

'How did you become aware something was wrong?' Sophie handed Don a mug of tea. 'There'll be some breakfast shortly.'

'What? Oh, thanks.' The man passed a hand over the hairless part of his scalp. 'I heard her moaning in the tent. I was sleeping just outside. She seemed to be choking and she didn't answer when I asked if she was okay. So I went in and found her. She said her arm was burning, then sort of passed out. Not all at once, she was mumbling and moaning and getting worse by the minute, so I woke up Luke here.'

'Was she on a camp bed?' Connor asked. 'Not that it'd make any difference. Anything that crawls . . .'

'Yes. But she wanted the tent unzipped. She liked to watch the stars . . . I suppose whatever bit her got in that way.'

It was a long wait until the first faint hum of the plane sounded. The sun was up by then, drenching the land with light. Breakfast was over, although neither Don nor Luke had eaten much beyond toast and tea. Jane moaned occasionally and mumbled, her face flushed and sweating. Luke, watching her, chewed the nails of his right hand until Tilly gently caught his wrist.

'Don't. It's most unhygenic. Come with me. You can help with the joeys.'

'What?'

'It'll give you something to do.'

'Yes, go on, Luke,' Sophie commanded. 'There's still the work to get through.'

They had just finished the feeding when the drone of the aero engine sounded.

'Thank Christ!' Luke abandoned his task and sprinted for the house.

Five minutes later he, the patient and her father were on their way to the airstrip. Presently Tilly, back sterilising bottles and sweeping the kitchen floor, heard the deeper note of the plane engines running up in preparation for take-off. She stepped out onto the verandah, followed by Connor, to watch the King Air's wings catch the sun as it arrowed away to the south.

The door opened and Sophie joined her, holding a second mug of tea. 'Never a dull moment,' she observed. 'I hope the girl'll be okay. Luke's really taken with her, isn't he?'

'He seems to have lost his heart,' Tilly agreed. 'So, lunches today, anyone?'

Matt emerged from the house. 'Not for me. I'll be in the shed. Vehicles to service,' he said, heading off.

'Are the whipper snippers fuelled up?' Sophie called after him, then continued as he nodded. 'Just me and Luke then, thanks. We're working on the walking tracks,' she explained.

'Ah.' Tilly nodded. Nature was a relentless force. 'What about you, Connor?'

'No thanks. Is it okay if I take the boat out this arvo, Sophie? It's the easiest way to check the river bank growth.'

'Yes, of course.' Binboona had inherited the former station's tinny for emergency use in the Wet, though, Tilly privately thought, you would have to be mad to put it into the Nutt in flood.

Remembering then, she said, 'I'd almost forgotten the mail plane. At least the strip's already been checked. That'll save me time.'

'I'll be here and free – I can collect the mail for you,' Connor offered. 'What time?'

'Would you? It's due about half ten.' She smiled her thanks. 'The mailbag will be on the table there. That sounds like Luke coming back now.'

It was. Don stopped briefly to let the young ranger out, then drove the station wagon back between the sheds towards the camp.

'He's gone to pack up,' Luke announced, bursting into the room. 'And I'm catching the mail plane out if I can get a seat.'

'Whoa, slow down a bit.' Sophie looked startled. 'What did the doctor say about Jane?'

'An extreme allergic reaction to something in her system. He thinks she'll be okay. *Thinks!*' he said scornfully, eyes flashing. 'And what if she isn't? I have to go to her. Don'll be forever reaching Darwin dragging that trailer. Six hours if he speeds, so I'm taking the plane.'

Tilly said, 'But Luke, what are the chances of there being a spare seat?' The mail plane serviced a dozen stations, any one of which could be sending or receiving travellers that day. 'They're nearly always booked out – with freight, if not people.'

'There's got to be,' he said stubbornly. 'You don't understand – none of you do – she could *die!* Anyway I'm going.' This last said with a challenging look at his boss.

'Okay,' Sophie said mildly. 'Take a couple of days. Though how you'll get back, short of waiting for the next plane . . .'

'I'll worry about that later,' he muttered and rushed from the room. Shortly they heard the sound of doors and drawers opening and slamming closed as he packed.

Sophie shrugged. 'So, that'll be just the one lunch then.'

Luke's impatience had him and Connor out at the airstrip twenty minutes before the first faint note of the plane's engine was heard. A few moments later it was overridden by the rumble of a vehicle pulling up before the homestead. Tilly, stepping out onto the verandah, was surprised to see Don Wellaway coming up the steps.

'Don – I thought you'd be long gone.'

'Well I would've been'—he looked both harassed and irritated—'only the young fellow that was travelling with us seems to have vanished. I can't wait any longer, so I thought I'd better leave word. God knows where he's got to! I'd've thought that giving a lift to someone means they have an obliga—'

'Wait.' Tilly shook her head. 'I'm not following. I thought there was just you and Jane?'

'Yes, yes – but he was there at Alloway. The roadhouse back down the track? A uni kid relying on hitching to get around. We gave him a ride in and the arrangement was he'd come back out with us. I hitched often enough myself when I was young, so I like to help . . . He had his own camp and gear, so I didn't see much of him, but he seems to have gone. Maybe somebody offered him a ride out? If so, you'd have thought he'd have had the decency to let me know. As it is, I've wasted half the morning hunting for him.'

Tilly caught her breath, overcome with sudden certainty. 'What did he look like? Was he sort of skinny, with longish fair hair? Did he wear a baseball cap?'

'You've seen him then?'

'If it's him, he left yesterday with another traveller.'

'Well, the bugger might've told me.' Don said, his irritation plain. 'I could be a hundred kay down the road by now.' He turned back to his vehicle, calling over his shoulder, 'Thanks, er, Tilly. You were great, you all were. Being here, getting the doctor for Jane. Tell the others too, won't you? I won't forget.' He slammed the cab door on the promise.

'That's all right. We're happy to help.' Tilly lifted her hand and stood, watching in a state of wild surmise as the dust shrouded his departing vehicle.

# *Chapter Eleven*

At ten o'clock Matt turned up for morning smoko, bringing with him the sharp reek of diesel on his clothes.

'Where's the freeloader then?' he asked, stirring his mug of tea.

'What?' Tilly eyed him in surprise. 'Do you mean Connor? Why would you call him that?'

'Well, ain't he?' His glance slid off hers in his habitual fashion. 'Swanning round the place. Hardly call what he does work, would you? Poking his nose in where it ain't wanted. Butter wouldn't melt – I seen him charmin' you, Tilly.'

She flushed, saying coolly, 'Even if that were true, I can't see it's any of your business, Matt. As to where he is, he ran Luke out to catch the plane. And his work *is* important, you know. Just as much as what you do.'

'You reckon?' Matt's lip curled. 'Funny thing about your hotshot botanist – yesterday I asked him what the tree was – the big 'un out back – but all he could come up with was some rubbish in Latin.' He snorted. 'I reckon he wouldn't know it from his big toe. We've only got his word he's even who he says he is.'

'Why wouldn't he be? Is he supposed to carry his degree around with him?' She'd bridled at that *your* and, rising, tipped her undrunk cup of tea away. 'Botanists learn Latin names, Matt,' she said coldly. 'It's how they classify plants. Look, you plainly don't like him, but that's between the two of you – I don't want to know. Now, if you've finished,' she added, snatching the plate from which he'd just lifted the last of his cake, 'I've got work to get on with.'

Seething, she busied herself at the sink until he'd gone. How dare he suggest that she had the slightest interest in Connor – or he in her! On the other hand, perhaps the exchange had made her lack of partiality for Matt himself plain as well? Though it should have been obvious to him anyway. God, she hoped he wasn't one of those blinkered obsessive types who only see what they want. He *was* a little odd socially, with his long silences and furtive glances that she'd hitherto assumed only to be the result of shyness. Tilly sighed. Why did life have to be so damn complicated?

She heard the plane take off and, a short while after, Connor's step on the verandah. He came in carrying the mail-bag, hanging his hat on the peg by the door. Searching the empty space behind him, Tilly said, 'Luke got a seat then?'

Connor nodded. 'Mind you, I think he was prepared to hang onto the tail if that was the only option.'

'Well, I'm glad for him. For Jane too – it'll be nice for her to wake to a friendly face. Don won't make Darwin today unless he drives all night, and that's without hold-ups. He's already had one of them, poor man. Would you like a cuppa?'

'Please, if it's no trouble. But wouldn't you rather check the mail out first?'

'Oh there's never anything for me.' Taking the bag from him, Tilly tossed it aside. 'Sit down and I'll make a pot. It's been a morning, hasn't it? To quote my mum, I really feel that I could do with the cup that cheers but won't inebriate.'

Connor laughed. 'Good Lord! What's that, a Temperance slogan?'

'Actually,' she said, 'I think it was advertising for the middle classes.' She rinsed the pot, made the tea and piled mugs, sugar and a handful of biscuits onto a tray. 'Shall we go outside? It'll be nice in the sun and I can keep an eye on the road.' And too bad if Matt happened to spot them from the shed. It would teach him to keep his nose out of her affairs.

It was pleasant on the verandah, the air so still that the flutter of wings from the bird basin sounded clearly. Connor squinted at the river bank. 'You can just glimpse the water. You certainly picked a peaceful spot when you came here. Do you get many repeat visitors?'

'Oh, yes, according to Sophie. Some even have their preferred camp sites and ask for them. And many of the first-timers tell us they'll be back. Though, maybe,' she added ruefully, 'the Wellaways won't be among them.'

'Perhaps not. Though the girl could just be super-sensitive to the toxin of whatever bit her. Have you ever had a centipede nip you?'

Tilly grimaced. 'Once. Very painful. One of the fishermen told me to cut an onion and rub the juice on the spot. It helped. I felt a bit sick, but nothing like poor Jane.'

'Well, she's in good hands now. Though her father'll have a worrying day. You said he'd already been held up – what was that about?'

'Oh.' The incident with Matt had temporarily eclipsed what she had learnt that morning. Tilly had already debated telling Sophie and decided against it. Her cousin would either question her sanity or worry about her emotional strength. Matt's behaviour had ruled him out as a confidante, and Luke, who must by now have met or spoken to all the campers, wasn't available. Connor, however, was a disinterested presence, and she did want to talk about it, she realised. If just to be convinced that her mind was playing tricks. 'Something a bit odd,' she said hesitantly, then went on to explain.

Connor heard her out in silence, then frowned. 'That can't have been very pleasant for you,' he said sympathetically. 'How good a look did you get at him? I mean, is – was – your husband very distinctive in appearance?'

Tilly raised her hands helplessly. 'Gerry was very good looking. Sort of . . . rakish and carefree, if you know what I mean. He had dark, wavy hair and an infectious smile. Easy to recognise. The way he held his head and wore his hat, I could have sworn . . .' She paused. 'It was such a shock but of course it wasn't him – I know that. But I also know that the other man wasn't the same as the first man—' She stopped, sighing. 'If that makes any sense?'

'It's certainly odd.' Connor drained his cup and paused to pick a tea leaf from his tongue. 'It could have quite a simple explanation, of course. Maybe the first guy wanted to stay longer, while the young one – you said he was young?'

'Yes, years younger than Ger— than the other,' Tilly agreed.

'Perhaps he'd had enough and wanted an early ride out?'

'The first man's likely to be stranded here then,' Tilly objected. 'Most campers haven't enough room to give rides.

It's why we see so few backpackers. They have no way of getting here.'

'Mmm. I suppose he must've thought of that. Tell you what,' he continued after a moment's thought, 'why don't I run you down to the camp this arvo? Just to take a look at who is there. What do you say?'

'Oh, but that's not necessary.' Flustered by the offer, Tilly suddenly doubted herself. 'Half the time I think I imagined seeing him, and the same person came out. Besides, you've got your own plans – aren't you taking the boat out this afternoon?'

'I can do that tomorrow. Look, it's upset you. It's only a few minutes to run down and check, and if it puts your mind at rest, well, isn't that worth the time? I was only little when my dad died, but for what seemed like ages, my mum used to see him everywhere. She'd go pale and afterwards she'd cry. Gramps told me it was about laying ghosts to rest. Something you had to do, he said, when you lost someone.'

The memory he offered smoothed Tilly's confusion. She said, 'You're very thoughtful, Connor, and your grandfather was right. So thank you, yes. It's silly, but I'll take you up on that. Straight after lunch then?' It felt right. And it would put that recurring *once* and all its connotations permanently to rest.

He smiled. 'It's a deal.' Settling deeper into his chair as she collected the tray, he drew a small piece of wood and his stock knife from his pocket and began idly to whistle, scraping at one end of the wood.

Intrigued, Tilly paused at the door to watch. 'What are you doing?'

'Huh? Oh, whittling. Bit of a hobby of mine. Good for stress.'

'Oh you certainly need it then,' she quipped and went indoors smiling. Anyone less stressed than Connor was hard to imagine.

Lunchtime was quickly over, for which Tilly was thankful; she found Matt's disapproving silence at table unwarranted and irksome. The two men ignored each other and she gave up pretending not to notice, eating her salad and answering Connor's occasional remarks. Afterwards Matt returned to his work, and once she had cleaned up, Tilly climbed into Connor's vehicle with a feeling of defiance, ridiculous though that was. She could do as she pleased, she told herself. Still, it was hard not to picture Matt observing her from within the black shadows of the workshop. The whole exercise was a waste of time – she had convinced herself as much over lunch – but Connor was being kind and the least she could do was to see out his offer since she had, after all, accepted it.

The camp was full, only Don Wellaway's site unoccupied. People sat on folding chairs or lay on camp beds in the shade. They were reading, dozing, chatting together or listening to their radios. One swung in a hammock, a leg draped indolently over the side. Women were busy at the laundry tubs, bird watchers wandered about with binoculars, people carrying cameras returned from the river, and three young children shrieked with glee as they ran through the sprinklers on the grassed area about the ablution block.

Tilly, observing them all, lifted her hands. 'What was

I thinking? I can't line up the people to inspect them. And we don't even know if they're all here.'

'Why don't we just mooch around the camp sites – see if there's a single anywhere?' Connor suggested.

So they had done so but without success. Every camp site had a vehicle parked in it, and glimpses of open tents, or the paired chairs outside caravans all bore witness to more than one occupant.

Back at their starting point, Tilly turned to her companion. 'Obviously I was wrong. I must've been thinking about Gerry and imagined the whole thing. None of the campers are remotely like him, and anyway, they're all couples or family groups. Let's go back, Connor. I've wasted enough of your time.'

'Whatever you want, Tilly. Look at it this way – if nothing else, you've set your mind at rest and incidentally saved the rangers from mounting a search. I mean if someone *was* missing . . .'

'Well, he isn't, because he was never here.' Feeling foolish, Tilly climbed into the vehicle, thanking her stars she hadn't spoken of the matter to anyone else. 'Can we just forget all about it, Connor? And please, don't mention it to the others.'

'Of course not.' He drew two fingers across his lips. 'Your secret's safe with me. By the by, do you know what's got into Matt? He seems very unfriendly all of a sudden.'

'He's probably cheesed off at Luke,' Tilly lied. 'He'll have to do his chores till he gets back.'

'Ah, I did wonder if it was me.'

'Don't be silly,' Tilly said hastily, 'Why would it be? Anyway, thanks for humouring me today. At least the matter's settled. It never would have arisen in the first place if it hadn't been for that sergeant insinuating . . .' She left the sentence unfinished. They rode back in silence to the homestead where she took a quick glance at the sun and said brightly, 'You've still got time to take the boat out.'

'There's no hurry,' he reiterated comfortably. 'I'll do it tomorrow.'

Home again, Tilly assauged her vague feelings of embarrassment with work. She tidied the games cupboard, a task long put off, and mopped and dusted the lounge. The mailbag caught her eye and, having hung the mop to dry on the clothesline out back, she sorted the mail, stacking the business letters on Sophie's desk and carrying the newspapers through to the kitchen. There was a birding magazine for Luke, several circulars and the usual handful of advertising handouts from Darwin's shops and supermarkets. Why the post office kept including them, she could never work out. Last of all was a grubby-looking letter addressed to herself.

Deeply surprised, for she received little mail beyond official notifications and the occasional note from her mother, Tilly turned it over but found no return address. The postmark was smeared, the address written in block capitals. Intrigued, she used Sophie's paperknife to slit the envelope and slid out a single sheet of cheap, lined paper only to find that it was completely blank. Tilly stared at it, puzzled, then peered into the empty envelope and studied the stamp, trying to make out a name. Only the initial letter of K was legible – for Katherine or Karumba, or Kathmandu? Not the latter, the stamp was

Australian. So who . . .? God, her life was being taken over by mysteries.

Thoroughly irritated, Tilly snatched up the junk mail, added the letter and the detritus from the games cupboard (old scoring sheets, a broken box that had once held mah-jong tiles, and empty photo folders) and marched out to the incinerator. Whoever was being funny at her expense would discover that she wasn't about to play. As far as she was concerned, anonymous communications could remain just that. She piled the papers onto the steel mesh in the blackened half-drum where the rangers burnt their rubbish, and lit the empty carton. The flames caught at once and she stood there, watching the pieces burst into flame, the junk mail and yellowed paper burning first. The blank sheet of the letter lay on the top above the envelope, whose corners now began to crisp. The draft of heat as it burnt lifted the sheet of cheap paper, and as it did so, writing appeared on its surface.

Tilley's hand flew to her mouth and she felt the blood drain from her head. She snatched instinctively at the letter, smelling the fine hair on her wrist scorch as the paper caught alight, crumpling to ash even as her fingers reached it.

'No,' she moaned. Shock made her heart pound as if it would break from the cage of her ribs. This time there could be no mistake. She might have doubted that she had seen Gerry in the flesh, but she would recognise his distinctive penmanship amid a thousand others. And that single brief glimpse had engraved his message into her brain.

What did it mean? she wondered wildly. The letter couldn't have been posted two years ago and have reached her only now. Besides, how would he have known where she would be?

There had been no redirection on the envelope. Shock and fury battled within her. If he still lived, how dare he do that? The words danced before her inner eye, browning into view even as the paper that held them crisped and burnt. Telling her nothing save that he was alive. *I'm sorry, babe,* the words coruscated blindly before her mind's eye. There had been no salutation and no signature at the end, just the initial *G*.

# *Chapter Twelve*

Hardly aware of having moved, Tilly found herself back inside. For a long moment she stood in the laundry, her head a whirl of fragmented thoughts, not allowing herself to hope. How and why scarcely mattered against the clamour of the overriding question: If Gerry still lived, could Francie also have survived? Was it possible? Tilly's heart burnt again with a sick longing for her daughter. What exactly was Gerry sorry for? For having deceived her and the rest of the world by faking his death? For failing to save Francie? For whatever he was mixed up in that required his removal from the world and a communication that, but for the merest chance, she would never have read?

She found that she was panting and wanting badly to scream. That would achieve nothing. Taking a deep breath, she walked through the house to the kitchen, seeking the coolness of water and the balm of familiar surroundings.

She stood at the sink to fill a glass and drank it, then dabbed a wet hand over her face, taking deep, slow breaths. The clock ticked loudly in the silence and a peewee's strident call pierced her ears. It called again and again, the noise like a drill in her head until she rushed to the door, flapping her hands, crying, 'Shoo! Go away!'

Too late she realised that Connor still occupied the chair where earlier he had sat whittling. He still was, for a shower of shavings fell from his hands as he rose, startled, to face her. 'Something wrong, Tilly?'

'No,' she said. Then, 'Yes . . .' Her throat worked but the words seemed lodged there, unable to come out. She suddenly realised that she had no proof. The letter, envelope and all, was gone and nobody but she had seen it. It was like her glimpse of Gerry – for she was perfectly certain now that it had been him in the vehicle, however he had managed to vanish again. And he must have also seen her, for how else would he have known where she was?

'I can see you've had a shock,' Connor said. 'Here, sit down.' He guided her to the chair he'd vacated. 'Just breathe, and when you're ready, tell me what the problem is. Or not. It's up to you. Should I make you some tea? Would you like that?'

His thoughtfulness undid Tilly. She would never have let go otherwise, she later told herself, sniffing furiously and wiping her fingers over her eyes. 'No tea.' She shook her head, the words muffled as if answering his query was the most pressing need of the moment. 'I just – I want . . . I got a letter . . .' And then it all poured out: the blank sheet, the fire in the incinerator, seeing the message magically appear only to vanish as the blaze consumed it. She could still smell the singed hair on her wrist. 'Why would he do that? *How* did he?' she demanded. 'There was nothing on the paper until then.'

'It's quite a common trick,' Connor said. 'Most kids

know it. You write the message in lemon juice – or urine,' he added. 'Little boys, playing at being spies. It's the acid in the medium, you see. You apply heat to make it visible. My mates and I, we held the paper over a candle. You don't actually have to burn it.'

Tilly rubbed damp hands on her shirtfront. 'But *why?* If he was going to write to me, why hide it? If I'd crumpled the paper up, I've never have seen it. How could he know I wouldn't just throw it away?'

'Maybe he thought you knew the trick too? And he might have worried about your mail being intercepted.'

Tilly stared at him, her voice sinking to a whisper. 'So, it's true. He's done something wrong. That's why the police came. Is that why my daughter is dead . . .?' This time the tears brimmed and ran over in a stream until she sobbed. 'I thought, when I saw the message and knew it was from him, that if *he* had somehow escaped death – then Francie might've too . . . That maybe she wasn't dead? But he wouldn't keep her from me. Gerry was never cruel.'

She hung her dripping head, shoulders shaking as the tears continued to fall, then felt Connor's hand on her arm. 'You poor kid! I'm sorry. Here, I'll just . . .' He rose and vanished to return a few moments later with a length of paper towelling from the roll on the kitchen bench. 'Sorry,' he repeated, 'couldn't find any tissues. You've had a nasty shock and I really think you should have some tea.'

'What, and that'll make everything better?' she blazed.

'I only meant—'

'I know.' Tilly felt a rush of shame for her rudeness. 'I'm sorry. That was uncalled for. You've been very kind.'

She blotted her face with the sodden paper. 'I— it was stupid of me to even think . . . It's worse when you hope, you know. You can learn to accept things but if hope steps in again . . .' She sniffed, firmed her trembling lip and tried to smile. 'Do you know, I think you're right after all, about that tea.' It was one way to be left alone and that, just then, was what she most desired.

'I'll put the kettle on,' Connor said, turning back to the kitchen.

All too swiftly he was back, saying, 'I don't know how you take it but I've made it sweet and hot.'

She pulled a face but drank it anyway, staring silently before her. When she finally spoke, she said almost wistfully, 'If I just knew *why*. I think I could handle it better if . . . Why would a man *do* that? I really thought he loved us, but to let me think . . .' She trailed off, looking at her hands.

'Maybe to him it seemed the only way,' Connor suggested tentatively. 'You said he owed money?'

'Yes, but you don't have to pretend to kill yourself for that! You can declare bankruptcy, can't you? People go broke all the time.'

'I suppose it might depend on who you owe the money to. Was he a gambler? If he owed one of the big syndicates . . . I've heard they're not very forgiving of debts. And from what you've said, he hadn't much collateral.'

'No,' she agreed. 'The house was mortgaged, the boat only leased and the payments were behind there too. But if he gambled, wouldn't I have known?'

'You said yourself that you didn't know about the debts.'

'No.' Her hand stole up to her cheek as she raised her gaze

to his. 'But even if he decided to, to skip out on us and pretend, because of the debt, it still doesn't explain the police interest. Surely debts are a civil matter? They're not *criminal*.'

'Not unless you steal to cover them. And he obviously didn't or they'd have been paid off. Perhaps he was involved in something because the debts made him vulnerable? He might've been blackmailed. Maybe vanishing for good seemed the only way out,' Connor suggested. 'Just a thought, Tilly.'

'Then why risk exposure by sending the letter?' she asked. 'It doen't make sense!'

'Loneliness? A drunken urge, or spur of the moment remorse? It must be difficult to ditch your whole life. If you turn it around,' Connor said gently, 'he has lost as much as you, and he did it to himself.'

'But how? I mean I saw him lift Francie into the boat! It was my last glimpse of them both. If he lost contact with it, if the tide took it out or he couldn't climb in, how did he survive?' Before Connor could hazard a guess she suddenly straightened in her seat, remembering her earlier thought. 'I didn't imagine seeing him then! Because the letter was addressed here, to Binboona.'

'Which raises another question,' Connor pointed out. 'Two, actually. Why did he come to the camp and how did he leave it?'

Tilly, however, was following her own train of thought. 'I wish I hadn't burnt it now. Only I thought . . .' She didn't bother to finish the sentence, because if she hadn't burnt it, she would never have seen the message at all.

*And would that have been such a bad thing?* a little voice in her head asked. Gerry had done this to her, and the most he could come up with was a three-word apology written in a kid's code that he didn't even know she could decipher. He was *sorry*? Well, so was she! Sorry she had ever met the man who had deserted her and proved himself to be a conniving crook wanted by the police.

Her anger suddenly felt good, subsuming the helplessness and despair she feared. She would *not* return to that dreadful place she had occupied in her early (supposed) widowhood. She had grieved his loss, believing him to be her other half, a person of worth – not someone who had lied and deliberately deceived her. Ignoring Connor's last remark, she stood decisively, collecting mug and the crumpled kitchen paper.

'Thank you,' she said stiffly, 'for listening. I don't usually . . . It was just the shock. I'd be grateful if you didn't mention this to anyone. It's a private matter and I'd like to keep it that way.'

'Of course.' Connor hesitated. 'You don't think you ought to let the police know?'

Tilly's hackles rose at the thought of Sergeant Burns. 'I wouldn't tell that man if he was on fire,' she said tartly.

'Ouch. Remind me never to annoy you.' He smiled then, a little lopsided movement that coaxed an unwilling laugh from her before he pressed again. 'Seriously, you're sure about that?'

'Yes.' Tilly was adamant. 'Whatever Gerry's done, he's still my husband.' She brushed the wood shavings littering the table into a heap and for the first time noticed the little carving in their midst. 'Oh, that's clever!' Picking it up, she saw that it was a shaky-paw lizard no longer than her forefinger, its tiny head held sideways and right foot raised in its signature wave. 'It's beautiful, Connor. So lifelike. You're very clever.'

The wood was as smooth as oil to touch, the eyes and mouth of the little reptile exquisitely carved.

'You have it,' he said. 'For me the pleasure's in the making.'

'Oh thanks, but I couldn't.' She replaced it, swept the shavings into the empty mug and returned indoors.

In Tilly's preoccupied state, the rest of the afternoon seemed to pass in a flash, and long before she had decided whether or not to confide in Sophie, the head ranger's vehicle was chugging up the track. Having already told Connor about the letter, something she now regretted, it seemed somehow disloyal to keep the news from her cousin, especially if there was any question of Gerry's still being around. Except, she now realised, that he must have left the property in order to post the letter. Unless he had an accomplice? The word reminded her again of the police. Ordinary people had friends, mates, acquaintances to help them – only criminals had accomplices.

'Oh, I don't know!' In her frustration Tilly had spoken aloud. She snatched a quick look about the empty kitchen as if fearing to be overheard before carrying on mixing the joeys' formula. Should she just forget the whole thing? *Yeah, some chance,* she mocked herself. Then the noise of the returning vehicle broke across the bugling call of a trio of brolgas passing overhead and the decision was upon her. If she was going to do it, then it would have to be at once, before Matt knocked off, while they had the house to themselves.

The vehicle's motor echoed briefly off the shed walls, then died. Sophie entered the kitchen carrying her empty lunch box and thermos, which she dumped on the sink. 'Hi, Till.

How's things? You wouldn't believe how full the camp is! Do you think you could give me a hand with the slide show tonight? I've had that many enquiries about it today, and with Luke AWOL . . .'

'Yes, of course,' Tilly said. Looking at her cousin, she knew then that she didn't have a choice. Sophie, as she had promised, had walked with Tilly every step of the way along her painful road of recovery, her patience, strength and cheering presence always available. Her sturdy arms had cradled Tilly as she wept, her blunt, workmanlike hands had soothed away the nightmares plaguing those early months . . . The very least she owed her cousin now was the truth.

Drawing a strained breath, Tilly said, 'Anything, Soph, but first there's something I have to tell you . . .'

# *Chapter Thirteen*

On the third day after the flying doctor had flown Jane Wellaway out, Luke returned to Binboona. He arrived sharing the back seat of a twincab HiLux with the two young sons of a tourist couple who were towing a camper trailer around Australia. Having waved them off and hi-fived the two boys, who plainly regarded him as their personal property, Luke set his small carryall down on the old verandah planks and stretched.

'Good to be home.' An unfamiliar stubble darkened his jaw. 'Hiya, Tilly. That last bit of road's getting in an awful state. Time it was graded again.'

'It's seen lots of traffic,' Tilly agreed. 'How did Jane get on? Is she okay now?'

'Yep, the hospital discharged her yesterday. She and Don left for the Alice this morning.'

'Did the doctor work out what it was that bit her?'

'Best bet is a centipede or a scorpion. A very severe reaction, they said, so she either got a lot of the venom or she's highly allergic. She's okay now though, but a bit off camping.'

'Well, that's understandable.' Tilly locked the cashbox. 'Come and have a cuppa, Luke. So where does she live? Can you see her again?'

'New South Wales.' He grimaced, picking up his bag and following her into the kitchen. 'We'll write to each other, and I'll visit her when the camp closes.' Dumping the bag, he gave her a clear-eyed look. 'I know, I know – you're thinking it won't last. A month or two and the letters'll stop. But I'm serious about her, Tilly. I've never met anyone quite like her before.'

Quashing the urge to tell him that in six months' time he would barely remember her face, Tilly nodded sympathetically. At his age, what did Luke know about love, how it could rip your heart in two, turn on you, betray you? *Once* . . . She shook the notion away. 'Twenty-two. That's very young to be thinking of a permanent partnership,' was all she said.

'And you're Lady Methuselah, right? Come on, Tilly, how old were you when—' He caught himself. 'Sorry, I wasn't thinking.'

'That's okay. I hope it works out for you, Luke, I really do. Being apart makes it harder, that's all. If you're truly in love, I mean. On the other hand, when it's just attraction, well, it's a case of out of sight, out of mind.'

'Yeah? Isn't absence supposed to make the heart grow fonder?'

'For a hermit,' Tilly agreed, 'or maybe an eighteenth-century sailor. They didn't have much choice, did they? Didn't really apply to their sweeties back in town though.'

Luke looked hurt. 'When did you get to be such a cynic?'

'I'm sorry,' she said penitently. 'Of course she'll wait

for you. I don't mean it, it's just we do that here, don't we – argue for the sake of it? Otherwise we'd run out of things to say. You keep the faith, Luke. You deserve to be happy.'

'So do you,' he said soberly, stirring his tea, 'but things don't always work out the way they should.'

*Not if you choose badly*. The words almost escaped her. Biting her lip instead, she asked, 'See anyone you know in town?'

'Nope. I was at the hospital, then down the caravan parks looking for a lift out. So where is everyone?'

'Well, Connor's gone. And Matt and Sophie are at the camp. She's planning on doing your night walk this evening. Matt's fixing the pump.'

'What's wrong with it?'

'It's not working. He said something about – do pumps have glands? It seems unlikely, but that's what he said.'

'Search me. When you say Connor's gone – gone where?'

Tilly shrugged. 'Away. He left early yesterday.' She had come back from feeding Harry and the joeys to find him carrying his bag down the steps.

'I made my lunch,' he'd said. 'Hope that's okay. I'll be back but I'm not sure when. I'll let you know though.'

'Right. Bye then.' A little surprised, for he had said nothing about leaving, she waved him off, then climbed the steps. She would miss him, she realised. Visitors broke the isolation of their lives. Not that you could call them isolated with forty-odd people camped only five kilometres away, but the four of them didn't share much of their time or their thoughts with Binboona's customers. Unless you counted Luke's recent romance, of course.

Placing the bottles in the sink, Tilly had seen that Connor had cleaned up after himself. The breadboard was in the wrong place though. Reaching automatically to right it, her hand stilled, then went instead to the windowsill where he'd left the carving of the little lizard sitting on the torn margin of a newspaper. On it he'd written, *Thanks for everything, Tilly.* Had he carved it because he was leaving, she wondered, or was it just a generous afterthought? Like a bunch of flowers delivered to a hostess after a guest's departure. In which case, shouldn't he have addressed the little carving to Sophie?

'Oh,' she said now, dragging her thoughts back to the present. 'We've got another patient. The cutest little sugar glider, Luke! I'd only ever seen pictures of them before. Sophie found him at the foot of a tree along the river walk. He's very weak – she's not sure if it's age or malnourishment. He did have ticks though. We got them off and I'm feeding him glucose and sugar water.'

'Umm, where is he? Let's have a look. Good thing you deticked him – they certainly wouldn't have helped his condition.'

'I put him in a box in the laundry.' Tilly led the way. The tiny marsupial, whose fluffy tail seemed larger than its body, was curled up in the corner of a shoebox lined with shredded paper. The creature's eyes opened when the lid was lifted but that was all. Tilly busied herself tipping glucose and sugar into a tiny saucer, which the glider readily lapped up. 'I used an eye dropper at first,' she explained, 'but he seems happy enough to drink it himself. He's very tame as you can see. What do you think?'

'Weak, not tame. The ticks were probably doing for him,' Luke said. 'See how pale his gums are? They must have been sucking the life out of him. He's only young. You might have caught him just in time. Where did the saucer come from?'

'A kid's teaset. I picked it up at the old dump. There would've been children here once, I guess.'

'Yeah, probably. Well, just keep on with what you're doing. Build his strength up and he should be right.' He turned back to the kitchen. 'I'll head down to the camp. No need for Sophie to lead the walk tonight.'

'Not without your dinner,' Tilly said firmly. 'Wait five and I'll get you something in a dish that you can warm up later.'

That evening, having watched three television programs without taking in a word, Tilly went to her room, closing the door firmly on her companions. Luke's door was open and a glance as she passed by had shown him back from his hike with the tourists and scribbling busily away – a letter to Jane, she surmised. Sophie was in the office and Matt had the ever-present chessboard out at the table, but if he was hoping for a partner she had made plain her disinclination to join him.

Alone at last, she could let her thoughts turn to Gerry. She had said 'he's still my husband' as a reason for not dobbing him in to the police – did that make her an accessory to whatever crime he was wanted for? She tried to imagine what he might have done. Surely nothing very dreadful, and yet, the voice of reason asked, wouldn't it have to be bad if his only recourse was to fake his own death? A state that could have nothing to do with Gerry, who was so full of life with his charming smile and full-throated laugh. An ache of sadness rose in her throat at the thought of all that he had tossed away. She had been proud to partner him, proud of his looks and virility, scarcely able to believe that, considering all the women he could have had, he had instead fallen for her.

Tilly thumbed through memories like old photos: Gerry, suited and handsome on their wedding day. His dishevelled panic in the delivery room when Francie was born. 'I can't do this, babe, I can't!' he'd blurted, heading for the door. Until all five feet of a tiny nurse had got in his face yelling, 'You get back there and hold her hand, buster. It's your baby too!' They had laughed about it afterwards. She saw him, proud as punch with a watermelon grin on his face, as he'd swept open the door of their new home. 'All yours, babe. Paradise with mod cons.' She remembered asking then if they could afford it and the careless way he'd laughed as if money was no object. 'You let me worry about the dough, babe.'

So she had – and about everything else too: the restuarants they'd frequented, the business, his time out on the boat. She had questioned none of it, and see where that had led! To fire sales and repossession, leaving her, as her stepfather would have put it, without a pot to piss in. How could she have been so blind? There must have been signals that all was not well. Surely no one could be that deeply in debt and act as unworried as Gerry had seemed. Looking back, he had been edgy at times with the occasional flare-up of temper, but he'd been quick to apologise and blame it on work. Tilly had believed him because she had seen it with her stepfather. The sea was a hard mistress, and fishing as unchancy a livelihood as you could well find. Temporary crews, bad weather, light nets more often than not, and the gruelling nature of the work itself. Men came ashore dog-tired from the boats, and it was understandable that they should occasionally be out of sorts.

That was how she had dismissed it, Tilly thought. Gerry had spent his time on the water, so whatever he was wanted for had to be connected to the boat or the sea. Had he been running drugs? People smuggling? No, that was absurd. Where would he take a cargo of illegal refugees? You couldn't just dump them ashore in croc-infested country – they'd be bound either to perish or be discovered. And he could hardly sail into Darwin Harbour with them. There must be checks – Customs officers, a Port Authority, something – at the docks. It was the back door to Australia after all: the government wouldn't leave it wide open, not with all the refugee boats heading this way. But if Gerry were just the transport, she reasoned, his cargo could have been met ashore by some other member of the gang and trucked to a dispersal point, couldn't it? Tilly had no idea how people smuggling operated, only that it happened.

She cringed, thinking of the misery of the desperate folk involved in such ventures, paying their life savings over to unscrupulous operators. How many were caught and sent back, or spent the next decade in detention? Why would Gerry do it? Surely not just to fund the lifestyle they had enjoyed. She had been as content with him in the tin shed of their fishing camp as in the fancy townhouse in Cairns. Had she ever given him reason to think otherwise? Could those nameless, hopeless refugees from the world's worst trouble spots have suffered on her account? The thought was insupportable.

She considered the alternatives, shying away from any involvement in drugs (not that, it was too wicked!) to robbery – but robbing what? There were no banks in the wilds of northern Australia, no armoured vans to hold up and electronic embezzlement wasn't an option if you could barely get a radio signal. Anyway, if he'd had access to stolen money, why wouldn't he have paid what was owing on the *Esmerelda*?

Gerry had loved that boat, joking that she was his mistress. 'There's you, babe, and then there's my best girl.' It had almost precipitated their first row until Tilly had realised that the shapely body and sweet bottom he continually spoke of belonged to the *Esmerelda*. He'd maintained a running tease about it when kissing her and Francie goodbye each time he left to head out to sea. 'Off to my best girl now, babe. See you in a week . . .' Or ten days, or whenever – it depended on the weather and the season. Sometimes he was away longer and the catch would still be lighter, but Tilly, making sure that a meal was ready and the donkey heater working to ensure a hot shower, never asked for details of the trip. The job didn't end at the dock. The iced fish had to be stored, transport organised, hands paid off, fuel and stores replaced . . . When he came wearily back to their camp, the last thing he needed, she'd told herself, was a lot of questions.

Because she loved him, and he was putting in the hard yards to keep her and Francie, and to run the business, she had swallowed her own needs to see to his. She had often been lonely in the camp when the boats were out, and occasionally bored, with long days to fill and only a toddler for company. And there were the little daily worries with Francie: the fever she had once run, the fall which had cut her lip, precipitating a screaming fit that had terrified Tilly into believing she had sustained not just a superficial cut, but a real injury. She had worried too about her daughter's isolation, whether she should be interacting with other children at this age. Doubts and fears that she had borne alone in order not to bother Gerry with them.

And all, it now seemed, to allow him to deceive her, to lead a double life doing whatever it was that had led to his present situation. She had been a fool, suspecting nothing, blinded by her love for him, her absorption in domestic matters and raising their daughter. How he must have scorned her simplicity! Shame at her own gullibility scalded her. Nobody respected a person so easy to hoodwink. It was as if she had collaborated in her own deception.

So should she tell the police? Tilly bit her lip, staring sightlessly at the night beyond the lighted window. Was she risking her own freedom by keeping silent? Did it make her an accessory – or was there some dispensation against spouses being forced to inform against each another? Her anger urged her to tell, but the memory of Sergeant Burns and her own innate loyalty tipped the balance. There was no actual proof of wrongdoing. She would continue to act the widow because, in her heart, that was how she regarded herself. Anything she and Gerry had once shared was over.

# *Chapter Fourteen*

The following morning, as Tilly left the house carrying the joey bottles, Sophie picked up the dish of diced meat that was Harry's breakfast and followed her across to the animal enclosure. There, she lifted the second joey onto her lap, feeding the long teat into its eager mouth, and looked searchingly at her cousin before she spoke. 'Have you decided about the letter then?'

Tilly shook her head. 'I won't be reporting it, Sophie. Keeping this secret is the last thing I'll do for him. He chose to be dead – well, as far as I'm concerned, he is.'

'I see. It's your decision, Till. You did tell Connor though.'

'It was the shock.' Tilly stared at her cousin, forgetting to monitor the milk flow. 'Reading those words was like – like having his ghost appear before me. I almost passed out! And it was all so quick, I barely had time to take them in before the paper burnt away. Anyway, I asked Connor not to mention it and I don't think he will.' Briefly she wondered at her confidence in him. She'd known him only a few weeks but felt an implicit trust in his word. He had said he wouldn't tell and she believed him.

Sophie frowned. 'That's all very well, but it means you're not free. Suppose the police don't find him, and down the track you want to marry again? What then?'

'Right now that's the last thing I have to worry about.'

'Yes, but one day . . . You might,' Sophie said carefully, 'want another child, Till.'

Tilly shrugged. 'Plenty of couples have kids without marrying. Anyway, you can have someone officially declared dead if they vanish for long enough. I'll find out about that if I need to. I'm going to revert to my own name too – Mum's maiden name, I mean. I was never Tilly Williams, so I'm not using that one. I'm sick of lies and pretending.'

'You might hurt Elaine's feelings if you do.'

'And what about mine?' Tilly demanded. 'I didn't ask for any of this! My stepfather never did more than tolerate me, my husband deceived me, my daughter—' Her voice broke momentarily but she swallowed hard and recovered, saying flintily, 'So just excuse me if I'm not too concerned about anyone else's feelings right now.'

Sophie lifted her hands, one holding the now empty bottle. 'Whatever you want, Till. I'd kick the bugger myself if he was here. The thing I don't like about this is that he was here at all. Why? He's supposed to be dead, so why is he doing the tourist thing?'

It was a question that had not occurred to Tilly. Frowning, she said, 'I can't imagine. I spent hours last night thinking about what he could've been up to and the most feasible, given that he had the boat, seemed to be people smuggling. But what could that possibly have to do with Binboona?'

'I can't see a connection,' Sophie admitted. 'Here'—she

passed the dish of meat to her cousin—'Harry's feed. I'll see to the bottles. And I just might ask the boys to keep their eyes open for anything odd about the place. Don't worry, I won't mention Gerry, but if something funny's going on here . . .'

'We keep a record of everybody that enters Binboona,' Tilly objected. 'And there's only the camp to come to. It would be tantamount to murder to dump refugees out in the bush.'

'That's what I'm hoping. Maybe Gerry was just hiding out, thinking it was safer than town. After all, he couldn't have known you were here. It must've come as a helluva shock to see you. If he did, of course.'

'He did,' Tilly said. 'Well, somebody did and told him. Or else how would he have known where to send the letter?'

She stared blindly at the dish of meat, saying slowly, 'Maybe I should leave. Not just Binboona, but the north – just go and leave the whole mess behind.'

'But—' Sophie checked her protest and said instead, 'Where though? Not back home?'

'No, I couldn't. Mum's got enough on her plate. I'd have to find a place of my own, and a job.' Her lips twisted derisively. 'Doing what? I'm not trained for anything – that's the trouble. If I hadn't been in such a rush to get away when I finished school . . . But I'm a bit old now to start anywhere as an apprentice.'

'You could start here,' her cousin offered. 'Become a proper qualified ranger.'

'But *here* is the problem, don't you see? You're out all day and I'm cooped up in the homestead with nothing to do but go over and over things . . . Oh, don't think I'm not grateful for the job,' she hastened to add. 'I am, Sophie, truly! Only now, knowing Gerry's alive, and worrying about what he's done—'

'That's his problem. *He* did it, not you. And having cost you everything, I don't see why you should lose your job over it, or your accommodation,' Sophie said sternly. 'What you need is variety, Till. I should have seen it myself. Why don't you think seriously about becoming a ranger? I mean it, girl. Doing the stuff Luke and I do. You're halfway there already – you know the bush, you can drive, handle sick animals, you've done your first-aid courses. Also you've learnt the birds, and can name quite a number of the trees. It's not a bad job. There's good tenure, the pay's not great but it's more than you're drawing now, and you get to wear this fancy shirt.' She plucked at her own khaki model with its stylised sugar glider on the breast pocket, surmounted by the capital letters *WPA*. 'You could start today, Tilly. Make your lunch and go with Luke – he can mentor you. Best that I don't, because of our relationship, so that later on there can be no question about your qualifications. Then I'll inform head office that they've got themselves a new recruit.'

'But what if they don't . . . I mean, you run things here, but can you just take on someone like that?'

Sophie nodded. 'The company's actively looking for new people at the moment – they've been advertising for expressions of interest for the past three months. Anyway, why wouldn't they want you? There aren't too many women willing to take on the job. So, do you fancy the change?'

'Yes, but . . . What about my current work? Won't we still need a housekeeper? Who's going to take the camping fees and keep the logbook and do the cooking and washing?' she blurted.

'We'll just go back to how we were before you came. Everybody takes turns, including you. So you'll have three days in the field getting your hands dirty and one at home cooking and feeding animals and logging the campers in and out. You'll be so busy you won't have time to worry about what Gerry's up to.'

'And you really believe I could do it?' Tilly asked doubtfully.

'On your ear,' Sophie asserted. 'It's just common sense and hard graft. You'll have to write reports, and maybe swot up some facts because you'll be helping with the slide nights and the nature walks, so you'll need to be accurate in what you say. And put in the hours of course. Still, you're pretty fit, so the physical side shouldn't worry you.'

Tilly drew a breath and said cautiously, 'Will the boys be okay with it? Luke, yes, but what about Matt? I've already had a disagreement with—'

'It's nothing to do with him,' Sophie said briskly. 'Matt's support staff, he's not a ranger. That's why you'll be teamed with Luke.'

'Oh.' Tilly was surprised. 'I thought he was. He's never said . . . I mean, he never says much anyway, but he hasn't once corrected me on it. And he's heard me tell people he's one plenty of times.'

'Yeah, well, he's on the books as a mechanic and handyman. So, what are you thinking, Tilly? Are you really serious about leaving?'

'No, not if you believe I can do this.' Tilly was suddenly filled with a sense of anticipation for the days ahead. 'Thank you,

Sophie – for the chance and the support. Somehow, whenever I get to a crisis point in my life you always seem to be there with an alternative.'

'Said I would be,' the other woman replied gruffly. 'Hurry it up then. I'll try to catch Luke before he leaves.'

Connor returned to Binboona two days later. Tilly, dusty and dog-tired, for she and Luke had been working on the walking paths up the cliffs that formed the Nutt River gorge, recognised his vehicle as they drove in at sunset.

'Looks like our wandering botanist is back.' Luke pulled on the handbrake and let the diesel engine idle down before switching off. Tilly, glad enough to sit for a moment, nodded. Luke grinned. 'How's the shoulders? We must've shifted half a tonne of rock today – you still want to be a ranger, Tilly?'

'Ah, but think how beautiful the paths are now,' she retorted tiredly. 'A blind man could find his way along them. It's hard work,' she agreed, 'but more interesting than cooking and cleaning. Speaking of which, I wonder what Matt's made us for dinner? I'm so hungry I could eat a horse – and raw at that.'

'Well, it won't be horse but I wouldn't guarantee it's not half raw or burnt black,' Luke said darkly. 'He's worse than me in the kitchen and that's saying something.'

Connor must have been of the same opinion, Tilly thought, for the next morning he announced his intention of moving down to the camp. 'I've imposed on you all long enough,' he told her as she cleared the table, it being her turn today for house duties.

She grinned. 'It wouldn't have anything to do with that truly frightful meal last night? By the way, Connor, thank you for that little carving. It's lovely.'

'You're very welcome, Tilly. So, you're going to be a ranger – how come?' Hastily he added, 'Not that I mean to pry, but—'

'Oh, that's okay. I suppose I just needed a change. Besides, it's an opportunity. I've only ever had odd jobs, never a career.' Save that of wife and mother, she thought. 'Something to put on my resume, if I ever need one,' she said lightly. 'What about you – have you ever thought of changing what you do?'

He paused for a moment as if considering the question. 'Maybe I'll go back to nursery work one day, run my own business. Grow things instead of just driving around monitoring them.'

'Speaking of growing, I'd better get the sprays started on the garden,' Tilly remembered. 'Just a few days away from it and I'm all out of routine.' Dumping a handful of cutlery in its drawer, she made for the door, pausing to say, 'No doubt I'll see you round the camp then. You should try some of the walking paths we've been working on. They're worth the effort, though I say it myself.'

'Maybe I will. I'll see you around.'

That evening, Sophie sighed with completion as she finished the excellent beef curry Tilly had made. 'That was great. I've had an idea, guys. What if Tilly picks out half-a-dozen simple recipes in her cookbook – something not beyond our capabilities – and we try following them when it's our turn to cook? She can tell us what we've done wrong each night and that way we might actually learn something.'

'I'll second that,' Luke said. 'Matt?'

He shrugged. 'Yeah. Whatever.'

'Well, come on! Are you saying your efforts couldn't stand improvement?'

Matt shot him a dirty look. 'You worry too much about your belly. Me, I'd just like to know who's been messing with my stuff.'

Tilly stared at him. 'What do you mean?'

'Someone's been through my room. A couple of times, actually. If it wasn't you lot, then it had to be Doyle.'

'Connor?' Sophie raised her brows. 'Are you sure, Matt? Is something missing?'

'No,' he said grudgingly. 'But my gear's been shifted around, like somebody's had a good poke through it. You know where you leave things. I do, anyroad. And if they ain't where you left 'em, it means somebody's gone and shifted 'em.'

'I can't believe that Connor's responsible,' Tilly protested even as she acknowledged to herself that Matt would certainly notice if anything was changed. He was obsessively neat, and she had cleaned his room often enough to know it. Something niggled at the back of her mind, the memory of coming home to find her own things displaced – the hairbrush out of place, the shoes pushed beyond reach beneath the bed. At the time she had put it down to haste on her part. Suspicion flickered for a moment before she banished it. Connor wouldn't! Though he had been in residence at the time, she remembered, and home before her that day. Still, why would he? It was ridiculous even to think it.

Luke was of the same opinion. 'Nah, you're dreaming, mate!'

'You think?' Matt retorted. 'What do we know about the bloke anyway, eh? He rocks up here, acts like he's entitled to be housed and fed, and snoops around the place at his leisure. I caught him in my workshop one day. Lookin' to borrow some pliers, he said. Only he weren't nowhere near the toolbox at the time.'

'He'd just have been interested,' Sophie said. 'Sheds, you know – tools and junk. Men love poking around in them. But getting back to what I was saying – you reckon you could do that, Till?'

'What? Oh, the recipes . . . Yes, no problem. Simple, foolproof, easy to follow. Right you are.' She grinned at her table mates. 'Dinner for dummies then. I'll make a list and write up the page numbers. You'll all be chefs by the end of the season.'

'Or dead from food poisoning,' Luke said dolefully.

Only Matt failed to join in the laughter.

# *Chapter Fifteen*

Tilly had almost reflexively dismissed Matt's accusation about Connor, but later that evening, as she sat up in her bed brushing her hair and ruminating idly over the day's events, she recalled his words and felt the growth of a faint uneasiness. It was no good telling herself that Matt had imagined somebody getting into his gear; Binboona's mechanic lived in a world of facts, not fancy. He wasn't the imaginative sort. It made him predictable, and yes, boring, even if his inability to invent was his main strength. What was, was, with Matt. Like the game that he was so enamoured of, she reflected. Chess rules were immutable. There might be a million moves to be made about the board, but when the king was checkmated, that was it. So if he said his belongings had been rifled through, then somebody must have done it, and Connor was the only candidate.

Was simple curiosity reason enough? But why should he have the slightest interest in Matt? The two men were as good as strangers, having barely, to Tilly's knowledge, spoken more than politeness demanded. Matt had ignored Connor, apart from the occasional comment to Tilly, prompted by apparent jealousy of a wrongly percieved understanding between them. Totally wrong, Tilly reiterated to herself. Still, Connor *had* been curious. All those questions he'd asked her about herself and the others – their backgrounds, their tasks at Binboona. Surely it was just a natural interest in one's chance companions – but you couldn't say the same thing about searching through those same companions' belongings. *If* he had, she reminded herself.

Something else Matt had said echoed in her head: *What do we know about the bloke anyway, eh?* It was a fair question, and in all honesty, the answer was very little. Connor had identified himself through a message he himself had left on the phone. She must check with Sophie, Tilly thought, but she was pretty sure that her cousin hadn't actually spoken to anyone at the university about the field trip he was supposedly undertaking. Which meant that no third party had vouched for him. He had represented himself as being who he was. And of course she believed him. She did. Only some faint tinge of suspicion she wished to banish lingered in her mind. The simplest way to do it, she thought resolutely, would be to ring the uni and ask for the whereabouts of Connor Doyle, botanist.

Momentarily pausing the brush, Tilly wondered whether she should take this step. Doing so, even contemplating it, gave body to the nebulous disquiet she felt, but it was more than that. Her hand moved again but the bristles, meeting the hair wrong, got caught and she winced, carefully disentangling the strands, brow creasing in a little frown. Checking up on him implied that Connor mattered to her, and she wasn't yet sure that she wanted this to be so. She would have to think carefully about it. It was too late tonight anyway, and there would be no chance in the morning with the others around. Which shouldn't matter, Tilly told herself severely, but somehow it did.

A spurt of exasperation made her grimace. Indecisiveness seemed to be becoming a habit. It was a simple matter, for God's sake! Either Connor was nosy to the point of transgressing the rules of hospitality, or he was hiding something. Her reaction should be as clear cut as the problem – check it out, or forget it. Laying the brush aside, Tilly wriggled lower in the bed and pulled the covers up, then lay for a long time staring at the ceiling before reaching over to switch off the bedside light.

The following day and the one after that, Tilly worked with Luke on the cliff path. The second evening was a slide night and they ate their warmed-over dinner – a surprisingly good tuna bake of Sophie's making – at the camp.

'You can do the intro this evening,' Luke said. 'I've been taping birdcalls so we'll make it a bit different tonight. Show the slide, then play the call. Then, if enough people turn up, we might try a quiz at the end. Play the calls again and see how many they can recognise. What do you think?'

'I don't know,' Tilly said dubiously. 'I've never done any public speaking. What do I say?'

'Whatever you can think of. Birds are great, birds are wonderful, great variety, they come in all sizes – you know, that sort of stuff. I meant, is the quiz a good idea? I don't want to bore them.'

'It can't hurt. And nobody *makes* them turn up, so they must be interested.'

'That's true,' he said, visibly cheered.

Tilly made a discovery. 'You're nervous, Luke! Remind me – how many times have you done this?'

He pulled a face. 'The slides and the talk are fine. I just wondered about the quiz thing, that's all. I always hated it at school, you know. Being singled out and put on the spot by the teacher.'

'Yes, well, you are the teacher now. There'll be kids – ask them first. They love attention.'

'Okay. And if nobody else answers, you can. Deal?'

'Deal,' Tilly agreed, collecting their dinner dishes. 'It must be about time to get over there and set up.'

The evening went well with plenty of interaction from their audience, at least half of whom lingered on to talk afterwards. Tilly, packing the slides carefully into their boxes, jumped when Connor spoke at her shoulder. She hadn't known he was present; it was too dark to see beyond the single cone of light angled away from the screen, by which they'd operated.

'Evening, Tilly. I didn't expect to see you here.'

'Oh.' She was flustered, suspicion warring with her liking for him, making her words sound offhand. 'No big mystery there. You know I've changed jobs. I'm a trainee now and keeping the tourists busy is all part of it.' Why, she wondered wildly, had she said 'mystery'? She might as well have told him to his face that she suspected . . . She was being ridiculous. Abruptly she asked, 'So, what have you been up to?' The words came out like an accusation.

He shrugged. 'Just the usual stuff, collating, photographing, collecting. Someday I hope to publish a book on the trees and shrubs of the Top End, which means trips like this are useful for research as well as work. So how are you liking your new job?'

'It's different,' she said shortly, fitting the projector into its battered box. 'More physical, and there's plenty to learn. Some of it I already know, but Luke's knowledge of the country just amazes me. Seems I've lots of catching up to do.'

'There's always more to any job than the outsider thinks,' he agreed, and yawned. 'Time for my bed. I enjoyed the show, by the way, if you'd tell Luke?'

'I will. Goodnight.' She wondered if her curtness had driven him away, but she wasn't able to pretend the ease she had previously felt in his company. And if he *had* been spying on them all, then she had no wish to spend time with him anyway.

'Was that Connor?' Luke asked. 'Nice of him to come. I didn't know he was interested in birds.'

'Mmm. He told me he enjoyed it. Luke,' Tilly said suddenly, 'do you think Matt meant it, about Connor going through his stuff?'

'Huh?' The young ranger looked up from the tricky task of collapsing the screen. 'Nah. Give me a single reason why he'd want to. Between you and me, I sometimes think old Matt lives in his head too much. All that chess. It's like he's always expecting a pawn or one of those horse thingies to sneak up on him.'

'Knights,' said Tilly. 'They're called knights.'

'Uh-huh. Well, maybe he ought to get out more. Can you grab the legs and fold 'em in for me? There's a clip at the bottom holds them closed. That's it. Damn thing weighs a ton.'

Irritated by his easy dismissal of her problem, Tilly picked up the slide box, tucked the cassette recorder under one arm and aimed the torch ahead of their feet. 'Got everything?' she said brusquely. 'Let's go then.' It was not that she *wanted* to be convinced of Connor's villainy, she told herself, but surely the question deserved more than two seconds' thought! Of course, Luke's entire being was probably consumed with thoughts of his Jane. She huffed out an exasperated breath. Men had no curiosity. The sky could fall, and they'd just pick up the bits and never think to wonder what brought them down.

When the chance came to do her own asking, Tilly found herself reluctant to take it. The homestead was hers for the day, the others dispersed about the property. She fed the animals, loaded the washing machine, swept the floors and, having made herself a cup of tea, sat eyeing the phone. All she had to do was punch in the number on the slip of paper beside her mug, then ask to speak to Connor Doyle. The receptionist – did universities have receptionists? – would apologise for their inability to comply, would say he was away from the uni just now, and that would be that. So why was she hesitating?

Because it was sneaky to be going behind his back, the little voice in her head observed. *Yes?* she mentally replied, *And searching other peple's belongings isn't?* But you don't know that he did, the voice argued. *Then why*, another voice – the voice of reason – nagged, *are you even thinking about it?*

'Oh, for heaven's sake!' Tilly grabbed the handpiece and stabbed fiercely at the numbers.

*

A few minutes later she put the phone down and sat staring at her empty cup. The receptionist had been quite sure. No student, mature age or otherwise, was registered under that name. They had no faculty member or visiting professor called Doyle in the university and no, no research grants were being funded at present – definitely not. Was Ms Hillyer quite sure that she had the details correct?

'Perhaps it was Adelaide he meant, not Darwin, and I got the wrong end of the stick,' Tilly had mumbled. 'No, no, that's fine. Thanks for your trouble, it wasn't really important.'

She rose from the table and, tipping her half-drunk tea into the sink, went to the door to stare at the distant waters of the Nutt glinting between the jungle growth of the river bank. Matt had been right. If Connor *was* a botanist, he certainly wasn't the one he was pretending to be. What possible reason could he have for lying to them, and what, if anything, should she do about it? Was it even her business? There could be a perfectly innocent explanation after all.

*Like what?* the annoying inner voice asked.

'Well, I don't know, do I?' she exploded, venting to the empty air. 'That's the problem!' Should she tell Sophie? She was in charge, after all, and it was her trust that had been exploited. Or she could simply confront the man himself and demand an explanation? Yes, she thought, she would do that first. And spill the beans after – if he had no reasonable excuse to offer.

No sooner had the decision been made than Tilly heard the approach of a vehicle from the camp. It was early for the others to be returning, and the pace of the Toyota made her heart jump in sudden dismay. She ran to the verandah's edge just as it slowed to a stop before the shed. Luke jumped out, followed more slowly by Sophie, and both hurried into the building to return a moment later, hefting the heavy collapsible ladder between them.

Tilly jogged over as they struggled to lift it onto the cab of the vehicle. 'What are you doing, guys? What's going on?'

'Ask those bastards!' Luke said furiously. He was balanced on the bullbar, hauling the bulky ladder forward. 'Tilly, there's a rope near your foot. Can you chuck the end up to me?'

She obeyed, shading her eyes. 'What's that for?'

'To check the nests, not that there's likely to be anything left in them. Go round the back, will you, and help Sophie. When I sing out "hang on", make sure you do.'

'Okay.' No wiser, Tilly did as she was bidden. She heard Luke yell, 'Now!' and the ladder jerked suddenly in the two women's hands, then Luke was there with a second rope, tying the lowest rung to the ball of the towbar at the rear.

'Right. Secured front and back. We should take the chainsaw too, boss. If there's a chick left, we won't reach it. The nests are usually at least a metre down inside the tree.'

'Get it then,' Sophie replied, then turned to Tilly. 'There's been wildlife traffickers working the place. Luke found some vehicle tracks out near Blooms Rock and we followed them. Whoever it is has been trapping black cockatoos and God knows what else. If they had birding nets—' She was as angry as the young ranger, Tilly saw, her lips compressed and a hard light in her eyes.

'But – cockies?' Tilly was incredulous. 'Who would want . . .? Can't you just buy them? And black ones aren't even that special.' There were droves of them in the north. She saw them every day, winging home above the river, their harsh discordant calls a feature of evenings at Binboona.

'They're protected, and worth anywhere up to forty thousand dollars a pair overseas on the black market,' Luke said tersely.

'*Forty* thousand!' Tilly blinked. 'But, I mean, they're a big strong bird. How—'

'It's breeding season,' he said. 'They've chicks in the nest. The smugglers use a ladder and carry a net to cover the hollow. Then they bang on the trunk and the parent bird panics and goes straight up into the net. All they have to do then is hang about until the bird's mate turns up and catch him too. Then they bugger off and leave the chicks to starve.'

'That's dreadful! So where are they now – these men?'

'Long gone,' Sophie said briefly. 'We can't spend time chasing them if we're to have any chance of saving the chicks. And we need to work backwards from the first nest we found – there could be more.' She pulled the door open as Luke also got in. 'See you later, Tilly.'

'Right.' Bemused by the rapid turn of events, her own worries temporarily subsumed in this new concern, Tilly watched them speed off. Sighing, she returned to the house to hang the washing.

# *Chapter Sixteen*

It was late in the afternoon before Sophie and the young ranger returned. Matt, who had spent the day grading the back roads, beat them home by just five minutes, and was hearing about their discovery when Tilly cocked her head to listen. 'Here they come now.'

'I hear 'em.' Matt smacked his hat against the one of the posts guarding the vegetable garden; his upper body was coated in dust, for the cab on the old grader was no more than a roof over a worn seat. 'A bad business,' he grunted. 'If the buggers are still about, I hope they ain't mucking around with my grader. I left 'er sitting out there at the end of the river track.'

'Did you?' Tilly said vaguely. She turned off the hose, her eyes on the vehicle and those emerging from it. They must have rescued a chick, because Luke was cradling something wrapped in a grubby towel.

She hurried to his side. 'What did you find?' He folded the material back to disclose not one but two ugly little bodies, all beak and eyes, only partially fledged. 'They're awfully young, aren't they? To rear, I mean.'

'Probably. They're maybe five, six weeks old. I'll have to try.' He didn't sound hopeful and Tilly touched his hand consolingly.

'It won't be your fault if you can't. Do you know if they visited other nests?'

'We didn't find any,' Sophie said, 'but we followed the tracks back almost to the river and saw where they'd had birding nets out.' Noting Tilly's blank look, she explained tersely, 'Very fine nylon with a tight weave. For little birds, finches and wrens and such. They can't see it so they get caught and tangled up in it. Like fish. Only, tiny birds are fragile things – they die easily from shock, or maybe the speed at which they hit it. It's said that about twenty per cent of those caught that way perish. We found the bodies, so we know the net was there.'

Tilly felt a flush of anger. 'That's wicked!'

'Yes,' her cousin agreed. 'I'll ring the police in Darwin, but there's not much chance of catching anyone now.'

Later that evening her prediction was borne out by her brief conversation with the Darwin station.

'What did the cops say?' Tilly asked as she dished out the meal. 'Who did you speak to?'

'Some sergeant. Who as good as told me not to hold my breath waiting on a conviction.' Sophie sighed. 'Of course, it's not easy for them. Travellers must outnumber locals in Darwin at this time of year. Then the birds could be transported by road or plane or sea. And the hell of it is, it doesn't matter to the criminals if they lose half of them – their thinking is there're plenty more to be trapped. It's not just birds either.

They smuggle terrapins, lizards, snakes . . . Anything that's protected, which is all our native fauna now.'

'How are the chicks?' Tilly asked Luke. 'If they're so valuable, why didn't they take them too?'

'Too much trouble feeding them. I'd better stop with 'em tomorrow, boss, see if I can get them to eat. We've got ordinary birdseed, which isn't ideal – they'd be getting ground eucalyptus nuts from their parents, plus whatever enzymes they'd have in their crop. I'm not very hopeful,' he finished gloomily.

'I can see to the camp stuff myself,' Tilly volunteered. 'I've got it down pat now. Clean the ablution block, rake out the ash beneath the donkeys, light the fire, restock the wood supply, empty the rubbish, check the tank and the pump . . .'

'Okay,' Sophie said, nodding. 'But be careful at the river, won't you? I noticed the supply of leaflets was low in the box too, so take a few extra. My turn to cook tomorrow – where are you up to, Matt?'

'I'll be getting back to the grader.' He frowned. 'Just hope no buggers been at it. Ain't much of a step from stealing wildlife to nicking a battery or damagin' something. I'd've brought it back if I'd known.'

'Let's hope they were too concentrated on getting away,' Sophie said heavily. 'They'd have come in and left on the old mining tracks, I expect. Right, I'd better report it to head office. Is it worth asking them for special parrot-chick feed, Luke? They could contact a zoo, I suppose, find out if such a thing is available.'

'It's a nice thought, but not unless there's a private jet involved. The chicks'd starve before it got here. I'll see what I can do with what we've got. Is there a rolling pin, Tilly?'

She raised her brows at him. 'Uh-huh. Why on earth—?'

'I thought maybe if I crush the seed, mix it with something – got any ideas? It needs to be sort of sloppy, but not too much so.'

Mentally running through a list of the cupboard contents, Tilly said doubtfully, 'You could try glucose syrup, perhaps. It's sort of gluggy, and isn't it used to rehydrate patients? It works for the glider, after all.'

'Worth a try,' he decided and she went to find it for him.

Both chicks survived the night. The following morning, Tilly, carrying her lunch and thermos, stopped in at the animal enclosure on her way to the shed and found Luke bent patiently above the new arrivals, using the finger and thumb of his right hand to simulate a beak, while the other held a pellet of food ready to poke down the chick's gullet if and when it opened its mouth.

'Getting anywhere?' she asked.

'Morning.' He looked tired and unshaven. 'Let's just say it's a battle. The smaller one's fairly weak, but I think this chap's starting to get the idea. You off, then?'

'Yes. Do I need to fuel up?'

'Always,' he said definitely. 'Never take a vehicle out unless the tank's full. You dunno where you might end up, and you don't wanna walk the last twenty kay. And watch yourself at the river. Remember the big salty's still in there.'

'I will,' she promised. 'Good luck with your babies, Luke. Don't forget to feed the little glider, will you? I'll see you tonight.'

*

By now Tilly was practised at the domestic part of the job. She parked beside the ablution block and began methodically on the chores, scrubbing the concrete floors with a stiff brush, cleaning toilets, heaving the day's allocation of wood off the vehicle's tray and spading yesterday's ash into the bucket, before starting a modest fire beneath the donkey. She replaced the shovel and broom in their simple cabinet, slid the padlock closed and turned to heft the bucket of ash onto the vehicle. Movement behind her caught the corner of her eye, and she swung quickly around to see Connor approaching.

'Here, let me get that,' he said. He swung the receptacle into the circle of the spare tyre. 'Morning, Tilly. Where's Luke today?'

'Busy.' Dusting her hands off on her jeans, she eyed him, her dislike palpable. 'So who are you really, Connor Doyle?'

His gaze flickered for an instant, the easy smile momentarily frozen in place. 'I beg your pardon?'

'I mean, seeing that you aren't a botanist and there isn't a research grant, we'd really like to know who exactly the WPA has been housing and feeding. And by the way, there are camp fees due before you push off.'

Connor held still with only that betraying flicker of the eyes; she could almost sense his mind scrambling for a plausible explanation. 'Listen, there's some mistake—' he began, but she cut him off contemptuously.

'Don't bother. I've spoken to the uni who, you won't be surprised to learn, have never heard of you – or your research. It was a nice touch, I must say, carrying an orchid handbook in the glove box. Very professional! You lied to us, wormed your way into our lives and you searched our rooms. You even went through the sheds, Matt said. For all I know, Doyle's not even your real name.'

'Well, it is,' he said flatly. 'And I did study botany, though I admit I didn't come away with a degree. And I'm sorry about going through your things, Tilly. I felt bad about that. I had no right but it was necessary at the time. I—'

'You certainly hadn't,' she said fiercely. 'What are you, some sort of pervert that gets off on sneaking into women's panty drawers? I should—'

He raised his hands. 'Please! It wasn't like that. I would never . . . If you'd just give me five minutes to explain.'

'And I'd do that so, what? You could spin another lie? I haven't the power to throw you off the place, more's the pity, but I *can* report you to the police, so maybe that's just what I'll do—'

'Wait!' He'd raised his voice into a bark of command and Tilly stiffened, casting a rapid look behind her. It was still early but there must be somebody stirring in the camp. She'd scream if he took a single step towards her, she promised her suddenly thudding heart.

'Sorry, sorry.' Connor must have sensed her unease for he made dampening motions with his hands. 'I didn't mean to yell, only you mustn't ring the police, or tell anyone. I mean it, Tilly. Please, just let me explain. I'm not a crook, if that's what you're thinking, but it's important that nobody else tumbles to the truth.'

'Oh yes.' She folded her arms. 'I expect this is where you disclose that you're ASIO or something, chasing a spy who's made off with the blueprints for a new superweapon or a better set of pram wheels, maybe. If that's the case, save your breath.'

His lips twitched involuntarily as he shook his head. 'Nothing like that. I'm a Customs officer working with Sergeant Burns and a handful of other coppers trying to break a drug ring. We know the stuff's coming in across the Straits, so there has to be boats involved, but it's not being funnelled through the port of Darwin. Which is why we're checking other options. Like Binboona.' He took a breath and finished with a blunt pronouncement. 'We have reason to think your husband is part of it. That's why I'm here, because we have never believed that he's dead. Now please, just let me explain.'

'No,' Tilly said vehemently for the third time. 'Not drugs. Gerry wouldn't do that. All right, he's lied. I know that. He's alive and hiding out, and he's obviously involved in *something* clandestine'—she couldn't bring herself to say *criminal*—'but not drugs. I've never known him to touch them.'

They were sitting on folding stools under the flyrig at Connor's camp. A small double-handled tin sat next to the fire, the edges of the water within it just beginning to bubble. Connor rose to drop tea leaves into it and lift it from the flames.

'What is that thing?' Tilly asked, distracted.

'Quartpot. Stockmen carry them on their saddles. Quicker than a billy.' He tapped the side with a stick, waited while the leaves settled, then poured half the contents into a tin mug. 'There you go – sugar?'

'I don't want tea.' She took the cup and immediately set it aside. 'I want to know what your coming to Binboona to spy on us has to do with running drugs.' The moment the words left her mouth, she made the connection and her hands flew to her mouth. 'It was *me*, wasn't it? You thought that Gerry – that I . . .? That's why the police came that day. And then you turned up, after.' Her eyes went wide as she remembered.

'Burns got impatient. He wasn't willing to wait. Once he'd got you offside, though, he had to leave it to me. He came back only because we couldn't think of any reason for me to have those photos you looked at.'

'I was going to refuse,' Tilly said contemptuously, 'only you turned up to play the good cop and convinced me to do it. That was well orchestrated, I must say.'

He said quietly, his words confirming her guess, 'I haven't liked deceiving you. And strictly speaking, I'm not a cop. But Customs play an important role in the country's defence, so I'm not ashamed of the job I do. And in fact, I'd exonerated you of any involvement only a day or two after we met.'

'So why were you still searching? Matt said you were in the sheds and you can't have suspected Sophie of importing drugs, for God's sake!'

'Somebody is, Tilly.' He looked at her across the blackened quartpot, and she absently picked up her own cup and took a sip. 'But it's not just Binboona we're checking out. There's a young Stock Squad copper in the camp at Spadgers Creek, keeping an eye out there. They have coastal access too, so theoretically the drugs could be run ashore on their country. Somebody at the station could be involved. That, by the way, is classified information, so I'm trusting you to keep it between us – all right?'

'I suppose,' she muttered. 'Did you say you had sugar?'

'Here.' He reached behind him and handed her a lidded tin.

'There's a spoon it it. So do the other rangers know about me being a ring-in yet?'

'Not yet. I only rang the uni yesterday while they were all out, then Luke and Sophie came rushing back for the ladder, and everyone was so upset about the birds it didn't seem important—'

Connor looked bemused, his tea forgotten. 'Ladder?'

She told him about the birders and the rescued chicks, and he nodded.

'Yeah, that's something else we watch for. Look, I'm going to ask you not to say anything about me. To anybody at all, and that includes the police.' He hesitated, 'You're going to ask, so I have to tell you. Burns suspects that some of his fellow cops are dirty, and if they catch even a hint of our operation it will fail and months of work will be wasted. Also your life could be at risk. In this case, ignorance is the safest path. I'm serious, Tilly. Drug runners are ruthless bastards. If there's a loose end, a thread that could lead to their capture – like, for instance, you knowing that your husband isn't dead . . . Well, they won't hesitate to kill.'

Ice seemed to fill Tilly's veins even as she protested vehemently. 'I've told you Gerry isn't . . . and anyway, he would never let me be harmed!'

'He mightn't have a choice,' Connor said grimly. 'There're billions at stake here and at best he's a foot soldier, as expendable as any frontline trooper. So will you promise me, Tilly, please? For your sake? Not a word to anyone.'

She rocked forward on the stool as if she were in pain, closing her eyes as the gravity of his words and manner sank in. *Once* . . . there was a time when she had a child and a man she loved and thought she could trust. When she had a future and believed in happily ever after – and see what had come of it! She wanted to howl her loss for fairytales that weren't true, for faith smashed on the anvil of reality. Gerry had done this to her, had tossed a grenade of lies and deceit into her life and then vanished, leaving her alone in the wreckage.

'Tilly?' A tentative hand touched her shoulder and was withdrawn. 'Are you okay?'

She straightened, blurred eyes blank and dark with grief. 'No,' she said bitterly. 'I'm not. And yes, I won't tell.' And with that admission of belief in his warning, she felt the last vestige of her love for Gerry die. Now she truly was the widow the world believed her to be.

# *Chapter Seventeen*

Over the following week the smaller of the two black cockatoo chicks grew gradually worse, then, just when Luke had pronounced that it couldn't live, made a remarkable recovery. The sugar glider too, having thrived on its diet, was to Tilly's secret regret returned to its habitat, disappearing up a tree with a whisk of its extraordinary tail.

'It's so cute,' she lamented to Luke, as she watched it vanish. 'Another week and it'd be as tame as a kitten.'

'Which is not what we want,' he reproved her. 'They're wild animals, not pets.'

'I know.' She sighed. 'Only we can't have pets at Binboona. Not cats or dogs, anyway.'

'There's Harry and Mickey – they'll never leave.'

'Oh, birds.' She wrinkled her nose. 'They're not exactly cuddly. I know, you think they're God's greatest creation, but I prefer the furry things. So, what next?'

'We'll take a run out to the springs. I want to check the track. Seeing Matt's got the grader halfway there, it might be worth his while to grade into 'em – if it's dry enough.

We'll head back first, make our lunches, grab a cuppa and go. Maybe the mail'll be in before we leave.'

Tilly nodded. 'How's Jane these days?'

'She's good, thanks.'

'You're still counting the days to the Wet?' That was when they took their breaks away, with Binboona's staff reduced to care-taker mode for the monsoon.

'Yep, can't wait.' He looked so young and hopeful that Tilly felt a momentary ache of anxiety for him. Dreams were so easily crushed. She hoped that Luke's would last. It was hard for her to view him objectively because he was so like a younger brother, but surely most girls would think him quite a dish, especially with the added allure of being a rugged outdoor type. Though could you really call his beanpole frame rugged?

'Have you gone into a trance, Tilly?' he demanded then and she came back to herself with a jolt.

'Huh? Oh, sorry. Ready if you are, then.'

Sophie was sorting the mail when they returned. She handed two letters to Luke, and Tilly, busy with their lunches while the kettle whistled, saw him tuck them into his breast pocket with a smile. He'd read them later, in private, where he could dream of their author, she thought. The shriek from the stove continued and she leant over to poke him with the handle of the bread knife. 'Who's in a trance now? Can you fill the thermoses, Luke?'

It was the first time that Tilly had been in the southern area of the property, and she was amazed at the tangle of old overgrown tracks leading every which way through the ridge country fronting the distant escarpment. She knew some, like the one they followed, were the original station tracks leading to old yards and watering points. Here and there the remains of fences still showed, or the rotted footings of a tank, but the rest of the tracks seemed a mad tangle with no discernable purpose.

'Mineral exploration,' Luke said when she asked. 'The Mines Department had geologists crawling all over the north back in the fifties. They bulldozed their way through the country, and this is what's left. You can still scc their old camps dotted about.'

'Didn't the stations object? They owned the land, didn't they?'

'They leased it,' he corrected. 'It actually belongs to the Crown. And mining rights take precedence over grazing. It's not all bad though, we use some of their roads – the station probably did too. On the other hand, they make it dead easy for the traffickers. Without these tracks they couldn't get around half so well.'

'So, a mixed blessing then.' Tilly winced as the front wheel fell into a hole and her elbow banged against the door. 'You sure you don't want to go back? There's bound to be bumps you missed.'

'Very funny. We'll collect 'em on the way home.'

The springs, Tilly learnt, were at the foot of the escarpment, in a gentle vale whose southern side rose to the rugged cliff face of fragmented ochre rock. Some time in the distant past, large sections of it had collapsed, forming a broken ridge of slabs and boulders through which a scrub of wattle, ironwood and grevillea had sprouted.

'It doesn't look awfully safe,' she said, eyeing the rockfalls. 'Isn't this the same cliff we were working on with the path?'

'Yeah, but that's back where it parallels the river. Nobody's got plans to scale this lot, and you'll notice the track keeps well clear of it, mainly because the ground's so boggy. The water spreads underground for hectares here. We'll have to walk in. Basically, the whole area is one big spring, it's just that the actual water's only visible here and there.'

'So why don't we let the campers come here?'

'Too difficult to set up facilities and control it. It's fragile country. A lot of the vegetation is unique to the springs, and it'd be tramped down, the ground would compact under foot traffic because people'd want to swim . . . Sophie's got plans for supervised day visits, but the road has to be upgraded first and some sort of fencing done, maybe a boardwalk to protect the flora. There's all sorts of wildflowers too. The WPA mightn't be willing or able to fund that much infrastructure. It's not as if we get tens of thousands of visitors to pay for it.'

'We got over four thousand last year,' Tilly pointed out.

'Mmm, and what do you reckon a kilometre or two of boardwalk would cost? Not to mention labour and the freight involved getting it here.'

'I see what you mean. With that and the road . . .' As she spoke, they encountered another fallen tree across their path. Luke pulled up. 'No way we can drive around with that gully blocking the side. We'll have to clear it.'

'I'll get it.' Tilly hopped out, grabbing the hook from the bullbar's winch, and towed the line out and looped the steel cable about the trunk. She stuck her thumb up at Luke, who engaged four-wheel drive and then, chin on shoulder, backed up until he reached a point where he could tow the fallen tree off the road.

'That's the second one,' he said, shoving the low gear into neutral as she regained her seat. 'Must've been a helluva big wind that came through here.'

'It's not a blow-down,' she said. 'I thought it had burnt through, but it's been chainsawed.'

'What?' Almost as soon as the words left his mouth Luke was out of the cab, striding over to the blackened stump. He bent to examine it, then eyed the fallen bloodwood, scratching reflectively at his neck. 'No hollows, so it's not the traffickers. Damned inefficient way of getting birds anyhow. If it was young corellas say, or galahs, you'd be more likely to kill 'em in the fall.'

'When was it done?' Tilly had rejoined him. 'Before the rains? There's no sign of fire except on the stump.'

'Not so long,' Luke disagreed. 'Weeks, maybe a couple of months. Looks like they built a fire beside it hoping the stump would catch and burn to disguise the saw work. Only it was too green. There's shoots coming out at the back there, and that doesn't happen overnight. Well, nothing we can do here, so let's go.'

A kilometre further on, they left the vehicle and walked towards the forest of brilliant green vegetation that hugged the foot of the cliff. The dark trunks of the pandanus lifted their spear-sharp tops of vivid green above the duller clusters of sandpaper fig and myrtle clumps. Bare sheets of rock glinted ochre and orange in the early morning sun, seamed by cracks and shallow horizontal declivities, which were in turn intersected by the bare roots of the occasional stunted trees clinging to the face or top of the cliff.

'See that big bulge over there just below the dead finish?' Luke nodded to the right at the mass of flowering native boronia clinging to the rock. 'There's a heap of Aboriginal paintings under it. Hand prints mostly, but there's barra, and wallaby, and human figures in corroboree. Very old – almost gone, in fact. The colours have faded back into the rock. Old middens too. You can see the bits of chert and the holes in the sandstone where they must've mixed the ochre. There's a bit of an old fence – the station must've put it up, though God knows why, there'd have been nobody round back then. Maybe it was to keep the stock out.'

'Can we have a look?' Tilly asked.

'Yeah, why not? But it's something else that'd have to be protected if we opened the site.'

Tilly, listening to the silence broken only by the piercing ring of bird calls echoing back from the cliff, and the soft squelch of their boots on the sodden soil, said, 'Shame really to disturb it. Places like this – they're sort of like church, aren't they? Not something to be trooped through as if it was a sideshow.' She stopped to watch a pair of kite hawks gyring overhead until the brilliance of the sky dazzled her retinas, forcing her to shut her eyes against the blazing light. The scent of the land came to her then, damp and flowery with base notes of dust and her own sweat. She sniffed deeply. 'What's that smell, Luke?'

'Some of the scrub'll be flowering. Wattle, maybe, or the myrtle. There's always something in blossom here. It's the water does it. Careful now, the rocks get slippery from this point on.'

Here the water had broken through the soil in little runnels trickling endlessly through mossy stone, spreading into shallow pools over which coloured dragonflies hovered. Tiny ferns uncurled in the damp and a hum of myriad insects – everything from water beetles to march flies, as Tilly discovered when she felt the red-hot wire of a bite on her wrist – filled the air. A deep crack several metres up the cliff face disgorged a slow stream of water that fell into a deep rock-fringed pool where young pandanus were clustered amid thigh-deep bladey grass. A mass of vegetation surrounded the whole area: thickets of wattle, and spring bloodwood, wild plum and ti-tree, some overgrown with wild passion vine, their foliage alive with birdcalls and the occasional glimpse of fluttering wings.

Tilly stared about her, entranced. 'Oh, look at the flowers, they're so tiny! What are those little red ones, Luke?'

'Where? Oh, sundews. They're carnivorous. See the little sticky beads of moisture on them? That's how they trap insects. The bodies dissolve, and the plant gets the juices.'

'I see.' Tilly rubbed her burning wrist. 'I wish they'd eat a few more march flies then.'

She squatted, laving her wrist, then cupping the hand to lift water to her lips, finding it sweet and cold. A glimmer of movement caught her eye within the depths and she saw an angler fish, just as Luke had said. 'How did the fish get in here?'

Luke shrugged. 'Washed in as eggs, or maybe babies. The whole valley would run water in the Wet.'

'I suppose. No crocs either. I can see it would be an ideal camp site – and very quickly loved to death. That's an awful lot of water, Luke.' The pool had to be five metres across and she could see smaller ones dotted about. 'If it were to open, you'd need kilometres of boardwalk to protect it all. Which way to the paintings?'

'Follow me.' He led the way, heading back towards the dry ground.

'Is this as far as the track goes?' Tilly asked.

'Nope. It takes a loop around to the caves, but that's too far for today. They're a bit out of the way, and there's nothing much to see, really. Just holes on the cliff. I daresay we wouldn't get there more than a couple of times a season. Though somebody's been poking around – there's old vehicle tracks under ours.'

'Didn't Connor visit? I'm sure he said something about it,' Tilly replied.

'Well, I can't see a botanist chainsawing trees, even if it wasn't done months back,' Luke said dryly.

'No.' He didn't know and she felt obscurely guilty that she couldn't tell him, so changed the subject. 'Look, it's well past noon. Why don't we take our lunch over to the paintings and eat it there?' She slapped wildly at another march fly. 'Hopefully there'll be fewer insects away from the water.'

'You took the words outta my mouth,' he said. 'Let's go.'

# *Chapter Eighteen*

Over dinner that evening, Sophie, apprised of the chainsawed tree, frowned and said, 'Probably the traffickers, Luke. It's another good argument for opening the spring country to paying customers. Less opportunity for clandestine operations if we had a ranger stationed there and people coming and going. Thieves need isolation to work in.'

'Whoa back, boss. Now you want to add a residence to the list? The WPA will never go for that!'

Sophie sighed. 'I know. But are you going to volunteer to live in a tent? I think not. Protection comes with a cost. Either we're willing to pay it or . . .' She trailed off.

'It'll be a one-off,' Matt said dismissively. 'Ain't worth spending a fortune on. If you were to open the joint you gotta think of the road as well – keeping that up won't come cheap.'

'I know.' Sophie sighed. 'Nothing does.'

'I think I'd rather see them stay as they are – the springs,' Tilly said. 'It's so beautiful there. Unspoiled, you know? That would all change with people and their noise and rubbish. You'd have to have smelly engines for water and light—'

'And of course you'd rather live in a cave,' Luke teased, 'and flog your washing on the rocks.'

'Well,' she said spiritedly, 'at least I'd hang it properly, not just chuck it at the clothesline. Shirts aren't meant to be pegged up by their cuffs, you know, Luke. And speaking of caves, when do we get to visit them?'

'Huh! Who'd want to? Chuck us the butter, will ya.' Matt reached a hand to receive it. 'Ta. It's a hole in the hill crawling with wallaby ticks. Good place to keep away from.'

'They can't be much worse than march flies.' Tilly eyed the red lump on her wrist. It burnt and itched still, but only if she touched it.

'That's what you think,' Luke supported Matt's argument. 'Tick bites irritate for months, especially if you just pull the body off and don't get the head out. They're tiny and damn near transparent so you never notice 'em till they've latched on.'

'And they live in caves?' Tilly quizzed, suspecting her leg was being pulled.

'No, but wallabies hang around dry, shady spots like the country around the caves, so Matt's right. It's a good spot to pick 'em up.'

'So – how do you avoid them?'

'Don't go there,' Matt offered. 'Knew a bloke once had a allergy to ticks. Damn near died from a bite.'

'Just wear boots and tuck your pants into your socks,' Sophie joined in. 'And if you get a tick, don't try to pull it off. Dab a bit of metho on it instead.' She glanced around the table with a little smile. 'I've got a surprise for you. I tried my hand at a pudding today. Who wants some?' A silence followed as everybody waited for someone else to respond. Made cross by their hesitation, she snapped, 'Well, don't all speak at once.'

'I will, Soph,' Tilly said. 'I'm sure it'll be great. What did you make?'

By midnight Tilly had cause to regret her loyalty. The pie pastry had been almost inedible, resulting in a ferocious bout of indigestion that woke her and prevented further sleep. Despairing of it passing, she switched on her torch, found her slippers and made her way cautiously through to the kitchen in search of a remedy.

There were antacid tablets somewhere in the pantry cupboard, but the tidy shelves that she had maintained were now a jumbled mess. With a hand pressed to her burning chest, Tilly peered between cornflake packets and sauce bottles until she located what she sought, then moved to the sink for a glass. A mopoke called from the darkness, the sound drifting on the wind, and she shivered in the icy air of the kitchen.

She wondered dolefully how much of the pie remained and whether she could tactfully get rid of it. It was Luke's turn to cook tomorrow, so she would be doing the camp by herself again. Maybe she could take a huge slice for lunch and ditch it somewhere? It was probably Sophie's first attempt at pastry, and Tilly devoutly hoped it would be her last. Turning away from the sink, she caught the faint sound of a motor and cocked her head, wondering if it was her imagination. But no, there it was again, a quiet, steady hum below the soughing of the wind.

Flicking off her torch, Tilly stared through the closed louvres, hoping that it wasn't another emergency. Calling the flying doctor in at this hour would necessitate lighting up the strip, but it was very late for any traveller to be abroad. Then, still waiting for the headlights to appear, she glimpsed the dark shape of a vehicle creeping past the homestead. Only the brief shine of starlight on the duco gave its presence away as it slid gently between the sheds and vanished into the night. The sound died with its going, and for a brief moment she wondered if she had imagined the whole thing. She briefly considered waking the others, but whoever it was she could find out for herself tomorrow just by checking the regos in the camp. And it was too cold to stand around now. Her body shaking with chill, Tilly hurried back to the warmth of her bed.

Over breakfast Tilly told the others about the midnight traveller to a mixed reaction. Sophie simply tutted at her description that the traveller had 'crept past like a thief'.

'Somebody probably had a breakdown, Tilly. Should have made it in daylight and was just being considerate about not waking us. You can see whoever it is this morning.'

Luke frowned. 'Yeah, but why would they drive without lights? Having them on's not gonna wake us. I reckon Tilly's right – it wants looking into.'

'Well, I can't today. I'm off to Darwin, remember? And you've got kitchen duties.'

' 'S'okay,' Matt said. 'I'll check it out. If he ain't in the camp, I'll find him. The grader's at Kileys' Yard and I'll be bringing it back today. If someone's heading through on the back roads, our paths oughta cross.'

Sophie nodded. 'Do that. You'll be right for the camp chores this morning, Till?'

'Yes, of course. What'll I do after that?'

'Take the rest of the day for yourself – do your washing, teach Luke some culinary skills.'

'Huh!' he muttered sotto voce. 'There's more than me that needs 'em.'

So she wasn't the only one to have suffered last night, Tilly thought. She had forgotten her cousin's upcoming trip. Subterfuge was no longer necessary – she could just dump the whole pie, if Luke didn't beat her to it. Unexpectedly then, she remembered her mother's favourite saying: 'There's an upside to everything, pet.'

She hid a smile, reflecting on how true that was.

Sophie left immediately after breakfast, slinging a modest bag into the front of the vehicle. 'I'll ring from Alloway,' she told Luke, 'so you know I've got that far. Once I hit the bitumen I'll be right – plenty of traffic if I have a breakdown. With a bit of luck I'll be back by Thursday.'

'You've got the costings, boss? Five dollars says they'll nix the idea.'

She tutted. 'I've got ten says they'll come out for a look first.'

'You're on. Safe trip.' He watched her drive off, then grabbed the bottles and bird feed. Both cocky chicks seemed to be thriving under his care, and the larger of the two joeys no longer used his bag. He nodded at Tilly. 'Time you weren't here.'

'I know. Matt's just coming.' He would drop her off at the

camp on his way to work. 'Hang on – he'll be gone all day, so how do I get back?'

'If somebody's leaving, they might give you a lift,' Luke suggested. 'Otherwise I guess you'll just have to wait. Connor would probably drive you, if you asked.'

'Okay, I'll do that, so expect me when you see me. Have fun, and Luke, if you're going to use the oven today, it needs cleaning first.'

Matt dropped her at the gate and Tilly, carrying the cooler containing her lunch, walked into the camp, heading straight to the ablution block to begin the daily cleaning. It was just after dawn with the first glow of gold visible above the river timber. Most of the tourists were still abed, so she had the shower and toilets to herself. The ashes below the donkey boiler were cold; she raked them out and as before, when she turned from the task, it was to see Connor, this time with a towel slung over one shoulder, ambling around the corner of the ablution block to greet her.

'Morning, Tilly. Alone again today?'

'Luke's turn to cook,' she said, 'and Sophie's off to meet with the WPA directors, so there's only me left.' She cast an eye over the diminished wood pile. 'I don't have a vehicle, so I hope that wood's going to last till everyone's showered.'

'How did you get here then? Surely you didn't walk?'

'Matt dropped me off on his way out to the grader.'

'I see. Well, we can take my vehicle and get a load if you like. Just let me wash and get my breakfast first. You fancy a cuppa when you've finished?'

'Okay. That would be great. I must admit I didn't give the wood a thought – besides, Matt was in a hurry. There was a vehicle that sneaked past us in the night, and he wanted to find where it went. The tracks didn't come through the gate so whoever it was is probably up to no good. He thinks it could be a shooter, or shooters.'

Connor shook his head. 'Never a dull moment out in the boondocks, eh? Come to my camp when you're ready.'

The tea was welcome, as was the folding seat Connor had set out in preparation for her. Tilly, with the mug warming her hands and her face turned up to the early sunshine, drew a satisfied breath. 'Lovely. Funny how you forget how chilly the nights and early mornings are.'

'You should try the desert in July. I camped at Chambers Pillars once and woke up with frost in my eyebrows. God, it was cold! So, this vehicle that went through last night – did anyone see it, or did they just notice the tracks?'

'I was up.' Tilly told him about her indigestion and what it had led to, adding, 'Luke didn't seem that concerned, and Sophie's concentrating on her plan to get another section of the country opened to camping – she's been burning up the phone lines for days costing things. Anyway, whoever sneaked in set me thinking.' She told him about her visit to the springs and discovering the chainsawed tree. 'It just seemed a bit too pat where it had been felled. I mean, right beside a gully with no way across with the road blocked? Of course, we had the winch and just pulled it clear, but your average camper would've had to turn back. And I wondered if maybe that's *why* it was felled?'

Connor frowned. 'But you got through and went to the springs, and presumably Luke didn't notice anything different?'

'If he did he didn't say.'

'Okay, so does the track end there or . . .?'

'It goes on to the caves, Luke said. And back behind them'—she waved a hand in the general direction—'are the old mining tracks that run into the sandstone formations they call the "Lost City". It's half a kilometre of rock pinnacles, or so they tell me. But that's beside the point, which is that these same tracks can take you south into the national park, or east to link up with the Savannah Way, the highway that runs across the top all the way to Darwin. Of course the tracks are terribly rough and overgrown in places, but it is doable, and the wildlife traffickers apparently know it. They could,' she said, frustration plain in her tone, 'be stripping the place of anything – birds, reptiles, possums – and we wouldn't have a clue about it.'

'I didn't see any caves marked on the map,' he said thoughtfully. 'Maybe it's something I should be investigating. How far away are they?'

Tilly drained her cup. 'Luke didn't say, only that there wasn't time to go on the day we went to the springs because the track was rough, and it was well past noon at the time.'

'I see. Maybe it's worth checking out all the same. What else do you have to do this morning, Tilly? Do you fancy guiding me out there? It's just past eight, so there's plenty of time. We could scrounge a bit of wood first, and you aren't going anywhere without a vehicle, are you?'

'Nope. I either catch a lift back with someone leaving, or wait here all day for Matt.' Anticipation stirred in Tilly.

'I'd love to go with you. There's only the pump and the wood left to do, and the day is mine.'

'Good.' He took the two mugs and his breakfast plate, rinsed them off with the remaining tea in the billy and set them aside. 'Let's get started then. Oh, and bring your lunch, it could take a while.'

# *Chapter Nineteen*

Firewood could only be collected beyond a five-kilometre radius of the camp, which meant they had to drive to find it.

'And we only put out a day's supply at a time,' Tilly explained, dusting off her hands, 'so I think that'll be plenty. Of course, the sensible thing, if the WPA was starting the place from scratch, would be to have the rangers actually living at the camp. It would save all this ferrying of stuff to and fro.'

'So when did Binboona switch from cattle station to protectorate?' Connor asked.

'Oh, twenty-five years ago at least – maybe longer.' Tilly frowned. 'I know they took the cattle off in sixty-eight and started ripping down some of the fences a couple of years after that, but the camp wouldn't have opened immediately. And when it did, the staff would have been operating from the homestead – because it was there, I guess. It mightn't be exactly where you'd want it, but the company wouldn't put itself to the expense of building more accommodation. I know Sophie's always on about keeping costs down.'

'It's an expensive world,' Connor agreed, tossing a rope

across the load of firewood and tying it off on the siderail. 'Especially out here – distance, freight . . . Right. Got your lunch? Shall we go then?'

They drove east with the morning sun glinting on the windscreen and warming the cab. Tilly donned sunglasses and shed her jacket, enchanted by the crisp newness of the day. The tracks of Matt's vehicle stood up in tiny patterned rills on the road, and the leaves of trees shone in the sunlight. Viewed through her dark lenses, the sky had a purple tinge and the wildlife they saw – a feeding wallaby, one ear lopped back to his surroundings, a skein of ibis rising above the timber, a plains turkey-cock with his throat bladder enlarged – looked like exotic cut-outs against a painted background.

'If Matt's on his tracks, your night driver seems to be heading straight through,' Connor commented. 'From memory of Sophie's map, this road will get him onto the wet-weather track that crosses the river.'

'Will it? I've never been that far,' Tilly said. She stared at the passing scenery. 'I think we're getting close to the turn-off to the springs. When Luke and I came, I remember it was all graded along here and the escarpment looks about right too.'

'Yep, coming up. We turn at the bloodwood there – hang about.' He slowed and braked, and Tilly saw that while Matt's vehicle tracks continued straight ahead, the set beneath his had plainly turned right onto the ungraded road to Sandstone Springs, where they themselves were headed. 'You said he was going to follow them.'

'It's what he told me.' Tilly pulled her shades off as if disbelieving what they showed her. 'The tracks are as plain as print! Even I can see he's turned off, but Matt's just driven on. I wonder why?'

'Well, let's find out. They went in but they haven't come out again. Either Matt's lost them – and I don't see how anyone with eyes could miss that – or he knows something we don't about the country and is trying to cut them off by going straight for the river?'

Tilly shrugged helplessly. 'I can't tell. I don't know enough about the roads.' She wished she had paid more attention to the map.

Connor's shades flashed as he turned his head towards her. 'Let's see where they go then.' The back wheel crashed into a hole and he winced. 'Sorry. Pity the grader didn't make it this far.'

The vehicle lurched and bumped its way along, with Connor skirting around the first fallen tree as Luke had also done, and Tilly pointing out where the second one had been deliberately felled. 'You can see we wouldn't have got past without the winch to tow it away.'

'Looks like somebody was trying to discourage travellers,' he agreed. 'So that green patch way over against the cliff – that's Sandstone Springs?'

'Yes. I thought you'd been here before. There were certainly tracks under ours when we came – we thought they were yours.'

'No. Something came up and I didn't make it out after all.'

His voice had changed – he almost sounded guilty, Tilly thought – and a sudden memory made her ask. 'That wouldn't be the day you turned those people back from the shed, would it? The ones with the dog?'

He shot her a quick glance. 'Could be.'

'Only they didn't have a dog, or at least not according to Matt, when he gave them a hand with a flat tyre. So, which of you is telling porkies?' she demanded.

'All right, it was me,' he said unhappily. 'They were coppers. I didn't want them blundering in on the op. They weren't pleased about me warning them off, but I told them if there was a leak or anyone worked out who they were, the chief inspector would have their guts for garters. I'm sorry about the lie, Tilly, but I thought it necessary at the time. If it had happened today I'd have told you straight off.'

Strangely, she believed him. 'Was it because you didn't trust them personally, or . . .?'

He shrugged. 'They were straight enough, as far as I know, but cops are like anyone else. They talk about stuff, about ops that are running, and it could get to the wrong ears. This one's supposed to be watertight, on a strict need-to-know basis. I rang the inspector straight after they left – he'll have had a word with them, so hopefully they've kept their mouths shut. One of them was actually from the op, so he's solid. He was showing initiative, I guess.' He was gazing ahead at the spread of vivid green bush. 'Hmm, pretty big area by the looks of it. A lot of water then?'

'Tons of it. Coming straight out of the cliff face. Luke says it dries back to a trickle but never actually stops flowing, even late in the year. The ground's quite boggy all around the perimeter. You have to walk in, starting from about where those anthills are.'

'We might give it a miss for now, unless our quarry has stopped. Doesn't seem to have though.'

'No.' The tracks ran straight on, following the rudimentary road as it curved south-west along the face of the escarpment, the height of which gradually decreased, running low to the horizon in a series of yellow and ochre hills bearing none of the grandeur of the cliffs along the Nutt River. The soil changed until they were driving on red gravel, which glittered in the sun. A family of wallabies broke from their camp beneath a wattle bush, and Tilly remembered what Matt has said about ticks. She reached to pull her socks over the legs of her jeans and then pointed at several dark hollows in the hills. 'Is that them?'

'Looks like it.' Connor scanned the surrounding barren slopes and low scrub, then leant out his window to study the tracks. 'They stopped here, and yep, headed for the caves. Then they've gone off over the ridge there. What's out that way?'

'I've no idea. A place they call the Lost City is somewhere behind the range, but why would they go there?'

'We'll follow them and see. But first, let's find out what they were up to here.' He pulled up and pushed his door open, then pointed at the tracks. 'Two men, see? Been back and forth a few times – fetching something, or leaving it here. So let's have a squiz. There's a torch in the glove box – can you grab it?'

'Of course.' She handed it to him and they stood for a moment inspecting the hillside. The opening of the closest cave was quite small – she'd need to stoop to enter it, Tilly thought, and Connor would be bent double. The entrance looked black in contrast to the yellowed rock. She felt a momentary reluctance at forsaking the bright day for the gloom within, but

Connor was heading for it and she followed him willy-nilly. She'd *wanted* to be here, she told herself, so it was silly to be intimidated by mere darkness.

The first thing that struck her was the surprising size of the hollowed area once they were within it, for the roof rose and the sides widened almost immediately. There was an earthy smell and the air, surprisingly, was oppressively warm and heavy with humidity. 'Whew! It's stifling!' she exclaimed. 'I thought caves were cold.'

Connor was playing the torchlight over the walls, the moving beam glistening on the rock. 'It's wet.' He touched it, then peered closer. 'Must be constant seepage. It accounts for the humidity – that and the small entrance, I suppose. There's moss and liverworts growing, and some sort of fungus that gives off light.' Without warning he switched the torch off, plunging them into darkness. Tilly gasped but then she could see it too, a faint, barely discernable bluish glow, almost not there in the stygian blackness. She felt the sweat beading on her face and gasped in the soggy air.

Abruptly the beam of light returned. 'Boy, sure is muggy.' Connor was moving away, deeper into the cave as he spoke, his footsteps muffled. 'The mass of the hill must hold the heat in. The stone soaks it up and releases it inwards, I guess.'

'How far back does it go?' Tilly hurried after him, resisting the urge to grab his arm. She liked nothing about this place – not the darkness, nor the booming echo that followed her question, or the sudden flurry of leathery wings above her head. She swallowed a cry, managing only to squeak, 'Bats!' They were harmless, she told herself firmly, as Connor flashed the light up on the whirring cloud of tiny creatures they had disturbed from their roosts on the rocky ledges and roof of the cave. 'Luke would love this,' she said, determined to act like a proper ranger. 'We've got flying foxes, of course – thousands of them – and we see ghost bats sometimes when the moon's full, but I've never noticed little ones before.'

'They're common enough around Darwin.' Connor sounded preoccupied. 'What were they up to? They've been back and forward, all over the place.' The torch beam jerked down at the muddle of footprints across the guano-laden floor, then suddenly stilled on a hump parked on a ledge jutting from the side of the cave. 'What's that?' Stepping towards it, he stumbled on something, swore and jerked the torch down to disclose a household brick. 'What the hell's that doing here?'

'Connor!' Tilly hissed. 'It's moving.' She strained forward to see and, as the torch light returned, jerked back with a cry of alarm. 'It's a snake!'

'Yes, I see. But it's okay. It's just a python – it's come in after the bats, I expect.'

It was a big one, its body as thick as Tilly's wrist, the pattern on it slipping through the yellow beam of light as it slid away. She stood rooted, but Connor was moving after it, his gaze on a dark object further back on the shelf.

'Come and see,' he called and reluctantly, her skin prickling against the touch of imaginary reptiles, Tilly stepped forward.

'What is it?'

'A box. A cage. I think this is where both that brick and the python came from. Look at the top. It's hinged but there's no latch – that's what the brick was for, to hold the lid down, only the snake was stronger and must've shoved it off.' Connor moved the torchlight along the shelf. 'Yeah, the impressions are plain as print. That's three, six, eight, I count, without this one. They've been using the cave as a depot, bringing them in until they had a full load to shift. Right under your noses, the cheeky bastards.'

'*What?*' Tilly demanded. 'What are you talking about?'

'Your wildlife traffickers,' he said. 'That's who was here. See the marks where the other cages have stood? They were sneaking through in the night because they came to pick 'em up. The cockies and finches and lizards – whatever it was they had. Nine cages full. They'll be long gone, and your wildlife with them, I'm afraid.'

Tilly stared at him. 'But how could they keep them here? Birds, animals – they need food and water every day. Well, maybe snakes don't . . . If they left them longer than overnight, there ought to be vehicles coming and going every day. There's no point stealing them if you can't keep them alive.'

'I know. It's a bit of a puzzle.' Connor stepped further in, waving the torch about to find the back of the cave. 'Here's where it ends. All in all it's a pretty large space.' The beam lit on the python again, its head lying flat on its coils at the base of the wall. 'Okay, old fella, stay there.' He moved back towards Tilly and added, 'I think we should check out the other two caves while we're here. Not that there's likely to be anything in them.'

'Whatever.' Tilly wiped her streaming face and pulled at the damp cotton of her shirt. 'I just want to get out. It must be forty degrees in here.'

His assessment was correct. The next opening in the hill was no more than a split in the rock that ran only a metre or so deep. Like the larger cave, it dripped moisture and due,

Tilly thought, to the greater amount of light it received, it had a lusher supply of ferny growth on its walls. The third was a shallow shelter with a wide opening and a sloping roof that met the floor within a half-dozen paces, the space between threaded with the twisted roots of trees growing on the hillside above.

'Just the one possibility then,' Connor mused, rubbing his chin with the end of the torch. 'Makes you wonder how they came to stumble across it. The racket could've been going for years, of course. Does your husband have much bush savvy, Tilly? Could he find his way around this sort of country?'

'Gerry's a fisherman,' Tilly said. 'I suppose that our fishing camp was in the bush, but he isn't Crocodile Dundee. Anyway, I thought you suspected him of running drugs, not poaching.'

'No reason why he couldn't do both. And we know that he's been at Binboona recently.' He turned aside. 'Well, what do you think – lunchtime? My stomach seems to think so. Do you want to go back to the springs to eat?'

'No,' she said definitely. 'Too many march flies. We can eat in the vehicle, then I think we should follow those tracks as far as we can. Like they say, knowledge is power and prevention's better than cure. If we can find out where and how they're getting away, then maybe we can stop them.'

'Under that ironwood tree then,' Connor said, adding with a little smile, 'You see, I do know the timber and a lot of the plants in the area. It's why I chose to pose as a botanist.'

'Well, you didn't convince Matt,' she retorted, handing him his sandwiches. She hesitated. 'He's a bit of an oddball, suspicious of anything different. He's a hard man to know with his prejudices and silence.'

'But you do?'

She shrugged. 'I'm not so sure any longer. Me changing jobs seems to have, I don't know, annoyed or upset him. Lord knows why, but some people seem to like pigeonholing folk . . . Like life is static, when it's anything but. The world would fossilise if it wasn't always changing, and that includes people.' Tilly took a bite from her sandwich, chewed and swallowed before adding, 'It might just be that he liked his meals well cooked and on time, and his washing done for him. None of which is happening now. Well, too bad. It's quite ridiculous that most men don't learn to look after themselves. I haven't met one yet that didn't eat.'

'Hey, don't look at me.' Connor put up his hands. 'I make a mighty mean curry, and I can do you an omelette, and whip up a rice pudding as well.'

'It's more than Gerry could,' Tilly said. 'He was hopeless. He could barbecue – if you didn't mind meat with third-degree burns – and make the coffee, and that was about it.' It was easier to speak of him now that she knew he still lived. 'Of course, he always had a cook on the boat – my step-dad did too. It's a full-time job running a fishing boat, so you couldn't cook for a crew as well.'

'Could your stepfather cook?'

'I don't know,' Tilly said blankly. 'Isn't that odd? I never thought about it. Mum did all the meals – she topped her class in domestic science at school. She always said that she wasn't clever but she could cook. She had me wrapped in a pinny, standing on a box at the table and mixing things for her when I was five. I could make a souffle by the time I was ten. I loved it when it was just us at home in the kitchen, especially in winter.'

'She certainly succeeded in passing on her skill,' Connor said.

Tilly smiled and inclined her head. 'Why, thank you, sir. You know, I think Mum might've gone on to become a chef if she hadn't fallen pregnant with me. She had such a feel for the chemistry of food. It's funny, isn't it, the things that can happen to turn your world upside down? She wanted a career, my mum. Whoever it was who said life was uncertain was dead right.' Especially in her own case. In the still place in her heart, Tilly heard again the echo of *once* and hastily gulped down the rest of her tea. 'I suppose we should be getting on?'

'Yes.' Connor seemed to be turning something over in his mind. 'I imagine you're going to tell your cousin and the others about the cave?'

'Well, naturally. Why?' She shot him a quick look. 'Is there some reason I shouldn't?'

He shrugged. 'Call it paranoia of the job. We like to keep things quiet when we can. Could I ask you not to mention it to the tourists, then? You don't know who might be doing what, and you've said you get repeat campers. One of them could be involved. Seriously. The people responsible would have to have someone on the ground for it to work. How else could they avoid both campers and rangers?'

Tilly said thoughtfully, 'Yes, I see that. But campers? Nobody stays the whole season through, Connor. It's a week, maybe ten days if they've a particular interest, like a twitcher desperate to see a Gouldian finch, for instance. They're endangered now, so it's rare to sight them. He might hang around hoping – but not for a month.'

'No. But the thieves could time it. Work out when they mean to hit the place and send somebody in a day or two beforehand. Lots of tourists travel with two-way radios. They could have a channel and a code. They'd need to pick the breeding season for the bigger birds, but they could net the smaller ones or hunt the reptiles any time. At most they'd need a week, but probably only a few days.'

'I suppose.' It gave Tilly an uneasy feeling, but she had to acknowledge the possibilities inherent in his words. After all, Gerry had been in the camp, however briefly, though whether to lie low or to act as Connor had suggested it was impossible to say. She gave a little shiver. 'I don't think I'll ever view any visitor in the same light again. They've always seemed so friendly, thrilled to be here, you know?'

'And I'm sure most of them are dinkum tourists. Suspicion's the curse of police work,' he admitted ruefully.

'I'm sure.' She wondered what it would be like to see everybody as a possible suspect – as he had her, she reminded herself. But not without reason once the authorities' belief that Gerry still lived was vindicated. In the light of that, the suspicion became less a terrible injustice and more an inevitable conclusion. Tidying the detritus of the meal into her esky, she stood up. 'I'm ready.'

'Let's go then. We mightn't get far and we're not going to catch them up, but just finding their route will be helpful.'

At first the tracks were easy enough to follow, running parallel to the low range of hills, but soon they crossed a saddle between ridges and joined one of the old mining tracks. Tilly had thought the property roads she was familiar with were rough enough, but this topped them. Whole sections were washed out, and every declivity became a deep gutter to be negotiated with extreme care. Connor pushed the gear into low range as they crawled along, swapping from one overgrown track to the next while she clung to the grab bar and tried to avoid hitting her head over the roughest bits.

After nearly an hour of bouncing and jolting, Connor stopped. 'It's not worth it, Tilly,' he said. 'At this rate we'll do an axle. Besides, look where the track's heading.'

Her whole attention had been upon their progress, but now, raising her eyes, Tilly saw that they were heading straight for a massive spread of tall weather-worn pinnacles in varied shapes, interspersed with a heavy growth of timber, above which the rock fingers rose like fantastical towers.

'My guess,' Connor said, 'is that the track ends there. No way is anyone driving into that, so they've must've bush-bashed a way around it. That'd have to be the Lost City. It was marked on Sophie's map, but no roads were shown near it.'

'Yes,' she said. 'It's why I've never seen it. Luke said it was hiking only and you'd have to carry your camp, because you wouldn't get there and back in one day – not if you wanted to see anything. Isn't it amazing? Do you think, now we're here, that we could have a quick look? On foot, I mean. I don't want you to risk your vehicle.'

'Why not?' He got out, pulling a backpack from behind the seat and shrugging it on. 'Water,' he said and glanced at her jeans-clad legs. 'Mind the spinifex. Roses have nothing to learn from its spikes.'

'I'll be right.' Tilly pulled her hat down and they set off. It took twenty minutes to reach the outlying pillars, and for half an hour they wandered the cool sandy-floored canyons between the rocky towers, marvelling at the weird sculpting that time and weather had produced. Bird calls rang in the still air that was elusively scented by a scrubby, purple-flowered shrub.

'Turkey bush.' Connor had halted to pull a water bottle from his backpack. He offered it to Tilly and glanced at the sun. 'We should be heading back soon. See that flatter shape over there? It doesn't look too bad a climb. Think you could make it?'

'Of course!' Tilly eyed it. 'Plenty of handholds. What are you hoping to see?'

'Well, how far back these pillars run, for starters. Be interesting to know how wide a detour our poachers had to make.' He received the bottle back, swallowed a few mouthfuls himself and stowed it away. 'If you're game for it, let's go.'

It was a harder climb than it looked, steeper than it had appeared from ground level. Connor arrived first and reached a hand to pull Tilly up beside him. She clung to him for a moment for balance; the wind was stronger and the weathered rock more uneven than she had expected.

'What a view!' She released him and turned carefully, the rush of air cooling the sweat on her body as her gaze slid over the forest of rocky towers that stretched half a kilometre or more away to the south.

'It must've been a cliff wall a few hundred thousand years ago,' Connor mused, staring down at the crenellated rock, 'then the sandstone started to break down and this is what's left. Maybe in another thousand it'll all be gone. Who knows?'

Tilly wasn't really listening. She'd spotted the dust cloud rising behind the community of pillars, and her mouth fell open as she grabbed his arm. 'Connor! There's a vehicle.'

He reacted to the urgency of her tone, stared where she pointed and then snatched the binoculars from his backpack.

'And a graded road!' Tilly exclaimed. 'Out here? How . . .? That dust cloud's heading back, not away. Who . . .?'

Connor said wonderingly, 'There's a logo on the door. I can't make it out at this distance but it looks very like – Good Christ! Was it really that simple all along? Not Luke – he's cook today, you said. And Sophie's heading for Darwin. It's Matt. Right under our bloody noses! The one who drives the grader. And he's graded the bastards an exit road. I'm betting that's how your husband left the camp without you seeing him, Tilly. And I'm afraid it's where your wildlife will have gone, too.'

# *Chapter Twenty*

They discussed their find in quick, broken sentences while making a hasty descent to the ground and back to the vehicle. They needed to beat Matt to the camp.

'Because the last thing we want,' Connor said urgently, 'is for him to get wind that we've rumbled him. That *you* have. It's too dangerous, Tilly. He mustn't ever know that you've even seen the pillars. Crooks are born suspicious, and I want you safe. I wish you weren't going back at all, but I suppose that might alert him too.'

'It should be okay,' she soothed him. 'He said he was bringing the grader home today. That'll take hours – if he really did leave it at Kileys' Yard, of course. If you just run me back to the homestead, I can tell him I got a ride back with a tourist, and I'll check the book first to make sure someone did leave this morning. What?'

Connor was shaking his head. 'And if Luke should mention me bringing you back? Just in passing? It could happen. Tell him you hung around the camp until I offered to drive you. It's lies that catch you out, Tilly.'

She shot him a look that he missed as the front wheel crashed into a hole. 'I expect you'd know. Is the job always like this?'

'No. We – Customs, that is – are only involved because of the boat aspect. Mostly it's straightforward inspections of ship manifests, or stop and search operations. This is a one-off.'

'And when it's over? If you catch Matt and his mates, what then?'

'Oh, back to the paperwork and the high seas.' The vehicle nosed over the ridge and thumped down onto the track before the caves. 'Thank God for that! Now we can make a bit of time. Yes, more manifests, but not before a break. I'm due some leave, and I should like to spend it with you, Tilly. Not crashing around chasing crooks, but enjoying ourselves. I'm thinking a nice restaurant in Darwin, maybe the Night Markets, a stroll along the Esplanade. I know a pub with a karaoke bar . . . So, what are my chances?' He snatched a quick glance at her, one eyebrow raised enquiringly, before turning back to the road.

Flattered, and a little flustered by his directness, she said, 'That last one's not quite my scene. Are you a Caruso in disguise? It sounds lovely, Connor, but I'm not a free agent. I mean, I have a job and it's the middle of the season. I—'

'Well, in theory then – is it something you'd like? Spending time with me? You could find out about my singing ability, and other things too.'

Tilly felt the heat in her skin and found that her heart was doing strange flip-flops. Their eyes met in the driving mirror and she flushed. 'Yes,' she said simply. 'I'd like that. Very much.'

'Whoo!' He blew out a long breath. 'Great! I haven't been so nervous since my first date. Thank you. Now, hang on tight while I get you home.'

Matt arrived with the grader a little after four o'clock.

'How'd you go?' Luke asked, looking up from his magazine as he entered the kitchen. Tilly, sipping coffee in the bird-watching seat, raised the glasses to her eyes, glad that Luke had spoken.

'Waste o' bloody time. Knew it would be,' Matt grunted, feeling the side of the kettle. 'I reckon the driver was just wantin' a shortcut through to the border. He's long gone. I followed 'im to the river, then quit. Once he's that far, there ain't more than ten kay before he's off the place. It was damn near midday before I got the machine serviced and movin' as it was.'

'That's that mystery solved then. If Sophie rings tonight, I'll let her know.' Luke returned to his magazine.

'I forgot to say'—Tilly hoped her words sounded natural, although to her they felt as stilted as if she were on a stage—'that we left without the wood for the camp donkey this morning, Matt. But it's okay. I asked Connor to cart some, so the hot water hasn't been an issue.'

Matt grunted again. 'He's some use then. Anything to eat? It's a bloody long way back to lunch.'

And further to the truth, Tilly silently thought. 'They would need somebody on the ground,' Connor had said, and it seemed horribly certain that his guess was correct and that somebody was Matt. Thinking back, she realised that he had been absent from the homestead every day save for his turns as cook since Luke had discovered the disturbed nests. Grading, he'd claimed, but how much time had he actually spent on the machine, and – apart from Binboona's regular tracks – where else had that grading been done? She wished there had been more time to explore the topic with Connor. The shock of their discovery was so great that, her mind now prey to uncertainties, she hesitated to tell even Luke. Though nobody could suspect *him* – or could they? In that moment, she truly understood Connor's remark about the curse of suspicion. Of course the young ranger would never be embroiled in anything that threatened his birds! But an hour ago, she would have been prepared to swear the same of Matt.

Groaning to herself, Tilly shelved the dilemma by deciding to say nothing until Sophie returned. Let her make the decision about whom to tell. At least Connor, she thought wryly, would approve her silence.

Sophie returned on Thursday, as expected, but not alone. Tilly, whose turn it was in the kitchen, was setting the table for the evening meal when the vehicle arrived, and a quick glance through the window showed both passenger and driver doors opening when the engine died.

'Looks like you lost your wager,' she observed as Luke came into the room.

'What wager's that?'

'Something about the WPA not listening to Sophie's plan? She's brought someone back. Look at him, he's wearing a tie. I'll bet he's the company's money man come to see the project firsthand.'

'Bugger,' Luke said mildly. 'I've gotta say, I never thought they'd go for it! Anyway, it's not a project yet, just the faintest possibility.'

'You still lose. Just as well Connor's room is made up.'

'Connor's?' He lifted one brow at her, an annoying mannerism that she had never been able to imitate. 'He doesn't own it, does he?'

Flustered, she said, 'You know what I mean. Anyway, your dinner's wrapped on the hob. Hadn't you better get going? Those kids I mentioned were really looking forward to your talk tonight.'

'Yeah, right. I suppose I'll hear all about the WPA in the morning.'

Graeme McGuire described himself modestly as the Wildlife Protection Association's bookkeeper. He looked to be in his mid-forties, his hair greying and his body thickening through the waist, though still trim overall. He had the tanned appearance of an outdoors man and was deeply wrinkled about the eyes. He had come, as she had surmised, to look over Sandstone Springs and study the problems and expense that their development would entail.

Sophie looked tired from the long drive, but she was keyed up too, taking the first opportunity to stop for a private word with her cousin. 'Thank the Lord you're on today – I don't want him starting off with indigestion. Look, could you bear to stay in the kitchen while he's here? Please, Tilly? The house is always nicer when you're running it – the boys never get round to sweeping or tidying stuff up.

I need him relaxed and positive, not cracking his neck to get away.'

'Yes, of course, if you think it'll help. What was his initial reaction to your idea?'

'Well, he's here,' Sophie said. 'I think that alone is hopeful. It's a huge amount of money, but building anything here in the north costs double anywhere else. He did say the company's books were in good shape though, so maybe there's spare money,' she added hopefully.

'But he's not just an ordinary bookkeeper, is he?'

'No. He's the financial director of the whole shebang. Which is another reason why I think he might really go for it. He wouldn't have come if the company meant to turn the idea down flat. I'll take him out there tomorrow morning to get him the overview, and then I thought Matt'd be best qualified to give him a tour of the rest in the afternoon. I mean, roads and machinery are his thing. Graeme'll need a breakdown of equipment costs and structural work. It'll be guesses at best, but Matt's would be closer than either Luke's or mine, and Graeme has to have a figure to start from, even if it's way out.'

'Mmm.' Tilly hesitated. 'Look, I can't tell you why now, but maybe don't say anything to him about Matt until we've had a chance to talk? You might want to change your mind.'

Sophie's brows knitted in puzzlement. 'Why would I?'

'Just don't.' Tilly could hear steps in the hallway. 'Trust me. I'll tell you later. It's important, Soph.' Then their visitor entered the room, rubbing his hands together.

'Something smells good! I could eat a horse – or a good part of one, anyway. The boys tell me you're a great cook, Tilly.'

She smiled, hoping Sophie would heed her words. 'I try. And you'll be happy to know we can do better than horse.'

Her cousin, Tilly thought, had taken her warning seriously, for over dinner Sophie talked about Binboona and her ideas for it if the Sandstone proposal went ahead, asserting that Graeme would see why she was so keen on it when she took him out in the morning. She said nothing, however, about any plans for the afternoon.

He may have been the financial director of the company, but it was obvious that McGuire had spent time in the ranks as well. He had been with the Tasmanian Wilderness Society in the early eighties, working with those protesting the Gordon-below-Franklin Dam. He was knowledgeable about birds and had lived in his share of wild places, curdling Tilly's blood with an account of once waking up to find that he was sharing his swag with a brown snake. She had closed her eyes in horror, muttering, 'God! I'd have died of fright regardless of whether it bit me. It didn't, did it – bite you?'

'Thankfully no. It was a long way back to town.'

'Shoulda had a greenhide rope with you,' Matt said. 'Old stationhand trick. Lay it down and make a loop around your bed with it, and the snake follows it round but won't cross it.'

'Really?' Tilly was doubtful. 'Does it work?'

He shrugged, his gaze sliding away to the pepperpot. 'There's blokes who believe it.'

'And if it's never been tested, they assume it's true.' Luke nodded sagely.

When the meal was over, Sophie and Graeme removed themselves to the lounge, while Matt took a torch and went out with a muttered word about the generator and Luke stayed to wipe up for Tilly.

She lifted her brows at him. 'What's brought this on?'

'I'm being tactful, letting the bosses get on with it without the help hanging over their shoulders. Besides, I'm damned if I'm going to bed just to stay out of their hair.'

'Very diplomatic. How's Jane these days?'

His face softened into dreaminess. 'She's good, thanks. As a matter of fact, she's coming north again as soon as her mid-year exams are finished. She and some uni mates are heading for Darwin. She's planning to fly out on the mail plane. I thought – well, I hoped – you might put in a word with Sophie, see if she can stay in the homestead? It'd only be for a week,' he added cajolingly.

'Aha, now I see why you're wiping up.'

He started to protest, then caught sight of her grin. 'You'll ask her then? Think she'll agree?'

'I don't see why not. And if another guest should turn up, Jane can share with me. Or'—she raised her brows—'with you?'

'We haven't got that far yet,' he admitted. 'Anyway, I don't think Sophie'd like it.'

'Probably not.'

'Thanks, Tilly.' He blew out a breath in exaggerated relief. 'You're the best. I've been wondering too, if we ought to send the cockies back with Graeme. They're old enough to go to a proper bird sanctuary. If we keep them here, they'll wind up domesticated and unable to live in the wild.'

'I guess it's worth asking,' she said. 'Would it matter though if they did – become pets, I mean?'

His boyish features gathered into a frown. 'I don't like to see it. Especially in birds who live a long time like the parrot family. It cripples them in a way. They're meant to live their own life, free and natural. Not dependent on man.'

'When you put it like that . . . Look, that's it, there's only the pan now. It'll take a while and I can wipe it, so your duty's done. Thanks. Oh, and Sophie's asked me to stay on kitchen duties until Graeme's gone, so you'll be doing the camp work yourself tomorrow.'

'I see. Well, much as I dislike cleaning dunnies, I'll do it for the sake of your meals.'

'And because you don't have a choice,' she agreed affably. 'Go write to Jane. I might drop Mum a line too – it's time she had a letter.'

It was an hour or more after the letter was finished before a tap on the door heralded Sophie's arrival. She came in yawning, wrapped in her dressing gown, and perched on the end of Tilly's bed.

'I'm bushed,' she said, yawning again. 'It's been a long day, so what's so important, Till? That was a great meal by the way.'

'Glad you liked it.' Tilly sat up, heaving the doona higher against the chilly air. 'I'll keep him well fed while you charm him, and maybe he'll see things your way. But never mind that. There was a vehicle that sneaked through here last night. I just happened to be up . . .' She told the tale succinctly, including

Connor's real purpose, adding anxiously, 'But you have to keep that to yourself, Soph. The point – and the reason you should keep Matt away from Graeme – is that we're now pretty sure that he's involved with the traffickers. He's grading roads for them, after all. And if he is, he'll try to sabotage your plans for Sandstone Springs.'

'No way!' Sophie straightened where she sat. 'I find that hard to believe. Matt's dedicated to the job. He's been here three, going on four years now, and there's never been any suggestion—'

'How do you explain the new road then? We both saw it, Soph. And we followed that vehicle within a spit and whistle of it. The driver certainly knew it was there! Anyway, how well do you really know Matt?' Tilly pressed. 'Would you say, for instance, that he was a good bushman? That he can track?'

'Well, of course he can. He—'

'Then why is he pretending that vehicle drove straight through to the river? Even I could see where it turned onto the Sandstone road. There's no way he could have missed it! Not when his main purpose was to follow the wretched thing. And, now I come to think of it,' Tilly said slowly, 'he's been trying all along to discourage me from going anywhere near the caves. Talking about the dangers of ticks and the sores they leave that won't heal. You know how I've wanted to see both the caves and the springs ever since I heard about them. I've often spoken of getting out there one day, but he's always said how bad the road is, how easy you can bog there. And then going on and on about the ticks – well, you were there.'

'He was just having fun, teasing you.'

'Matt doesn't tease,' Tilly said flatly. 'It's business or silence with him, you know it is. And I've just remembered that it was the workshop Connor chose to search. Not the sheds or the engine room, but the one place, apart from his room, that is Matt's domain. Like maybe he always suspected him. Connor started out looking for drug dealers. Who's to say Matt's not into that too? And consider this: to be efficient, wildlife traffickers would really need a man on the ground to tell them when the coast was clear. Matt's perfectly placed for that, isn't he? That's why you shouldn't let him talk to Graeme – not if you want Sandstone to be developed – because it's the last thing *he'll* want.'

Sophie looked torn. She said, 'But he's *good* at his job. He cares about what we do here.'

'Or he pretends to. And don't forget he knows every inch of the country. Stands to reason with the amount of time he spends out on the roads. Who is better placed to tell the poachers about a handy cave where they can stash the animals they steal until they're ready to collect them? And when the rangers are somewhere else for the day?'

'You could say the same about Luke,' Sophie retorted. 'He knows the country equally well.'

'Can he drive a grader?' Tilly asked. 'Anyway, can you see Luke killing and terrorising birds?' Exasperated with her cousin's unwillingness to believe, she rolled her eyes. 'Remember, I was there today. I *saw* him on that road – well, one of our vehicles, which comes to the same thing! I saw the cave where the cages had been, not to mention that damned great snake and the box he got out of. Look, Connor wants to keep the whole thing quiet and let it play out until they can nab the lot of them – but I thought you ought to know.'

'Well, thanks – I think. All right, I'll bear it in mind. And I might have a word with your Mr Doyle too, when I see him next. I'll give him botany!'

'He's not mine,' Tilly said sharply. And then reminded, she added, 'By the way, Luke's Jane is heading this way soon, for a week apparently. He wondered if we could house her? She's coming on the mail plane so she won't have camping gear.'

Sophie got tiredly to her feet, smothering another yawn. 'Oh God, why not? Undercover agents, stray girlfriends . . . I might as well be running a pub.'

# *Chapter Twenty-one*

In the morning, Tilly rose early to make a batch of rock cakes (the cake supply tended to dwindle between her turns as cook). She packed some, still warm, with Graeme's lunch, mentally thanking Providence for the tender supply of corned beef in the fridge as she made his sandwiches. Somebody had got it right at last – half-done meat seemed to be the metier of her fellow cooks. Luke had refuelled Sophie's vehicle, and Graeme and Sophie left straight after breakfast, him with an impressive-looking camera slung about his neck.

Luke, having fed the cocky chicks, was the next to go, which left only Matt still at table.

'Will you be needing your lunch today?' Tilly asked. She found it hard to speak naturally to him and was relieved when he nodded.

'Yeah. I'll be workin' at the camp. Ain't worth drivin' back just to eat.' She felt his eyes on her and looked up to see them slide away. 'What was the big confab about last night then?'

'With Graeme and Sophie? I've no idea. I was clearing up.'

'Later,' he grunted. 'I saw Sophie go into your room.'

'Oh.' Tilly, taken aback, searched for an answer. 'Really, Matt, wouldn't that be my business? If you must know,' she improvised wildly, 'I've suggested to my mum that she come up for a visit. Sophie agrees she needs a break and we were working out how to present it to her.'

'Right, well. What d'you reckon about this McGuire bloke? Think he'll go for it?'

'I've really no idea,' Tilly said primly. 'Could you make your own lunch? I'd like to get on. That vegie garden looks like it hasn't had a weed pulled from it in weeks. And I see there's some laundry waiting as well.'

Once he too had left, Tilly was glad to have the place to herself, the tourists coming and going hardly counting, their interruptions only brief as they signed in and paid. She mopped and tidied, worked in the garden and pegged out washing while half her mind played over the previous day's events and the rest, caught by the idea she had plucked from nowhere to satisfy Matt's curiosity, wondered if her mother could be coaxed north for a visit.

Elaine, Tilly knew, had served her husband faithfully and submissively for nearly thirty years, so surely she was due a break. A week or ten days in respite care shouldn't be too much to ask of a man who, according to her mother's rambling accounts of her daily life, couldn't even recognise his wife half the time. She could travel by bus if the airfare proved too expensive, and either be met, or catch the mail plane out to Binboona; Tilly herself could help with that fare. It would be a well-deserved break for Elaine, while to have days of her mother's company would be an unalloyed treat for Tilly. Except when he was at sea, the shadow of her stepfather had always come between mother and daughter; not exactly threatening, Tilly mused now, but crowding the edges of their intimacy until his presence subtly succeeded in separating them. This unacknowledged silent pressure had, she realised, been mainly responsible for her leaving home when she did.

Then there was Jane's upcoming visit to factor in. There was only the one spare room, but Luke had said she would only stay a week, so her mother could come immediately after. She might even cook for them. Tilly smiled at the thought; her mother certainly wouldn't care to eat anything that Luke, Matt or Sophie could produce. She found herself keenly anticipating Elaine's arrival, momentarily forgetting that so far the idea lived only in her head and that both Sophie and Elaine would have to agree to make it happen.

Connor arrived in the early afternoon, pulling up at the shed and walking across to find Tilly busy in the vegie patch.

'Just coming,' she called, without looking round. She smeared a gloved hand across her hot brow and rose saying, 'Welcome to Binboona. It's only – Oh.' Looking up, she saw him and gave a little laugh. 'Connor. Sorry, thought you were another tourist. What can I do for you?'

'Luke said you'd pulled kitchen duties,' he answered, 'for the duration of your guest's visit, I gather. I just thought I'd drop by on my way through.'

'You're leaving us?' Tilly was surprised at the intensity of her disappointment.

'Overnight trip, that's all. I need a word with my man at Spadgers Creek.'

'I see.' Tilly remembered then and enquired somewhat guiltily, 'Have you seen Sophie today?'

'Yep. She's not best pleased with me,' he said ruefully. 'Words like *deceit* and *weasel* spring to mind.'

'I'm sorry, but I had to tell her. Oh, you don't know the latest, do you?' She stripped off her gloves. 'Come in, and I'll put the kettle on and tell you all about it. You'll see then why I had to give you away.'

'It's okay,' he assured her. 'And I do understand why she was upset. It's human nature not to want to feel that you've been used or made a fool of. Which was not my intention.'

'No, of course not.' Tilly led him inside. 'Take a seat, I'll be right back when I've washed.'

Seated across the table with the tea things between them, Tilly told him Matt's version of the previous day and his low-key but persistent opposition to her earlier desire to visit the caves. 'Of course, he doesn't know that I did. I had to tell Sophie about that and it's made her even more determined to have Sandstone Springs made accessible for tourism. Having the public there will protect the caves too – even just the workmen being there would be enough. So,' she finished, belatedly realising that she hadn't made plain her reasons for telling Sophie about him, 'I had to warn her about Matt. Because she was going to let him show Graeme – he's the company's money man – around the place. And of course Matt would have done his best to talk him out of it.'

'But would this Graeme have listened? Sophie's in charge, isn't she?'

Tilly gave him a pitying look. 'And Matt's a man, and understands machinery and the costs and difficulties of keeping roads open in monsoon country. What do you think?'

'Ah. Well, she chewed me out pretty well this morning but

has agreed to keep quiet about who I am. I have to admit I've had my eye on Matt all along. Because if Binboona's strip of coastline was being used, then *somebody* here had to be in league with the bad guys, and on the surface he's the most likely candidate. And now we know I was right. Of course, Sophie's simplest course would just be to sack him – not that we want her to do so.'

'She can't do that,' Tilly protested. 'I mean, not without proof. She's only got our word for it after all.'

He raised his brows. 'And she wouldn't believe us – you?'

'Yes, but she has a boss too, and he'd be harder to satisfy. He'd probably fear a backlash for unlawful dismissal. And think how Matt could twist it if he chose to. I don't expect he would, because he wouldn't want to draw official attention, but he might claim it was a put-up job, that I orchestrated it to get rid of his attentions to me. Because I do think,' she said hesitantly, 'that he's attracted to me a little, so there are grounds there if he wanted to use them.'

'I'm a bit at sea here.' Connor's eyes narrowed. 'Is it that you actually care for him?'

Tilly's colour rose again. 'No, I don't,' she said vehemently, then added more moderately, 'not at all. In fact I had no idea until . . . Anyway, I doubt that Sophie's about to sack him. Apart from anything else, this place would be lost without a mechanic. Luke can change a tyre and that's about it.'

'Good. It means I shouldn't have to worry that he'll disappear on me. Look, thanks for the tea and the chat, Tilly. I'd better get moving. I hope you all succeed in talking your visitor round on the springs. That whole area is certainly worth exploiting. The tourists will love it.'

'We think so too.' Tilly walked to the verandah with him and stood to watch him leave, then checked the pleasing growth of her seedlings in the tubs at the foot of the steps and returned to her weeding.

Sophie and Graeme arrived back mid-afternoon. Luke was home by then, and Matt arrived soon afterwards. He had been fencing, it seemed. Luke helped him load a supply of timber posts for next day, and while Graeme showered, Tilly pounced on her cousin. 'Well? How did it go?'

'Pretty well, I think.' Sophie was cautious but there was a gleam of excitement in her eyes. 'He was definitely impressed, and he said he could see the potential. Turns out he's got a real interest in birds too, so tomorrow I think I'll get Luke to take him down to the coast along the river road. There'll be plenty of wading birds to look at, and with a bit of luck, he'll see jabiru and fish eagles too.'

'Birds?' Tilly raised her brows. 'What's that got to do with Sandstone?'

Sophie shrugged. 'If zebras were his thing, I'd do my damnedest to find some of them for him. I want him to love the place, Till. What resources get allocated to the various properties the WPA owns isn't just up to him. He has to go back and convince the board, or shareholders or whatever, that it's worth spending here. I want him to root for Binboona. It's a truckload of money we're asking for.'

Tilly nodded. 'That makes sense. I've made pasties for his lunch tomorrow, and he'll have croissants for breakfast.'

'You're the best! Anything interesting happen today?'

'Connor came through and I told him about Matt. He said you chewed him out properly. He's really sorry, you know, about having to deceive you. You didn't actually call him a weasel, did you, Soph?'

'I believe the phrase was "weaselling his way into the place",' she replied. 'Why couldn't he just have explained to us?'

'How? He's working undercover! There's also a cop in the stock camp at Spadgers Creek. I bet Bruce Hansen isn't aware of that either, so don't mention it.'

Sophie shook her head. 'Lord, the things that go on.' She sniffed. 'Something smells wonderful – what's for dinner?'

The following morning, Graeme entered the kitchen to find Tilly staring through the binoculars at the bird basin. She looked up and beckoned, saying quietly, 'Quick, come look. Gouldians. It's the second time in a month that I've seen them.'

He took the glasses. 'Oh, wow! Isn't that something. Whose idea was the basin?'

'Luke's, of course.'

'That figures. Sophie said he was keen on birds. The finches certainly like it. Man, I can see some crimson, some double-bars, and long tails . . . And those two. You can hardly believe they're real, can you? Such colour.'

'Oh, Binboona can turn it on.' Tilly spoke eagerly. 'We had the cutest little sugar glider a while back. Very weak and covered with ticks. I'd never seen a real one before. We were able to nurse him back to health, which was very rewarding. And there's Harry the brolga, and the joeys . . . Have you seen Luke's black cocky chicks?'

He spoke with the glasses still to his eyes. 'Not yet. So, why did you decide to become a ranger, Tilly?'

'It's an interesting job. And worthwhile – I like doing something, however small, to help the environment. And I love the tranquillity of the place. Oh, the climate's extreme but it's very beautiful country. It's become home to me.' She smiled. 'I'm a transplanted southerner, you know. Once we discover the north, I doubt we ever leave.'

'Ah, they've gone.' Graeme lowered the binoculars. 'Never mind, I understand we're going bird-watching today. I envy you, Tilly, with all this for a backyard.' A circular sweep of his arm took in the open slope to the timber-fringed river bank with the sparkle of water beyond. 'It's a bit different to the city.'

'It's certainly that,' she said. 'How are you getting back to Darwin, Graeme?'

'I'll fly out tomorrow on the mail plane. Then I'm heading across to Halls Creek. The company has a property there. Thank God for aviation, eh?'

'Better than bulldusty roads,' Tilly agreed. 'Breakfast is ready when you are.'

Later in the day when Luke and Graeme had left, with Sophie on camp duties and Matt occupied with something in the shed, Connor returned. Tilly was again in the garden, watering this time, and turned off the hose at his approach.

'How's it going?' she asked. 'Did you get your errand done?'

'Hi, Tilly.' He ran an eye over the vegetable plot. 'You've certainly got a green thumb. That all looks good enough to eat.'

She laughed. 'Vegetables are meant to, or what's the point? But no special credit is due. Everything grows up here, and there're no pests. I haven't seen a cabbage moth in two years. Would you like some greens? There's plenty to share.'

'Well, if you're sure. I suppose a bit of fresh stuff in my diet wouldn't hurt. Actually, the reason I stopped by was to give you this.' He held out the jar that had been half concealed in his hand. It was full of a golden liquid with something floating within it.

'What is it?' She eyed it curiously, lifting it to eye level.

'Just a little carving I thought you might like. You should leave it to cure in the bottle for a month or so, because the wood's green and it'll split if it dries too quickly. And as you seem to be the one who looks after him . . .'

'It's Harry!' She looked from the jar to him and back again, marvelling at the detail. 'Good Lord, you can see every feather! It's beautiful, Connor. Thank you. Though why—'

'It's all in the timber,' he said, cutting her off. 'That's got to hold the shape before you start. You can't, for instance, get a horse out of something that's plainly holding a dog. Birds are simpler. There's plenty of them lurking in branches everywhere.'

'Well, I think you're very talented and I do thank you. You must have spent hours getting it so perfect. It's Harry to the life! He's even got a broken beak.' Tilly was awed by the work's perfection.

'Yep. It's a warts and all job with me,' Connor agreed. 'I carve what I see. I'm glad you like it. Making things passes the time for me, and right now there's a lot of it to pass. Incidentally, I think that your stolen wildlife may have left the country. My mate at the station says there was a boat in the inlet – came in last evening and was gone again by daylight before the Customs vessel could get there to intercept it. The timing fits with that stray vehicle. So they collect the cages, make a loop via that new graded track and drive back to Spadgers Creek, where they lay up in the scrub until dark.' He sighed and scratched at his jaw. 'You can see the Gulf waters from the homestead verandah, but it's too far to hear a motor. Which doesn't rule out them meeting the boat's runabout on the western edge of the inlet. It's just too damned easy. They load up the cargo – you'd get it all in a dinghy – and you're home free. Back at sea by daybreak and no one the wiser.'

'I see. Not much to be done about it then. So they'll wind up in Asia, the cockies and whatever else?'

'For starters,' he agreed. 'Maybe even New Guinea – and who knows from there? America, Europe . . . The world's a big place. They'll go where the price is highest.'

'It's wicked.' Setting the jar carefully aside, Tilly stooped to pull bok choy and lettuce from the soil. 'You want some radishes too? I'll just rinse these off and find a bag. Can you stay for a cuppa?'

'Anytime.' He followed her housewards. 'So, how's the campaign for Sandstone Springs going?'

She grinned. 'Deviously. I'm wooing his stomach, Sophie his brain, and Luke's out with him now hopefully finding plenty of birds. Turns out he's a twitcher too, which is a stroke of luck. The idea is to make him love the place so much he'll want to go to bat for us.'

Connor gave such a shout of laughter that it brought Matt out of the shed. Tilly grimaced to herself and reluctantly waved, calling, 'Cup of tea, Matt? I'm just putting the kettle on.'

# *Chapter Twenty-two*

Binboona had lived up to Sophie's hopes, providing a smorgasboard of birds for Graeme's viewing. Most of the dinner talk concerned birds, and Graeme willingly agreed to deliver the black cocky chicks to a suitable home, providing the mail plane would accept them as freight. After the meal he and Sophie retired for a private word in the office, leaving the others in the kitchen.

Luke, once again wiping up, said, 'He's a good bloke. Think he'll go for it?'

'Fingers crossed.' Tilly swiped suds from the splashback. 'There were a pair of Gouldians on the basin again this morning. Did he say?'

'Yep. They were the icing on the cake, because we saw just about everything else today from fairy wrens to jabirus.'

Matt, at the table behind them, looked up from his chessboard and snorted. 'Birds! You think he's gonna spend a million bucks on the place because of birds?'

'Having them can't hurt,' Tilly said lightly. 'Luke, when is Jane coming?'

'The boss is okay with it?'

'Of course. I'm hoping that I can get Mum up for a visit after Jane's gone, but it'll take a while to organise things her end.' Sophie wouldn't object, and the more Tilly thought about it, the more she realised that she wanted it to happen. 'So if Jane's visit is close, I might write tonight.' She wouldn't phone – Elaine would say no automatically and then not budge on the decision – but if Tilly laid it all out and let her think about it, she might agree.

'I'll ring her later and let you know,' he promised, polishing a pot. 'She only had one more exam to go last time we spoke. That was a smashing dinner tonight, Tilly. Can your mum cook?'

'She taught me.'

'I'll take that as a yes.' His blue eyes were suddenly hopeful. 'Maybe she'd cook on days when you don't – do you think?'

She laughed. 'You probably couldn't stop her.'

'Really? In that case I'm gonna be begging her to stay for a year.'

Tilly pulled the sink plug. 'Don't get your hopes up. First I have to convince her to come at all.'

Graeme left the following day. Sophie, who saw him off, returned from the airstrip without the cocky chicks, the pilot having agreed to take them.

'So what do you think?' Tilly asked. 'Do you reckon the WPA'll go for the plan?' She hadn't passed on Connor's news about the suspected poachers' boat, reasoning that there was nothing Sophie could do by knowing. Somewhat guiltily, she acknowledged that keeping silent also helped prevent Matt from learning that his part in it had been uncovered.

Sophie shook her hair back, her plain, suntanned face thoughtful. 'Realistically? I think we've a good chance of getting the go-ahead. Outback tourism is growing every year, and the public is more aware these days of what's been lost, so they're interested in seeing what we're managing to save. Which means there's a good return for expended dollars. The WPA might mainly be about the environment, but the board are business people too. So it's obvious to Graeme what a drawcard the springs could be. He agreed with me that the place would pack people in.' Sophie spread her hands. 'He seemed genuine enough, Tilly, didn't you think? I doubt he would have said that unless he favoured the development.'

'I liked him too.' Tilly nodded. 'I suppose it's a matter of wait and see. Incidentally, Jane will be flying in next week. And I wondered, Soph, what do you think about me seeing if Mum could come up?' She went on to outline her plan, not neglecting to slip in the bit about getting Elaine to cook for them, adding, 'Mind you, I doubt I'll manage to persuade her, but I think it's worth a try.'

'Of course it is,' Sophie said energetically. 'It'd be good for you both. Respite care is there to be used, and so I'll tell her. You write, then I'll give it a week and ring her, just to help make up her mind.'

'Bless you, Soph!' Tilly gave her cousin a hug. 'I really hope she'll come. I've been thinking back, and I don't believe I've seen her more than three or four times since my wedding – and not too often before, either.'

'It'll be good for you both,' Sophie declared. 'Heaven knows Elaine must need a break. Her life can't be easy.'

'No.' Guilt smote Tilly. She had been so focused on her own tragedy that she had forgotten her mother's. Watching the slow destruction of a spouse through dementia was probably worse than losing that spouse outright. From now on, she promised herself, she would be more mindful of the fact. Just because she had no love for her stepfather didn't mean that Elaine hadn't. Could you still love the husk, she wondered, once the mind that made it a person was gone? Were memories enough, or was it simply duty that kept the habit of caring going?

Sophie broke into her ruminations. 'So what's Luke got planned for today?'

'Oh, he volunteered to do the camp duties this morning, then he's going to pick me up and we're heading out after lunch.' She grimaced. 'Working on that old fenceline near Blooms Rock, which means rusty wire again.' It was something that the rangers toiled at between other duties. 'Matt's got the kitchen today.'

'Be sure and take gloves then. And it wouldn't hurt, next time you're in town, to check if you need a booster shot for tetanus.'

'It's on my list,' Tilly said. 'Meanwhile, I think I'll prepare Jane's room. Save myself some time later.'

The day, long awaited by Luke, finally dawned and Jane arrived. She was every bit as pretty as Tilly remembered and seemed a pleasant, conversable person. Her unfortunate experience hadn't turned her against the bush either. Tilly, asking how she felt about camping now, received a laugh and a brilliant smile from her.

'It couldn't happen twice,' she said. 'I admit it put me off a bit at first, but I decided I was being silly. Like never getting into a car again because you once ran into a post. Luke says nothing's ever worried him and he never uses a tent.'

Love was not only blind, Tilly thought, but infinitely suggestible. 'So,' she said, 'you know I'm a trainee ranger now under Luke? Which means – I'm sorry – but I'll be playing gooseberry when you two go anywhere.'

'Yes, it was in his letters.' She grinned impishly. 'He's told me a lot about you.'

'Really? Like what?'

The girl tipped her head considering, her brown eyes sparkling. 'Well, that you're a marvellous cook, you have absolutely no sense of direction, and you're really good with hurt, and baby, animals.'

'No sense of direction! Just because I got lost and drove the wrong way once,' Tilly said indignantly. 'You do know there are about fifty million tracks all over Binboona? And not a signpost among them? I bet Daniel Boone'd get turned around too.'

'Are there?' Jane was intrigued. 'Why so many? Do stations need lots of roads? Luke said it was a cattle property once.'

'About thirty years ago,' Tilly agreed. 'But the roads had nothing to do with the property owners. Some mining company made them for mineral exploration. They stop and start and run in all directions. What makes it confusing is that the station incorporated bits of them into their own roads – which we use – so you can be driving along and there's a sudden choice of tracks. Luke,' she added bitterly, 'says you ignore the ones that aren't headed east or north or wherever you're going. Huh! All very fine if you happen to know which direction that is.'

'I see.' Jane nodded. 'That's like my dad – he always knows which way to unscrew nuts and jar lids and I never do. It must be a male thing. Never mind, Luke thinks you're great anyhow.'

'He's not bad himself,' Tilly said and was rewarded with a brilliant smile.

Jane was only staying for a week, so Tilly spent most of her time with her and Luke, except when it was her turn in the kitchen. Wearing gloves, their visitor gamely collected wood, helped roll up long strings of rusted wire, filled and lumped away buckets of ash from the donkey heater at the camp, and learnt to feed the youngest joey.

'You all work really hard. I had no idea,' she said one evening, trimming split and ragged nails. 'I feel like I've run a marathon today.'

'Oh, you toughen up after a while,' Tilly answered. 'I'm just coming good now myself. You should clip your nails really short – even the gloves won't stop them breaking. So, just one more day. When will you two lovebirds meet again?'

'Christmas, I guess.' Her pretty mouth drooped. 'It's a long time to wait.'

'But it'll pass,' Tilly encouraged. 'It's only six months. You do know Luke is absolutely crazy about you?'

'He's wonderful,' she said, sighing. Tilly, eyeing her wide brown eyes and the delicate flush on her cheeks, felt a pang for her youth and ignorance of what life could do to dreams as the girl continued. 'We're getting engaged at Christmas. He said we'll marry when I finish my degree. I'd chuck it tomorrow, but he said no, it's important and I have to finish.'

'It's good that he's prepared to wait,' Tilly agreed. 'Patience is one of his strengths.'

Jane giggled. 'Like silence is Matt's? Does that man ever manage more than a sentence at a time?'

'Not often.' Matt had been mostly absent during the week, hauling fuel from the Alloway Roadhouse, at the station collecting meat, or digging a pit for the new set of toilets that were going in at the camp. He was present for breakfast and dinner and gone for the rest of the day. 'He's not a ranger,' Tilly explained, 'so his work is different. Oh, we share the chores – the cleaning and the wood, stuff like that – but he mostly looks after the machinery, keeps things running about the place.'

'Mmm.' Jane got up to peer through the window, Matt's character forgotten. 'I wonder what Luke's doing? He said he'd only be five minutes.'

'And it's been all of six.' Tilly smiled. 'He won't be far.'

The following morning when the three of them finished at the camp, Tilly dried her hands and dropped the towel back behind the seat. 'That's practically walking,' she said, wrinkling her nose. 'Remind me to put it in the wash tonight. So, what next, oh master?'

'The fenceline again, but first,' he added, cutting off both hers and Jane's groans, 'I thought we'd take a quick swing by Sandstone. Show Jane the springs and the caves. She knows about Sophie's plans and wants to see the place. Maybe next time she comes north it'll all be done and we can stay there. There's an old track near the caves that'll bring us out pretty close to the fence, so we might as well have a squint at it in passing. It'll only take an hour. What do you reckon?'

'You're the boss.' Tilly shrugged over Jane's eager rejoinder.

'Oh, yes, please. I've heard so much about them. I'll just check how much film I have left in my camera.'

'And I need to find my sunnies. I left them here somewhere yesterday,' Tilly said. She found them near the laundry tubs and quickly returned to the vehicle.

Making shooing motions at them, Luke headed for the driver's seat. 'All aboard then.'

# *Chapter Twenty-three*

Grading, Tilly mused, certainly made a difference. They sped along quickly to the point where the road diverged, then lurched and twisted over the narrow side track, getting ever closer to the line of cliffs until the green blob of Sandstone Springs appeared at their foot. Jane eyed them, impressed, the yellow and ochre of the rock face vivid in the morning sun. 'Wow! Look at the colours. I bet you'd get a view from up top.'

'It's not as high here as the river escarpment,' Tilly observed, studying it. 'I could climb that. Why don't we, Luke? If the scheme goes ahead, maybe we could have a marked trail to the top for those who want to hike. Something you could suggest to Sophie.'

'Or you could,' he said. 'Your idea.'

'You're the ranger – for now I'm just the help.'

Jane grabbed his arm. 'Oh, let's climb up. It'll make a marvellous photo.'

'After I've had a dekko maybe,' Luke squinted upwards. 'I don't want either of you falling.'

'While your natural male superiority is going to see that you don't?' Tilly teased. 'Get over yourself, mate. Let's go.'

The view from the top proved to be worth the effort. The back of the cliff rolled downwards studded with snappy gum, boulders and spinifex, for all the world like a huge mound that had been sliced in half. The path they found was relatively easy; the exposed rock lay in broken sheets that made for steep but safe climbing.

'Like a neverending staircase for giants,' Jane panted, as they neared the top. She wiped sweat from her flushed face and paused to snap a quick photo. 'Whose mad idea was this?'

'Well, not mine,' Luke said. His breath, Tilly noted, was annoyingly under control. 'You okay, love? You want to stop?' He took Jane's arm to help her on.

'Course not!' She flashed him a grin. 'We're almost there.'

A cool blast of wind hit them as they made their last steps, and Luke whistled as they all stared about at the distant range and the pewtery gleam of the river glinting far over like a fugitive thread between the trees. Below, the ground debouched into a valley carpeted with red gravel from which the sunlight glinted.

'They look man-made.' Jane pointed down at shrunken, straight-edged sections of ground, their edges marked by lines of yellowed feed.

'Mining tracks,' Luke said.

Tilly shot a covert glance south-east but the pinnacles of the Lost City were little more than a smudge on the horizon.

'They're everywhere. They go to the old camps and, I suppose, prospecting sites.'

'Sometimes you see overgrown pits beside them,' Luke added. 'Dunno why – too big for rubbish pits – so maybe they were testing the ground, or digging up specimens.'

Making the whole network a boon for poachers, Tilly thought, wondering who had first seen the possibilities it presented. Was it Matt? He had been here three or four years, Sophie had said. But if he'd worked long in the north, he could well have known about the roads and applied for his job because of them. She must mention the idea to Connor when next they spoke.

Luke was getting restless; he was always conscientious about time. 'Seen enough?' he asked. 'Let's go down.' He glanced at his watch. 'We might have lunch, then head on for a quick look at the caves before we start work.'

Tilly groaned. 'I think he *likes* pulling down fences,' she confided to Jane. 'Are there any more after this one?'

'Nope. And there's only about thirty kay of wire left in it. That's the good news. The bad news is that the last ten of them are through thick wattle scrub. That'll be really hard work.'

'I believe you.' Tilly sighed.

It wasn't until their vehicle braked to a stop outside the main cave that Tilly remembered the snake. Finding no way to mention it without relating the whole saga of her visit with Connor, she just hoped to God it had found another home. She alighted reluctantly from the cab saying, 'That's an awfully dark-looking hole. I don't suppose we have a torch?'

'Under the seat,' Luke said. 'Not that it matters – there's nothing to see except bats. And I'm warning you now, it's like a sauna inside.'

'You've been here before then?' Jane asked.

'I had a quick look once, but it was summer and there was a storm brewing. Really, I just stepped inside and out again – I didn't even see the bats, just heard them moving around. You're not scared of them, are you?'

'No-o,' Jane said stoutly. 'I mean they won't fly into us, will they? You hear about them getting into people's hair. And don't they carry disease? I wouldn't like to be bitten.'

'You won't be. And anyway that's fruit bats.' He clasped her hand. 'Got the torch, Tilly? Lead the way then.'

'I'd rather you did.' She handed it over and, taking a deep breath, followed behind. She'd once seen Luke pin the head of a red-bellied black snake and bag it for later release, rather than kill it. In the face of that, she couldn't afford to gibber with terror at meeting a python, which might not even still be there. Rangers, she reminded herself, frequently handled bush-fires, crocodiles and stroppy tourists. A non-venomous snake should be a doddle.

The mugginess of the cave was again immediately apparent, and this time, for some reason, the smell of bat guano was stronger, or perhaps she just noticed it more. Tilly's head jerked nervously about, seeking the shine of scales in whatever the torchlight lit upon.

'It's bigger than I thought.' Luke sounded surprised. *Thought . . . thought* echoed back and he laughed. 'Hear that?' Powdered guano dust rose as he strode forward, the light bouncing over ledges and up the walls of the cave. 'Moisture,' he said. 'See the walls? I thought that glitter was mineral last time, but it's damp. It explains the humidity.' He went closer. 'There's moss and even some sort of lichen growing here,' he marvelled, 'and the light's absolutely minimal.'

'Listen to the bats.' Jane's hushed voice sounded nervous. She tilted her head at the increased activity of wings and minute squeaks coming from above them.

'Hand me the torch,' Tilly said. 'There's something . . .' She shone it along the ledge, but the box that had once housed the python was gone.

'What?' Jane said sharply, the word creating a echo. 'What did you see. Are there . . . are there snakes?'

'No. It was just a shadow that looked a bit like a box.' Tilly flipped the torch higher and a positive storm of wings and beady eyes erupted from the cave roof, whirling distractedly above their heads. 'Oops, sorry. Seen enough, Jane?' The brief glimpse she'd had of the girl's face had shown it to be pale.

'Yes,' she said thankfully. 'Can we go, Luke?'

'In a minute, love.' He was staring at the silhouettes the bats made against the light from the cave mouth as they whirled about. 'You got your camera there?'

'Yes, but the flash doesn't work, so I can't—'

That's okay,' he said. 'Tilly, shine the torch on the roof, would you? Stir 'em up again. I want to see . . .' She obeyed and from the corner of her eye saw him crouch and suddenly leap, swiping at the air with his hat.

'Got ya!'

'What in the world?' In the torchlight she saw him pinch the felt brim carefully together as he came towards them.

'I need a pic of this little fella,' he said. 'I want to check him out. Come over where the light's better, Jane. Let's try for a really clear shot. Take several.' Tilly watched him wriggle his fingers into the hat, heard the muttered, 'Shit! Little bugger bit me!' then he pulled the hat away, the tiny mammal held firmly between his fingers, one of which was bleeding. The bat was pale brown above, with a funny-shaped nose, and light-coloured belly fur. Luke positively beamed at it. 'What a little beauty! Haven't seen you before, mate. We'll just find out what you are.'

'How?' Jane, clicking away, had recovered her colour.

'We have a pretty good reference library at the homestead,' Tilly said. 'You'd better disinfect that bite, Luke.'

'Yeah, in a minute. Right, that should do it.' He opened his fingers and the bat shot away into the darkness behind them. 'Okay, tour's over. That was interesting, wasn't it?'

When they returned that evening, tired and dirty from their afternoon labours, Tilly said, 'You have first go at the bathroom, Jane. I want to check the garden.' Neither Sophie nor Matt were particularly good at remembering to water it.

'Thanks, I'll be quick.' Clasping her camera, the girl hurried off as Tilly made her way around the back. Luke went straight indoors, and when she rejoined him half an hour later, he was paging through *Native Mammals of the North*. He glanced up at her arrival. 'Come and see. Do you reckon this is the bat we saw, Tilly? Far as I can tell the colour's the same, though if there's a difference it could be age related. And the nose is definitely the same . . . What d'you think?'

She scrutinised the picture, trying to recall the exact

shape of the little mammal viewed in the faint daylight at the mouth of the cave. 'It looks about right. They're all the same though, aren't they – only bigger or smaller? It was tiny so it might've been a baby.'

He sighed. 'There are thirty-odd species so no, they aren't all the same. And it wasn't a baby, not if I'm right. I'll have to wait for the film to be developed to be certain, but I'm pretty sure this is the one.' He tapped the picture. 'Which makes it a leaf-nosed bat.'

'So? I thought it had a weird-looking face, but I've never seen one up that close before,' Tilly admitted.

Luke tutted. 'You need to study the native species,' he said seriously. 'It's part of the job, Tilly. And if I'm right, that cave is rather special because the leaf-nosed bat has only ever been found in Arnhem Land. Which would make this one a separate colony and maybe different. A new species, in fact.'

'Really? Wow! You'll be famous, Luke, if you're right. We'll have naturalists from all over swarming the place, wanting to see and study . . .' Her thoughts leapt ahead, dismissing caution. 'And once the WPA hears it'll be bound to guarantee the Sandstone project, wouldn't you think?'

'Maybe,' he said cautiously. '*If* I'm right. But it would also mean they're very rare – maybe the only colony in existence – so they'd need protection. The first thing I'd be advising would be a gate to keep them safe. To keep people out. It's not like they have a choice of habitat round here if they're chased out of their home. Theirs is the only cave in the region.'

'Have you told Sophie?'

'Not yet. She's feeding the joeys, and I wanted to check the books and your recollection first.'

'Well, I'm sorry I can't be more help, but you probably *are* right. It pains me to admit how often that happens.' He grinned at that and she said, 'Congratulations if it's true. And now I'm bagging the bathroom.'

There was a lot of speculation over dinner as to what Luke's discovery, if it panned out, could mean for Binboona. *Native Mammals of the North* was passed around, and Jane, for one, was willing to swear that the illustration was a perfect match for the creature she had photographed.

'I'll finish the roll and put it in for developing the moment I get to Darwin,' she told Luke. Then her face fell. 'Damn, it'll be after office hours, won't it? Well, first thing next morning then. I'll give them your address so they can post the pics straight out once they're developed. You'll ring as soon as you have them, won't you?'

'Of course. Thank you, sweetie.' Excitement gleamed in his blue eyes. 'I'm not counting on it, mind. There may be a difference I didn't notice . . .' But it was clear, Tilly thought, that he didn't believe it.

'They might name it for you,' Sophie said. '*Aldyce-onia something*. You never know. If you do the studies you've planned, it won't harm your career prospects at all.'

'Seems a lotta fuss over nothing,' Matt said sourly. 'Bats! There's millions of the buggers and they all stink. Try livin' with fruit bats and you wouldn't be so keen on 'em.'

'Well, I didn't like the cave much,' Jane confessed, 'or the bats. But I'm glad we went. It was a fabulous day, Luke.'

'And we even got some work done,' Tilly said wryly. 'Only

another twenty-five kay of tangled fencing wire to go,' she said, rising to clear the table.

Later that evening, Tilly sought out her cousin for a private word. Sophie looked up from a report sheet and pulled off her reading glasses. 'Something up, Till?'

Tilly perched a hip on the edge of the desk, her eyes on the open door, and spoke softly. 'I didn't say anything at the time because Luke doesn't know the traffickers were using the cave, but they've been back – or somebody has – since my visit with Connor. The box they'd left behind has gone. Do you still think Matt can't be involved?'

Sophie sighed and screwed her eyes shut for a moment. 'I don't know what to think except that I wish your mate Connor would *do* something more than just sit in the camp like some horrible great spider. If he suspects Matt, why doesn't he just question him? Sort it out somehow? The whole thing is intolerable! Suspecting workmates, having to consider every word you say . . . It's not who we are, Tilly. The job's hard enough – we *need* to be able to trust each other.'

'I don't like it either,' Tilly said helplessly, 'but we have to let Connor handle it his way. I promised that we would.'

Sophie sighed. 'Then I suppose we had better hope like mad that Luke is right about his bat. That way we could legitimately ask the company to put up a barricade, a lockable steel gate. Nobody could use the cave then.'

'It wouldn't necessarily stop the poachers. They'd just find another spot to stash their catches.'

'When did you get to be so damned logical?' Sophie demanded. 'Of course you're right. On another subject, Elaine rang for you today. I told her to try again tonight. It's all arranged – she's putting your stepfather into respite care for ten days and flying up. Said that, in the long run, bussing it would cost as much as the flight itself, what with the ticket, meals and accommodation. She sounded quite excited about coming.'

'That's wonderful! It'll be the first break she's had since—' Since Francie's death, Tilly thought. If you could call her mother's brief rush to her daughter's side a break. She thrust the thought determinedly aside. 'Thanks, Soph, I'm sure your words clinched the deal. She was trotting out all the reasons she couldn't come when I spoke to her.'

'She just needed a gentle push,' Sophie said, adding unexpectedly, 'She carries a lot of guilt, your mum – about her marriage. Feels she owes a debt, you know. Which makes me think that maybe it hasn't been as smooth a sailing as she makes out. I always wondered if she really loved your stepfather. I mean, it's not like it'd be easy, a misanthrope like him.'

Tilly looked struck. 'Really? I thought they were okay, that I was the problem.'

Sophie shrugged. 'The onlooker sees most of the game, you know. I suppose she did what she thought best at the time, as we all do. Now, I really have to finish this report if it's to catch the mail tomorrow.'

'I'll say goodnight, then,' Tilly said and left.

# *Chapter Twenty-four*

The following day it was Matt's turn again in the kitchen. Tilly, taking a look at the hard fried eggs congealing on a plate on the stove, opted for cereal and toast instead. Luke and Jane were already at the table, sitting close together. Jane's eyes looked a little pink, and Luke's habitual cheerfulness was absent.

Tilly suspected that they had spent the night together, perhaps not for the first time, which would only make the coming separation harder. She said kindly, 'I'll do the camp this morning, Luke. And I'm going to miss you like crazy, Jane. It's been fun having you around.'

'I've loved being here.' Jane smiled below woebegone eyes. 'Thank you all for having me. I'm going to miss it all so much.'

'You can always come back,' Sophie replied. 'Really, I feel we ought to be paying you for the work you've put in. Has everybody got their mail in the bag? Good, I'll lock it then. Don't forget to pick it up, Luke.'

'When have I ever?'

'There's always a first time. Especially when your mind's on other things. I'll be down the coast today, Matt, so if anyone rings for me, ask them to call back tonight.'

Matt's brown gaze fixed on her. 'You expecting a call then?'

Sophie shrugged. 'Be pointless trying to guess. I'm just saying – in case.'

At the camp, Tilly unloaded the day's supply of wood, then drove to Connor's camp only to find his vehicle missing. Disappointed beyond reason – after all, she had only wanted to report the missing box in the cave – she drove back to the ablution block and set about the day's chores. Once she had hauled off the ashes, she walked down to the river to start the pump, but after anxious moments with her ear pressed to the delivery line – 'Always be sure the water's actually running, or you'll burn the pump out,' Luke had instructed – she switched off the solar-driven pump with a heartfelt 'Damn!'

'Now what?' The pipe was definitely empty. Could the foot-valve be jammed open? She eyed the opaque face of the water, corrugated into ripples by the wind, and visions of crocs filled her mind. No way she was setting foot in that! What would the boys do? she wondered. Well, for a start they'd know how the system worked. She only knew it by rote.

Hands on her hips, she considered the matter. The pump floated on a raft, which was tethered to a post planted firmly in the sloping bank. If she were to pull it closer, she could step onto the raft and maybe raise the foot-valve to investigate it without entering the river, but what then? How did you get water back into the line? Because, as far as she could see, the lack of it was the root of the problem. The action of the pump pushing the water along the pipe opened the foot-valve to drag more in, according to Luke. Only air in the line would stop it, in which case you had to bleed the air out and replace the water. It was just a pity that she didn't know how to accomplish this.

Sighing, Tilly decided she could do no more. Much as she hated to appear useless, she would have to get help. Luke would be taking Jane out to the plane about now, and Sophie – who would certainly fix it in a flash, she thought wryly – had left, which meant asking Matt. And the matter was urgent. It wouldn't do for the camp to run out of water.

She had just reached this conclusion when Connor's voice hailed her from the top of the bank. 'Tilly, they said you were looking for me?'

'Oh, Connor.' She turned thankfully to see him scrambling down the steep bank. 'Yes, it was nothing much, I just stopped by your camp on the off chance . . . Look,' she said hopefully, 'you wouldn't know anything about pumps, would you? This one's stopped working.'

'Let's have a look then. What seems to be the problem?'

'Well, there's no water coming through when I switch it on. I know there has to be water in the line, that the pump sucks it in, but it doesn't appear to be doing it. Could the foot-valve be the trouble, do you think?'

'Most likely.' A strong hand reached past her to grasp the mooring line and pull the raft in to the bank. 'Hold this while I check it. Maybe it's sucked some weed in and jammed the valve.'

'Thanks,' Tilly said. 'I really didn't want to have to ask Matt, but he's the only one home just now.' She tried to see past his body as he hauled the tail pipe up. 'Is it that?'

'Half a mo.' The foot-valve came up with a splash, trailing

a length of thin nylon rope and she heard him grunt. 'Yep, it's jammed open. Picked up a bit of rope that must've been floating past. I'll get rid of that so it doesn't happen again, then the pump'll just need priming.' He freed the loop of cord and dropped the valve back into the water, then pulled at the rope, which seemed to resist. 'Must be caught on a log.' He heaved again and the hemp rose, bar taut surrounded by ripples. 'Feels like the log's coming too.' Suddenly his voice changed. 'What the hell?'

'What?' Tilly craned forward as Connor knelt perilously on the pump housing to fish something from the river. 'Don't fall in!' she called in alarm. 'There's a big croc slide just upstream.'

'I'm fine.' He was heaving up a heavy plastic canister, as big as a twenty-litre drum. 'Well, look at that.' With a carefully judged leap he landed beside her, the canister shedding river water over his jeans leg as the movement banged it against him.

'What in the world? Is it somebody's rubbish?'

'I doubt it,' he said, 'but first let's get your problem sorted. Have you got a bucket or a jug – anything that'll hold water?'

'There's a bucket in the tool shed.' Tilly climbed the bank to the little tin hut at the top where spare polypipe, a wrench and some spanners were kept. 'Here,' she said, returning breathless from haste. 'Is this any good?'

'Just the ticket.' Connor took the half bucket, one side of which had been squeezed into a pouring lip, and began to fill the pipe through a plug hole in the line. 'It's called priming,' he explained. 'The pump impeller thrusts the water up the pipe, which creates a vacuum, which sucks at the valve to draw more water in. There.' He screwed the plug home, jumped back to the bank and gave the raft a push with his foot. 'You can start it up now.'

Tilly did so and heard the almost immediate rush and gurgle of moving water. 'Thank you, Connor.' She spoke with heartfelt relief. 'I'll remember that next time it happens.' She eyed the container as if it contained a nest of spiders. 'Are you going to open that?'

'Sure am. We'll take it up to my camp. But first, let's see where the other end of the thing goes.'

It took just a moment to learn that the rope was tethered to a dee ring bolted to the end of a steel fencepost, which had been driven full length into the mud of the bank about a metre from where the pump raft was tethered. The length of steel had been pounded out of sight, the result being that the end of the rope was also buried.

'Not meant to be turned up by accident,' Connor mused. 'But nobody comes down here, do they?'

'They're not supposed to,' Tilly agreed. 'The path is fenced off, as you'd have seen, and there's a *No trespassing* sign on the shed. So it's really only us.'

'And Matt's responsible for the pump?' Connor used a pocket knife to tease open the knot securing the canister.

'We all take turns starting it, but yes, he services it, puts it in, takes it out for the Wet.'

'So it's a fair bet that this is his work.' He tapped the plastic drum, which gave back a heavy, dull sound as if it were full of water, then shortened the rope by a metre and began shredding the cut end with the knife.

'What are you doing?'

'A precaution,' Connor grunted, straining at the tough strands, 'against him finding it gone. Don't want to spook him into doing a runner. There – you reckon a croc might've done that, or a boat's propeller?'

'Umm.' Tilly pounced on the inference. 'You think, whatever it is, it's dodgy?'

'Know any other reason for it to be there?' he said. 'Come on, let's go back and find out.'

At his camp he wiped mud off the drum and fetched what looked like an extremely sharp blade from his tent. 'Fishing knife,' he explained as Tilly eyed it from her seat under the flyrig. 'I don't think my pen knife'll cut it. No pun intended.'

'Just do it,' Tilly said. 'I can't imagine what it could be – and that's worse than not knowing.'

The heavy plastic yielded grudgingly to the knife blade as Connor sawed at a spot below the shoulder of the square drum. 'The whole top's been removed, then replaced – see the welded seam here? Which means the contents didn't go in through the bung. Can't be pills or powder – he could've just poured those in.' He paused to flex and rest his hand before resuming his labour.

Tilly forced her lips to silence and waited tensely on her camp stool until the last bit of plastic was cut. The top of the drum fell away and Connor let out an astounded whistle.

'What? What is it?' She was on her feet, staring, her mouth dropping open. 'My God! Is that all money?'

'Looks like it. Here, better get it out of sight.' Hoisting the drum up, he kicked the tent flap aside for her to enter and followed her in. A camp stretcher filled the back of the space and he dumped the drum's contents onto the grey blanket covering it. It tumbled out in thick stacks, each individually wrapped in plastic. They fell helter-skelter across the stretcher and a few onto the canvas floor. Tilly stooped automatically to retrieve them.

'God in heaven!' she said faintly. 'There must be hundreds, thousands of dollars here.' She turned one of the bundles in her hands. 'These are all fifties. Are those the same?'

Connor squatted by the bed and examined the bricks of money. 'Looks like it. Okay, Tilly, you're my witness. Just wait till I grab my camera. I'll document it, count it and get you to sign something to verify the amount. Jesus! Looks like I was right. There's more than a bit of poaching going on around here – you'd need a bloody zoo of animals to make half of this little lot!'

It took a while to reach a total, but once the bricks had been stacked up on the stretcher, photographed, and one of them opened to ascertain its value, the counting began, with Tilly keeping a running total on the back of a flyer advertising pizza.

'I make it sixty thousand.' Connor straightened his back. 'Some of 'em are hundred-dollar bricks. Wouldn't have fit otherwise. So the racket pays – in spades, I'd say! And it tells us something else about Mercer too.'

Mercer, Tilly belatedly remembered, was Matt. 'What's that?'

'That he's not casual help. Remember I said they'd need a man on the ground to keep track of the rangers' movements? I was thinking of hired help, but no way – Mercer's running the show. He's the boss.'

'Because of this?' She indicated the now re-packed drum. 'Isn't it a fairly risky strategy, keeping it in the river? Supposing a croc *had* snapped the rope? Why not bank it? It would be safer surely?'

Connor nodded. 'Safer, but a bit hard to account for. Dirty money has to be laundered or held in cash. The last thing your villain wants is for the tax man to find vast undeclared sums in bank accounts. They tend to notify the cops.'

'Yes, of course. I hadn't thought . . . So what happens now?'

He smiled at her. 'A cuppa first. Then I'll get you to sign something verifying the amount of cash and the circumstances under which you saw it recovered. After that,' he said, glancing at his watch, 'I'll head for Darwin to hand it over to my superiors. And you can't—'

'I know,' Tilly sighed, 'I won't say a word. Not even to Sophie, I suppose?'

'Better not,' he agreed soberly. 'It's not that I don't trust her, but when you know something damning about a person, it's hard not to show that you know. And crims have good antennae. Besides, if he finds the money gone – hopefully he won't – but if he does, you musn't give him any cause to think it anything but an accident.' His gaze and tone were serious now. 'Be very careful, Tilly. I don't want anything happening to you.'

'I'll make sure it doesn't,' she replied, her mind running on ahead of her assurance. 'He must meet with somebody – some sort of messenger for the gang – fairly often, don't you think? How else would the money get here? He hardly ever leaves the place.'

'No reason why he should. Anyone could pose as a tourist to meet him and pass it over. It's an ideal set-up. He's on the spot, but at one remove from the action. The goods, whatever they are – parrots, people, drugs – are passed and the payoff comes back to him in untraceable cash, which he plants. I wonder how many more caches he might have around the place?'

'Good Lord!' Tilly said faintly. 'I never thought . . . You don't really think there could be another drumful somewhere?'

Connor shrugged. 'Depends. Is this lot a season's work, or two, or five? Till we know that, we can't even begin to guess. I've got to admit it's a sweet deal, though. If things were to go belly-up for him, he can grab the swag and run.' He coughed awkwardly. 'I reckon it's a pretty big organisation to generate this sort of dough, and I think your husband's a part of it. He pretty well has to be, given that he turned up here and then vanished overnight, as it were. I'm sorry, but that's the way it's looking.'

Tilly swallowed. 'I know. And he's my husband in name only, now – whatever we had is over. I want nothing further to do with him.' She stood up. 'I'd better be getting back. Oh, I've just remembered. We were at the cave yesterday – Luke and Jane and I – and that box the snake was in?' He nodded and she continued, 'It's gone. So somebody's been back for it. And last night I just suddenly thought, what if the poachers are getting ready to catch another lot? It would explain taking the box. They could be coming back.'

Connor frowned and glanced behind him at the money. 'It's possible. I wish I wasn't going – but I must. Look, try not to worry, Tilly. I'll be back as quick as I can. Just be careful around Matt, eh? Forget this morning ever happened.'

'I'll be fine. You're the one carrying the cash. God! What if you were robbed? It doesn't happen much out here, but if it did! The baddie'd think he'd lucked onto a travelling bank.'

Connor laughed. 'Not gonna happen.' He was packing the tea-making utensils away as he spoke and zipping the tent flap closed. 'I'll head off then. But I'll be back as soon as I can. Anybody asks, I'm busy chasing orchids in the wilds of Spadgers Creek.'

'You'd better let Bruce Hansen know then,' she suggested. 'Matt's leery of you, doesn't totally believe in your botany. It'd be just like him to check, and he's at the station often enough to do it, too. We get our meat from them, and our supplies are left there. It's his job to fetch them.'

'Good thinking. I'll do that. Bye then, Tilly.'

'Take care.' When she'd reached her vehicle, she glanced back in time to see him heaving his swag into the back of his own. She hoped he treated the money less cavalierly, then, with the thought of facing Matt knowing what she now did, wished treacherously that he wasn't going. Which was ridiculous. It wasn't as if she would be alone with him – Sophie would be there, and Luke. She would just immerse herself in the details of her mother's visit, she decided, talk about nothing else and make endless plans for when she arrived. And if Matt *was* in the habit of checking his hidden stash, then finding it gone should similarly occupy his thoughts until he wouldn't notice if she were to paint herself blue.

# *Chapter Twenty-five*

Once back at the homestead, the day continued without incident. Luke was a little down in the mouth after Jane's departure, but a discussion started by Tilly about the bats diverted his thoughts from his missing sweetheart. He calculated how long the photos would take to be developed and returned, and had recourse again to the reference books to pore over and re-examine the information it contained.

'You'll find out soon enough,' Sophie said placidly. 'This is the north, mate. It's pointless wishing for speed in anything.'

'I know. I just want—' The ring of the phone cut off the rest of his words as he bounced to his feet. 'That'll be Jane. She said she'd ring after seven.'

He returned shortly, beaming. 'She got the film in to the chemist. It'll be on its way on tomorrow's plane.'

'That's great,' Tilly said. She calculated flights. 'So you should have the pics back by the mail after next. My mum'll be here next week. Maybe we could take her to see the bats, Luke? Just in case they're a major find that'll make you famous.

Then she could tell all her friends that she knew you when you were just a humble ranger.'

'You'll keep.' He wagged a finger at her. 'There's lots of old fence wire still to roll.'

'I see your botanist has finally cleared out,' Matt interjected curtly. 'Run outta weeds, has he?'

'Gone?' Sophie looked up. 'Did you collect his camping fees? We are charging him, you know.'

'You better send a bill then,' Matt sneered. 'He never stopped, just roared through.'

'He hasn't gone,' Tilly defended the absent Connor. 'At least only for a few days. He said he was heading down to Spadgers Creek, on an orchid hunt I think. I noticed his camp's still there.' Better to keep it vague, she thought; it might prevent further questions. The idea seemed to work, for Matt simply grunted and, to her relief, let the subject drop.

The following night was a Thursday. Tilly again found herself running the slide show for the campers. The bird names she now mostly knew by heart, needing to call upon Luke only to differentiate between such species as the greater and lesser egrets. When she had run through them, he slipped another loaded holder into the projector and clicked the first slide into place to display an emu-apple tree.

'Okay,' Luke addressed the audience in his easy way. 'Anyone recognise this?'

A man in the audience gruffly sang out the name. 'Very good,' Luke said. 'Now, some facts about it – anybody? And this includes you, Ranger Tilly. What do you know about its uses, timber strength, seeds?'

'Um,' Tilly hesitated, hoping she'd got the scrap of lore

right. 'Its name comes from the fact that its fruit has to pass through an emu's digestive system before the seed will germinate?'

'Correct. A gold star for our Apprentice Ranger. Its habitat is the sandstone country, and you can use the bark to catch fish. How about that?'

'Really?' Tilly wasn't the only one to voice scepticism for the claim.

'Perfectly true,' Luke said. 'There's a toxin in the bark that de-oxygenates water. The fish can't breathe, so they drift to the surface and lie there waiting to be picked up. It's just temporary, with no lasting ill effects. Something to remember if you're stuck without a feed or a fishing line. Now this next one – I'll bet everyone recognises this . . .' It was a wattle. He told them how the seed pods could be used as bush soap, then ran on through a medley of different species, all of which grew on Binboona, each with their peculiar characteristics and uses. His audience clapped loudly at the end and Tilly, helping to pack up the gear, commended his performance.

'That was really interesting, Luke. You know such a lot.'

He grinned. 'You will too, by the time you're a fully fledged ranger. Seriously though, people interested enough to visit here should take the trouble to learn all they can. It's their heritage after all. Wildlife Reserves are meant to be an experience, not a fun park.'

'You really love your job, don't you? I wouldn't be surprised if half the kids who hear you leave here wanting to be rangers.'

'They could do worse.' He shouldered the screen. 'You got

the torch? I mean, fresh air, mozzies, heat, mud – be like joining the army, only nobody shoots at you.'

Poker-faced, she interjected, 'You forgot about pulling down old fences.'

He snorted with laughter. 'Not really – I'm saving that up for tomorrow.'

Connor returned on the weekend. Tilly, whose turn it was to cook, heard the vehicle coming and stepped out onto the verandah ready to register the newcomers. She recognised the vehicle and watched, disappointed, as it slowed but failed to stop. Connor simply waved as he drove past. Well, she could see him tomorrow at the camp, not that she had any need to. He'd obviously delivered the money, and she had nothing to report. Matt had been his usual silent self, so plainly he had yet to discover his loss.

Irritated with herself, Tilly clicked her tongue as she returned to her task of filling the smoko tins. It was pointless – shades of Sophie! – pretending to herself. She cared for the man, she might as well admit it. Her heart beat faster in his company and she was pretty sure the feeling was returned. When she was with him she'd felt a steady regard emanating from him – she couldn't be wrong about that. And he had helped her in lots of ways when he could just have walked by: with the pump, for instance, and restraining that odious police sergeant. They'd had a nice day out at the coast that first time, and surely he didn't go around giving his carvings to every woman he met? No, there was definitely a connection.

Besides, she reminded herself, she had no reason to feel

guilt. It wasn't as if she was still mourning her husband. Far from it! Gerry's coldblooded deception had killed her love, making a mockery of the long months of grieving she had done for him. He had abandoned her in her grief, a grief he should have shared for their lost daughter, and that was a betrayal she could never forgive.

Sophie, coming into the kitchen at that moment, found her young cousin standing staring raptly through the window. 'You taking up meditation, Till?'

'Huh? Oh, no I was just . . . woolgathering. Actually,' she contradicted herself, 'I was thinking about Connor. He just returned. I feel – well, I like him, Soph. Quite a bit, and I'm trying to convince myself it's okay to do so. In my circumstances, I mean. How do you stop loving someone? Can you? Because I have. I feel nothing for Gerry now, just a sort of tired sadness over how it's all turned out.' She pondered a moment. 'It's not hatred, that's too strong a word, but I despise him, and love can't live with that. I know you can love someone even if you don't always like them – that's human nature – but when they've acted despicably . . . Well, it's hard to come back from that.'

'I don't see why you should even try,' Sophie said bluntly. 'I wouldn't. There was something – I don't know – facile about Gerry. You want the truth? I never liked him. He was always too smooth, too accommodating, like nothing really mattered enough to him for it to be worth his knuckling down and scrapping for it. That's not how life works. Not as I know it, anyway. You've got to do the hard yards – in a job, a relationship, anything. You don't get to skim over stuff and just select the easy bits.' She touched Tilly's hand, saying slowly, 'I don't want to hurt you, love, but when I learnt he was alive, I wasn't all that surprised. Little Francie died, but sooner than face up to that, and you – and I suppose his creditors – he just made himself scarce. Typical of the behaviour I'd seen in him.'

Tilly looked surprised. 'You never said.'

'No, well, he was your pick, and I didn't see that much of either of you, remember.'

'So you think it's okay that I fancy Connor?'

'God, yes! Not that it's anything to do with me, or anyone else. You fancy the pants off whoever you want. He seems a decent bloke, if a bit on the sneaky side, but the sort to stick, if this job he's on is any yardstick. Do you think he fancies you back?'

Tilly blushed. 'I do, a bit. And I really like him, Sophie. He's clever and kind, and thoughtful – and not bad looking either.'

Her cousin rolled her eyes. 'Dear Lord! First Luke and now you.' She dropped the banter. 'Seriously? I'm pleased for you, Till. You're overdue a bit of happiness, and you don't owe that husband of yours a second thought.'

Tilly nodded and sighed out a little breath, adding inconsequentially, 'Mum'll be here in a few days.'

'Will you introduce them to each other?'

'I was thinking about that. I . . . Oh my God! The biscuits!' She dashed to the stove, where a curl of smoke was issuing from the oven and the question remained unanswered.

The following Wednesday, Tilly was at the airstrip to meet her mother. As the pilot gave her a hand down from the plane,

Elaine Williams thanked him, then gave herself a little shake as if to confirm her feet were back on solid ground and opened her arms to her daughter. 'Tilly! You look well, love. It's such a treat to finally be here. My, it's warm isn't it?'

'Yes, the days are lovely here now,' Tilly agreed. 'I'm so glad you've come. It's a long way. How was your trip?'

'That was my first small plane.' Elaine shuddered. 'I think I like them bigger.' She lowered her voice. 'Back in Darwin, there was a girl flying one of them.'

'Women drive trains these days, and fly jets, Mum. I imagine a Cessna would be a piece of cake. How's Dad?' Tilly asked dutifully.

'Oh, much the same, love. He created a bit about going into care – I think the room being different upset him.' She took her suitcase that the silent pilot pulled from the rear door, along with the mailbag, which he exchanged for the one Tilly held.

'Thanks, Mike. See you. Come on, Mum.' Tilly grabbed the case and shepherded Elaine towards the vehicle. 'Hop in. No, leave the window up. There'll be clouds of dust when he starts moving.' She slammed her own door and sat waiting for the plane to taxi away, then begin its take-off run. 'We have to see him off the ground,' she explained, starting the engine as the Cessna flew off. 'We're not far from the homestead. I've been really looking forward to this. How long can you stay?'

'Ten days including travel – one to come and one to go – so that's eight here. I wanted to leave on a weekend, but they told me the little plane only flies on Wednesdays. Why's that?'

'It's mail day, Mum.'

'What – only once a week?'

Tilly looked affectionately at her mother's indignant expression and nodded. 'Yep, this is the back of beyond. The tourists all say that too – well, the ones from Sydney and Melbourne, anyway.'

'It doesn't seem right! Why, I remember when the postie came twice a day.'

'And I'll bet there're a few old timers up here who remember when they got their mail once a month,' Tilly said. 'You get used to it. Mail days are a treat – that's the way to look at it. Same as anything – scarcity adds value.'

'It wouldn't suit me.' Elaine gave her daughter a searching look. 'But something obviously agrees with you. You look so much better than when I last saw you. Happier too. I'm glad, love.'

'It's been two years, Mum,' Tilly responded as she turned off the road and slowed before the homestead. 'A lot of water's gone down the river since then. New home, new life, new job. Well, here we are. Sophie's home today, so we'll have a cuppa and catch up, and you can settle in at your leisure. You've got eight days to do exactly as you please, and I'm going to see that you do. God knows you've earned a break.'

Elaine smiled at her daughter. 'Take Two and cocoa after dinner?'

'If that's what you want,' she replied, nodding at the figure that had emerged onto the verandah. 'There's Sophie waiting for us now.'

# *Chapter Twenty-six*

Luke's first question as he stepped through the door that evening was whether the photographs had come on the mail.

'Of course not,' Tilly said. 'It'll be next week at the earliest. Luke, this is my mum, Elaine.'

They shook hands. 'Nice to see you here,' he said. 'Tilly's been looking forward to you coming. We all have. She told us you were a wonderful cook.' The last was said hopefully.

Tilly rolled her eyes at him. 'What he means, Mum, is that when you've eaten some of the meals he makes, you might want to take over the task.'

'But isn't that your job?' Elaine looked puzzled.

'We share the cooking now, Elaine,' Sophie explained. 'Didn't Tilly tell you that she's training to be a ranger?'

'Oh, yes, but I thought that was just studying that she did of an evening.'

'On-the-job training,' Luke said, 'and our stomachs suffer for it.'

'Well, of course I'm happy to help out. I love cooking.' Elaine smiled.

'You're on holiday, Mum,' Tilly protested. 'I want you to see more of the place than just the kitchen. It's really beautiful – there's the beach and the river walks. We could take you out to Sandstone too, that's a spring at the foot of the escarpment . . .'

'I'm sure that with a bit of organisation we could fit that in,' Elaine said. She cast a judicious glance around. 'You seem to have quite a good set-up and plenty of freezer space. Does the plane bring your fresh provisions in? I didn't see anything unloaded today.'

Sophie shook her head. 'Too expensive. We have hens, the station supplies our meat and we grow fresh vegies. Well, Tilly does mostly. Before she came, we lived on tinned stuff and a bit of bush tucker. Luke's our fossicker.'

'Oh.' Elaine looked doubtfully at the young man, visualising who knew what, Tilly thought. She turned to ask the silent Matt, 'And you're a ranger too?'

He met her gaze only long enough to shake his ginger head. 'Nope. Handyman, that's me.'

'He keeps things running, and grades the roads.' Tilly grasped the opportunity to speak of, if not to, him. 'We couldn't operate without Matt.'

'That's a fact,' Sophie agreed. 'And like Luke and me, he has no particular talent with the pots and pans, so if you'd like to help out in that department, Elaine, we'd all really appreciate it. And I'll see to it that you have time to get around the place as well. And what's more'—she sent a minatory glance around her co-workers—'we'll do the washing up. *All* of it, guys. Least we can do.'

There was a murmur of assent. Tilly said, 'Well, that's torn it, Mum. Just keep it basic, hmm? Or they might wind up kidnapping you.' Moved by a sudden impulse, she leant across from her chair and hugged her mother. 'I'll do breakfast. You look tired, so you're going to start your holiday with a nice lie-in and a cuppa in bed, okay?'

Elaine, the odd silver hair glinting through the brown, looked lovingly upon her daughter, the delicate skin about her eyes creasing as she smiled. 'Oh, but it's good to be with you again! Don't spoil me too much or I'll never want to leave.'

In the morning Elaine, as promised, rose later than the rest to find her daughter humming as she moved about the kitchen sterilising a feed bottle and chopping up meat for the birds. 'I had such a lovely sleep,' she announced. 'Where's everybody?'

'Sophie's down at the vehicle shed, I think. Luke's gone off to do the chores at the camp and Matt was heading for Spadgers Creek – the station. It's our next-door neighbour. They're killing today, he said.'

'Killing what?' Elaine looked startled, then concerned.

'A cow, I suppose. Or a bullock. I'm not sure. For meat. There aren't any butcher shops out here, Mum.'

'Oh.' Elaine looked relieved. 'You had me worried there. So what would you normally be doing?'

'Helping Luke. But just now I'm making you breakfast. Toast and a soft-boiled egg? With coffee?'

'Sounds lovely. As a matter of interest, who cooked last night's tea?'

'Sophie. It was her turn. Ghastly, wasn't it?' she said cheerfully. 'I've given them simple recipes to follow, but I really think she's worse than Matt. He at least gets his spuds cooked through.'

'Well, I'll see what you've got presently and work out tonight's menu. Actually, it'll be a treat. Your dad eats very simply these days, so it'll be a chance to spread myself a bit. What's the meat you've got there for?'

'We've a couple of injured birds – it's for their breakfast. And we have two joeys, with one still on the bottle. We've just got rid of two black cocky chicks, and I nursed the dearest little sugar glider . . . Oops, the toast is ready and the egg's coming. Sit down and I'll get the coffee. Then I'll have to head out for a bit.'

Tilly attended to the morning chores and returned to find Sophie and her mother talking companionably over the washing up. She left them to it to work in the garden, weeding, watering and picking some early tomatoes. An hour or so later, the first of the campers departing Binboona began to appear, and by noon, new travellers were coming in.

A red Toyota towing a dust-shrouded camper trailer pulled up at the house and, while his mate stayed in the cab, the driver got out, introduced himself as Gordon Chant, and asked to speak with the boss.

'That would be Sophie Barker, the head ranger,' Tilly said. 'Hang on and I'll get her.'

She found her cousin in the office. 'Somebody asking for you, Soph. Just turned up – I don't know what he wants.'

Sophie went out to speak to him while Tilly watched unobtrusively through the louvres of the tiny verandah office. Presently her cousin turned back to the verandah steps to yell, 'You there, Till?'

'Yes?' She appeared framed in the doorway.

'Come and meet Gordon. Looks like we'll be seeing a bit of him. He builds stuff, and right now he's heading out to Sandstone to see the layout there and work out a quote for the boardwalk. It seems that the WPA have made a decision on the springs.'

'They didn't let you know?'

'It'll be in the next mail for sure. The company would want something in writing, for the records. Right, I'm off. I'll lead them out. Is Luke home?'

'I haven't seen him. He was taking a group on the river walk this afternoon.'

'Okay then.' She grinned, slamming a fist into her other palm. 'Hot damn! I never really thought . . .' She trailed off and bustled away to the shed.

'What's happening?' Elaine looked up from her task as Tilly returned indoors.

'Looks like we might be getting the Sandstone Springs opened. You remember I wrote you about them? Mmm, something smells good. What are you making?'

'Honey and cinnamon cake. The honey's very dark. Is it local stuff?'

'You could say so. Luke found a sugarbag nest last month. That's the hive of the native bee. Bit messy to get, but worth the effort.' Tilly sat at the table watching her mother decant the steaming cake onto a cooling rack. 'Tell me about Dad. How bad is he really? I mean, is he likely to die? What does the doctor say?'

'Oh, he's good for a while yet,' Elaine said, setting the tin down and going to the kettle. 'I'll make us some tea. It won't be the dementia that kills him, but his blood pressure is very high, and I worry about strokes. He gets very disturbed at times – I never know what sets him off, but it's risky, Dr Peter says. Though how you can keep somebody calm when you can't communicate with them, I don't know.'

Tilly rubbed her hand. 'I'm sorry, Mum. You've had a pretty thankless time of it.'

'And you haven't, love? It's all right. It's different now, of course. Mostly he's like an angry stranger, but I manage. I don't forget what I owe him and that helps.'

'Marriage shouldn't just be about duty,' Tilly said. 'If things had been different, if you hadn't had me, you'd never have looked at him.'

'And what would life be without my daught—?' Elaine bit the words off. 'I'm sorry, love. I forgot about Francie when I spoke.'

'It's all right, Mum.' Tilly's smile slipped as *once* echoed again in her heart. 'It still hurts to remember – it always will – but I don't want to forget her either. And lately I've felt more accepting of things . . . not that I have any choice. But life does go on. I suppose it must if one is to survive.' She wondered briefly if she should tell her mother the truth, that Gerry still lived and was almost certainly engaged in criminal activity. But why wreck her peace of mind? Instead she said, 'And as a matter of fact, just recently I've met somebody I rather like. I'm not saying we'll ever have a relationship, but just being interested shows I've given up grieving, doesn't it?'

Elaine abandoned her tea-making task to give her daughter a hug. 'I'm glad to hear it, love. No, stay there, I can find stuff.'

When both were seated with their cups before them, Tilly

turned hers in its saucer, saying slowly, 'Then you don't think it's wrong?'

'Of course not. What an idea! The heart knows, Tilly. And we all need love. Am I going to meet him?' A thought struck her. 'It's plainly not Luke – he's only a lad.'

Tilly laughed at the idea. 'And madly into a gorgeous student called Jane. And before you ask, it's not Matt either.'

Elaine's face cleared. 'Good. I shouldn't say it, but I haven't really taken to him. I thought him a bit shifty.'

'Oh, he never meets anyone's eye,' Tilly said, understanding perfectly, 'but he's okay. A hard worker, just not very social.' The last thing she wanted was for Matt to suspect dislike or caution in her mother's manner towards him. Unless he was a very good actor – though, of course, he must be, Tilly mused – he had yet to discover that his stash in the drum had vanished.

'So?' Elaine prompted.

'He's a botanist and his name is Connor. He's staying in the camp and yes, I expect that you will meet him. But no embarrassing questions, okay? In fact, no questions at all, Mum. I want you just to act as though you've never heard his name before. He is not to become a talking point with you and Sophie hatching plans.'

The blue eyes, so like her own, twinkled at her. 'I shall be the soul of discretion,' Elaine promised. 'No wonder you look so much better. I didn't think it was a good idea for you to stay out here, but Sophie was right all along. I shall have to tell her so. But she probably knows that already. Even when we were self-absorbed teenagers, very little got past her.'

# *Chapter Twenty-seven*

If Elaine's words did nothing to calm her daughter, Sophie was, in any case, far too preoccupied with excited plans to worry about Tilly's love life.

She and Luke would head back to Sandstone first thing tomorrow, she said. They had to decide where best to site the new ranger's quarters, and to choose a layout for the projected camp. Gordon had calculated that his own assessment, which involved pegging the route the boardwalk would take, should occupy him for a week, even with his mate Adam's help. Luke was scratching out a rough map from memory, talking all the while: the water table was going to be a problem for the builders; they would need height as the valley was a floodway in the Wet; the station itself would probably be a small kit-home, certainly the most affordable when it came to freight and the labour of erecting it . . .

Tilly listened, bemused by the speed of it all, though she doubted they'd see much progress beyond the planning and perhaps ordering of supplies this season. The monsoon took a big chunk out of the year and no contractor would risk being wetted in for months at a time. Still, 'It's really going to happen,' she said.

Sophie beamed at her. 'Yes. Do you mind hanging on here tomorrow and seeing to the customers? I need Luke out there with me. We'll have to service the camp on the way – unless Matt could fill in? That would free you up.' She turned to him but he was shaking his head.

'Sorry. My towbar's cracked and needs welding. I gotta get it to the station.'

'Why, are we out of oxy?' Luke asked.

Matt cast him a pitying look. 'Oxy weld won't do the job. Needs arc. I'll run the coastal road on the way back,' he offered.

'Yes, that's an idea.' Sophie nodded. 'Sorry, Till. Looks like you're stuck with the washing up.'

'That's okay.' She had been hoping to pull camp duties, which would give her a chance to see Connor and perhaps learn the outcome of his Darwin trip, but it would have to wait. 'We'll cook, Mum. Get a few meals in the freezer so you can have a day or two out. Maybe see Sandstone Springs for yourself. It's an amazing sight, the ferns and flowers. Like an exotic garden with the waterfall trickling down the cliff.'

'And that's another thing, speaking of water.' Sophie made a note. 'We can't just plunk a pump and engine on the main hole. We'll have to run the tailpipe back into the scrub, have a discreet little shelter shed. And some way of shifting it at need. Maybe a hoist? We can't go cutting a track into it for vehicular access.'

'Getting it in will be the hard part,' Luke said. 'The weight of it, I mean, given you could bog a D4 in that ground . . .'

Tilly shook her head at Elaine. 'Television in the lounge? Or Take Two? It'll make more sense to you than all this.'

Friday saw Luke and Sophie back at the springs for the day, knee-deep in sketches and rough maps of the site. They needed to get something on paper for head office in order to have proper plans drawn up for the builders to follow, Sophie said. Tilly volunteered for camp duties, delegating Elaine to feed Harry while she loaded the day's supply of wood.

Her mother eyed the eager bird with some trepidation. 'He's awfully big. Why's he opening his wings like that? He's not going to attack me, is he?'

'Of course not! He's just impatient for his breakfast. Chuck him some meat and he'll settle down. He couldn't attack a beetle with that beak, and that's the trouble. It's why we have to feed him.'

'If you say so.' Elaine, sounding unconvinced, obeyed and then gasped in admiration as the brolga adroitly caught and swallowed the double offering. 'He's so quick!'

'Well, he has to get it from the air because he can't pick it up. Throw it one bit at a time.'

'Oh.' Pity captured Elaine, instantly changing her caution into partisanship. 'You poor thing,' she cried. 'Here, have another. You're really quite a handsome fellow, aren't you?'

Grinning to herself, for she'd banked on the change, Tilly called, 'Right, I'm running way late, Mum, so I'm off. Nobody's likely to come, but if they do, just get them to sign in and pay – you know the rate. I'll be back in an hour or so.'

*

The camp was astir by the time she arrived, and she'd barely started unloading before Connor was there, heaving the firewood off for her.

'Thanks. How are things? Any developments?'

'You look happy,' he commented. 'Did your mum get here?'

'Yes, on Wednesday. She's got eight days all up so if you're around, you'll get to meet her. So, no news of villainy?'

'Not from my end. My man at the station said there's been vehicles using the coastal road lately. Would they be yours?'

She was surprised. 'They shouldn't be. Matt was going to check it today.'

'Yes? I wonder if he's meeting somebody.'

Head on one side, Tilly considered the proposition. 'How would he arrange that? I mean, the other guy would have to know where and when, wouldn't he?'

Connor shrugged. 'Matt could have a wireless. There's no point him being here if he can't direct the rest of the gang. They *must* be able to communicate.'

'But on the air – couldn't anybody hear them? The stations might have phones now, but I understand they still use wireless in their stock camps.'

'On the normal channels, I agree, they could. So they'd use a different wavelength, set a particular time, have code phrases. Maybe keep changing wavelengths.'

'I suppose.' Tilly had been working as they spoke, and now he pulled the filled ash bucket away as she relit the fire under the donkey.

'What's next?'

'Cleaning, then checking the tank and the pump. Then I'd best get back.'

'Has Matt already left?'

Tilly glanced at the sun. 'Oh, yes, an hour or more back. I'm awfully late today. What's the time now?'

He glanced at his watch. 'Nine. Bit after.'

'He'd have been gone by seven,' she said, and he swore lightly.

'Damn! With a headstart like that, there's no point following him. I'd very likely meet him returning, and that might make him nervous. Particularly if he's not buying my cover story.'

'Or it could be he just doesn't like you,' Tilly suggested, 'and pretending you're something else is a way of, I don't know, sneering at you? He seemed to think it was significant you giving him that Latin name for the shade tree at the house. As if you were trying to, you know, baffle him with science.'

'Did he?' Connor snorted in amusement. 'Genus names are something you learn in a nursery. I daresay I knew 'em better than my times tables because Pops started me off on them at five. Good thing, as it turned out.'

'Yes, I told him it proved your case,' Tilly said. 'He didn't like that, so perhaps he does just have it in for you for sort-of showing him up. He hasn't much education, you see.'

'That was very loyal of you, Tilly.' He smiled at her and she felt the blood heat her skin. 'Look, why don't I dump this'—he indicated the full bucket at his feet—'then head up to camp and put the billy on? You've time for a cuppa after you've finished here?'

'That would be lovely. But I mustn't stay long. Mum's holding the fort. She was making friends with Harry when I left, but I dread to think what might happen if the old goanna that hangs around the animal enclosure was to make an appearance. He's a giant of his kind.'

'She's not a city woman, is she?'

'No, but the biggest wildlife she's ever encountered before today was probably a dead fish.'

'Ah. Well, maybe she'll like wildflowers? I could take her for a drive while she's here,' he suggested. 'Better, of course, if you came too.'

'That would be kind of you. We'll have to see.' Her heart gave a little skip and she smiled at him before busying herself with the cleaning equipment.

At the camp, he had the tea made and was busy turning the last of a pile of flat little cakes on a small metal plate placed atop the flame of his stove.

'Pikelets?' Tilly sat under the awning on the camp stool awaiting her. 'I didn't know you cooked.'

He gave an aw-shucks grin. 'Just trying to impress. So what's happened to your stepfather while your mother's up here?' He poured the tea and passed her the enamel pannikin holding a small quantity of milk.

'Thanks. He's in respite care till Mum gets back. Thank God for places like that, or carers would never get a break. It's a life sentence when a spouse has dementia – unless the carer can afford to pay for help. It's four or five years since the diagnosis and this is only the second time, to my knowledge, that's she's spent a day away from him. She flew up when Francie . . . when my daughter died.'

He dabbed jam onto a couple of pikelets and passed the plate across. 'Try one, tell me if you think it's terrible. That must have been hard for you both. Had she seen much of her granddaughter?'

'Not really. I took her home once, before she was twelve months old.' Tilly bit absently into the pikelet, tasting the sweetness of jam and the fluffy lightness of the batter. 'Hmm, tasty. But Mum missed out on a lot – hearing her speak, her first steps with her little arms flapping . . . Of course I sent photos, but it's not the same. Pictures can't capture the . . . the essence of a baby.' Her heart lurched to the echo of *once*. She sipped her tea. 'The little things you never forget. Their warmth when you hold them, their smile that's just for you. You love them so much it hurts.' The sweetness had turned to ashes in her mouth. She swallowed past an aching throat and felt her eyes tear. 'I'm sorry, it's . . . I don't think you ever get over losing a child. Sometimes I dream that I hold her still and when I wake, I just want to die.'

'I'm sorry.' He came to squat beside her, and placed a solid, comforting arm about her shoulders. 'I shouldn't have brought it up, only I want to know you, Tilly, and your daughter is such a big part of your life. I should have waited. Please'—she felt his lips on her hair—'I didn't mean to upset you.'

'It's okay.' Tilly gave a watery sniff. 'I don't want to forget her,' she reiterated fiercely, 'but sometimes the hurt and the guilt is nearly unbearable, knowing, in those last moments, that she would've been so frightened.' She let herself lean into his strength, feeling again the comfort of having somebody hold her, the tension leaching away with the contact. 'I should've jumped in myself, not left it to Gerry.'

'You can't go there. "Should haves" have broken more hearts and wrecked more lives than you can count. Regret is the cruellest thing, my dear, because you can't change it.'

'I know.' She ran a finger below her eyelid to catch a vagrant tear. 'What did you call me?'

'My dear. Because you are becoming increasingly dear to me, Tilly. I'm sorry – am I presuming too much?' He pulled back to look at her, his brown eyes intent as they searched her face. Using his thumb, he wiped away another tear by her mouth. 'I've fallen for you, Tilly. I expect a lot of men do. But if you're not ready, or have a violent dislike of my job . . . I mean, I came to you under false pretences. And there's your husband.'

'No.' She straightened to face him. 'I never want to set eyes on Gerry again. Even if I'd never met you, that is over.'

'So, there's a chance for me?'

He looked so eager and hopeful that she couldn't help but smile and tease him a little. 'Well, there might be. I do feel a connection between us. Is it just loneliness because we've nobody else in our lives? I think the only way to be sure is to see more of each other. So, will you be around for long, Mr Doyle? Hang on, it is Doyle, isn't it?'

'It is.' He was smiling too. 'And a little bird told me that you're Matilda.'

'Yes. A stupid name, but that's mothers for you.'

'I like it. It's rare and different. It suits who you are. And as to being around – yes, I shall be, until I've swept you off your feet. And speaking of mothers – may I meet yours?'

'Anytime. In fact, why don't you come to dinner tonight? You can do your undercover stuff with Matt, quiz him about his trip today. And hear all Sophie's plans for Sandstone,' she added. 'You know she's got the go-ahead for opening the place to campers? She and Luke are out there right now with a contractor. He's doing a – what do they call it? – a feasability thing for building a boardwalk. I shouldn't think it'll be done this year, because of course there's more to it than a boardwalk. They'll need the road fixed and ablution blocks and a ranger's house. Somebody will have to be on site twenty-four-seven, after all, and they'll have to have somewhere to live. It might suit Luke,' she added judiciously. 'He's getting engaged at Christmas and could well be married by the time the place is ready.' She gave the sun a guilty glance and stood up. 'I have to go, Connor. I told Mum an hour and it's closer to two. Will you come tonight?'

'You try and keep me away.' He had taken her hands in his and now leant forward to give her a quick, light peck on the lips. 'Just an earnest against later canoodling, Ms Matilda.'

'You mean this sort of thing?' Tilly grabbed him, her arms going around his neck as she kissed him passionately. He seemed to freeze for a millisecond, then she found herself enfolded and the kiss being enthusiastically returned. For a long heady moment they clung together before he released her and stepped back.

'That's more or less what I had in mind,' he agreed. 'Drive safely, dear one, and I'll catch you later.'

# *Chapter Twenty-eight*

Tilly, hands and feet automatically performing their tasks, remembered little of the drive home. She felt as giddy as a young girl and simultaneously longed both to tell somebody and to keep the matter secret. Her thoughts swooped dizzyingly between the joy his words had produced – *I've fallen for you* – and wondering how a love affair could be managed when both of them lived such different lives. When the undercover operation ended, what then? He was based in Darwin and her life was here at Binboona. Still, that was for later. Right now, remembering the electrical charge of that kiss, she could think only of being wanted, of being loved and of anticipating their next encounter.

Driving into the shed, she was in time to catch the first travellers of the day as they pulled up behind her. 'Morning,' she sang at the newcomer, bestowing a flashing smile upon him and what she could see of the others within the vehicle.

'Well, somebody's in a good mood,' he responded. 'Ben Carson and family. We booked last month.'

'Ranger Tilly,' she replied. 'Isn't it a beautiful day? If you'd just step up to the office, we'll get you signed in.' She could see Elaine hovering at the door and waved her off. 'It's okay, I've got it.' She'd make Connor something special for dessert and maybe the two of them could sneak off after dinner while the others were washing up? Her heart sang at the prospect as she turned another blinding smile on the customer before her. 'Sorry, what did you say your name was again?'

Matt was the first to get home, arriving mid-afternoon. He had a cup of tea in the kitchen while complaining of a puncture, then put on a load of washing; they all did their own now that Tilly no longer house-kept. Later she heard a repetitive banging in the shed, deducing from it that he was repairing the tyre. Sophie and Luke came back in the last glow of daylight, when the dust of their travel hung in an amber haze behind them and the river glimpses shone dully like wrinkled pewter. The camp was full again and between Elaine's arrival and the general excitement over the Sandstone project, they had completely forgotten the weekly slideshow and talk.

She reminded Luke as he came up the steps between the now-blooming tubs of marigolds that Connor had helped her fence in.

'Have to be tomorrow night then.' He yawned widely, dusting his hat against his jeans. 'We've got the plans just about sorted, so that'll work.' He sniffed eagerly at the aromas from the kitchen. 'Boy, that smells good! I could eat a horse, saddle and all. What is it?'

'Ask Mum. I hope you're showering before we sit down. I can smell the dust on you from here, and you look like you've waded in mud.'

Luke sniffed ostentatiously at himself, then leant towards her. ‘Probably because I have. Is that perfume? You’re looking mighty bright-eyed, Tilly. What’s going on?’

‘We have a guest for dinner and Mum wanted to make an occasion of it,’ she lied shamelessly. ‘She loves entertaining.’

‘A guest? Who?’

‘Connor.’ She flushed as she met his gaze and he smirked.

‘Oh. Like that, is it? Nice shirt thingy.’

It was a good one that she’d last worn in a bistro in Darwin, having lunch with Gerry, and actually not a shirt at all but a soft blouse with a tie neck, in shades of blue and cream. She had left her hair down, curling inwards on her shoulders, for it was months since it was last cut, and added the faintest trace of pink to her lips. Nothing over the top, she had told herself, but Luke plainly wasn’t fooled by her attempt at casualness.

‘I can get out of working clothes sometimes.’ She let her irritation show, but he simply grinned annoyingly.

‘Yum, yum. And I reckon our botanist won’t be meaning dinner.’

‘You’re impossible,’ she said crossly. ‘Why don’t you go and shower.’

Connor arrived on time, without his usual hat and dressed in clean khaki. He greeted Tilly with a smile and her face pinkened as she replied and introduced him to Elaine.

‘Ah,’ he exclaimed, smiling as he shook her hand. ‘The lady who taught Tilly to cook. I was a houseguest here for a bit. You’ve quite a talent, Mrs Williams. I would’ve brought flowers had there been any available, but I carved this for you instead. A little thank you for tonight’s meal.’

‘You’re very welcome. I—’ Flustered, Elaine accepted the

token, while Tilly craned to see what she held and heard her mother gasp in surprise, or delight. 'Oh! Why, Connor, it's beautiful. Look!' She held it up for them all to see, a cameo of a flower the size of a twenty-cent piece. 'Every petal's as plain as. It's a rose, isn't it? One of those flat old-fashioned ones with the wonderful scent. Thank you. You carved it yourself?'

He shrugged. 'A bit of a hobby of mine. You can stick a pin on the back and wear it as a brooch, but it needs oiling first. Tilly knows how.' With practised ease he turned to Sophie. 'So, I hear you've had good news about Sandstone Springs. How's that going?'

It was a wonderful evening for Tilly. She felt Connor's awareness of her like a physical touch as he ate and chatted, slipping the occasional comment or question Matt's way, while being attentive to Elaine and listening to Sophie's and Luke's enthusiasm over future plans and present progress at the springs. She was content to watch and listen, filling her eyes with the sight of him. There was a scar on his chin she hadn't noticed before, and one thumbnail had split and regrown over itself, which could only be the result of a nasty injury. She flinched inwardly on his account and yearned to ask about it, but now was neither the time nor place.

The meal was delicious and when the dessert came out – a chocolate mousse, served in individual glasses, each decorated with a net of spun barley sugar – Luke predictably exclaimed, 'Wow! I must've died. This is food heaven.'

'Tilly's work,' Elaine said fondly.

Sophie clapped. 'Double wow! It looks too pretty to eat.'

'Not to me, it doesn't,' Luke said reverently, lifting his spoon and demolishing the decoration, eager as a child at a party. Connor smiled across the table at Tilly, the look as intimate as a kiss.

'Nice to be appreciated,' she said.

Luke and Matt did the dishes while the rest retired to the lounge with coffee.

'So, how long will you be here, Elaine?' Connor asked, passing the sugar.

'Till next mail day. I'm flying out on that awful little plane.' She shuddered. 'And apparently it goes *everywhere*, so it'll be a long trip.'

'Other places need their mail too, Mum,' Tilly reminded her.

'Well, in that case . . . How would you like a drive tomorrow? I could take you down to the coast. A different sea to the one you know. What do you say? Maybe Tilly could come too?'

'Yes, take a day, Till,' Sophie seconded. 'I'll be home. We've done what we can at Sandstone, and I need to draft a report with my recommendations for the site.' She looked hopefully at her aunt. 'You said you were cooking ahead? Is there something in the freezer I could defrost for tomorrow night?'

Elaine nodded. 'Beef casserole. I'll get it out in the morning. Thank you, Connor. That would be lovely. So, lunch? Or is it a short trip?'

'Nothing's short out here, Mum. You'll see why tomorrow. Make a time, Connor, and we'll be ready. And thank you. It's very thoughtful of you.'

'Not at all, ladies,' he said, right eye dropping in a wink at

Tilly. 'I hope you'll enjoy it, but the pleasure will be entirely mine.'

'It's early days, but I must say I like your man,' Elaine confided the next morning as she and Tilly worked on the lunches. 'Is he Irish? He's got a sort of blarney charm about him.'

'With a name like Doyle it's very possible. Maybe his grandparents, or their grandparents.'

'He has a kind manner,' Elaine decided. 'A botanist – that's different. So what's he doing out here, or is he on holiday?'

'Research work. Some land development thing through the university, I think,' Tilly said vaguely. 'He studies vegetation for them, tracks the spread of noxious weeds. Something like that. I haven't really been into it.' If her mother wanted more detail, then Connor would have to tell his own lies. She had better not say anything that he might later contradict. Changing the subject, she said, 'It was a lovely dinner. A great evening, in fact. I'm sure the others thought so too. Connor certainly did.'

'You were a long time saying goodnight.'

'I'm not a teenager, Mum!'

'No, of course not.' Elaine smiled lovingly at her daughter. 'I hope he's good for you. I think he will be. Maybe it's experience, but you're not so anxious to please this time, and that makes for a more balanced relationship.'

Her words gave Tilly pause. She had been young with Gerry, but looking back, it was true – she had always striven to foresee his wants. Out of love, she had told herself at the time, to save him hassle. It had seemed a laudable sacrifice then, making her own wishes and needs secondary to his. Something that he had initially found charming and then taken for granted, she now realised. And it had left her in ignorance of the hidden life he had pursued, the debts he had incurred. No, there had been nothing balanced about it. She wondered how much longer her compliance would have lasted if the tragedy hadn't occurred – ten years, twenty? Perhaps it wasn't the extra years, but grief and loss that was responsible for the change in her.

Looking at her mother, she wondered if Elaine's own marital experience – for she too had spent her life attempting to please her own husband – had made her able to recognise the same foible in her daughter. Gratitude was no basis for marriage, she thought, but the sixties had been a different era. And if Les Williams hadn't married Elaine, in all ignorance of her condition, then Tilly might well have grown up in an orphanage. So maybe he deserved the gratitude and service his wife had given him through the years. But it wasn't the same as love. The relationship, flawed by Elaine's deceit, had cheated all three of them of that.

'Mum,' she said with sudden decision, 'why won't you tell me my father's name? You always said he didn't matter, so who can it harm? I'm no longer a child and I think I deserve to know.'

Elaine looked startled, then sighed resignedly. 'Oh, Tilly! I thought we were past all this. It still doesn't matter. How can it? There's nothing of you in him.'

'Well, that's not true. Half my DNA is his. I don't want to meet him, or claim him, Mum, if that's what's stopping you. I just want to know.'

'Very well then.' She folded the last sandwich into its wrapper. 'But you'll be no wiser. I don't know his name. His mates called him Benno. It happened at a teenage party. We were drinking. The adults had left us downstairs quite early in the night, and some of the boys had sneaked in some grog. I got squiffy and giggly, and Benno was there.' She flushed. 'It sounds cheap and horrible – and stupid. It was. A quick fumble in the dark with a boy I hadn't met before. I was sixteen and curious, and everybody said you couldn't fall pregnant the first time. I never saw him again after that night, or learnt his surname, or even what Benno stood for – Benjamin, Benedict. Maybe his surname was Bennet . . . It wasn't a meaningful or romantic act, just a stupid one. That's why I didn't want you to know.'

'I'm sorry.' Penitently Tilly took her mother's hand. 'I shouldn't have asked. You were just a kid – it's not fair to have your whole life ruined for one little mistake.'

'Who said anything about ruin?' Elaine demanded. 'I got you, didn't I? Do you really think that I would wish that undone? Shame on you, Matilda! You have always been reason enough for everything.'

'Oh, Mum.' Touched, she hugged the older woman to her. 'I love you too. And I should know better than to try and judge,' she said thinking of Gerry. 'Nobody outside a marriage really understands it.'

'Well, you're right about that,' Elaine said. 'And quite a few spouses don't understand it, or each other either. Now, do you think we need cake as well? And what about a thermos?'

'Definitely cake, but Connor will boil the billy. I'll clean up,' she added with a glance at the clock. 'Then he ought to be just about here.'

# *Chapter Twenty-nine*

Connor was on time and, having loaded up, they took the road to the coast, leaving the main route to the station to turn onto a single vehicle track heading due north.

'Where are you going?' Elaine clung, aghast, to the hand bar in front of her as the vehicle shook over the potholes.

'It's the most direct way,' Tilly explained before Connor could defend his driving. 'If we went round by the station, that's an extra two hours' travel. This is a slower road, but shorter.'

'Well, I'm glad you called it a road. It's like something out of a Mexican Western,' her mother said forthrightly. 'Why doesn't your company mend it, or make a new one?'

'It all comes down to money, Mum. Matt grades most of the roads, but this one isn't driven that often, so I suppose he thinks it has a low priority.' Or maybe, she thought, catching Connor's eye in the mirror, it was more about discouraging the rangers' use of it. Movement off to the right caught her eye and she pointed. 'Look, brumbies!' The mass of brown and bay bodies flashed through the scrub in a burst of moving legs and flying manes.

Elaine clapped her hands, thrilled. 'You never told me there were wild horses here.'

'I suppose I'm just used to seeing them about. Heaven knows there're plenty of them.'

'And they just run wild and free? That's nice.'

'Only because wildlife's protected here,' Connor said. 'Some of the stations trap them, and sell them for pet meat.'

'That's horrible,' Elaine cried.

'It's economics,' he said. 'They're a pest. They foul the waterholes, break fencing, eat feed – there're thousands of them. The graziers have to protect their livelihood.'

'Well, I wish you hadn't told me. How come they're here, anyway?' Elaine asked.

'Binboona used to be station country and it was all open range back then. No fences. So the stock – all the stock – cattle, buffalo, brumbies, wild pigs, spread right across the north. They—'

'Oh, look,' Elaine interrupted him. 'Emus! Four, five – no, seven . . .' She twisted in her seat. 'Oh, I wish I'd brought a camera. Why didn't I think of that?'

Binboona, Tilly thought, was really turning it on for her mother. She nudged her, nodding ahead. 'Hang on now. This creek is a bit rough. Don't bounce or you'll hit your head.'

At the coast they found the same tamarind tree as before. Connor boiled the billy in its shade, and they ate some of the cake Elaine had packed with their cuppa.

'So where's the sea?' she asked.

'Just a bit further on. We'll drive along the coast track,' Connor said, 'and see what we can see. The Gulf is pretty flat, so it's not very spectacular. Not like the WA coast with its big tides. Still, the trawlers work it. Tilly said your husband was a fisherman?'

'Yes. Cold water though, and a lot of bad gales. Not an easy life.'

'No,' he agreed. 'So many occupations aren't. Everybody finished? Shall we then?'

They started off again, driving slowly, with Connor pointing out the first glimpse of blue to Elaine. He was looking, Tilly knew, for Matt's tracks from the previous day. She kept a sharp eye out and was first to spot the flattened area of coarse grass where a vehicle had turned around.

'Somewhere here,' she said, meeting his eye. She jerked her chin just as he trod on the brake, exclaiming as he did so.

'What is it?' Elaine asked.

'I think I've just seen a particular plant. Stay there, I won't be a sec.' He got out, leaving the engine running, and headed for the thin scrubline that screened the beach.

After a moment Tilly pushed her own door open. 'Think I'll visit the ladies while he's away. Just wait here, Mum. Once Connor gets into plants it can take him a while.' She skipped behind the vehicle, made a detour beyond her mother's sight and, jogging, caught him up where he squatted, examining a slew of bootprints in the sand.

'Tide must've been in,' he said, glancing up at her and then across the shallow bay. 'They'd have motored in in the runabout, waded ashore. Two men, and that'—he pointed—'the T-boot there, is what Matt wears. Question is why? A meet up with the boss, or something more?'

'Like what?'

He shrugged, his brown eyes, netted in faint creases, intent upon an inner vision. 'Could've delivered a pay-off, or a few kilos of drugs, I suppose. Maybe even slipped an illegal into the country, though that's not very likely.'

'No. Highly unlikely, I'd have thought,' Tilly said. 'What would he do with them?'

He grinned. 'That's my practical girl.' Then abruptly he sighed and stood. 'I shouldn't have got you mixed up in this, Tilly. They're just tracks in the sand now, but these men are dangerous. And if involving you isn't bad enough, I brought your mother along as well.'

'Speaking of which, you'd better grab a few samples off a bush and get back to her before she comes looking. After all, wasn't this'—she waved at the empty beach with its betraying tracks—'what you came for?'

'Not entirely. There was this too.' His arms swooped around her, drawing her in for a kiss. 'Good morning, my dear. And then I wanted to please your mother too. Three birds with the one tank of petrol, you could say.'

'Well, she is pleased. She thinks you're charming and suspects an Irish background because of it. Or possibly because of your name. But she totally buys your cover, so let's not make you into a liar, hmm?'

'You're right.' He released her reluctantly and went to break off a section of a straggly shrub with yellow pea-shaped flowers.

'What's that?'

'Broom bush. *Jacksonia ramosissima*. Or very similar. You usually find it further east. The flowers here are a bit different to the ones I'm familiar with,' he said, examining them, 'but they'll do, anyway.'

Back at the vehicle, he snapped off a small piece holding the most blossoms and presented it to Elaine. 'Sorry about the wait. This was what I spotted. I haven't seen it growing in these parts before.'

'It's pretty. What is it?'

'It's a species of broom bush. I'm not quite sure of the variety though. Have to look it up.'

'It's a lot to remember, all those names. I suppose you know the Latin ones too?'

'Oh, he does,' Tilly said dryly. 'Tell her the name of the big shade tree back at the house, Connor.'

He complied and Elaine laughed. 'Sounds like a gastric problem. Well, since you know them all, what's that dusty-looking bush over there?'

They arrived back at the homestead a little before dark, when the light was fading on the river and the flying fox colony there had begun to stir.

'Just in time for the evening feeds,' Tilly said. 'Well, Mum, you can't say you haven't seen a different slice of the Top End.'

'I had a lovely day. Tiring, but it was really interesting.' Still clutching the wilting broom sprig, Elaine climbed from the vehicle and stretched. Her face and arms had pinkened from the sun, and wattle pollen dusted her hair and shoulders.

'Thank you, Connor. And now I'm going to shower and lie down for a bit to settle my back.'

'No, I want to thank you, Elaine, for your company and the delicious lunch,' he responded, but found he was talking to her back as she made for the steps. Low-voiced, he added, 'Well, that was quick. I haven't offended her, have I?'

Tilly giggled. 'Don't be dense. She probably wants the loo. And she's giving you the chance to kiss me goodbye.'

He grinned. 'I don't need telling twice.' He swept her into his arms and complied. 'She's all right, your mum. Okay, my sweet, I'll be back tomorrow. I need to report to my lot, and if I can phone from here, it'll save me the drive to Spadgers Creek. What will you be doing?'

'I *should* be working. But sometime this week we're taking Mum out to Sandstone. It'll depend on Luke's schedule. Oh my God! We're doing an extra slide night tonight and I'm supposed to help. I have to go.' She snatched another brief kiss and fled up the verandah steps, turning at the top to wave goodbye before vanishing indoors.

The following few days fled by. Tilly spent them cooking, sightseeing with Elaine, stealing interludes with Connor, and doing brief stints of labour with Luke. Gordon Chant, the contractor, submitted his quote, along with an initial list of materials the job would require, then departed. He was gone when they took Elaine out to the springs, where a forest of ribboned stakes outlined the position of the proposed boardwalk.

'The campground will be over there,' Luke said, pointing, 'and the ranger's quarters further over, and much higher.' He waved a hand at a rocky rise not far from the section of lower cliff where the Aboriginal paintings were. 'The plan is to scrape the top off that ridge, level it, and then raise the building higher still on metal posts to maybe a metre above the ground. The paintings haven't been flooded, so that should make it safe enough.'

'And will they fix the road in?' Elaine rubbed her back. 'Because, honestly, I can't see too many people willing to suffer over that even for such a beautiful spot as this. And what about the camp site itself? If, as you say, this all goes under water in the monsoon?'

'There won't be anything to be damaged,' Luke said. 'The ablution blocks will be demountable buildings we can load and remove at season's end. Then we cap off the septic tanks – they're underground anyway – and the water flows over the top. Bit of tidying and mowing at the end of the Wet, bring the buildings back and hook 'em up, and we're in business again.'

'And the road will be fixed, Mum,' Tilly said. 'But even the way it is, it's worth the trip, don't you think?'

'Oh, yes.' Elaine sighed with pleasure. 'When I'm back home, I'll remember today – sitting here listening to the water, with the ferns and moss all around, and the dragonflies like . . . like aerial rubies.' She smiled a little at her own conceit. 'It's wonderful. Balm to the soul.'

'I'm glad. Do you want to see the caves? The road gets worse from here on, I'm afraid.'

Elaine shook her head. 'Caves don't do much for me. And besides, you couldn't top this. If we could just stop a little longer?'

So they stayed, before driving back to the homestead through the tawny dust of evening. On the way, Tilly spoke of Luke's bats, as she had come to think of them, and the question hanging over their identity, which they hoped would be settled one way or another by the next mail.

And then Wednesday and leave-taking was upon them. Elaine, determinedly cheerful, hugged them all save Matt who, seeing her coming, proffered a hand and mumbled something with averted eyes. Tilly watched her mother suck in her breath before stepping gamely up into the little plane, and saw her face twist in the anguish of parting as she waved a frantic goodbye through the window.

Sophie had seen it too and put her arm around her cousin. 'She'll be fine. When does her flight go tomorrow?'

'Twelve-thirty.'

'Gives her time to see a bit of Darwin first, then.' She hefted the incoming mailbag. 'Right, back to the treadmill for us all. Whose turn is it in the kitchen today?'

'It had better be mine,' Tilly said, adding dryly, 'The shock to our stomachs might be a bit much if we start with either of the men.'

# *Chapter Thirty*

The first words out of Luke's mouth as he entered the kitchen that evening were, 'Did they come?'

'Right here.' Tilly handed him the package from the chemist. 'How was your day?'

'Hmm? Oh, you know.' He ripped the packet open and was flipping through the photographs, giving a brief crack of laughter at one, frowning at another. 'Not enough light,' he muttered. 'Shit! That – ah! Got ya! That's a good clear one. Okay, now let's see . . .'

He vanished into the lounge, reappearing some ten minutes later and saying triumphantly, 'I knew it! It *is* different. Look, Tilly. You compare them, tell me I'm not dreaming.'

Holding the spoon she'd been stirring the mince with, Tilly studied the two pictures. 'They are similar, but yes, I can see a difference. The nose shape is less pronounced. Wait, though – what if it's just a gender thing, or age? I mean, if an alien compared a teenage boy with a man, it might not realise they were the same species, don't you think?'

'In the matter of colour, possibly, but I can't see how it

would affect the shape of their ears, say. Every species has a pattern it grows to, and unless I was unlucky enough to catch a freak . . .'

'You're probably right then. So what will you do now?' Tilly dipped the spoon again and stirred, before lowering the gas. 'Dinner's about five minutes off.'

For once food failed to interest Luke. 'I'll ring Darwin – somebody at the university will know who to contact. I'll send him the pic, but I reckon they'll need a live specimen to be certain. Maybe I should start figuring out a bat trap? I daresay they'd have ideas on that too.'

'Very likely. I'm about to ring the dinner bell, Luke. Just warning you.'

'Huh? Oh, right. Where's Sophie? I'll get her to check it out. She—'

He darted off, leaving Tilly to cast up her eyes and turn off the heat. Dinner was plainly going to be late.

The following day, Matt, despite his grumbling, was rostered onto kitchen work.

'Which fits nicely,' Sophie said, 'because we'll be getting a load of steel out and you can show the men the best place to unload. Somewhere it'll be easy to get at, Matt. It's the supports for the boardwalk. It seems that the company's moving pretty quickly on the project. I thought it would be months before they decided anything.'

Luke looked up. 'Maybe they haven't, except that it should go ahead. I mean, whoever builds it will need the same materials, and they'd likely want to get them in before the Wet. Graeme would tell them about that – how the roads close and the country shuts down for the duration. There'll be another visitor too. Land Resources is sending a chiroptologist out once they contact him. Might take a few days, they said.'

'And a chiro-whatsit would be . . .?' Tilly asked.

'A bat man. The bloke I spoke to sounded quite excited, so they're not waiting on the photo – well, unless they can't get hold of their fella before it turns up.'

'Lotta bloody fuss over a flying mouse,' Matt said. 'Can't see how it matters myself.'

'You soon would if there weren't any,' Luke replied. 'The insects'd carry us away, for starters. They're great pollinators too, you know.'

'Huh, that's what we've got bees for.'

'You can't convert non-believers,' Sophie said briskly. 'Slide night again. Maybe you could include bats in your talk this evening, Luke?'

'It's an idea. Tilly and me, we'll mostly be in the camp today. There are a couple of walks booked. I'll do the gorge trail, and she can handle the other one.'

Trepidation seized Tilly. 'I can?'

'Course you can. I told those for the river walk a nine o'clock start. It's simple. Stick to the trail. If there are kids, make 'em behave, and then just answer everybody's questions. You can handle that. You know enough about the birds and vegetation now. And don't forget to invite them to the slide show.'

'Got it,' Tilly said faintly. She had gone along and helped on previous walks, admiring the effortless way Luke had controlled the group. He had the attributes of a good sheepdog, she thought, keeping the stragglers up with the rest, and being polite but firm even with those who thought they knew better. And entertaining them to boot. 'Right,' she said, hoping she sounded confident, 'so we'll need our lunches then?' A happy thought occurred to her. Connor might be free; if he was, she could ask him to join the group. It was enough to put a smile on her face as she pulled out the bread to begin making sandwiches.

As it turned out, the morning's efforts, though initially nerve-racking, stood Tilly in good stead for the evening's performance, which Luke again insisted she share. 'You need to get comfortable with it,' he said. 'Who knows? You could be doing it all next year. I mean, once Sandstone's up and running, we're going to have to split forces, aren't we? And you've plenty of local knowledge, Tilly. It doesn't have to be birds. You can talk about the country's history, industry, climate. I've jotted down a few dates and facts on a sheet for you. The year the WPA started up here, and why these sanctuaries are necessary. Then there's rainfall – you've been through a Wet here, so tell them about it. There's Sweetheart, the biggest croc ever caught in the Top End – I've noted down his weight and length – and they can even go and see him in Darwin. They love hearing that sort of stuff. It's also a good reminder not to ignore the no-swimming signs.'

'Okay. Dear God! It says here he was over five metres long and he attacked boats! If I'd known that, I'd never have taken Mum on the river.'

'Well, he's in a tank in Darwin now, so she was perfectly safe. How did the walk go this morning? I had a bugger of a kid on mine. I could have happily dropped him off the cliff, and his mother with him.'

'It was good. It helped that we saw an old tarpot slithering along in the grass. Nothing like sighting a snake to keep people on the path, even if it is only a python.' She grinned.

He gave her a wink in return. 'Sure thing. Let nature work for you, I say.'

Despite her nervousness, the evening talk went well. Making discreet use of her torch, Tilly was able to check the facts on her cheat sheet, and in a moment of inspiration spoke of her own introduction to the breathtaking difference of the country: the wet hush of tropical dawns, the jewelled colours of the insects – iridescent beetles, ruby-red and sky-blue dragonflies – the cuteness of the shaky-paw lizards and the novelty of barking geckos. She was roundly applauded at the conclusion, not least by Connor, whom she hadn't known was in the audience.

'You had them spellbound,' he said, sliding his large hand around her smaller one. 'Cuppa at my camp?' He brushed a kiss onto her cheekbone. 'It could lead on to other things if you want.'

'You think so?' Tilly's heart lifted as she swayed towards him. There was, she told herself, no reason to hold back. 'Mmm, you know I might consider that. How big is your bed?'

'Big enough. It's a swag, well padded too.' His hand cupped her bejeaned bottom. 'And I'll keep you warm.'

'And breakfast? Would that be included in the deal? I have to work, you know. I'll probably be pulling down fences tomorrow.'

His lips nibbled at the skin below her ear, sending little pulses of excitement through her. 'I think I could probably find something adequate in my tuckerbox,' he murmured.

'You might have to drop me back home quite early,' she warned. 'If you can manage that, we're on.'

'A very modest request, dear heart, and entirely doable.' He linked their hands, his thumb massaging the side of her finger. 'I'll walk you up.'

'After we help carry the gear,' she demurred.

He gave a martyred sigh, but heaved the screen rig onto his shoulder, leaving the box of slides for Luke. It gave her the opportunity for a murmured explanation to the young ranger. 'I'm spending the night in the camp. Tell Sophie. I'll make a start on the chores, and you can pick me up there in the morning, rather than me coming back, okay? Don't forget my lunch.'

The dark hid Luke's expression and any surprise he may have felt. 'Okay,' he agreed. 'So, the lovebug bites again, hey? Must be something in the water round here.'

'Besides crocs, you mean? Well, you should know,' she quipped. 'And surprise! The young aren't the only possible victims.'

# *Chapter Thirty-one*

Tilly woke with an ache in her right hip and a heavy weight across her shoulder. It took a second to remember, then she stretched luxuriously and rolled towards Connor, dislodging his arm and waking him. 'Good morning.' She kissed his chin, feeling the bristles there. 'I have to tell you, sir, that you got me here under false pretences.'

'Yes?' He pulled her closer, his hand roving down her bare back. 'How is that, then?'

'According to my hip, your swag is lined with rocks. That said'—she smiled into his eyes, blowing a stray strand of hair from her face—'the rest of the night lived up to its billing.'

'Well, that's a relief. We could,' he said hopefully, 'stay here a bit longer? It's cosy, not really that rocky and we're both naked—'

'And Luke will be along before you know it,' she said, thrusting the blankets back and yipping at the cold. 'If there's still hot water to be had, I want a shower, and breakfast, so stir your stumps, my dear. Feeding me was part of the bargain, remember?'

He sighed, but sat up, the blankets pooling around his waist. 'Brr! You're a hard, mercenary woman, but eminently kissable.' He suited the action to the word, releasing her reluctantly. 'Did I tell you I adore you, Tilly Hillyer? Because I do. Last night was . . .' He shook his head. 'Let's just say that right now I could die happy.'

She laughed, but her heart sang at his words and she leant to kiss him again. 'I'd rather you cooked breakfast, handsome. I've work to do and I suspect you have too. Up and at 'em, boyo.'

A very quick shower later, for the water had been just lukewarm, Tilly sat down to cereal, pancakes and tea. They ate in the little annexe out of the wind, and she lifted her face gratefully to the newly risen sun.

'I should've brought gloves. Never mind, it'll warm up soon enough. So what are you planning for today?'

'I might head out to that new road, and lay up somewhere out of sight. Ideally we should have a twenty-four-hour watch on it, but that'd mean pulling Des away from his post, and maybe missing movement along the coast.'

'You will be careful,' she said, alarmed by the idea. 'I mean, the poachers seem to travel in pairs. You won't tackle them alone?'

'I'll be fine, Tilly. Ten to one I'll twiddle my thumbs all day for nothing. What about tonight? Can you—'

Regretfully she shook her head. 'My turn in the kitchen tomorrow, so I'm afraid not. We'll just have to wait. And now I'd better go clean my teeth because if that's not Luke I can hear, then someone's abroad very early. I told him I'd start on the chores too.'

'Till later then,' he said, standing. He pulled her into his arms for a final kiss. 'Don't work too hard, my love. And thank you for last night.'

'And you be careful,' she admonished. 'I mean it. You're always telling me how dangerous those men are. So no tackling, hmm?'

He grinned. 'Only pint-sized women then. And only if they look like you. Okay, okay. Later then?'

'That's a promise,' she vowed and went.

Luke was at the ablution block unloading the day's supply of wood when she got there.

'Sorry.' Tilly grabbed the ash bucket and shovel from the lock-up. 'I got a bit caught up. Cold enough for you?'

'Eight degrees by the verandah thermometer,' he said, inhaling. 'Nice brisk weather, so who's complaining? It must've got colder than this back in Victoria.'

'This is the north.' Tilly rubbed her freezing fingers together. 'What's Matt up to today?'

'Getting on with the posts, I think.' Sophie had come up with a plan to replace the rocks that prevented vehicles from driving across camp sites with sturdy posts. 'Oh, and he wants to check something on the pump, so he said not to start it up. He'll see to it later.'

'He picked a good day for it.' Tilly shivered. 'Nobody's going to be having long showers. It was icy in there this morning. I was afraid of getting frostbite.'

'I've just the job lined up then.' Luke grinned evilly. 'Ve haff vays to keep you varm, madame. We're going to extend the cliff walk, and that means clearing scrub. I've brought the whipper snipper and the brush hook.'

'Oh, goody,' Tilly said. 'Did you bring the lunches?'

'Nope. I thought we'd go home. No need to finish it all today.'

When midday arrived, Tilly, remembering Luke's words, doubted that the job could be finished within a month. There wasn't much growth along the escarpment's top, but what there was had no intention of yielding without a fight. Luckily Luke had put work gloves in with the tools or she hated to think what the wiry, deep-rooted shrubs would have done to her hands. Metre by metre, they grubbed a winding path through turkey and booran bush, and past the odd, stunted gum, rolling aside the larger rocks to clear the painted lines Luke had sprayed on either side of the proposed walking track.

'I just hope our tourists appreciate what we do for them,' Tilly panted, sinking onto the latest rock she had heaved aside. 'I'll have Mr Universe arms by the time we're through.'

'Take a break.' Dropping down on his heels, Luke wiped a palm across his face. 'About time we headed back anyway. But hey, on the plus side, you're no longer cold, are you?'

'Exhausted, hungry and my arms are dropping off, but cold? No. How did you guess.'

'Ve haff strange powers, madame. Okay, let's pack up for now. Tomorrow – no, I'll be cooking, so the day after – will be soon enough to come back.'

'Glad to hear it.' Tilly rose with a groan to face the long

trudge back to the vehicle; they had left it half a kilometre behind them at the foot of the cliff.

Back at the homestead, the table was still set despite it being an hour past their normal lunchtime. Sophie, looking pleased with herself, pulled a dish from the oven and presented it with a flourish.

'We're a bit low on bread,' she said, 'but I found this recipe and it seemed simple enough.'

'Quiche? That's nice,' Tilly said, keeping her reservations about the pastry to herself. She glanced around. 'Where's Matt?'

'He came back from the camp in a bit of a mood. I think he might've had a run-in with a camper – he muttered something about the river. There's always some idiot who won't listen to the safety regs. Anyway, he made himself a sandwich and left. That's when I realised how low the bread supply was. I had some of the quiche,' she said encouragingly. 'It's not that bad. And by the way, Luke, your professor rang from the road-house. He's had fuel trouble and reckons he won't get here before dark.'

Luke grimaced. 'He's only at Alloway? Does he want help? I could drive—'

'No, he says he'll be fine, just late. The mechanic's draining the tank and cleaning out the whole system as we speak, but it could take a while. How did the trail-making go?'

'Slowly.' Tilly sawed at the pastry, gave up and concentrated on the quiche's filling. It was surprisingly tasty. 'The vegetation on that hill could out-stubborn a mule. A really, really pig-headed one. My arms will never recover.'

'Course they will.' Luke shovelled in a mouthful of quiche,

case and all, and chewed. 'Right then, Sophie, I think I oughta head out to the cave and catch a couple of those bats. It'll save a heap of time if Leary can take live specimens back with him. You know how these things go. They never allow enough time for the trip, which means they want to leave almost before they get here.'

'It's an idea,' Sophie agreed. 'Just how did you plan on catching them though?'

'Same as last time. That was probably pure luck, but you never know.' He laid his fork down. 'What about that birding net we found that time? That'd work. Any idea where it's got to?'

Sophie shook her head. 'That's history. Matt got rid of it last year, along with the old trawling net. Said he was sick of falling over them. I suppose they were in his workshop and it wasn't as if we were ever going to find the owners of them to lay charges against.'

'Pity,' Luke said. 'Never pays to chuck stuff out. That man's just too damn tidy for his own good. Well, for mine, anyway. Back to plan A then – it'll have to be the hat. We'll need to find a box to put the critters in. You up for it, Tilly?'

'Yes, of course. And I have a shoebox, one that opens at the end. That should do.'

'Great.' Luke concentrated again on his food. 'Soon as we've finished, we'll head off then.'

Driving out half an hour later with the shoebox on her lap, Tilly wondered uneasily whether Matt's reported mood was due to discovering his cache of money missing. Never given to small talk, he seldom interacted with the campers, so Sophie's supposition about the river seemed a little unlikely. But would he return tamely to work if he had realised it was gone? On the other hand, what else could he do? No man in his right senses would risk entering the river to investigate. He might, she supposed, grapple for it with a hook on a pole. Perhaps he was doing that now, but the Nutt was a strong force and you couldn't reasonably expect that anything landing in its muddy depths wouldn't, sooner or later, be swept away.

Shelving the thought, she fell to remembering last night and the pleasure she had found in Connor's arms as her body had awakened to his lovemaking. From that she passed easily to wondering how he was getting on now, planted somewhere in the scrub by the secret road in the (probably) vain hope that a vehicle would pass by. His job seemed to consist of waiting, which, she thought, must be incredibly boring.

'You seem pretty happy about something, grinning away like a Cheshire cat.' Luke's voice broke the silence. 'Am I to suppose it's your hunky botanist?'

'What?' Tilly said blankly, then as her brain assimilated his words, 'Suppose what you like, my friend. Maybe I'm just amused at the idea of you preparing insect dinners. Have you thought how we're supposed to feed these critters we may or may not catch? Didn't I read somewhere that they need to eat every night?'

Luke frowned. 'It would be a problem if we were keeping them. Hopefully Leary will turn up early enough to do the business tonight. I can release them then, so it shouldn't be a worry.'

'You can't just let them go, can you? Binboona's miles away. Won't they get lost?'

'I'd take them back, of course.' He slapped the steering

wheel. 'Yeah, that'd work. Leary could come with me and see the place for himself. He'd probably want to if they *are* unique, because he'd write it up, and the WPA would likely want his recommendations about the habitat. A brand new species would need protection and they'll certainly be listed as endangered, unless someone finds another colony or two.'

'That's not very likely, is it?' Tilly grabbed the crash bar as the vehicle lurched into a hole, hitting with a thud that rang in her bones. 'I wish Matt'd get out here with the grader!' she said crossly. 'Why hasn't Sophie got him onto it?'

'No point till the actual work starts. Costs come first, last and always – you know that. The rains'll be here, I expect, by the time the WPA have organised it all – the blueprints, the material, the workforce – so it's good economy to leave the grading until next season.'

'I suppose.' The answer came grudgingly as she rubbed the elbow she'd banged against the door. The cliff face loomed ahead, and now she could see the dark green patch of vegetation outlining the area of the springs.

'I wonder what your mum's doing?' Luke said apropos of nothing. 'I think of her whenever I see that.' He nodded at the sandstone cliff. 'She loved it, didn't she? I've never known anyone to respond that way to a place. Peace just sort of settled on her, like a flower opening.'

Tilly was touched. 'Why, Luke, that's quite poetic. But yes, you're right. I think the expense of the trip was worth it, just for that one day.'

'And her cooking.'

'Of course,' she agreed dryly. 'By the way, do you know what Jane's like in the kitchen?'

'No, well, she shares accommodation. Student meals, I guess – noodles and take-aways, cup-of-soup, chips – that's what I lived on at uni. When we're married maybe you could give her some tips?'

Tilly grinned derisively. 'Huh! Hasn't helped you much. By the way,' she said, for they were now passing by the overhang where the paintings were, 'what's the go with the artwork? I forgot to ask before.'

'Graeme's organising that. The old fence will go – it'll be railed off and have a boardwalk for protection, and he's going to see if there's an elder from the area he can contact. Maybe there'd be somebody willing to guide the tourists, tell 'em the stories behind the paintings.'

'Looks like next year will be an interesting one, especially if your bats turn out to be a real find. Maybe you could specialise, Luke? Become a well-known chiro-whatever – bat fancier. Write books, be on TV talkshows, earn big bucks.'

'I like the job I've got,' he said mildly. 'Professor Leary might get himself interviewed, but I can't see that— Hang about!' He was slowing for the series of gutters just before the cave, and now Tilly saw it too, the back end of a closed, long-wheelbased Land Rover pulled off to one side in the scrub. 'Who's that? They must be in the cave. What the hell is going on here?' Luke stamped on the brakes, switched off and sprang wrathfully from the vehicle even as Tilly was stuck wrestling with her seatbelt that had jammed shut.

A dreadful premonition gripped her as she tore herself free and thrust the door wide. 'Luke, wait! Don't go in there!' But he was already on his way. His lean form vanished from sight, then she heard a shout, too muffled to tell if it was Luke's or someone else's, and then nothing. The seconds crawled stickily by, filled only with the buzz of flies as she hovered indecisively by the vehicle, but in the end she couldn't not know. Her heart in her mouth, she pulled the seat forward, searching feverishly for anything that could be used as a weapon, and settled for the unwieldy jack-handle, which she grabbed from its metal clasp.

Wishing that Connor was there, or that she could forget his warning – *these men are dangerous* – she swallowed hard and headed resolutely for the cave, discarding all alternatives. The WPA didn't run to satellite phones, and going for help was obviously out of the question. By the time it came, the traffickers – for there was no doubt in her mind as to who the interlopers were – would be long gone, and very likely, Luke along with them.

# *Chapter Thirty-two*

The narrow entrance was lighter than Tilly remembered. It halted her for the moment it took to realise that the glow must be coming from a torch, and, gritting her teeth, she crept forward, gripping the jack-handle, her palm sweaty against the smooth metal. The floor was smooth and the combination of dust and guano muffled her tread so that she was inside before the cave occupants heard her, or her eyes had made sense of the tableau confronting her.

It wasn't a torch but a pressure lamp, and by its white glare she saw two figures bent over a third one slumped against, and partly screened by, a stack of crates. A horrified gasp escaped her as she realised it was Luke. He sat swaying on the floor, with a trickle of blood dripping through his hands, which held his head.

The stocky figure nearest her whipped around at the noise she made. Unsurprised, she stared at Matt's familiar features. 'You! You traitor!' she yelled, just as Luke groaned and pitched sideways to lie in a boneless heap amid a little explosion of dust. 'Oh, God,' she cried, starting forward. 'What have you done to him?'

The sound of her voice triggered the second figure, at whom she'd barely glanced, to turn towards her, his eyes widening to mirror Tilly's own shock. 'Gerry!' she stammered. 'What . . .?' It was him – there was no mistaking that handsome face, even with its two-day stubble and his generally dishevelled appearance. The jack-handle slipped, forgotten, from her nerveless fingers. 'So it's true! Everything the police said – you're just a dirty crook. What have you done to Luke?'

He winced at her tone. 'Babe, I'm sorry. I'm sorry. I couldn't . . . I never meant to hurt you—'

'Shut up!' she said fiercely. 'I don't want your excuses or apologies. I couldn't care less about you. All I want is to know what happened that night – why you let Francie die?'

'I didn't!' he protested. 'The runabout tipped over. She was safe in it, and then a wave came and rolled it. I tried . . . I really tried, babe'—he shook his head, face twisting as he lifted his hands towards her—'but I couldn't find her in the dark and the tide was taking us. It was like a rip out there.' He shook his head again, and dropped his hands. 'There was nothing I could do.'

'Except save yourself. You managed that,' Tilly said bitterly.

His eyes, once so bright and full of life, met hers, the light in them dulled. 'I got washed against the runabout, and climbed on top. Rode it for hours, then Stefan picked me up.'

'Who?'

'Nobody you know. He was bringing stuff in that night. Chance in a million, really, that the runabout crossed his path. He hauled me aboard and scarpered, to dodge the search vessels we knew would be out.'

'You didn't look for her? You . . . you . . . She was your *daughter*, Gerry! She was only two, for God's sake! How could you just go off and leave her?' Tilly shouted furiously.

'She was dead.' He spoke with flat finality. 'And if it came to insisting, Stefan would've had me back overboard to join her. Easy for you to talk, but you don't know him. I'm sorry, Tilly, I am. But kids die, and ours did. What the hell are you doing up here anyway? Why didn't you go home?'

'What home? Oh, you mean the one sold up to pay your debts? I'm earning my living, seeing you left me penniless, you worthless piece of—' A quavering groan interrupted her and she turned from Gerry to drop on her knees beside Luke.

He had fallen twisted, and she rolled him carefully onto his back, patting his slack cheek and bending to speak in his ear. 'Luke! Wake up, Luke!' The blood on his temple had run down into his eye socket, and his white face appeared even paler in the brilliant glare of the lantern.

'Save yourself the trouble. He's out to it,' Matt, who had held his silence till then, growled. He jerked his head at Gerry. 'If you've finished excusin' yourself, get loadin''. We've gotta get outta here PDQ. What're the two of you doing here anyway, Tilly? I thought that uni bigwig was comin' this arvo.'

She shot him a look of intense dislike. 'He's been held up. Luke!' she tried again, demanding fiercely, 'What did you hit him with? He could have a fractured skull.' She became aware of a discordent squawking as Gerry began lifting and carting the crates away, and caught a brief glimpse of avian eyes, of black and grey feathers and raised yellow combs. Cockies then, but she had no time to worry about them now. 'You won't get away with this, Matt. You're not as clever as you think. How many birds have you stolen anyway? And what else are you smuggling? Connor said—' She bit down on the betraying words but the sudden change in his expression showed that he had heard and understood.

'That bastard!' he snarled. 'He didn't fool me from the get-go. Botanist, my arse! So, what is he? Copper, Drug Squad? Answer me!' She hadn't seen it happen but suddenly there was a gun in his hand.

'You know perfectly well he's a botanist,' she flared.

'And I'm sodding Christ. One more chance, Tilly. Tell me the truth'—he pointed the gun at Luke's supine form—'or I swear you won't have to worry about him waking up any-time soon.'

The world seemed to freeze around Tilly. As from a great distance she heard the agitation of leathery wings and a myriad tiny squeakings overhead, and the subdued hiss of the pressure lamp pumping its light into the dark recesses of the cave. Her knees ached from kneeling beside Luke, and she felt the throb of her pulse in her fingertips. Sweat dripped from her chin, and a line of it tickled the small of her back as she stared into her erstwhile workmate's feral brown eyes until he broke the contact, his gaze sliding, in usual fashion, away from hers.

'What made you think he was Drug Squad?' she said, fighting to keep her voice calm.

'Answer me!' he yelled suddenly, and before she could open her mouth, he fired. She screamed, cowering over Luke's body, eyes pulled wide, and mind gibbering in terror as she searched his unconscious form for torn flesh and blood. There was none. Matt had fired into the roof, startling the bats into a whirring, squealing maelstrom that had him ducking and swearing, as Gerry burst back into the cave.

'What's happened?'

'Nothing yet. But this bitch is about to get it. Doyle's Drug Squad. He's been spyin' on us. And I'll bet the bastard's had the cash too. Frayed rope, my blind aunt! Who's he think that's gonna fool?'

'He's not!' Tilly cried desperately as the gun swung towards her. 'What cash? I don't know what you're talking about, Matt. Look, you've only stolen a few birds – that's not much of a crime, but killing—'

'There'll be no killing.' Gerry stepped forward and she breathed again. 'She's my wife, Mercer. Leave them both. Let's load and clear out. We can disable their vehicle, and you can see he's in no state to walk. No need even to tie them up. We'll be long gone before anyone comes looking for 'em.'

'So they just walk away with six months' worth of cash? I don't think so. As for being your wife – forget her. The bitch is sleepin' with Doyle, anyway.' There was jealousy in his tone and frustrated lust, she realised – so he *had* fancied her. His hand rose again and Gerry leapt forward.

'No! I don't care. I won't be party to any killing.'

'Grow up!' Matt sneered. 'You just want one hand dirty, is that it? A kilo or two of drugs, a few smuggled birds and lizards, but oh, no, Officer, nothin' bad. You're in this up to your neck, sonny, an' that includes that boatload of dead reffos. Two more ain't gonna make no difference to the sheet.' With that, he turned the short black barrel on Tilly and fired.

Terror had hastened rather than slowed her brain, and while he spoke, her hand had found and closed over the jack-handle.

It was a pathetic weapon but it was the only one she had. Her mouth opened in a fruitless cry of protest as she read his intent but she was given no time to utter it. The roar of the shot was magnified by the cave's echoes, and before she could wonder at hearing it, a heavy weight knocked her across Luke's prone body and Gerry's arm thudded down across her neck.

Tilly heard Matt swear and, turning her head, stared dazedly into her husband's dead face. He had thrown himself into the bullet's path to save her life, which, she thought hysterically, was only going to extend it by seconds. Matt had now fired the gun twice but it must hold more bullets than that. Panting, she tightened her grip on the steel she held.

'You stupid bastard!' Matt, bending over to check Gerry's body, dealt him a savage kick. 'Christ Almighty! What a turn-up. After she gave you up too. Well, one more stiff's neither here nor there,' he decided. And it was then, as he straightened to finish the job, that Tilly hit him with all the strength that fear and fury could give her.

She aimed, of necessity from her partly prone position, for his right leg and had the satisfaction of actually hearing the bone in his kneecap crack. He bellowed in pain and surprise and went down hard, hitting the floor on his back with his right elbow cracking crisply against the stone. She scrambled up and with another, less steady swipe, belted the gun from his hand, which had somehow managed to retain its grasp of it, then scampered after its clattering fall while he writhed, yelling in pain, behind her.

With trembling hands she examined her prize, terrified that it might go off. Tilly knew nothing about firearms. Gerry had kept a rifle on the *Esmerelda* – for crocs, he'd said – but she had forbidden him to bring it into their camp. Staring distractedly around while the bats wheeled and chittered above her, she spied a long fissure in the rock wall of the cave. Hyperventilating, she thrust an arm into its darkness and felt nothing but space. It would do. With a feeling of relief that helped steady her breathing, she dropped the gun into it and heard metal clatter on stone somewhere well beyond her reach.

'You bitch!' Matt was yelling. 'You'll pay for that. Get yourself over here now.'

'I don't think so.' She spoke as coolly as her thumping heart allowed. 'Your patella's cracked, Matt. You won't walk on that leg, much less drive anywhere, and you might as well face the fact. It's over.'

He must have been in considerable pain but he managed a grating laugh. 'I don't think so, bitch. Not unless you want our boy wonder dead. Get back here, take a look an' work out who's got the upper hand. Won't take me but a moment to do for 'im.'

His words filled Tilly with a sudden dread. She stepped cautiously closer, being careful to remain beyond his reach. As the harsh light revealed the truth, her shoulders sagged and the fight went out of her. While she had been disposing of the gun, Matt had wriggled himself about, probably with considerable pain, until he had managed to snag Luke's leg and drag his unconscious form close enough that the blade of the knife in his hand was resting against Luke's unconscious throat.

# *Chapter Thirty-three*

The surge of adrenalin that had powered her movements vanished, leaving Tilly sick and shaken. She had scarcely given a thought to Gerry's sacrifice, but now the sight of his body sprawled in death brought her to her knees and tears to her eyes. He had lied and cheated and done much worse, and he had deceived her and lost their child, but she had loved him once. And he must have still loved her to have flung himself into the path of the bullet that would have killed her. The sobs kept coming, not helped by the sight of Luke stretched insensible before her with that wicked blade threatening his life.

'Waterworks ain't gonna help you,' Matt growled. 'So shut it and gimme a hand up. You're gonna drive me out to meet some mates of mine. Try anythin' and you'll be dead meat. Upside is, behave yourself and Luke makes it home, always supposin' Gerry didn't hit him too hard. Got it?'

Hating him, Tilly swallowed a final sob. 'And then? You're going to let me go, I suppose?'

His lips drew back in a grimace – of pain or mirth, she couldn't tell. 'Yeah. You can walk back. Won't be much above ninety kay.' This time the grin was real and evil. 'We might have your shoes first, but.'

Even if he meant it, which she doubted, she would never make it. Her feet were soft; they might carry her a kilometre or so, but the stone and spinifex would defeat her. Besides, why wouldn't he just kill her? Eyeing the knife, she swallowed terror, but if she dodged past him now and ran, Luke would die. That was certain and when Sophie grew alarmed at their continued absence, and came looking . . .

Oh where, her heart cried, was Connor when she needed him most? Waiting in blissful ignorance in an ambush that would never happen while she was trapped here in the midst of death and destruction. She could have wept for the irony of a love so newly found and as swiftly lost. And for Luke, who could be dying even as he lay there, bleeding into his brain perhaps, from the damage inflicted by the brutal blow that had felled him.

Tilly said coldly, 'Let him alone! And I don't for a minute believe that Gerry hit him. It was you. I know it was.'

'Then you better believe I mean what I say. Now, get me up.'

Tilly shrank inwardly as she touched him, and when he was upright, sweating and panting with pain, she shuddered from the weight of his arm across her shoulders. He held the knife in that hand only a thumb's width from her throat as together, like a mismatched pair of three-legged racers, they lurched and staggered towards the Land Rover.

She had calculated her chances of getting away when they got to the vehicle. She would have to help him in, but he couldn't control her movements then. Only, if she took the opportunity to run, he was perfectly capable of dragging himself back into the cave to Luke . . . As if he had divined her thought processes, he waited while she opened the passenger door, then shoved her ahead of him.

'Get in. An' don't even think of it. I've got the keys. Now, pull me up.'

She obeyed, first negotiating the gear stick and getting some satisfaction from the yell he gave as his broken knee banged against the doorframe. The leg of his jeans was strained over the swelling, she saw once he was in his seat, hissing in pain, but his right hand still held the knife steady against her waist. He raised a sweat-stained face to her, his words coming raggedly. 'Under your seat. Gimme the phone there.'

It was a satellite phone, expensive to own and use. She remembered the wads of money packed into the drum she and Connor had found. Cost obviously wasn't a consideration. The conversation was brief. Matt said, 'Yeah, me. Somethin's come up. Meet me ASAP. End of the road. Yeah, I ain't. Whiskey, painkillers. See you there.' He dropped the phone into his lap and with his left hand dug keys from his shirt pocket. 'Right. Drive an' no tricks. Don't think I won't use the knife. You're no use to me dead, but it don't mean I can't maim you.'

Tilly didn't dignify the threat with an answer. She prayed that the road he'd mentioned was the new one. Connor was there. She didn't know how he could help, but he was her only chance of getting out of this alive, and getting help for Luke. She turned the key, engaged the gear and, with mentally crossed fingers and toes, headed back towards Sandstone Springs.

And the miracle she had asked for happened.

'Not there. Go right,' Matt barked, 'over the saddle.'

'But—' Deliberately she stalled the vehicle. 'There's no road.'

'Well, it ain't sign-posted,' he said scornfully. But it's there. Use your bloody eyes. Now get this heap movin' an' follow the tracks.'

There were none to be seen on the gravel, but proceeding hesitantly, more for show than need, Tilly soon picked up traces of wheel prints where Gerry must've driven in. She wondered where Matt's own vehicle was. Perhaps planted in the scrub at the springs, or somewhere closer, hidden from sight as he had been all these years. With malice, she drove carelessly, hitting the gutters a little too fast and dropping into the potholes until Matt jabbed the knife lightly into her thigh, drawing blood. She cried out in shock and from the pain of the slight wound.

'I'm warnin' you, bitch,' he snarled, fresh sweat gleaming on his face. From then on she took more care, driving so slowly that he snarled at her again to speed up. When the pillars of the Lost City came in sight, she remembered to stare and peer out the side-window as if it was her first sighting of them. She passed the point where she and Connor had pulled up, and from then on the track required her full concentration. They stopped only once. Matt made her hand over the keys and her shoes, then told her to get out and bring him the waterbag from the side rail where it hung behind a protective skirt of leather.

She slid out reluctantly, wincing as the cut in her leg smarted and her bare soles hit the rough ground, and moved down the vehicle's side. She wished she had some way of causing a puncture, but even supposing she could snap off the valve stem, he would know she had done it. Casting a longing look down at the back tyre, she noticed there was no cap on the stem and the idea was instantly born. Matt had twisted sideways in his seat and was watching her through the window, but her hands were out of sight. Stooping, she wrestled with the stiff buckles, muttering to herself, then bent to snatch up a length of grass.

It was the work of a moment to thrust the piece into the stem beside the valve and she was immediately gratified by the faint hiss of escaping air. It would take a while, hours maybe, but the tyre would go flat. 'And we'll see how you handle *that*, you sick bastard,' she muttered, wrenching the second strap through its buckle.

Back in the vehicle, Matt retained both the water and her shoes. He drank thirstily from the mouth of the bag, wiping away the spillage with his thumb. Hating to ask, Tilly did, knowing her body needed it. 'May I have some? I'm thirsty.'

'Too bad.' He settled the bag at his feet, where her shoes also rested. 'Drive. Maybe you can earn it by behavin' yourself.'

Soon enough they reached the road. She braked in feigned amazement at sight of the raw red ribbon of track and turned to stare at her captor. 'What's that? It looks new.'

'Drive,' he muttered irritably, and as she deliberately swung the wheel north-east, 'The other way! For Chrissake, haven't you learnt nothin'? You can't be that bloody dumb.'

Tilly allowed herself a burst of frustration. 'Well, I don't know where I am, or where I'm going!' She slammed the gear lever into reverse and backed up, turning the wheel to the right as they started off again. 'I've never even seen this road before. Where does it go?'

'Zip it, woman. Just drive.' He was sweating worse than

ever and his sun-splotched face looked flushed as if he had started a fever.

She said maliciously, 'You ought to check your foot. If it's swelling and turning blue, the blood supply might be interrupted. That causes gangrene. Displaced bones can do that, you know – block arteries. And I'm willing to bet your patella's not where it should be.'

He bared his teeth at her. 'Yeah, and I haven't forgotten who done it, neither.'

The threat inherent in his words silenced her and for a craven moment Tilly wished the taunt unsaid. She drew in a breath but held her peace; there was no point in trying him too far. She tried to calculate how far they had come. He'd said ninety kilometres, which, she presumed, would include the stretch from the cave to the new road. It must have taken a good hour to get that far, but the speedometer wouldn't have reached fifteen km/h on much of it, and she was only doing forty now. The track might be graded but it was a very cursory affair, more a clearing of bushes, anthills and fallen timber than a real grade. Still, it was clearly a boon to the smugglers, giving them egress from the property in a direction from which they couldn't be overlooked.

Curiosity overcame her and she said, 'How come we don't patrol this area? When it was a station, didn't the owners run stock out here? How did they manage during the round-ups without roads?'

He cast her a look of contempt. 'You a Yank? They're musters, not round-ups. And the country weren't used, because there ain't no water out here. You can think on that when you're hoofin' it home.'

She persevered, ignoring the comment, for any knowledge might help her in the fight for survival. 'So why didn't they make some? A bore, or a dam? It's a lot of country to waste.'

'Shut it,' he snapped. 'I dunno and I don't bloody care. What's it to you anyway?'

'I like to know the reason for things.' Tilly's voice hardened. 'For instance, why Gerry? He wasn't a bad man. How did you drag him into all this?'

'Not a bad man,' Matt mocked. 'Just weak. Gamblin' debts piled so high a buck roo couldn't clear 'em. And a greedy wife. You had to have the flash home, didn't you, all the fancy stuff? You think you get boat payments, a mortgage 'n' a couple of cars 'n' a kid outta fishin'?'

Tilly went cold, then flashed to instant heat. 'The house was his doing, not mine! He said we could afford it. He said—'

'Yeah, yeah. Nothin' the turn of another card couldn't fix. Then he's desperate, into the syndicates for big dough 'n' cryin' poor. A bit of dope, a few birds, no problem – I tell you,' Matt said viciously, 'he woulda killed without a blink if it'd got him outta the jam he was in.'

'No,' Tilly said weakly. 'You're lying! I know you are. He would never touch drugs.'

'I suppose he's too good for people smugglin' too?' Matt sneered. 'You can tell that to the fishes. I doubt they'll believe you, but.'

'What do you mean?' Her heart knocked unevenly and she felt sick. 'You said back in the cave . . . What did you mean about the "boatload of reffos" being on him too? You weren't smuggling people too?'

He gave a savage grin. 'Ain't smugglin' if they never got

there. Still, they paid up front 'n' this country don't need no more Muslims, that's for damn sure.'

'You're despicable!' The wheel pulled sharply under her hand and she straightened it. The tyre was flattening. Excellent. She'd run it for another kilometre, or until he noticed, let the rims chew the tube to pieces. Of course there'd be a spare, but changing it might give her a chance.

Tilly had no plan save to get beyond his reach. She would walk, barefoot if she must, following the road back and if, as she prayed, they had not yet passed Connor, he would catch up with her at day's end, which wasn't so very far off, she now realised. She had hardly noticed the afternoon passing; they had come perhaps thirty kay on the new track. That wasn't so far, Tilly told herself, quailing at the thought, and walking would warm her. The chill in the air had crept up on her unnoticed, hardly registering until now. Well, better beneath the night sky than a hot sun that would only exacerbate her thirst.

Then the wheel dragged again, the metronomic flap of torn rubber rising above the engine noise, and Matt swore. 'Jesus! Pull up, you stupid cow. You've got a flat.'

# *Chapter Thirty-four*

Before the wheels stopped rolling, Tilly's right hand flashed down to the door handle but Matt was quicker. His big freckled fist seized her hair, yanking her over the gear lever towards him. 'Not so bloody fast.'

Tilly shrieked in pain, clawing at the wheel for purchase and inadvertently sounding a long blast on the horn. Instantly she banged her inner forearm down again, repeating the blast until he ripped her hand free of its grip. 'Let me go!' Tears stood in her eyes from the pain of it.

'You're comin' out this side,' he said, 'nice 'n' slow. And don't be thinkin' of boltin', neither.' One-handed, he pulled the belt from around his waist and, releasing the grip on her hair, threaded the loop over her wrist. 'Right.' He gave it an experimental tug and showed her the knife. 'This way with you.' With a great deal of swearing and hissed breath, he got himself out and, standing on his good leg, hauled her after him. Sweat stood on his forehead and for a wild moment Tilly contemplated shoving him over and running for it, but the vehicle's frame supported him and she feared his strength. The buckle of the belt was cutting cruelly into her wrist; he had only to yank on it to have her helpless at his feet.

'Under the seat. Jack 'n' the tools, and rope. Get 'em.'

Tilly obeyed, wondering what the rope was for. She found out when he made a noose with it and slipped it over her head before reclaiming his belt. He gave the thin nylon cord a tug. 'You've got the idea. Slide the jack under 'n' get the brace on the lugs.' Dragging his bad leg, he hauled himself around the vehicle, keeping up the pressure on the rope as she followed his instructions, her hopes of freedom dashed. He kept the noose tight enough to prevent her yanking it free, and she feared his reaction if she dared escape and failed. Would he tie her up, or simply throttle her into submission? She clung to the hope that he still needed her, for his leg hung like a dead limb and the slightest movement brought a curse to his lips.

In the gathering darkness, he wrenched at the wheel lugs, teeth bared with effort, and eventually made her jump on the brace to loosen them. Tilly spun it out, deliberately losing her balance to slow the process for the onset of night gave her hope. If she could grab a tool, the jack-handle say . . . but he was too careful for that. Once the lugs were loosened, he made her lie down behind the wheel, then made his own careful descent beside her, the rope doubled around his fist as he laboriously wound the handle, raising the tyre.

Job completed, he lay panting, his eyes momentarily screwed shut. Tilly's hand crept towards the noose as she inched her head closer to his body to gain what slack she could, but as if her held breath had warned him, his eyes snapped open just as a voice called, 'Stay where you are, Mercer,' and a torch beam split the darkness around them.

Tilly gasped, recognising Connor's voice, but Matt's reflexes were lightning fast. Before she could move, he had rolled his body on top of hers and his hands were at her throat. She struggled furiously, trying to cry out but she got no further than 'Con—' before the strangling rope cut her off.

'Back off, Doyle!' The words were snarled almost into her ear as they lay in a quasi-sexual embrace, his weight pinning her top half. She was choking, her lungs starving for the air that came in minuscule sips through her tortured throat. 'Get that bloody light outta my face,' Matt yelled. 'Put it on 'ers. See that? Want me to yank it tighter? Back off or I will.'

Light speckled her vision and Tilly felt herself fading into blackness. She had to make one last effort before it was too late. Matt seemed to have forgotten the knife, which he had laid aside in order to wind the jack. She had no idea where it was, and neither the time nor strength to find it. Instead, she put everything she had left in her into a blind kick aimed at her captor's legs and by the sheerest fluke connected with his broken knee.

Matt screamed and jerked backwards, rolling off her. His body shrank into a fetal curl as Tilly tore the strangling rope loose and threw herself violently out from beneath the vehicle, smacking her head in the process. She scarcely felt the pain as she scrambled to her feet and was caught in Connor's grasp. His arms tightened around her, his hand frantically smoothing her back. 'Oh God, Tilly! Are you okay?'

'Yes . . . no. Gerry's dead. Matt killed him. And Luke's hurt – back in the cave. I couldn't—' She felt hysteria closing in and drew a great lungful of air in an effort to calm the trembling of her limbs. Pushing back from his clasp, she said, 'We have to get help to him, Connor. He—'

'Yes, and we will. But first . . .' He bent and grabbed Matt's boot, dragging him from under the vehicle.

'He's got a knife,' Tilly remembered, 'and I bashed his other knee – it's broken. He phoned his mates. They were going to meet him at the end of the road.' Matt snarled and aimed a punch at Connor, which he avoided before rolling Matt deftly onto his face and, using the choke cord Tilly had cast off, securing his hands.

'Where this knife then?'

'There!' The torchlight showed a glint of steel. Connor secured it, then played the light over the back of the vehicle.

'Room for him in there?'

'It's full of cages, birds, maybe reptiles too. Shouldn't we let them go?'

He shook his head. 'They're evidence. You said he phoned.'

She explained about the satellite phone. 'It's under the driver's seat. We've got to ring Sophie, tell her about Luke. He might've come round, but he'll have concussion at the very least. She can reach him faster than we can.'

'I'll see to it. But first . . .' Lifting the end of the rope he'd used to tie up Matt, he took a couple of turns about the Land Rover's tow-ball and knotted it securely. 'That should do it.'

'Bastard copper! You think you're so smart, but I was onto you from the start.'

'Hasn't done you much good then,' Connor retorted. He put an arm around Tilly's shoulders. 'Come on, love, let's make some calls. Oh,' he added, turning back to the tied figure hunched by the tow-ball, 'and it was me who found your stash in the river. In case you're wondering.'

Matt spat a string of filthy language at him as they retreated into the dark.

'Where's your vehicle?' Tilly asked.

'Fifty metres or so, up a ways. I was about ready to quit when I heard you coming, then you stopped. Next thing, the horn was blasting away so I came running. What, in the name of God, were you doing back at the cave? I take it you and Luke ran into them there? Why did he kill Gerry?'

'It was meant to be me, but Gerry threw himself in the way.' She shuddered at the memory, then pulled the phone out, handed it to him and flicked the dome light on.

'Oh, God!' He stared at her, face stricken in the sickly yellow light, and reached to touch her maltreated throat. 'You nearly died while I was twiddling my thumbs in the scrub. I should never have involved you.'

'You didn't,' she pointed out. 'It just happened. Now, please call Sophie. I'm really worried about Luke.'

He complied. There was a long, anxious wait until the distant ringing stopped and the dial tone resumed. 'No answer. All right, we'll have to go ourselves. But I need to let Sergeant Burns know about Mercer's mates. He can follow the lot who are coming to meet Mercer. I'll get a message to Spadgers Creek and have Des come through and collect our prisoner. We'll head for the cave, and should make it back to the homestead before he arrives.' He rubbed at his jaw. 'It'll take bloody forever for the other lot to get out from town, that's the trouble. Time enough for those involved to do a bunk when Mercer doesn't turn up. How sure are you about

Luke's condition? Not all bangs on the head are fatal, you know.'

'And none should be ignored.' Tilly said spiritedly. 'I've done first aid, Connor, and he was hit really hard. He was slumped on the ground, bleeding from the temple, then he pitched over and didn't move again. Oh, God,' she fretted. 'Where's Sophie? Why isn't she answering the phone?'

'It's okay,' he soothed her. 'We'll go.' He pressed more buttons, held a brief conversation, shut off the phone and swore. 'Jesus Christ! Is the whole world agin us? Burns and Wilmot left town hours ago. Heading out here according to the front desk.'

'Well, that's good, isn't it?'

He swore again. 'No, because I can't get hold of them and I don't know who else among the cops I can trust. I'm not even one hundred per cent sure of the inspector.'

'Ring the Alloway Roadhouse,' Tilly said practically. 'If they haven't got that far, you could leave a message. If they have – well, at least they're that much closer.'

He did so, and after a short conversation, his face cleared. 'Put him on, will you? Thanks. Ah, Wayne. I've a situation here . . .'

Tilly listened to his rapid outline of events and instructions, finishing up with, 'Great, we'll head straight back. Should be at the homestead by the time you arrive. See you then.' He sighed in relief and hung up the phone. 'He's got my number and can ring if there's a problem. Look, could you drive this crate back, do you think?'

'Not with a flat tyre,' Tilly pointed out. 'It's not punctured, or at least it wasn't till I ran it flat. I fiddled with the valve, you see. I wanted to get him out of the vehicle. I thought it was my best chance.'

'You're a living wonder, Tilly.' He kissed her. 'And I see it's already on the jack. It'll only take a moment to change. Hang on here and I'll bring my vehicle over. It'll be easier with the headlights than a torch.'

With the second vehicle in position and lights to work by, Connor swiftly swapped tyres, having first shifted Matt by securing his tied hands to the side rail.

'You'd be better off puttin' some distance between us, copper,' Matt sneered. 'My mates are comin' for me. Fancy your chances against four of 'em, do you? Yours wouldn't be the first body dumped out 'ere.'

'Oh, I think you'll find the sergeant and his constable practised at dealing with scum,' Connor said. 'Plus the copper from Spadgers of course. None of 'em like killers. And I'm Customs by the way, not police.'

Tilly, handing him the last wheel nut, said, 'Where was Burns when you were speaking to Wilmot?'

'In the gents. Dead lucky we caught them. Wayne said they'd be underway soon as he got out.' Connor wound the jack down and dismantled the handle. 'Right. You sure you'll be okay?' he asked and when she made no reply, 'Tilly?'

'What? Oh, yes.' Distracted by the twisted buckle on the tool roll, she nodded. 'Of course. Besides we can't leave those poor animals without water or food. Do you want to lead?'

'If you like.' He untied the rope and nudged his captive. 'Get in the Toyota. Not the front,' he said as the man hopped, teeth bared with effort as he hauled himself along the vehicle's body. 'Am I stupid? Round the back. Sit with your back to the passenger seat.' Mercer obeyed meekly enough, saying nothing even when Connor lashed his tied hands to the headrest.

The fight seemed to have gone out of him, or perhaps the pain was too great, Tilly thought. Still, his easy compliance made her narrow her eyes, and when Connor slammed the rear door, she beckoned him to one side. 'I don't trust him – he's up to something.'

'It'll be fine,' Connor said. 'Besides, he's crippled. You really did a number on his knee. And I'm a seaman of sorts, love. I know how to tie a decent knot.'

'Just promise me you'll be careful,' she begged.

'It's sweet of you to worry.' He kissed her. 'Follow as close as you can. I'll see what speed I can make, and we'll head for the caves. Sophie might even be there now, you know. She knew where you were going?'

'Yes.'

'Then ten to one she got worried when you didn't return and headed out after you.'

It was a reasonable hypothesis that Tilly was glad to adopt. 'Yes, she could well have done so. It would explain why the phone rang out. And if the professor turned up, she might've taken him along, so there'd be two of them to carry Luke. Let's hope you're right – it would be such a relief.'

'Only one way to find out.' He got in the vehicle and turned the key. 'Stick close,' he called and drove off.

# *Chapter Thirty-five*

The journey back seemed to take forever. The track, plain enough in daylight, was harder to follow by headlights, but at least there was little dust, due to its uncleared nature. Tilly bumped and crashed along, frequently changing gears as she tried to anticipate the gutters and half-glimpsed potholes, hearing the crates sliding and banging behind her, worrying equally for Luke and the wellbeing of her cargo. The land looked alien by night, the scrub like tattered skeletons, and the Lost City, when she reached it, looming under the starry sky like a cemetery of vast headstones.

It was a relief to finally recognise the stretch of gravel leading to the saddle on the far side of the range that held the caves. Tilly breathed out thankfully and let her stiffly held shoulders relax as she braked behind Connor's Toyota and switched off her lights. His were still shining, aimed at the cave mouth, and she slipped from her seat to jog to his side so that they entered the narrow entrance together.

'Okay?' he turned to ask her as he flicked on the torch. 'Hard to tell – there're so many tracks overlaid out there – but I think another vehicle's come by. Let's hope it was Sophie.'

'Luke's vehicle's gone,' Tilly said, and as his words penetrated, 'God! You don't think there could be more of them?' She was aghast.

He shrugged. 'There might be. It seems a big operation – more than just a few birds involved.'

'Matt did say something about refugees – a boat sinking somewhere. And he mentioned drugs,' she agreed unhappily.

'If there are and they were here, they're gone,' he said. 'Maybe you should wait out here anyway, while I check—'

'No.' Steeling herself, she followed him in, her gaze skipping over the space where Luke had lain. It was empty. 'He's gone,' she said blankly. 'And Gerry. He was just there . . .' She pointed.

'It's okay, I think.' Connor turned his torch on a dark shape against the cave wall. 'Sophie must've got here, because I can't see the other lot bothering to wrap a body.' He dropped to his knee and turned back the edge of the blue poly-tarp that shrouded the still form. 'Yep. Is this your husband, Tilly?'

'Yes.' She looked away from the face with its blank, dead eyes, prey to a thousand mixed emotions. Those eyes had smiled at her, admired her, won her heart. Those dead hands had loved her and had held their child, and she knew every expression that face had worn. Or she had thought she did. Something snagged at her memory and she suddenly gasped, thoughts of Gerry vanishing in the cold certainty of a terrible mistake.

'What? What is it, Tilly?'

Torchlight momentarily dazzled her as she clapped her

hands to her face. 'I think,' she began. 'You know when I told you Matt was up to something? It was his face, just a fleeting expression, when you said something about Constable Wilmot – that Burns was in the toilet. It bothered me then, but I forgot. It was satisfaction I saw, because it was Wilmot who had got the news. Don't you see, Connor? He's one of them! The crooked cops. Burns won't get the message. If Wilmot turns up at all it'll be on a rescue mission for Matt. *That's* what he was smirking about. Just for an instant and then – remember? He stopped fighting – he never said another word, because he knows his mates aren't going to be arrested, and that if Wilmot turns up it's to help him.'

Connor shook his head. 'Tilly, you're imagining it. Wilmot was checked out pretty thoroughly and he came up clean. There's absolutely no evidence to suggest he's ever crossed the line.'

'Maybe.' She was thinking furiously, casting her mind back. 'The day you were fuelling up and you turned those two people back, a man and a woman, remember? First you told me they were tourists with a dog, then later you admitted they were cops and you didn't want them treading on your op. So you sent them away. Was one of them Wilmot?'

'Well, yes. Wilmot and a young female cop. A new arrival at the station. He said he was mentoring her, showing her around. I told him he should've had more sense, knowing what he did. Why?'

'And did they have a lot of camping gear in the vehicle?'

He frowned. 'Why would they? They'd have got a meal at Alloway, and a bed if they'd wanted it.'

'Because Matt met them on the road and told me some

cock-and-bull yarn about helping them change a flat tyre. Said they were southerners, loaded down with brand-new camping equipment and had no idea how to handle a puncture. It was after that he started sniping at you, hinting you weren't a botanist. He *knew*, Connor, because that's when Wilmot told him. He must've – it was the only time they saw each other. When he was here with Burns before that, Matt wasn't home.'

In the faint glow of the headlights, she saw Connor's eyes flicker as her words sank in. 'And another thing'—she nodded, remembering back—'when Burns came first and was bullying me about knowing Gerry wasn't dead, Wilmot tried to get him to back off, like he might've been afraid that I'd admit to it.'

'There's an easy way to check,' Connor said. 'I'll ring Alloway. See if Wilmot left without the sergeant. If he did . . .'

The phone seemed to ring forever until it was snatched up and an irate voice said loud enough for Tilly to hear as well, 'Bloody hell, I'm coming! Alloway. Waddyouwant?'

She listened to the quickfire exchange and deduced the answer from Connor's grim look. 'Well, find him. And report it to the police,' he barked, and killed the connection.

'Seems you're right.' He sighed deeply. 'Shit! That was the owner. According to him, Wilmot left on his own. Told him he couldn't locate his mate, that he'd had an emergency call and couldn't wait. Then took off like his backside was on fire, to quote mine host.'

Tilly bit her lip. 'Do you think he's okay – the sergeant?'

'Who knows? He could be tied up, or lying somewhere with a bullet in him. These guys play for keeps. Okay, so the cavalry's down to Des, and I've no way of warning him about Wilmot.'

'And Sophie – is she safe?'

'I think she'd better take Luke and go to the camp. She needs to be among other people right now.'

'And Matt? Why don't we leave him here? Nobody's going to find him and he certainly can't shift under his own steam, even if he wasn't tied up.'

Connor considered it, then nodded. 'Only you'll have to bring the Land Rover along. If his mates trek all the way in here, we don't want to signpost the place with their own vehicle.'

'You don't think they would?' Tilly looked nervously in the direction of the caves.

'Unlikely. I'll just ring the homestead, organise Sophie, then I'll get Mercer out. Say nothing about Wilmot in front of him. Let him think he's still got a winning hand.'

'Do we?' Tilly asked, deeply worried. 'We've already got one dead man, possibly two if the sergeant . . . Wilmot can't afford to just walk away, can he? It's his job, his liberty, and he'll know that you found the money, so he'll have lost his share as well.'

'Some of it,' Connor corrected. 'There're more than two or three involved. They'd expect a better return than sixty thousand shared among 'em.' He was dialling as he spoke and now his voice quickened, 'Ah, Sophie. Connor here. Please listen carefully . . .'

Judging by the gabble that burst from the handpiece, Sophie didn't intend to listen. Twice Connor attempted to stem the rush of words but without effect. Finally Tilly took the handpiece from him and barked, 'Sophie! Shut up!'

There was half a second's silence before Sophie said, 'Tilly? What the hell's going on? Where are you?'

'At the caves – as Connor was trying to tell you. Is Luke okay?'

That started her cousin off again. 'No, he's not! He's not properly conscious and his pupils are all wrong. He's concussed, nothing he says makes sense. The doctor's on his way. For God's sake, what happened? Jesus, Tilly! Gerry's in the cave and this time he really *is* dead! He's been shot and—'

'I know. By Matt. I was there when he did it. When's the doctor due? Because you have to get out of the house, Sophie. All of you – I take it the professor came?'

'He did, he's here. He helped me . . . Why do we have to leave? The plane should be here in oh, half an hour, say.'

'Because you could all be in danger,' Tilly said flatly. 'There's a crooked copper on his way there – the constable who was with the sergeant when he came to grill me about Gerry. He'll be looking for Matt, and chances are he's already harmed his sergeant, so he hasn't much to lose. You should either get to the camp or go to the airstrip now. You'll need time anyway to set up the lights. When the plane leaves, head for the camp. We should be there by then. But whatever you do, don't go back to the homestead.'

Sounding somewhat subdued, Sophie agreed that she wouldn't. Tilly pressed the off button and handed the phone back. 'That's sorted.'

'Thanks.' His lips twitched. 'She's a bit like a tank in motion, your cousin. I didn't know that shouting worked.'

'It's about the only thing.' Tilly gave a faint smile. 'Have you a first-aid kit in your vehicle? Murderer or not, Matt needs painkillers.' He nodded. 'I'll see what you've got while you get him into the cave.' Taking the torch, she rummaged under the seats until she had what she sought. There seemed to be nothing stronger than paracetamol, so she tore off a strip and filled the thermos cap with water, then took them in to their captive, now sitting propped against the wall opposite his victim. Glaring at her, Matt nevertheless opened his mouth and she tipped them in, following them with a slug of water. He'd protested furiously about being left, loudly asserting that he needed a doctor and that he wasn't sharing space with no stiff.

'Tough,' Connor said flintily. 'You made him one. I'd call it no more than your deserts. And I daresay the police will see to your medical needs when they get here.'

'Bastard,' he roared. 'I'll sue you for this. I got rights like anybody else.' They began moving off and he yelled after them, 'You can't do this!' as they left him there.

Tilly was having second thoughts. 'Do you think we should leave him? He really does need medical attention for that knee.'

Connor caught her hand in his. 'And if it hadn't been for that poor sod under the tarp, I'd have been attending your funeral. Let's not forget that. His bloody leg can fall off for all I care.'

'You're very fierce,' she said, but her heart was warmed by his vehemence and she smiled in the dark. 'What about Gerry, Connor? It seems awful just to leave him. Shouldn't we take his body back with us?'

'No. The cave's a crime scene. The cops won't thank us for disturbing it any more than Sophie already has.' He hesitated, thinking about it. 'She must have reported it when she contacted the doctor, so I'm guessing there'll be a copper on the plane too. Let's hope he's not one of the crooks.'

Tilly strangled a yawn. 'At least this whole thing's gone past the cover-up stage now. I mean, there's you and me, Sophie, Luke, and now the professor as well – they can't kill us all. Particularly if the sergeant is really dead. That's far too many corpses—' She yawned again. 'Oh, dear.'

'There's that,' he agreed. They had reached the vehicles and his torch lit the way to the Land Rover's door. 'What a day you've had. You go ahead, love, and I'll see you at the camp.'

# *Chapter Thirty-six*

For Tilly, the trip back to the camp was a nightmare. The headlights threw strange shadows over the bushes and anthills by the track, and she was too tired and agitated to drive well. The Land Rover crashed its way through the potholes while her mind vividly replayed scenes from the last few hours. Gerry's cry of 'No!' as he threw himself at Matt; the terror of knowing her death was imminent; and then the heart-stopping struggle under the vehicle while he did his best to choke the life from her.

She was safe now, she told herself in an attempt to stop the horrors her mind conjured, but oh, God! It could so easily have gone the other way. She had no illusions about that. Matt was ruthless, and the proof of that lay back in the cave, wrapped in poly-tarp. Gerry had been weak and venal, and, if Matt was to be believed, had done dreadful things, but he must really have loved her. His actions had proved that. Perhaps he had even tried to get out of the criminal life he'd become involved in. For a man supposed to be dead that brief note had been a foolish thing – or had it been a subconscious cry for help?

Her love for him might have died, but she could feel regret for his death, and even, she thought, find it in herself to forgive what he had done.

The camp was fast asleep when she arrived. She pulled up by Connor's site, turned the engine off and sat shivering in the cooling cab until he coasted to a stop beside her.

'Okay?' He came to her door, which she opened to bring on the cab light, then tsked when he saw her. 'You're freezing! Come on, I'll find you something.' It turned out to be a navy jumper that hung on her slim form but was wonderfully warm. 'I'll boil up,' he said.

'Yes, tea would be great,' Tilly said tiredly. 'I don't see Sophie, Connor.' She was worried. 'You don't think she could have been silly enough to go back?' Her words were interrupted by the distant roar of an aircraft leaving the ground and she relaxed. 'Ah, that must be the doctor leaving – that's why. Seems a shame he'll have to be called back for Matt.'

'The cops wouldn't let him go without an escort,' Connor pointed out.

'And Gerry?'

'I don't know, love. They'd probably take a body by road. You know, you haven't yet told me exactly what happened. Why you and Luke were even at the cave.'

'It was the bats . . .' The story filled in the time while they waited, and telling it gave her a chance to order the events in her mind. She would have to go over it again, probably several times, for the police. Murder was involved, after all – quite a few murders, if a refugee boat had really sunk, and Tilly could see no reason why Matt would have lied about that. Not when he had had every intention of killing her. She had only just finished her tale when headlights appeared at the camp gate, and a few moments later, Sophie's vehicle rolled to a halt beside theirs.

She wasn't alone. The tall, thin middle-aged man with spectacles and a little grey goatee with her was introduced as Thomas Leary, and the younger, uniformed one as Constable Lapin. He at least didn't waste any time, cutting across Sophie's rush of questions with a curt demand of his own. 'So where's this body Ms Barker reported?'

'Not here,' Connor said unhelpfully. 'Which branch of the Darwin lot are you from, Constable? I thought I knew most of the officers, by sight anyway.'

'We haven't met,' he said curtly. 'I'm from Katherine. So where—'

'Why Katherine? I thought—'

'Oh, the doctor was already there when I put the call through,' Sophie said. 'He was picking up a patient, and they told me he'd come by us on his way back to Darwin, rather than make a second trip, you see.'

'That's right,' Lapin confirmed, 'and they needed a cop, they said, so I was it. And how the hell am I supposed to get back from here, and with a body too? Which,' he added, 'you seem remarkably reluctant to tell me about.'

'That's great news!' To Lapin's obvious amazement, Connor seized and shook his hand. 'Okay, if you'd just step over here for a minute, I'll put you in the picture. Sorry, folks,' he said, but was largely ignored for Sophie was urgently demanding the same from her cousin.

Tilly shook her head. 'First, how is Luke? What did the doctor say?'

'A bad case of concussion.' Sophie was succinct. 'His skull might be fractured. They'll do a scan and take it from there. What happened, Till? I've been going out of my mind with worry about the pair of you.'

'I'm sorry, Soph. Come into the tent and I'll tell you. And you, Thomas, seeing as you've been dragged into this too.' She and Sophie sat on Connor's stretcher in the glow of the pressure lamp that, already lit, filled the space with a warm glow, while the professor folded himself neatly onto his haunches against the canvas wall. 'Sophie's probably already told you,' she began, 'that Luke and I were intending to catch a bat for you, so you'd have a live specimen to study. He is quite certain, you see, that they're different to all the ones he knows. Only when we arrived, we saw light in the cave and Luke rushed in thinking it was someone mucking up, before I could tell him. He didn't know, and I feel bad about that, too. He—'

'Sorry, what didn't he know?' Leary interjected.

'That the cave was being used by wildlife traffickers. We discovered it a little while ago and I told Sophie but not the others . . . Anyway, it was full of cages – birds and maybe reptiles – and oh, Sophie, they're still caged in the back of the Land Rover, but Connor says they're evidence and we can't let them go yet.'

'Yes, well, never mind that now. Luke rushed in and—'

'I was going after him and I heard this yell. When I went in, he was slumped down beside the cages bleeding and holding his head, and then he sort of keeled over and just lay there.'

She told them the rest, her voice trembling when it came to Gerry's death and how Matt had almost killed her.

Sophie put her arm around her in response. 'That bastard!' she muttered. 'Years he's worked here and he could still do that to Luke? He might've killed him. So Gerry was mixed up in it, just as you thought?'

'And worse,' Tilly said. 'Drugs and people smuggling too, only that seems to have failed because the boat sank and they all drowned.' She ground her teeth. 'Matt said they'd paid upfront and the country didn't need any more damn Muslims anyway. I broke his kneecap while he was trying to kill me,' she added matter-of-factly.

'Go, girl!' A wide grin split Sophie's face. 'Elaine would be proud of you. *I'm* proud of you. So where is he now? He didn't get away?'

'No. We left him in the cave, tied up. When the tyre went flat, Connor turned up and helped me.' Her hand went unbidden to her throat as she relived that deadly struggle and her fight for air. 'So we came back thinking you might've come out to the cave, only you'd already gone, and that's when I realised that Constable Wilmot must be a crook too. It's why we didn't want you at the homestead – because he's on his way there now.' In a few rapid strokes she outlined the results of the Alloway phonecalls. 'It means the rest of the gang will probably get away, but Matt can be charged with Gerry's murder, and, if he's done no worse to the sergeant, Wilmot for complicity in the business and assault on a policeman. That's why Connor was so pleased that this cop'—she moved her head to indicate where the two voices murmured outside the tent—'is from Katherine. He must be clean. And the one at Spadgers Creek is coming too.'

'Good Lord,' Thomas said reverently into the silence that fell after she finished speaking. 'Does this sort of thing go on all the time?'

'Thankfully, no.' Sophie had turned to another problem. 'I suppose we'll have to lend him a vehicle.' Catching Tilly's blank look, she said, 'The cop – how else will he get the body away, or his prisoner?'

'Maybe Connor – I mean, he's part of it. Or he could call in reinforcements. He's appropriated Matt's satellite phone.'

'He had a *satellite phone*?' Her cousin sounded scandalised. 'Well, I hope Connor runs up a decent bill on his account. Those things cost the bloody earth.'

'They . . . Ssh, listen!' Tilly cocked her head. 'There's a vehicle coming. Oh, God, what if it's Wilmot? I must warn Connor.' She darted out only to find that he had heard the sound too.

'It's okay. It'll be Des.'

'How can you be certain? Wilmot—'

'The man hasn't got wings,' he said patiently. 'He was at Alloway. No way he's here yet.'

'Oh.' It was at least a three-hour drive from there, and some of the tension left her. 'I've told the others everything. So what next?'

'Keith, here, and I have been making plans. I've suggested he and Des collect Mercer and take him on to Alloway. I'll ring the RFDS to alert them, and when the doctor arrives, the two can accompany him to Darwin. Along with the body.'

'But you said it had to stay—'

Connor grimaced. 'Ideally, but with the heat in that cave, it's probably a better idea to shift it now. Another day . . .'

He trailed off and Tilly shut her mind to what remained unsaid. 'Besides,' he continued then, 'any evidence must've been tramped away with the number of bodies that've been in and out of the joint since.'

'Yes, I see.' Turning to the young policeman, she said, 'How will you find the cave?'

'Connor's drawn me a pretty good mud map.'

'And if you should run into Wilmot on the road out?'

'Not gonna happen,' Connor put in. 'You can bet Wilmot will come the shortest way, so they'll take the coastal track instead. Des knows it – he'll be on it before Wilmot gets here.' Headlights flashed through the timber as he spoke, and when the vehicle purred gently into the camp, he leant in to activate his own lights, switching them on and off again.

Tilly watched quietly as a chunkily built stranger alighted from the vehicle. He was wearing typical stationhand clothes of felt hat, jeans, boots and a sheepskin-lined jacket pulled over a checked flannel shirt. He nodded at Tilly and said, 'G'day, Connor. What's going on?'

'Got a job for you. This'—he tipped his head at the young uniformed constable—'is Keith. He's clean, from Katherine. We've got a prisoner to transport and a body. Keith's got the details, and he'll fill you in because you need to get started. Wilmot's dirty and he's on his way here, we think, to rescue the prisoner who's been injured. So you've got to get him away. Use the coast road, and I'll have the flying doctor waiting for you at Alloway. There's a good chance that David Burns is there, either dead or incapacitated. Mercer's tied up with a bust leg. He's responsible for the body. It's Gerry Hillyer, by the way. Shot at point-blank range.'

Des appeared to absorb the information much like a sponge, Tilly thought. He asked only one question. 'What'll you be doing?'

'Dealing with Wilmot,' Connor said tersely. 'He and Burns were at Alloway when I rang them. But the owner said Wilmot left alone because Burns had vanished. Seems to me to be the place to start inquiring after him.'

'I'll get onto it. Okay. Glad to meet you, Keith.' He leant across to shake hands. 'You got the location of the prisoner? Good. Let's go then.'

# *Chapter Thirty-seven*

Watching them leave, Tilly said, 'He seems very capable.'

'Yeah.' Connor was fishing out Matt's phone again. 'A good man. He's done a lot of undercover work. Suits him because he's one of those blokes whose appearance doesn't shriek "cop".'

'Who are you ringing?'

'The RFDS base. The doctor'll be sick of us. I'll just alert them that we'll need a pick-up at Alloway in about . . .' He held his watchface towards the faint light from the tent. 'It's midnight now. Say four am. That ought to give them enough time.'

'And it means you have no backup,' Tilly said anxiously. 'So how exactly do you plan on "dealing with" Wilmot? Don't Territory cops carry guns?'

'I think all cops do these days.'

'Don't dodge the question,' she said sharply. 'I don't want to be humoured, Connor. What do you plan to do? You're not armed, so what happens if he decides to kill you?'

'He won't, love. What would be the point? When he learns Mercer's been arrested and is out of reach, along with the body of the man he killed, I imagine he'll run for it. Especially if, as I fear, he's already done for Burns.'

'And you won't try to stop him?'

'Not if he's waving a gun at me,' Connor said. 'I'm not an idiot. Anyway if Burns *is* dead, the police won't stop till they've hunted him down.'

'So the rest – the ones Matt organised to meet him – will get away too?'

'Can't be helped.' Connor shrugged. 'Look, in an ideal world we'd catch all the villains, but crime would still go on. Now, you should try and get some rest, love. You must be exhausted.'

'While you do what?'

He exhaled patiently. 'I thought I'd poke down to the homestead. Wait for him there. It's what we arranged on the phone. Don't worry – I won't let on that we've rumbled him. I'll just tell him the doctor picked up Mercer too, when he came for Luke.'

It wasn't a bad plan, Tilly thought. Wilmot would be free to leave, but that was a small price if it kept Connor safe. 'Okay, that should work. But it would be better if we were there too, Sophie and the professor and me. He might get suspicious if you're all alone in an empty house. And the presence of witnesses should stop him doing anything stupid, like killing you.' *Unless he decides to kill us all.* She didn't say it.

He sighed, head tipped to one side. 'Are you always this managing?'

'It makes sense,' Tilly said stubbornly, 'and you know it lessens the risk. Anyway, I'm going if I have to walk.'

He gave in. 'All right. Get the others. We'll leave the Land

Rover here for now.' He checked his watch again. 'Another hour, hour and a half till he arrives, I reckon. We could even catch a bit of sleep.'

It was the last thing on Tilly's mind, but curled up on the lounge – she had refused to go to bed – with only the kitchen light on and Thomas Leary's hearty snores issuing from the spare bedroom, she finally dozed off, falling straight into a dream of pounding rain and crashing thunder. It was the Wet, she realised, the dark night hot and damp and full of menace. The mighty McArthur River had broken its banks and the rising water now threatened the fishing camp. Intermittent flashes of lightning lit the tin-walled room as she splashed through ankle-deep water towards the cot where Francie cowered, her face tear-streaked, little hands clamped over her ears.

'I don't like it, Mummy! I don't like it,' she sobbed as Tilly scooped her up.

'Hush, it's all right, darling,' Tilly soothed her as the child's arms snaked around her neck. She turned to the door, but the water was suddenly waist deep and Gerry stood there with the blood blooming over his heart and his blank eyes staring.

'Sorry, babe,' he said and slid bonelessly into the flood just as a huge crocodile surged towards them.

Tilly screamed, twisting away and bending protectively over the child as the monster lunged at her unguarded back. She felt the buffet of the water and glanced fearfully back, but it was Gerry who stood there now with his dead blank eyes and greenish scaly skin, wresting the screaming child from her arms. 'No!' She hit out at him and felt her fist connect, but he slipped away as she lunged furiously after him. 'No! Give her back to me! I won't let you take her!' But he and Francie had vanished and only mud remained. Her heart broke afresh and she wailed her loss as urgent hands shook her.

'Wake up, Tilly! Wake up, it's a dream. Only a dream, dear heart.' Connor was cradling her to his chest as she shuddered awake. 'What is it?' he asked tenderly. 'You were dreaming and crying in your sleep.'

'Oh.' She sat up, shuddering, and palmed her damp cheeks dry. 'An old nightmare about losing Francie. But different. I suppose it was seeing Gerry today – yesterday? He was dead in my dream, but he still took her.' She drew a deep breath, memory touching her. 'I felt myself hit something – that wasn't you, was it?'

'Yeah.' He rubbed his chest and grinned wryly. 'For a little 'un you pack a mean punch.'

'I'm sorry.' Then reality returned with a rush. 'What time is it? Why hasn't Wilmot come?' But even as she spoke, the faintest tremor in the air stilled her breath. 'Do you hear that?'

'Sounds like him now.' Connor stood up. 'Why don't you put the kettle on?'

'You're not offering him a cup of *tea*?' she said incredulously. 'He might be a murderer, Connor!'

'He won't accept,' he replied, 'and it's cover for your presence to explain being up at this hour.' He lifted his wrist to glance at his watch. 'It's after three, Tilly. So you woke, saw I was still up, and your tender heart got the better of you so you came out to make me a coffee.'

'Yes.' Tilly jumped up, caught sight of her clothes and whirled to the door. 'I'll put a robe on and some slippers. You light the gas, he'll be here any minute.' The snores in the bedroom stopped suddenly and springs creaked as though the professor had rolled over, before they began again in a deeper register. Sophie's room was quiet as Tilly feverishly pulled the scrunchy from her hair and dragged her dressing gown on over her clothes. The vehicle pulled up before the homestead, and she hurried back to the kitchen in time to catch the kettle as it began to whistle.

She heard Connor cross to the door and the faint squeak of its hinges. He said something, a mumble, then his words came more clearly as he turned back, 'Come on in, then. Though I'm afraid you've had a wasted journey.'

'What do you mean?' Peeping round the opened fridge door, Tilly saw Wilmot stop in his tracks. He looked tired and tense, stubble shadowed his lower face and his eyes had narrowed suspiciously.

Connor seemed oblivious to his reaction. 'Where's Burns? I thought he was with you.'

'Left him at Alloway.' Catching sight of Tilly, he said abruptly, 'G'day. Up late, aren't you?'

Caught off guard, she opened her mouth to answer, but Connor spoke first and she busied herself sweeping together the sauce, pepper and salt canisters, and sugar holder left out on the bench top. Sophie never put stuff away after herself.

'Why?' Connor said. 'I mean, it doesn't matter as it's turned out but—'

'Dysentery. He's stuck in the Gents for the duration, I reckon. Come on him sudden like. Then you ring like the house is on fire, so we reckoned I'd better just head over.' He ground the heels of his hands into his eyes and shook his head. 'And now you're telling me – what exactly?'

'Look, I'm sorry. Sit down, Wayne. You've had the trip for nothing. If I could've got hold of you, mate, to stop you, I would've, believe me. Tilly's just making me a coffee. She took pity on me pulling an all-nighter, and I reckon you could use one too. Thing is, when I realised the flying doctor had been called out for young Luke, and he had a copper on board as well, on account of the body Sophie found with Luke – well, it seemed too good an opportunity to miss. Mercer needed medical attention, and the plane had room for two stretchers, so . . .' He shrugged, accepting the cup Tilly brought him with a nod of thanks.

'What will you have, officer?' she asked.

He waved her off, saying blankly, 'What copper? And why – was Mercer hurt?'

'Broken leg,' Connor replied cheerfully. 'He'll be tucked up in hospital with a guard on the door long since. And slapped with a first-degree murder charge among the rest – drug-running, wildlife trafficking, people smuggling . . . He admitted to that one in front of witnesses. And he kidnapped and assaulted Tilly here, so that's on his sheet as well. With the amount of time he's facing, I'm betting he'll talk and we'll roll up the rest of the gang, so wasted journey apart, it's been a good night's work. And the blokes on the new road – you organised a reception committee for them, I take it?'

'Yeah – well, Burns said he'd see to that. When he could get out of the bog, that is.' Wilmot rubbed his face. 'Sorry, I'm too bushed to take it all in at one sitting. How did you call the roadhouse from this new track you were talking about? Just curious about that.'

'Mercer's phone. Sat job. It's been damn handy, I can tell you. Pity they don't give cops the same. Sure you won't have that coffee? You look all in.'

'I'm fine,' Wilmot said tersely. He sucked his teeth, obviously thinking. 'Right. Reckon I'll head down the road a bit and have a camp, then get going again and pick up the sarge. I'd better take that phone in. It's evidence. The tech boys might be able to figure out who Mercer was contacting. Where is it?'

Connor sat unmoving, as Tilly's gaze flew to the object in question. 'I thought I'd hang onto it for a bit. The constable escorting Mercer has the number. He'll be calling me with an update any time soon.'

Wilmot's voice hardened. 'He can call you here, can't he? It's evidence. Look, we appreciate all that Customs has done in the case, but basically it's a police matter, so I'm afraid you'll have to hand it over.'

So he could dispose of it, Tilly thought, or at least anything incriminating that it contained. She squeezed her fingers together, hoping that Connor would refuse, then the matter was taken out of his hands as the instrument in question gave its warbling call. Wilmot was startled, but cottoned on fast. He took two strides and grabbed it off the counter, pressing a couple of buttons. 'Yep?'

Des's voice broke into the room. 'Connor? Des here. Christ, we just found Burns! The bastard cut his throat and dropped him in the service pit in the shed.' His agitated voice bounced around the room. Wilmot, obviously unfamiliar with the phone's workings, had put it on speaker. Des never paused, the words tumbling over each other. 'He must've planned on being long gone before the body was discovered. If he turns up there, you've gotta stop him. I—'

The words cut off as suddenly as they'd begun. Wilmot dropped the handpiece and reached for his weapon. 'Right.' His voice was suddenly no longer weary, but cold and hard. 'That was unfortunate – or maybe not.' He aimed the gun at Connor. 'You've been playing me for a fool, Doyle? Who's this Des then, and where'd he call from?'

'He's an undercover cop, and the call was from the roadhouse at Alloway.' Connor replied readily. 'Best give it up, Wilmot – you won't spin your way out of this. He knows you're involved, that you've killed one of your own. You know cops. You don't walk away from that. They'll hunt you down, however long it takes.'

He sounded amazingly calm, Tilly thought, caught between fury and terror. She had *told* him this would happen.

'That being so I've got nothing to lose.'

Her blood turned to ice at Wilmot's reply. Her hand had closed convulsively over the pepper canister when the phone rang, and now she slid it into the pocket of her robe. It wasn't much but if she could get close enough . . . She swept the sauce bottle onto the floor and shouted, 'No!'

The policeman had plainly forgotten her presence. He jumped, then swung the barrel sideways in a beckoning motion. 'You! Shut your mouth and get over here.' She came around the counter's end and his face reddened with anger as he took in the jeans below the hem of the robe. 'A set-up,' he snarled, grabbing her arm and yanking her towards him.

Connor yelled something, and then everything happened at once as a deafening racket, akin to a jet engine firing, broke out on the verandah.

Tilly's free hand had been working at the canister in her pocket. Wilmot, momentarily distracted by the earth-shattering roar behind him, had loosened his grip. She tore herself free, held her breath and, scooping up a handful of loose pepper, flung it into his face.

Yelling 'Gah!' he reeled back and fired blindly. She felt the hot gases of the explosion on her neck, then Connor's terrified roar of 'Tilly!' that penetrated even the sudden deafness caused by the shot as he launched himself at the staggering Wilmot. Both men crashed to the floor just as the door opened and Sophie appeared, wild-eyed and pyjama-clad, holding a roaring chainsaw in both hands.

Wilmot's gun had skidded across the floor. Tilly gingerly picked it up, looked helplessly around, then ran outside and hurled it into the blackness under the house. When she returned, Sophie had switched off the chainsaw and Connor, with a red splodge on one cheekbone, had rolled Wilmot onto his front and was fixing the man's own handcuffs to his wrist. That done, he surged to his feet and went to her.

'Are you okay? God, when he fired I thought—'

'It's okay. I'm okay.' She rested her head against him, feeling the wild clamour of his heart match her own racing pulse. 'I felt the heat on my neck but the bullet missed me.'

'Thank Christ!' He kissed her, the stubble on his cheek rough against her face as he leant there for a moment, smoothing her hair with trembling hands. 'What on earth did you do to him?'

'Pepper.' She gave a little giggle, on the edge of hysteria. 'It was on the counter. Sophie never puts stuff away.' She turned to her cousin. 'You were brilliant! How did you think of a chainsaw?'

Sophie grinned sheepishly. 'It's true I'm not tidy like you. I was working with it, lopping the shade tree branches where they overhang the roof, and when I was done I left it out the back. I woke up and remembered it and thought I'd better get it in out of the dew. I was going to put it on the verandah for now. Then I saw what was going down . . . So I tried for a distraction. It was all I could think of at the time. Lucky it started first pull.'

'It worked a treat,' Connor said. 'Gave us our chance, so thank you.'

'Isn't he one of the coppers that came to ask you about Gerry, Tilly?'

She nodded. 'Yes. He's a crook, and a murderer. He killed the other one tonight, the sergeant. He—'

At this point Thomas Leary appeared in bare feet and rumpled sweats. Obviously confused, his eyes widened as they fell on Wilmot, writhing ineffectually on the floor. 'What was that infernal racket?' he demanded. 'I thought a plane was coming down on the roof. And did I hear a gunshot? What's going on? Is he a *policeman*?'

'Well spotted,' Connor said. 'If you're feeling charitable, you might like to wash the pepper from his eyes? Tilly threw it at him while he was trying to kill us.'

Leary baulked, goggled at him, then crossed uncertainly to the sink before gazing helplessly around at the cupboards lining the walls. 'What? Where . . .?'

'I'll do it.' Tilly filled a jug and bent over the swearing man. 'Open your eyes.' He did so to disclose bloodshot eyes that were continually tearing. He swore at her as she splashed water over his face and swollen cheeks. 'You're alive,' she snapped, 'unlike the men you've killed. And if you don't stop that language, your eyes can go unflushed. It's no skin off my nose.' He glared at her, the veins of his temple swelling, but the swearing stopped.

'What are we going to do with him?' she asked when she had finished her ministrations and had beckoned Connor to the far end of the kitchen.

'I've been thinking about that.' He yawned and stretched. 'For the moment, can you find a blanket? We'll leave him handcuffed and tether him to a verandah post till morning. That ought to hold him. Then we're all going to get some sleep. But first I want to speak to Des. He's the only one I can reach that I know I can trust. He'll be back in Darwin by dawn. I'll get him arrange a plane and take Wilmot in myself. They'll all know about Burns' murder by then, and every corrupt cop in the station will be ducking for cover. I'll contact a few of my own men just to be on the safe side. We might even hold him ourselves until the dust settles. We do have the facilities.' He yawned again and nodded. 'Yeah, that'll be the way to go. If any of the senior cops object – well, their dead sergeant's a powerful argument for doing it my way. Which reminds me, love, what became of his gun?'

'I threw it under the house.' Tilly said. 'I just wanted to get rid of it.'

'I'll retrieve it in the morning. It's evidence. I wonder where the bullet went?'

'Into the wall, or the china cabinet, though nothing's broken, so maybe not.'

'We'll check it out tomorrow. You'll be swarmed with police,' he warned, 'taking statements and collecting evidence.'

Sophie wandered over in time to hear this. 'What about my animals? Can I let them out of those damned cages?'

'Have you somewhere else to hold them?' Connor asked. 'They'll need to be photographed. If you could keep them captive for a few days . . .?'

'We could use the enclosure,' Tilly suggested. 'The cockies could go in the hen-house, perhaps? And the possum cage would hold any little ones. I don't know about the reptiles,' she said doubtfully.

'We'll fix something up. The professor can make himself useful.'

It suddenly struck Tilly. 'There's only you and me left, Soph! They'll all have to be fed on top of everything else. I wonder how Luke is, and when he'll be back?'

'Worry about it tomorrow,' Connor said. 'Can you get that blanket now? I'll secure our resident thug, and then we can all get some rest.'

# *Chapter Thirty-eight*

It was very late by the time they all retired. Connor took one look at Tilly's bed, and then pulled the mattress onto the floor. 'Not so far to fall if I roll over.' He stripped to his boxers and lay down. With a sigh, Tilly spooned in beside him and reached to hold the hand that held her snug against him.

'What a day!' She sighed and shuddered, remembering. 'I'll have nightmares about it for months.'

'Well, it's over now.' He kissed her hair and his arm momentarily tightened around her. 'And you're safe here with me. Sleep now. It's not long till morning.'

'You saved my life.' Her voice was drowsy as she pushed the words out against her closing eyes. 'I think I love you, Connor.'

'We saved each other. And I know I love you, dear heart.' It was a voice on the edge of hearing, no more than a whisper in a dream, but Tilly heard it. She slept smiling, the words a promise for the future.

*

The following day started late for them all. The caged wildlife had to be fetched back from the camp and released into their temporary homes, then fed and watered. When it came to the two olive pythons, Sophie waited until Connor finished photographing them and then propped the cages open.

'We've nothing to feed them on,' she said, when he eventually noticed their absence. 'If Luke was here . . . But he's not. If you want them back, you'll have to go catch them yourself.'

'They were evidence!' He was put out and showed it. 'Where'd they go? Which direction?'

'I wasn't watching,' Sophie said shortly. She too was suffering from lack of sleep.

When his gaze switched to Tilly, she held up her hands. 'Don't look at me! I might tackle baddies, but I'm not taking on snakes. Just so you know,' she added firmly.

By the time they were through with the feeding, and everyone, including their captive, had breakfasted, the plane could be heard approaching. Wilmot, handcuffed again following his breakfast, was hustled into the vehicle. Tilly slipped into the seat behind him, determinedly clutching the refilled pepperpot, which she showed him as a warning against trying anything. Another Customs officer was on the plane to take charge of the awkward business of getting Wilmot aboard without the use of his still-secured hands. Connor threw a small travel bag in after them and turned to take Tilly in his arms.

'You will be careful?' she said anxiously. 'How will you get back?'

'I'll work something out.' His eyes crinkled in a smile as he kissed her, saying, 'Take care, love. I'll check on Luke as soon as I get a free moment.'

'Thank you.' She kissed him back. 'Sophie'll be ringing about him now.'

When the plane lifted off, she drove home to find the professor watering the vegetable garden. Sophie, he said, had gone to the camp to attend to the chores there. She had left a message with him from the hospital reporting that Luke was concussed but thankfully had an undamaged skull. He would be released when his current drowsiness passed, possibly as early as tomorrow.

'Well, that's a relief,' Tilly said. 'How long are you staying Thomas? Not that we want to hurry you away. But I doubt the police, when they get here and that'll probably be late today, will let you anywhere near the cave.'

'I'll just have to adjust my schedule then.' He pushed his spectacles up his nose and directed the hose at the cabbages. 'I'm assuming that the past twenty-four hours aren't the norm out here, but it seems to me you must all do a lot of adjusting in your daily lives. So I'll hang around and I may even be able to help. Bottom line is, I do want a look at those bats, and even if it takes a week, then – as long as I'm welcome – I'll stay till I've done so.'

'I'm sure you'll be very welcome.' Curiosity got the better of her. 'Last night, it took you a long time to come out of your room. With all that racket going on, did you really not wake up?'

He looked sheepish. 'You probably notice I snore very loudly? It's to the point where it wakes me, so I use ear plugs. It means I don't hear alarms, phones, even people yelling. But it seems chainsaws will do it.'

'Ah. Well,' she considered, 'in terms of helping, do you

know anything about engines? The diesel will need fuelling. You have to pump it from a drum into the tank, and then roll another drum over from the fuel dump for next time. Matt usually did it on a Monday, so it must be about due.'

He nodded. 'I can manage that.'

'Thanks. I'll be in the house if you need me.' There was plenty to do. The laundry basket was full, the cake tins empty and she would probably be feeding extra that evening. She hoped that the police would come equipped to camp, and because it was the height of the tourist season there were still travellers to book in and out. The professor, for all his diffidence, proved a useful sidekick willing to pitch in, whether it was peeling vegetables or feeding the hens, who were temporarily locked out of their home by the visiting wildlife.

It was late in the afternoon when Des, still in jeans and shirt, and a young, uniformed constable turned up in a four-wheel drive loaded up with a swag and camp gear – presumably Des's. She was driving and Des, when he got out, yawned and stretched as if he had just woken. He probably had, Tilly thought as she greeted him, for he couldn't have slept at all the previous night.

Des, whose surname she had forgotten, introduced his companion as Constable Helen Prentiss. They had come to fingerprint and collect statements from the three of them. The fingerprinting, he explained, was due to the presence of firearms at the crime scene in the cave, and the fact that an officer had discharged his weapon here at the house. He also wanted the bullet, if it could be found.

'I can show you where it went,' Tilly said. 'Connor took Wilmot's weapon away. And the other one's still in the cave, though I don't know if it's recoverable. What's happening in town, Des? Has Matt been locked up, and Wilmot? I know Connor was worried about who he could trust at the station.'

'That situation's been remedied,' he said curtly. 'Officers have been stood down and a new superintendent sent in. It took a good man's death,' he added bitterly, 'but there's a proper shake-up going on now. And a few soon-to-be ex-cops'll be joining Wilmot in gaol.'

She made them tea and then they took turns at giving their statements. When she had finished hers, Tilly said honestly, 'The times and the distances might be out. I wouldn't swear to them. It all seemed to happen in seconds – Gerry getting shot, and then when I hit Matt and took the gun. I was so terrified. Maybe it was longer. And when we were driving, it seemed like hours, but it can't have been because we got back to the cave quite quickly. So maybe I exaggerated the time there.'

'That's perfectly normal,' Helen assured her. 'I think you kept your head very well.' She smiled kindly at Tilly, who smiled back.

'Have you spoken to Luke?' Tilly asked Des.

'Yes. His memory's patchy. He wasn't able to tell us much, so you're our main witness for Gerald Hillyer's murder. And we'll certainly be contacting the Indonesians about that refugee boat you mentioned. If we can find some evidence to link Mercer to that—'

Tilly broke in. 'But he admitted it. He came right out and—'

'Hearsay,' he said, cutting her off. 'Not admissible in court.' He capped his pen. 'Right, fingerprints, then if one of you could accompany us to this cave?'

'Not tonight.' Sophie spoke decisively. 'It'll be dark in half an hour, and none of us got much sleep last night. So dinner's on the agenda for us and bed, but we'll be happy to assist you tomorrow.'

The following morning, Tilly woke to utter stillness; even Leary's truly horrific snoring had ceased. All she could hear was the drip of moisture falling from the roof edges as she dressed swiftly and headed for the kitchen. A light mist hovered above the river and she lingered, staring, until the harsh cackle of a kookaburra shattered the silence. Des, who had rolled his swag out on the verandah, was already up. She saw the neat cyclinder of his rolled swag and his boot tracks in the sodden grass leading away to the river. Helen, lacking her own bedding, had slept on the sofa in the lounge. Tilly hoped it had been more comfortable than it looked.

Tilly herself had slept like the dead, untroubled by dreams – probably, she thought now, breathing in the fresh morning, because of Connor's late night call. Everything had gone well. The good guys, he had told her, were back in charge and the villains behind bars. Due to the nature of their crimes, neither Mercer nor Wilmot would be granted bail. 'Too big a flight risk,' he'd said. Of course, the men in the vehicle slated to meet up with Matt were still at large, but the video camera on the fuel pumps at Alloway had a record of all vehicles that had passed by that day, and it was only a matter of time before the driver, at least, was located.

'And Luke?' Tilly had asked. 'How is he?'

'Doing well. They're discharging him tomorrow. He remembers driving to the cave and then nothing until he woke up on the plane on his way to hospital. His main concern seems to be about missing his chance with the professor.'

'Oh, he hasn't. Thomas and I are heading out to the cave this morning with Des. He wants to try and recover Matt's gun. We'll ring Luke later and tell him so. When will you be back?'

'Soon as I can manage, love.' They had talked a little longer; she smiled now, remembering his words, then stretched, deliciously aware of a new energy and expectation in her heart. It was just as Sophie had promised her: life was good again. Humming a little tune, she went back inside to start breakfast.

They took two vehicles to the caves, the two police following Tilly and Leary out.

'The road seems a lot better than it did the other night,' the professor observed. He wore an air of expectancy this morning and had brought along a fine mesh net on a telescopic handle.

'Daylight helps,' Tilly agreed. 'It's a shame Luke can't be here. What will you do if it turns out that he has discovered a new species? Will you publish a paper?'

'Oh, yes, once the research is done. Probably in *Nature* magazine. Don't worry, your friend will get the credit of discovery. But,' he added, pushing at his spectacles, 'we're getting ahead of ourselves. Let's wait until we see what we've got.'

At the cave, Tilly pulled up and sat a moment before alighting. She felt the greatest disinclination to continue, but Des, parking behind her, walked briskly towards the entrance, waiting with obvious impatience for her lagging steps to catch up. He carried a large torch, prompting her to caution him about the presence of the bats.

'Don't shine it up.'

'Not until I say, anyway,' Leary said singlemindedly. He looked every inch the mad professor, his beanpole length echoed by the now fully extended net handle and the box tucked under one arm. He kept pushing at his spectacles, his eyes gleaming with anticipation.

'You'll not be entering yet, sir,' Des said firmly. 'You'll stay with the constable until we've located the weapon. Is that clear?'

Leary grudgingly agreed and, resisting the urge to clutch at Des's arm, Tilly followed him into the cave. It was as humid and smelly as she remembered. It was only her imagination, she told herself, that she fancied she could still catch the taint of death in the muggy air. The darkness was disorienting, and she stared about in bewilderment trying to picture where she had been when she threw the gun into the fissure. Des's prompting didn't help and in the end she said, 'Just give me the torch. I can't see anything while you wave it about.'

There was still the shape of one cage imprinted in the guano, the rest destroyed by foot traffic. She stared at it, picturing the stacked shapes next to which Luke had sprawled. She had hit Matt and run *that* way to secure the gun and distance herself from the horror of Gerry's corpse, so it must be somewhere here, she thought, moving along the cave wall, that she had spotted the break in the rock.

The rustle of wings sounded above her and the fine disturbed dust caught in her throat. Sweat beaded her forehead and her heart pounded with remembered fear. She would never willingly enter a cave again. Then the light lit on a deeper blackness within the glistening stone and she breathed out thankfully. 'Here. I dropped it down there. And I really don't think you'll get it out again.'

Des tried, but the cleft proved longer than his arm. He returned to his vehicle, rummaged among the load and eventually returned with a set of oven hooks, long sturdy lengths of wire with a hooked end that were designed to lift hot camp-ovens from campfires. Tilly waited outside with the professor while the two officers occupied themselves fishing in the cleft with their improvised tool. The echoes of a faint shout showed when they succeeded, and shortly they emerged with the weapon encased in plastic.

'Okay, the place is yours,' Des said.

Leary started eagerly for the entrance. 'I'll need a hand. Someone to hold the torch.'

'Not me,' Tilly declined. With all her heart she hoped that the tiny mammals within were a unique new species. It would almost certainly mean that the entrance would be barred, the habitat made inaccessible to people. Let the echoes of fear and death fade into the rock that held them. She would remember only the sacrifice. And even that was tainted with might-have-beens, like the ghostly *once* that haunted her heart. Gerry had died trying to save her when he could instead have chosen a life free of crime and been with her still.

She heard the voices and turned back to see the others exiting the hill, the professor like a jaunty schoolboy with the net hung over his shoulder, both hands cradling the box he had brought with him. He wore a beaming smile.

'Well?' Tilly asked as the other two peeled off towards their vehicle.

'Oh, I think your young friend may be right,' he said. 'There's certainly an excellent chance, anyway.'

'So it is a new species?'

'It's certainly different to any of the creatures I'm familiar with,' he said pedantically. 'At this stage all I'm willing to say is that the *Hipposideros inornatus* is probably a close relative – very close. It looked to be a healthy colony,' he said approvingly, 'but even so, it would need protection. You wouldn't be able to let people in. Constant disturbance . . .' He shook his head. 'It could force them to leave. And that would certainly destroy the colony.'

'Good,' Tilly said. 'Let's go home. And when we get there, ring Luke and tell him.'

# *Chapter Thirty-nine*

Connor returned at dusk the following evening, the dust-laden vehicle he drove nosing to a gentle stop before the homestead. Tilly rose from her seat on the verandah and came down the steps, past the blaze of orange marigolds, to greet him. She had reached the bottom before her eyes even registered the passenger door opening as Luke got out.

'Luke! I didn't see you there. How are you? Is your head okay?'

'It's fine, thanks.' A seam of tiny black stitches crossed his right temple where a bruise had bloomed in yellow and green, but he was smiling. 'Who's cooking today?'

Tilly laughed. 'I am, actually. It was just quicker seeing there was only the two of us to get round the chores. How was the hospital food?'

'Better than Sophie's.' He grinned now, looking more his old self. 'But that's not high praise. I suppose the professor's gone?'

'Left at daybreak, thank God! You should hear that man snore.'

'That bad, eh? Well, I could really do with a cuppa so I'll leave you to your man. Catch you later,' he said, heading to the steps.

Connor now rounded the vehicle, his arms held out. She stepped into them, kissing him hungrily. 'I've missed you. Everything fixed, paperwork done?'

'In triplicate.' His eyes creased and he held her back to search her face. 'You're okay, my sweet?'

'I am now. Whose vehicle is it?'

'A mate's. He's flying out Wednesday to collect it. The department's paying. And I've got a fortnight off.'

'That's wonderful. So were you planning on spending it here?'

He gave her an incredulous look. 'What do you think?' he asked, then grinned sheepishly as she smiled. 'Okay, you got me.'

'Just checking. Is there any news on Matt's mates? Did the police find them?'

'They've got the driver – traced him through his vehicle.' He shrugged. 'The cops'll work their way through his known associates, so they could get lucky.'

'And the refugee boat that sank – did they find out about that?'

'Des said they're liaising with the Indonesians, and the Malaysians – it could have come from either country. But, you know, it may not have been on a register. It had to have been a clapped-out old wreck in the first place for it to sink. It could well have been sitting on a mud bank up a tidal creek for years.' He lifted his shoulders, let them fall. 'When money matters more than human life . . .'

'Yes.' She shivered, and not just for the rapidly cooling air. 'I can't get past it, Connor, knowing that Gerry was involved in something like that. I can forgive him the rest, the trafficking of animals, even the drugs, but the callousness of that . . . It's wholesale murder, even if the victims were willing to chance it. Those men, including Gerry, sent them to their deaths as surely as if they'd shot them.'

Connor hugged her and she huddled against the broad warmth of his body, pressing one palm to where his heart beat like a metronome beneath his shirt. 'He saved you'—his breath stirred her hair—'remember that.'

'I do. It's the only reason . . .' She trailed off and lifted her head. 'I suppose I shall have to see to his funeral. There's no one else – some uncle somewhere but we never met. His mother's dead. She and his father split years ago and I've no idea where he is.' Then, as if the thought had triggered the reminder, 'And there'll have to be an inquest into his death. I expect I'll have to go to that too, as well as Matt's trial. I'll be a witness, won't I?'

'I expect so.' He took her hands in his, exclaiming, 'You're freezing! Let's go in. Think, love. We've got a fortnight in which to sort out all the stuff like that, and after that, a whole lifetime to order the rest of it – where we'll live, how we'll make our jobs work, what we'll call our kids . . .'

Tilly stopped him there, standing one step higher so that her gaze was level with his, letting her eyes learn the lineaments of his beloved face.

'Do you swear that, Connor Doyle?' she demanded.

'By the stars above, you suspicious wench, multiplied by all the galaxies you can't see.' He put his hand on his heart.

'My troth to you, my love. Now, come on.' He kissed her again and caught her hand, pulling her on up to the verandah. 'Dinner.'

# *Acknowledgements*

I would like to thank all the staff of Penguin Random House for their part in the production of this work. In particular, publisher Ali Watts, my superb editor Amanda Martin and the truly attentive proofreaders who sieve out all the inconsistencies and mistakes.

Great work, girls, and thank you.

# Discover a new favourite